Advance praise for James Villas and
Dancing in the Lowcountry

"Jimmy's fiction is like his cooking, wry and ribald, languid and laugh-out-loud funny. When you are from the South, as I am, these are the characters you wish were in your family. A wonderful novel from a wonderful man. The only better thing than reading it would be to hear the author read it out loud. His delicious sass fills every page. A real feast. Serve with some sippin' whiskey and enjoy!"

> Marsha Norman, Pulitzer Prize–winning
> playwright of *'night, Mother*

"James Villas has crafted an epic story steeped in the traditions and culture of the South. It's about family and secrets, memories and regrets, lifelong passions and the inevitable tragedies we all face. Ella Dubose is a complicated, courageous woman still living with gusto, still struggling over life's hurdles, still dancing in the Lowcountry with grit and grace."

> Cathy Lamb, author of *Julia's Chocolates*

"*Dancing in the Lowcountry* is a delightful and moving account of a certain kind of upper-middle-class life in the South of my own generation. I know of few, if any, novels that give such an accurate account of that life and of the rich and amusing language we've used for a long while now—whether we're white, black, or red."

> Reynolds Price, author of *A Long and
> Happy Life*

Please turn the page for more advance praise!

DANCING
in the
LOWCOUNTRY

JAMES VILLAS

KENSINGTON BOOKS
http://www.kensingtonbooks.com

KENSINGTON BOOKS are published by

Kensington Publishing Corp.
850 Third Avenue
New York, NY 10022

All Kensington titles, imprints and distributed lines are available at special quantity discounts for bulk purchases for sales promotion, premiums, fund-raising, educational or institutional use.

Special book excerpts or customized printings can also be created to fit specific needs. For details, write or phone the office of the Kensington Special Sales Manager: Kensington Publishing Corp., 850 Third Avenue, New York, NY 10022. Attn. Special Sales Department. Phone: 1-800-221-2647.

Kensington and the K logo Reg. U.S. Pat. & TM Off.

ISBN-13: 978-0-7582-2847-5
ISBN-10: 0-7582-2847-3

First Kensington Trade Paperback Printing: October 2008
10 9 8 7 6 5 4 3 2 1

Printed in the United States of America

To the memory of Jamie

Chapter 1

A FRESH PEACH

The week after Easter, Ella Dubose set about making preparations for her "incognito" jaunt in as normal a manner as possible for a Southern lady determined to fulfill a vital mission. She very attentively went through her wardrobe as she used to do so she'd have the right clothes for every occasion. She had Lucy give her a permanent at the beauty parlor on her regular day, then went to the bank to get plenty of cash. While Goldie filled the car with gas, went to the liquor store for booze, and refilled the prescription for Ella's heart pills, Ella dried a few marijuana leaves from the side porch in the oven, ground them finely in the blender, packed them firmly in a cigarette emptied of regular tobacco, and smoked a joint as part of her self-prescribed program to ward off glaucoma. She thought of everything, including getting the two old fishing rods and reels stored in the basement, checking to make sure the small gun in her pocketbook was loaded, and canceling delivery of the *Observer* so there'd be no newspapers in the drive to attract neighbors' attention. When, in fact, Goldie arrived the following Monday morning to pack the car, and the two finally got under way in the white Cadillac, it was as if Ella planned never to return to the house again.

★ ★ ★

Ella insisted on driving at least the first leg of the four-hour trip, and since Goldie was now wearing her hair in a long pigtail and sporting more exotic Indian ornaments, the sight of a slight, dignified, elderly lady in a pink silk blouse and pearl earrings behind the wheel and a stout, tan-skinned woman decked out in colored glass beads and flashy bracelets studying a road map was enough to catch anybody's eye—especially in rural North and South Carolina. At first, the two women had little to talk about, but the farther they drove through the flat, sandy Pee Dee countryside dotted with drab little farming towns, fields of young tobacco and cotton, and one Baptist church and trailer camp after another, the more Ella was inspired to tell Goldie about the region's history, and the giant watermelons and boiled goobers sold at roadside stands around Pageland during the summer months, and how she and Mr. Earl once stopped awhile in Bennettsville to witness a tobacco auction. Then, just outside Darlington, she suddenly slowed the car down and pulled off the road in front of a dilapidated wooden hut where an old black man was dozing in a lawn chair.

"What's wrong, Miss Ella?" Goldie exclaimed with alarm.

"Nothing's wrong, dear. I saw a sign back there that said PEACHES. It's still way too early, and I'm sure they're hard as rocks, but I'd give my eyetooth for a fresh peach."

With which she got out of the car with her pocketbook on her arm, approached the rack displaying small bags of yellowish pink, slightly fuzzy peaches, and squeezed one.

"Clings?" she asked the man.

"Yessum. Early Belles. The first."

"Any taste?"

"Yessum. Not bad. 'Course they ain't freestones, but not bad for this time of year."

Ella sniffed another peach, frowned when she squeezed it, but nevertheless dug into her pocketbook for money and paid for a bag.

Back in the car, she asked Goldie if she'd take over the driving, then, once they were on the road again, rummaged in the back-seat for a small knife she'd put in her liquor bag to cut lemons for her drinks. She then spread several Kleenexes over her lap, peeled what looked and felt like the ripest peach, cut and tasted a wedge, and handed one to Goldie.

"Still a little mealy," Ella said, "but that Negro man was right when he said they have some flavor."

"Miss Ella, you better stop using that word," Goldie informed her politely.

"What word?"

"Negro."

"Why, I don't know what you're talking about," she said, popping another wedge in her mouth. "That's a perfectly respectable term, and you know I don't have a prejudiced bone in my body."

"All I know is what I hear on TV, and I heard the other night that the blacks don't like to ever be called Negroes and now want only to be called blacks or African-Americans."

"Why, I've never heard of anything so absurd. First, they're not Africans, they're Americans, and if I'd called a Negro a black when I was growing up in Charleston, I'd have gotten the worst whipping of my life." She removed some pulp from her mouth with her fingers and placed it on the Kleenex. "Lord, these are mealy."

"I'm just telling you what I heard on TV," Goldie went on, taking another wedge that Ella held out. "And, you know, more and more of us Indians are now calling ourselves Native Americans."

Ella glanced over at her with a puzzled expression on her

face. "I know of no such thing, dear, and if you ask me, I think that really is crazy. I mean, you're an American Indian and should be proud of it. Plain and simple."

Goldie just laughed. "I really don't give it that much thought, ma'am."

"Honestly," Ella muttered dismissively, reaching for the map, "sometimes I don't know what this world's coming to." She studied the map, told Goldie to slow down so they wouldn't miss an important turn, then removed some more pulp from her mouth. "Yep, mealy, but Lord, there's still nothing like a fresh peach."

"No, ma'am," Goldie agreed, accepting still another wedge as she drove. "But I know how you love those Elbertas and Indian Reds."

"I certainly do," Ella declared, wrapping up the skins and pit in the messy Kleenex and cramming the bundle in the bag with the other peaches. "That wasn't bad; just what we needed to put us in the right mood. You know, I once met these folks up North who kept going on about their New Jersey peaches, and when I couldn't stand it one minute longer, I simply told them that there wasn't a peach in this country that could hold a candle to South Carolina and Georgia peaches. I didn't mean to be rude, but Yankees do have some strange ideas about what's good and not good. Of course, I have to admit that Mr. Earl and I used to eat wonderful peaches over in France—white ones almost as juicy as our Dixie Belles." She now appeared preoccupied with the memory, so much so, in fact, that she took her eyes off the map too long and failed to tell Goldie to make still another tricky turn on the confusing route leading into Florence.

"These roads are a disgrace," she huffed as they turned around. "You'd think that after fifty years there'd be a direct major highway from Charlotte to Myrtle Beach, but there's not been one iota of improvement since I began coming down here. It's a crime and disgrace, an absolute disgrace."

Her rant stopped when she noticed unexpectedly a magnificent antebellum home on a wooded rise in the far distance. "Lord have mercy, would you just look at that. Almost like some of our gracious old houses around Charleston—and stuck back here in this wasteland. I bet that place is two hundred years old. Sherman must have missed this area." She again seemed lost in her reveries as Goldie slowed down and tried to look.

"Now that, my dear, is what life was like when cotton was king and we had mansions all over South Carolina. Just look at that."

With no warning, a rusty tractor pulled out onto the two-lane road from a dusty drive that led to a crumbling shack with a glider on the porch, but before Ella could even gulp, Goldie had very expertly swung out around it.

"Crazy fool!" Ella yowled at the farmer. "You're a good driver, dear."

Since it was now coming on noon, and Ella feared the dining room at the Priscilla would be closed by the time they arrived and got settled, she told Goldie to begin looking for a respectable place where they could get a bite of lunch. Following a shiny black Buick on the approach to Marion, they both had just noticed the sign for a diner when, from nowhere, a large dog darted in front of the car ahead and was sent flying in the air to the side of the road.

"Oh my Lord, my Lord," Ella cried as Goldie slammed on the brakes and they watched the Buick simply drive on without so much as slowing down. Almost by instinct, and in a fraction of a second, Ella's eyes caught the number of the South Carolina license plate as Goldie uncontrollably bellowed "The bastard!" apologized for her language, and pulled over to the side.

"I got the license number," Ella said with rage in her voice, reaching above the visor for a pencil and jotting it down on the road map. "Go check on the poor dog and see if it's alive."

Blood was already draining from the dog's mouth when Goldie crept up on the motionless body, and it didn't take long to realize the animal was indeed dead. Anybody else, of course, would most likely have had a cell phone in the car to call for help, but since Ella's outmoded convictions precluded that possibility, all the two women could do was vent their anger. Almost sobbing with frustration, Ella sat still a few minutes longer, wondering what to do.

"This has to be reported, ma'am," Goldie said with conviction, "and there's gotta be a police station in that town."

"You're exactly right," Ella agreed as if she'd thought of the idea herself. "Let's go up there to that filling station and get directions to the Marion police."

In almost no time, they found the small, cinder-block building off Main Street and were standing in front of a high counter telling the uniformed, heavy-set officer what had happened.

"We'll take care of it, ma'am," the man drawled indifferently, eyeing Goldie suspiciously. "Happens all the time out there on the highway."

"Well, sir, I got the license-plate number of the car," Ella told him, pointing to the map, "and I'd like to know what you're going to do about finding the driver."

The officer ignored the scribbling on the map. "As I said, ma'am, we'll look into it and try to notify the dog's owner."

"Whoever did that oughta be arrested and put in jail," Goldie protested mildly at first, anxiously fingering one of her silver bracelets.

The man glared at the Indian. "I just said we'd check it out and notify the owner."

Ella's hand was shaking. "I don't think you understand, sir. Somebody in a big black Buick just killed somebody's dog and didn't even have the decency to stop to see if the poor animal was dead or alive. I call that hit-and-run, and we want that person prosecuted. We'll be happy to sign anything as witnesses."

The officer began shifting on his feet impatiently. "That won't be necessary, ma'am. It's only a dog, and we know how to handle these things."

"Only a dog?" Goldie then blared uncharacteristically, her dark eyes burning.

Ella now had real fury in her own eyes. "What do you mean, mister, only a dog? Just what on earth do you mean? A crime has been committed, an inexcusable crime, and if you can't assure me that it'll be fully investigated and this person found and made to pay . . . I want you to know I have every intention of following up on this, and if it means reporting the incident to the state highway patrol, or the ASPCA, or any other authority, rest assured that's exactly what I'll do."

"Now, now, little lady, just calm yourself down. No need to get so keyed up," he said, obviously aware that this cranky woman with the weird-looking Indian meant business and could cause a real commotion. "We'll put out a search for the car, don't you worry, and notify you if we need a statement."

"No, no, I'll contact you," she said, fumbling in her pocketbook for her tiny leather notepad and gold ballpoint and asking him to jot down his phone number. "I won't be easy to reach."

All this time, Goldie stood fuming, and when the two walked out of the station, the officer simply turned to a young woman with big dangling earrings smoking a cigarette behind a desk and, shaking his head, commented, "Some rich old city gal with a damn redskin raising hell 'bout a dead dog. Can you beat it? Boy, what you see these days. Better call Henry 'bout gettin' that animal off the road."

In the diner farther down the highway, Goldie ordered macaroni and cheese and iced tea, but Ella was still so shaken by what had happened that she had an appetite for nothing more than one of her sneaky minibottles of whiskey in her pocketbook poured into the plastic glass of ice water, and one cat-head ham biscuit with gravy.

"Good thing I'm driving, ma'am," Goldie said mildly as Ella emptied the small bottle.

"Oh, hush, woman," Ella snorted, reaching back into her pocketbook, this time for the gold cigarette case.

Although the two women were by now as accustomed to one another as two sisters might be, never would either one have assumed that the relationship was in the least way intimate. Not, however, that this prevented Goldie from bringing up questions occasionally about things that intrigued her.

"Miss Ella, I've always thought that was the most beautiful cigarette case I've ever seen and hope you won't mind me asking where you found it."

Ella sat perfectly still for a moment, then took a sip of her doctored drink. "Of course not, dear. Mr. Earl gave me this case many years ago," she lied, a nervous expression coming over her delicate face.

"Oh, I've never seen one like it and always wondered where you got it. Mr. Earl did have such a wonderful eye for beautiful things, didn't he?"

"Yes, Goldie, he did."

Goldie fingered her cheap bead necklace. "Bud gave me this not long after we got married, and do you know Mr. Earl once complimented me on it?"

"Well, he should have. It's lovely, dear." She took another long sip. "I'm sure you still miss Bud a great deal."

"Oh, yes, I do. Not a day passes that I don't think of him and John. I sing to them every night—a sky song I learned when I was young."

"He was a fine person, Goldie. And John was such a fine young man. Makes you wonder, doesn't it?"

"Yes, ma'am, though the Sacred Spirits have reasons for everything," she replied cryptically, her eyes still fixed on the gold case. "And I also remember Mr. Earl every single night. He was so good to everybody."

Ella patted the back of her silver hair the way she often did when caught off guard by any unexpected statement or question pertaining to her personal life. "Yes, Mr. Earl was special, a very special and good man." She turned her head and stared out the window between the moving traffic at a cotton field across the road that extended far in the distance. "And he always loved this drive down to the beach, and the area's history and people. Why, he could go on for hours about every crop, and major battle of the war, and barbecue, and the pulp industry, and all the old plantations. Mercy, I don't know where he learned it all, but for me and the children it was like one long history lesson every time we made the trip." She hesitated when the waitress placed the food on the table. "You know, we could be sitting at a sidewalk café in Paris, or shopping for antiques in London, or riding on a train to Venice when we did all that traveling in Europe, and Mr. Earl would eventually say he was about ready to feel sand between his toes again and eat peach cobbler, and I'd know then that he was ready to come home. Funny how I happen to think about that now, but that's exactly what he'd say: that he wanted to feel sand between his toes."

Goldie, to whom the travel references meant nothing, took a fork to her macaroni and cheese, but it was still too hot to eat so she blew on it. "I know just how he must have felt, 'cause when it's hot and crazy in Charlotte, and I have to drive around fighting for a parking place in the shopping center, I sometimes remember what it was like in the cool air back on the reservation when my brother and I would go riding in the Nantahala Forest and all I'd hear were birds singing in all directions—just the birds and the sound of twigs cracking under the horses' feet. I've thought about that so many times."

Ella cut into her biscuit and dragged a morsel in the gravy. Then, gazing down at the table while Goldie attacked the macaroni and thinking about what her companion had just said, her mind drifted involuntarily back to a late spring evening in Paris when she and Earl had celebrated her thirtieth birthday with dinner and glass after glass of champagne at La Tour d'Argent, after which he unexpectedly told the taxi driver to take and drop them off at an entrance to the Bois de Boulogne. Ella didn't know he was even aware of the massive park, but there he hailed a horse-drawn carriage for a ride down some of the romantic, tree-lined lanes, and there she experienced one of those moments in time that can never be forgotten. She remembered that she was wearing a fancy, hand-tailored, light green dress with a frilly, plunging neckline that Earl had insisted on buying for her at a shop on the rue Cambon. She remembered the steady clomp of the horses' hooves and the tweeting of birds in the trees overhead. But most of all she remembered his arm around her and the way he pulled her close to kiss her passionately, and how, under the coverlet across their laps, he gently but steadily caressed her thigh till she thought her entire body would explode. She could still almost smell the tangy sweet aroma of champagne on his breath, and just the thought of the prolonged, unbridled manner in which they made love back at the hotel still made her tingle. She knew, of course, that the charm of Paris and just being away sparked instincts in Earl that were much more restrained, or often nonexistent, when he was under the pressures of work at home, but she knew it was also true that, under the right circumstances, there was no man on earth capable of making her feel more like a desirable woman and satisfying her most fervent desires and needs the way her husband had that magic night in Paris.

★ ★ ★

"Looka there, Miss Ella!" Goldie suddenly interrupted the reverie, trying to talk with food in her mouth while pointing eagerly out the window at a long, slatted van loaded with hogs that, for some reason, had come to a halt in the road.

"Pigs," was Ella's only comment as she picked up the bill the waitress had stuck under the salt shaker and took cash out of her pocketbook. "Don't rush, dear, but I really do think we should be getting on our way soon if we want to arrive at the inn in time for a good nap."

Goldie offered to help her up from the table, but Ella fluttered a hand fretfully to indicate she could manage very well herself. "Mercy, woman, you're worse than the children."

Chapter 2

FLESH AND BLOOD

Ella had been as aware as everyone else of the sad demolition years ago of the majestic Ocean Forest Hotel and other landmarks at Myrtle Beach, and she remembered friends back in Charlotte also complaining about other modern changes over the past couple of decades that had transformed much of the entire Grand Strand into a major resort that now engulfed the hitherto independent small beaches of Ocean Drive, Cherry Grove, and Crescent. Nothing, however, could have fully prepared her for not only the sleazy theme restaurants, amusement parks, and strip malls that now lined both sides of Kings Highway but also the towering concrete oceanfront hotels and condos that had replaced most of the gracious old family cottages and inns. Of course, Goldie was awed by all the spectacle and glitz, but she kept her excitement to herself when it became obvious that Miss Ella was nothing less than shocked as they slowly made their way along Ocean Boulevard past one flashy high-rise after another, looking anxiously for a sign that read THE PRISCILLA.

Then there it was, the same pinkish white, shingled, dignified structure recessed off the road that Ella had known in the old days and that stood in noble defiance of progress and trendy vulgarity. Both the inn and its spacious parking lot were virtually camouflaged by old palmettos and tall, thick borders of well-trimmed myrtle hedges that guaranteed an optimum of privacy for the privileged guests, and when she looked up from the car, Ella noticed that every window was now graced by a neat blue awning with a small white *P* in the center of each. On the front was a long, white, bannistered porch with rocking chairs overlooking a wooden terrace and plush lawn between the inn and the ocean, and, as all the locals knew, the formal dining room inside still served what was without question the finest Lowcountry cuisine on the entire beach.

Pulling through the front gate to the main entrance of the inn, they were greeted immediately by an older, uniformed attendant, who opened Ella's door, directed them to the reception area, and said he would park the car and handle the luggage and fishing rods. Inside the quiet, wood-paneled hall, furnished with deep cane armchairs, a handsome bookcase, and tasteful seascapes on the walls, it was as if time had stood still, and when the familiar, salty aroma of fresh sea air swept through the front-porch doors into the vestibule, Ella had the strange, comforting impression that she'd been here only yesterday.

"Young man, when you've finished checking us in," she told the attractive clerk behind the desk, fishing in her pocketbook for a credit card while he glanced furtively at Goldie, "I'd like to have an important word with you."

"Yes, Mrs. Dubose, by all means," he acknowledged cordially in a thick Lowcountry accent, taking the card, running it through a machine for an imprint, and indicating where she should sign the registration form. Ella thought about commenting on the vulgarity of credit cards, but she'd learned that she was just wasting her breath ridiculing this modern phenomenon.

"Do you know what 'incognito' means?" she almost whispered, leaning up and touching the sleeve of his blue blazer.

The lad looked perplexed. "No, ma'am, I can't say I do."

"You don't? Well, I'll tell you. It means somebody who prefers not to be recognized, who's in disguise, and that's the way I'm traveling on this trip—incognito."

"Oh," he said, still baffled by what the elegant lady was trying to put across.

"You see, I and my family were coming to the Priscilla years ago—before you were even born." She stopped to laugh softly to herself. "And I'm now returning with my companion here mainly to rest and relax and not be disturbed—total privacy."

The clerk, his blue eyes wide open, remained quiet a moment, then said, "Oh, yes, ma'am, we try to respect the privacy of all our guests."

Ella frowned slightly, her hand still on his arm. "I don't think you fully understand, young man, so let me try to put it another way. As far as this inn is concerned, I don't exist, I never checked in here, and if there should be any phone calls for me, you've never heard my name. I have my own very personal reasons, and, take my word, there's nothing shady going on, but can you assure me that this request will be honored, and your telephone operator notified, and—"

"Don't forget about Mr. Tyler," Goldie interrupted quietly, nudging her arm.

"Oh, yes, my son from New York City, Mr. Tyler Dubose, will be joining us on the weekend for a few days—I believe you have his reservation—and he also will be staying here incognito."

By now, the poor clerk, who was trying to be sophisticated in accordance with his training, was so confused that all he could do was excuse himself, tap on an office door just off the reception area, and speak momentarily with a much older gentleman dressed in a beige linen suit.

"Good day, Mrs. Dubose," the man greeted, approaching the desk and eyeing the dark-skinned woman with the beads and bracelets before turning his full attention to Ella. "I'm Albert Glover, the general manager, and I understand that you'll not be accepting any incoming calls during your stay with us."

"That's correct, Mr. Glover. In fact, I'd like our registration—and my son's this weekend—to remain anonymous, if that's no problem. I have my reasons."

For an instant, the manager wondered to himself if perhaps the perfectly respectable-looking lady might be either a celebrity or a kook, but then he quickly determined that she was no more than a well-off, harmless eccentric with a peculiar companion who, for whatever reasons, simply wanted to be left totally alone.

"No problem, Mrs. Dubose," he assured in a friendly manner. "As you might know, we're still a very old-fashioned, traditional place and go out of our way to accommodate all our guests' every wish, so our lips are sealed if that's what you ask. And please let us know if there's anything at all we can do to make your stay more pleasant."

Once Ella had thanked him, the two women were shown to their adjoining rooms on the third floor, Ella's on a corner with sweeping views of the sea and coastline, and Goldie's much smaller connecting room on the side. The first thing Ella did was cut off the air-conditioning and open all the windows, and, after hanging up a couple of dresses and leaving the rest of the unpacking to Goldie, she looked down at the blue and white cabanas that were similar to those where she used to sit sewing and watching Big Earl and the children romp in the waves. She now felt tired and a little groggy, and as she gazed out over the ocean with thousands of small whitecaps reflecting the hypnotic afternoon sun, what came to mind first was the day so long ago when she and Jonathan frolicked up the beach in front of the Ocean Forest, and he held her tight around the waist, and she was so in love. Then she remembered worrying, years later, about Tyler one morning strolling

all alone up the beach while his father pitched baseball with
Little Earl, and how she caught up with him and they searched
together for beautiful shells. And next surfaced the vision of
pier fishing with Earl, and pulling in a large blue, and standing
back in horror as he ripped the hook from the struggling fish's
mouth while Little Earl and Liv cheered him on. One by one,
the disparate memories emerged and clashed, and if, sitting
there in a partial trance with the warm, familiar breeze blowing across her venerable body, Ella sensed a remote happiness
being back in her beloved Lowcountry, where important
chapters of her long, rather ordinary life had unfolded, she was
not so distracted by the promise of pleasure and relaxation to
forget the primary reason for this deviant trip. Nor could she
disregard some of the irritating family circumstances back
home that threatened to darken her entire mood.

"We're concerned, Mama, and not just about your physical
health," had been Olivia's exact words that day at Bull's Barbecue.

"When somebody gets to your age, there're changes in the
system that can affect everything we do, from making important decisions to . . . driving a car," had been Little Earl's added
two bits.

Not that Ella had really wanted to go to lunch with her
son and daughter on that hectic Saturday. It had been a trying
week, so much so that if one single thing else went wrong, she
thought she might reach for the gun in her pocketbook and
blow her own brains out. First, she was still recovering from a
nasty touch of the colic, most likely brought on by a strange
shrimp dish she'd ordered at Phoenix Garden when her old
friend Lilybelle Armstrong invited her out to celebrate Ella's
seventy-third birthday. Because of a terrible, really inexcusable
mix-up, the man due to clean the crystal chandelier in the dining room had yet to show up. Nor had young Billy next door
come over on Wednesday after school as promised to help

Miss Ella move one of the two heavy artificial Christmas trees on wheels from behind a large Indonesian screen in the sun room to a corner of the library.

All week long, her soaps on TV had been preempted hour after hour by the news of some factory or house or bus that had been blown up over in Israel. And as if that annoyance were not enough, Ella now had good reason to worry that the garbage man might start asking questions about the potted marijuana plant growing taller each day in a remote sunny area of the spacious porch that wrapped itself round two sides of the house. She had almost burned the bottoms of jelly cookies intended to be served at her charity league luncheon, then Lucy, sick as a dog with a migraine, had called to change the regular hair and manicure appointment at the beauty parlor. And what should arrive in the mail from up North but a copy of Tyler's new memoirs revealing not only certain aspects of his unusual life that should have been kept private, but also a few embarrassing details about the family that were not at all necessary.

All of which meant that Ella Dubose was not exactly in the best frame of mind when Little Earl called out of the blue to announce that he and Olivia would like to drop by the house on Saturday and take their mother out to Bull's Barbecue for lunch. Ella immediately suspected something shady since it just wasn't normal for her younger son and daughter to pay a visit together, much less pick a Saturday to eat barbecue when everybody in Charlotte knew how horrendous Saturday crowds could be at any restaurant. Maybe if Earl had said that he and Betty Jane, his wife, were simply planning to drive over to visit, Ella wouldn't have been so leery, but no, it just wasn't normal for the two of them to be coming together and wasting a good Saturday that could be and usually was spent with their own children or some friends.

"Son," Ella began to beg off, "that's awfully sweet of you

both, but to tell you the honest truth, it really doesn't suit this weekend. I've had a pretty bad week, and besides, much as I love it, I'm not one bit sure I should be eating barbecue after this little intestinal spell I've had."

"Oh, Mama, you know as well as I do that half of that's in your head," he had said in the nonchalant way he adopted when trying to sway his mother. "What you need is to get out of that big house and forget about your problems for a while. If you don't feel up to barbecue, you can always have a good bowl of Brunswick stew, and a few hush puppies, and plenty of iced tea, You know how much you love the Brunswick stew out at Bull's, and it might do your tummy lots of good. And Liv's dying for a barbecue plate."

Ella stood her ground. "Earl, honey, please don't try to humor me, for heaven's sake. As I said, this has not been a very good week, and I'm aware when my nerves are on end, and I certainly know what I should and should not eat after I've had a little setback. I also know that I have no intention, no intention whatsoever, of waiting over there for a table on a busy Saturday."

Earl could be as persistent and stubborn as his mother, not only at his company but when dealing with any of his kin. "Now, Mama, I think you've forgotten, I think it's completely escaped your mind, that I've known Bull Godwin ever since we started coaching Little League together, and that Bull will have me a table ready anytime faster than you can shake a stick. All it takes is a quick phone call, so you can't use that as an excuse."

"Son, I'm not going to argue with you till I'm blue in the face. Some of the girls from the church are coming over this afternoon to strip palms and make crosses for Sunday, so I don't have time to argue. Goldie's here now helping me fix tea sandwiches and roll nutty fingers, and we still have to straighten up the sunroom. If you and Liv want to drop by just for a visit, fine, but I'm not making any promises about going to Bull's. Just depends on my condition."

Ella had every right to wonder about her son and daughter coming over together to take her out to lunch on Saturday. Not that she'd ever had any reason to distrust her own flesh and blood. It was simply because she couldn't remember the last time just the three of them had gone out together to eat barbecue or anything else, and her maternal instincts told her that something odd was up—something peculiar that she could detect merely from the tone of Earl's voice on the phone. Of course, had she been a fly on the wall at his and Betty Jane's home the previous weekend while the two of them and Olivia sat around the kitchen table drinking cola or coffee and nibbling on snacks, she'd have known in an instant why any wariness was justified.

"Haven't you noticed some weird changes in Mama Ella's behavior the last few months?" Betty Jane asked Olivia, twisting a clump of tinted blond hair with her thumb and index finger.

Olivia, wearing a jersey with CAROLINA stenciled over the front, was sipping coffee from a mug with the figure of a blue ram on one side. Her short, auburn hair was flecked with gray, and it was obvious that one day it would be as radiantly silver as her mother's.

"Nothing Mama does these days really surprises me," she answered, snickering in a childish way.

"Well, we've noticed, and it worries the hell out of us," Earl said, popping another small cheese biscuit from a tin into his mouth and washing it down with Diet Coke. "And I think we need to talk about it before . . ." He stopped to listen to the TV in the den when there was a roar from the crowd at a basketball game. "Did B. J. tell you what Mama was doing just the other day when she drove over there to return some of her china? She was baking dog biscuits. Dog biscuits!"

Betty Jane, who couldn't have weighed more than a hundred pounds and dressed in expensive skirts and blouses even when at home, now had a stunned look on her face. "That's right. Baking dog biscuits for dogs in the neighborhood. Can you imagine?"

"Sounds more like something Goldie might do," Olivia uttered.

"Listen," Earl added facetiously, "if Mama decided to dynamite the Charlotte Coliseum, that damn squaw would be right there to light the fuse."

"Well, one thing that really does bother me is how Mama seems to be having more of her strange spells," Olivia said with more concern. "Haven't you noticed recently she sometimes just stares into space like she doesn't know where she is?"

Earl leaned back from the table, sucked in his ample gut, then ran a hand over the almost totally bald top of his head that betrayed his forty-nine years. "Honey, that's part of what's worrying hell out of me."

Olivia's expression became even more serious. "Lord, you're not saying you think Mama could be headed for something like a bad stroke or . . . Alzheimer's?"

"Who knows?" he grunted in exasperation, shaking his head and reaching for a handful of potato chips. "She's got that heart murmur, and Dr. Singer's been begging her for ages to have some more tests, but you know how bullheaded Mama can be when it comes to doctors and tests and all that."

"Have you talked to Tyler recently about this?" Betty Jane asked, pulling at the large, pear-shaped diamond ring on her finger.

There was another clamor on the TV, which moved Earl to jump up and peer around the corner for a minute to see what was happening at the game.

"Tyler?" he muttered as he sat back down, a disgusted frown on his slightly tanned face. "How could I talk to Ty when he and lover boy were living it up over in Paris? Last time I brought up the subject of Mama's health, he said Mama knew what she was doing and started to raise Cain, so I just let it drop. Of course, Big Brother sits up there in New York with all his fancy friends living high on the hog while we watch out for Mama and wonder what will happen next." He leaned back in the chair, trying to hear the sports commentary, then fixed his bulging eyes on his sister. "You know Mama can do no wrong in Ty's eyes, but, dammit, one day he's gonna have to face reality about what it's like for us down here. As if he ain't already brought enough disgrace to this family."

Little Earl made no pretense about the way he felt about his older brother—not to his sister, or his wife, or his mother, or anybody else in the family except maybe Tyler himself. Not that there'd ever been any real open strife between the brothers, or that the two weren't civil enough to one another in a respectful Southern way on the rare occasion, usually at Christmas, when Tyler flew home to North Carolina to visit his mother. But it was no big secret that Earl had little use for Tyler and his way of life, or that the two couldn't have been more different in their sophistication and even in their physical characteristics.

Happily married to Betty Jane for nearly thirty years and the proud father of a fine son and daughter, Earl was the president of Charlotte's largest and most prestigious printing and engraving company. Founded by his father and a partner when Big Earl and Ella moved to Charlotte back in the forties, Creative Graphics had been a highly lucrative success over the years, and from the day Little Earl began working at the company after graduating at State in Raleigh with a degree in business management, it was taken for granted that he'd inherit the whole enterprise when Big Earl passed on.

Little Earl knew everything there was to know about printing and engraving, and nobody could ever have accused him of not being even more ambitious and industrious than his daddy had always been. As a result, he not only commanded the utmost respect throughout Charlotte's business community and his health club, but he and Betty Jane enjoyed considerable social status at Christ Episcopal Church and Quail Hollow Country Club, as well as prized seats at Lowe's Motor Speedway and all NFL Panthers games. Although heavyset like so many Southern men who eat three square meals a day, he had always been called Little Earl within the family, not because of his size but to distinguish him from his daddy. Most friends simply called him Earl, but at the company he was respectfully addressed by employees as either Mr. Earl or Mr. Dubose, and at work he was never seen without a jacket and tie, much as he hated dressing up. Like many prosperous Charlotteans, he and Betty Jane had a weekend retreat up at Lake Norman near Davidson College, and that's where Earl could really relax in a pair of jeans, or cutoffs, or bathing suit without compromising his image as one of the city's more reputable citizens.

Tyler, on the other hand, couldn't have been less interested in family or civic activities, religion, social clubs, and certainly not sports and quaint lakeside cabins. Almost two years older than Little Earl and much more independent by nature, he had received a PhD in comparative literature at Duke in the early seventies, landed an assistant professorship at Princeton, and might well have become a leading scholar of English Romantic literature had an unfortunate and well-publicized indiscretion with a male student not suddenly ended his promising vocation and sent him fleeing to Manhattan to pick up the pieces of his life and try his hand at writing fiction. News of his disgrace that leaked back to Charlotte shocked and embarrassed Big Earl and everybody else except Ella, and even after

Tyler's first popular novel became a best seller all over the country and launched what would develop into a phenomenal career, most Charlotteans still chose to dwell with disapproval on the mostly fabricated gossip about his private life up North rather than on the hometown boy's literary success.

Rather elegant in demeanor and still remarkably handsome for his age, Tyler, no doubt, had spread his wings far and wide in younger days, as revealed in his new juicy book of memoirs. But the truth was that, for a number of years, he had been living rather conventionally with Barry, an intelligent, successful fine arts dealer originally from Chicago with whom he shared both a well-appointed duplex apartment on East 67th Street in Manhattan and a comfortable but modest home out in Amagansett on Long Island, where Ella would occasionally visit the two. What possibly caused the most resentment in his Charlotte family, in fact, was the deep affection that Tyler and his mother had always shown toward one another, a love and devotion that bordered on adoration and that many felt was simply based on their mutually rebellious, liberal, and downright eccentric personalities. Even as a teenager, Tyler had never been very close to Big Earl, since the two shared very few interests, and it's for sure that he never had much in common with his younger brother. As for Olivia, Tyler had always been rather protective of his sister when they were growing up, since she was never the most popular girl with the boys in her class, but after she eventually got married and began raising a family, the relationship with her older brother became more and more remote and impersonal.

Such friction had undoubtedly caused Ella some distress, not only because she loved every member of her family but because she considered the large family home on Colville Road to be a happy haven where she and Big Earl had lived since the fifties, the house where Tyler, Little Earl, and Olivia had all been reared, and the house where everybody should be able to gather together any time in total harmony. The white Colonial Revival structure was certainly not as grand as the stately mansions along Queens Road West or even some of the more modern spreads out in the Providence Plantation area of town, but it was a gracious, comfortable, two-story home with attractive grounds in a fine old neighborhood. Ella loved her house, and as long as she was physically and mentally capable of faring for herself, she planned to remain there till, as she often proclaimed, they carried her out feet first. And except for a slight heart murmur and the first signs of mild glaucoma, which she occasionally combated by secretly smoking a little home-grown marijuana, Ella was still more fit, energetic, and alert at seventy-three than many women ten years younger. It could even be said, in fact, that she could conceivably outlive Tyler, who, unbeknownst to everyone in the family and to practically everyone up North except his doctors and Barry, had been waging a nasty battle with colon cancer for much of the past year.

"Of course, you know what really drives me to distraction is Mama wheeling that big car all over Charlotte day and night—even when she's been drinking," Earl went on, popping the tab on another Diet Coke. "I mean, I don't know when her eyes were last checked, and all we need is for somebody to call and announce that she's just plowed into three or four cars and killed God knows how many people."

"Mama really shouldn't be driving at her age," Olivia said in her simple way. "Lord, what if she had one of her spells out on Independence Boulevard?"

Betty Jane chuckled. "Well, all I can say is I don't want to be around when somebody so much as suggests to Mama Ella that she should give up her white chariot."

"B.J., I don't find one thing funny about this," Earl scolded his wife. "The point is, we gotta have a long talk with Mama and try to convince her to at least go to Dr. Singer for a thorough checkup. Then we might have some clue to what we're dealing with."

Betty Jane pretended to fan her face with one hand. "Boy oh boy, the fur's gonna fly."

Chapter 3

DULL GOLD

Rising from her chair at the inn overlooking the sparkling ocean, Ella decided to take a nap before getting dressed and going downstairs with Goldie for drinks and dinner. But since the thought of that fretful lunch with her younger son and daughter back in Charlotte continued to prey on her mind, all she could do was lie wide awake on the bed, stare at the ceiling, and reflect further on that and the real reason she'd decided so compulsively to flee to the beach. Then, as if overcome by a strange urge, she got up and went over to the bureau, opened the top drawer, and nervously rummaged beneath a pile of carefully folded elegant silk scarves for the discolored package of tattered letters tied together with frail string that, back home, she'd kept concealed with other old mementos in a shoe box. Since the yellowed envelopes had been mailed from U.S. Army bases in England and France during World War II, there were no postmarks, and since the writing on the time-worn, creased pages was all in pencil, many words and parts of whole sentences were now too smudged or faded to read. Still, sitting at the foot of the bed, Ella opened a few of the letters at random, and as she began to scan the contents for the first time in nearly forty years, she was so gripped by a terrible wave of nostalgia and confused emotions that she could feel her heart pounding.

> *"My darling Ella, Tonight, in . . . seemed like a hundred years . . . in that pretty polka-dot dress as the train pulled out."*
>
> *"Over two dozen casualties to handle today, but we know the job must be done, and all we pray is the unit . . . before you know it."*
>
> *"My sweet Ella, Do you remember when you got that bone caught in your gum at Perditas? Well, yesterday when we were on patrol near Louviers, a very . . . farm woman offered . . . began laughing my head off."*
>
> *". . . promise when this hell is finally over and we're back together, we'll . . . teach me how to tango like Valentino. How I miss you. Always yours, Jonathan."*

For a while longer, she continued to look through the troubling letters, but when the exercise seemed to produce more anxiety than revelations that might help her carry through her self-imposed mission, she tucked them back into the drawer and purposefully distracted her thoughts back to the present by once again pondering the annoying implications revealed at lunch with her two youngest children.

When, in fact, Little Earl and Olivia had arrived at their mother's shortly before noon, Ella had still been wavering over whether her system was yet up to eating at Bull's. But after Little Earl coaxed and coaxed, and again mentioned the onion hush puppies, and added that he and Liv were both hungry as dogs, she had finally given in if for no other reason than to stop all the bickering and make her children happy.

And, just as Earl had promised, there was indeed a booth ready for the Dubose family, even though at least a dozen other customers milling about the lounge area were waiting patiently to be seated. Almost immediately, Earl and Olivia both ordered the chopped barbecue platter that included coleslaw, french fries, and a cup of Brunswick stew, and Earl told the waitress to bring also a basket of hush puppies and a pitcher of iced tea. Overcome by the aroma of smoky meat that filled the entire restaurant, Ella dropped all her defenses and decided to have a barbecue sandwich. Then, after asking the pretty waitress if she could have just a glass of ice water, she began rummaging in her dark green leather pocketbook and slyly pulled out a small silver flask that she furtively cupped in her wrinkled hand.

"Oh, Mama, you're not," Earl whined disparagingly, shifting his eyes to see if anybody close by was watching.

"I most certainly am," Ella said, "and I don't want to hear a peep from either one of you. You know I enjoy a little nip when I go out, especially when I'm getting over an upset, and if your friend Bull Godwin would have the gumption to get a liquor license for this place like every decent restaurant in Charlotte has, maybe I wouldn't be reduced to having to bootleg my own."

"Mama, what if the waitress notices the color of the water?" Olivia asked nervously, rubbing the front of her V-neck rose cashmere sweater.

"Well, honey, have I ever embarrassed you in public?" she answered indifferently in her rather raspy voice. "I'll simply tell her it's a medication I have to take before eating—that's what. Now, for heaven's sake, would you two just mind your own business and tell me what this is all about?"

Olivia, sitting beside her brother, glanced up at him.

"What's what all about, Mama?" he pretended confidently, laughing.

Before Ella could answer, there was a muffled beeping inside the left side pocket of Earl's jacket, and when he pulled the cell phone out, his mother frowned in disgust.

"Hi, Frankie," Earl drawled. "Naw, I'm busy this afternoon with my mama and sister. Maybe next Saturday. Yeah, I'll give you a call. Thanks, ole buddy."

"Lord, I hate those vulgar contraptions," Ella said as he rammed the phone back into his pocket. "Oughta be outlawed—like computers."

"Mama, why do you hate anything modern and practical?" he commented. "Cell phones are here to stay, so you better get used to them. If you'd let me get you one, you'd see how convenient they are—and what they could mean in a bad emergency."

"Over my dead body," Ella mumbled, feeling the side of her hair.

After the waitress returned with a pitcher of tea and the water, Ella very deftly poured from her flask into the glass of water, stirred the ice with a spoon, and took a sip.

"Now listen, you two, you don't both sacrifice a perfectly nice Saturday just to eat barbecue with your old mother—not without Betty Jane or Jesse or one of the kids. So what's up?"

"Oh, Mama, don't be like that," Earl said, reaching over and playfully popping her arm. "The three of us haven't been together by ourselves in a coon's age, and I don't think you realize how much Liv and I worry about you being over there alone in that big house all the time and not getting out more."

Ella put her glass on the table, reached again in her pocketbook, and took out a dull gold cigarette case with the engraved initials EPH barely discernable on one side.

Olivia looked surprised, almost shocked. "Mama, you told us—you promised—you'd stopped smoking those filthy things."

Ella lit a cigarette with a small gold butane lighter and took a long, delicious draw. "Oh, honey, I have—almost. I've been quitting for the past forty years, as you know, and now go days without smoking. But when I have a cocktail in a restaurant, or my nerves are really on end . . ." She took another drag, then picked her glass back up and gazed at Earl. "And, Son, I don't know what in this world you're talking about when you say I'm not getting out of the house enough. I mean, I go to the beauty parlor every Friday and to church every single Sunday, and have my charity league and Bible class, and go to the store with Goldie at least twice a week, and have lunch with Lulu Woodside, and Folly, and Jinks Ferguson, and . . . Why, the very idea that I don't get out enough. You two just don't know what all I do. I stay busy as a bee, and maybe if you called more often . . ."

Earl twisted his mouth to one side and said, "I've never understood what you see in that Mrs. Ferguson."

"Why, I don't know what you mean, Son. Jinks Ferguson is a very nice lady who devotes lots of time to the charity league."

"Well, I just don't trust any of those Catholics with all their sick hang-ups."

"Now, why would you make an asinine remark like that?"

"Well, we could start with Mrs. Ferguson breeding six children and then mention her love affair with the gin bottle, couldn't we?" He chuckled. "People at the club still talk about the night she got so tanked that one of her sons had to be called to come take her home."

Ella drew back indignantly like some startled exotic bird. "That is absolutely not true, not a word of it—just malicious gossip. I happen to know that, at the time, Jinks was still getting over her husband's tragic death, and that she was simply on the verge of a bad nervous breakdown. I'm sure Jinks enjoys a social drink from time to time like the rest of us, but I can tell you that at our meetings I've never seen her touch anything but a nice glass of sherry."

Earl twisted his mouth again smugly and raised an eyebrow. "Yeah, with a float of gin on top. Those Catholics are crazy people—just eaten up with guilt over everything."

"Son, sometimes I think you've lost your mind when you

make ugly remarks like that. None of that nonsense about Jinks is true, and, besides, it's not one bit of your business what she or any other of my friends do."

The waitress brought the food, and the second Little Earl saw the hot hush puppies, he popped one in his mouth without even buttering it. He asked his mother if she didn't want to taste the Brunswick stew, placing the small bowl in front of her, so she took a spoonful and pronounced the thick concoction to be excellent—as good as her own. She then asked about the grandchildren and wondered why she didn't see more of them. Earl, who had both a son and daughter, said that Carter was already showing great promise at the company, and that he and B. J. had every reason to think he and Lena Rose Hitchcock were much more serious about each other than they let on. As for daughter Bippie, well, Bippie had been spending more and more time helping some Italian guy from Monroe run the wine shop over in Sardis Mall, and all anybody could do was pray there wasn't more to that shady relationship than met the eye. Cameron Lee, Olivia and Jesse's only child, was still working hard to set up his podiatry clinic just off Park Road, Olivia informed, and while they couldn't be more proud of him ever since he finally finished all his training down at Emory, they did wish—they prayed every night—that he'd hurry up and meet the right girl and think as much about starting a family as playing golf every weekend and becoming a rich foot doctor.

Earl wolfed down his entire platter before Ella had taken three bites of her sandwich, but Olivia, who was always battling her weight, left some barbecue on her plate and didn't touch the french fries. Earl had never managed to take off the thirty pounds he put on after he stopped smoking some years ago, and, like most reformed smokers who tend to substitute food for nicotine, he was now fidgety with nothing more to satisfy his appetite than glass after glass of iced tea.

"As I was saying a little while ago, Mama," he resumed almost impatiently, "I and B. J. and Liv here worry our heads off about you over there in that house alone at night without so much as a cell phone in case of emergencies."

"Oh, please, Son, let's not beat that dead horse again. You know how I loathe all those modern gadgets and will not have one in my home. So would you please hush about that once and for all?"

"Okay, but we've been doing a lotta thinking, Mama, and we think we all need to talk about your health and well-being."

Ella put her sandwich down in her dainty way, took another slow sip of the whiskey in her glass, and glared at him as if the reality of the situation was beginning to dawn on her. "There's not one thing wrong with me."

"How would you know, Mama?" he blared. "You haven't seen a doctor in at least three years."

"So that's what this little get-together is all about. You two want me to go to Dr. Singer and let him give me the once-over. Right?"

Appearing more agitated, Earl poured more tea into his glass. "Well, frankly, Mama, you just haven't been acting like your old self lately—whether you're aware of it or not. And all we're asking, all we're begging, is that you go to Dr. Singer and let him give you a complete checkup the way any normal person does from time to time."

Ella began tapping her perfectly manicured red fingernails on the table. "There's not one thing wrong with me—nothing— and if there's anything I hate, it's a doctor fooling around with me, and making me take one pill after the next, and lecturing me about smoking and drinking. I've just had lots on my mind lately—that's all—and I will thank you both just to let me attend to my own affairs. I think you've forgotten who somehow raised you."

"Mama, you're not being very reasonable," Olivia chimed in, picking at a french fry as if debating whether to eat it. "What if they found something wrong?"

"If they did, my dear, I probably wouldn't do a thing about it—not at my age. I now believe simply in letting nature take its course."

When Ella lit another cigarette, leaving the rest of her sandwich uneaten, Olivia fanned the air, prompting her mother to exclaim, "Oh, for heaven's sake, child, stop being so silly."

Earl drew back in his seat and swept a hand over his stomach, which protruded well over his belt. "What about your heart condition, Mama? You know you have a bad heart, just like Paw Paw had."

"I have nothing of the sort. They told me it was just a slight murmur, and I don't classify a murmur as a bad heart. And besides, my daddy died of pneumonia, not a heart attack."

Earl reached over for Olivia's fries and dragged them through a small mound of catsup on the plate before stuffing them into his mouth in a single bite as his mother watched and frowned.

"And since we're here obviously not for just a nice Saturday lunch but to discuss health and doctors," Ella continued in irritation, "I could say that at the rate you're going, Son, I'll end up burying you long before I go to meet my maker."

"That's ridiculous, Mama," he said. "Sure, I'm a couple of pounds overweight, but I don't smoke or drink or stay up till the wee hours the way you sometimes do, and Dr. Singer told me just last month at my physical that I'm basically fit as a fiddle."

Ella slowly rubbed the gold cigarette case and sat very quietly for a moment. "Can we please just drop the subject and talk about something more pleasant?"

"But we're concerned, Mama," Olivia said. "And not just about your physical health."

Again, Ella didn't budge, debating whether to argue further or insist that they get up and leave.

"What are you implying, honey? That I'm going off my rocker? That I'm losing my mind?"

"Of course not, Mama. But you know as well as we do that when somebody gets to your age, there're changes in the system that can affect everything we do, from making important decisions to . . . driving a car. And remember, Mama, that Goldie's not always around to help."

Ella's expression suddenly became almost hostile. "So now you're saying I shouldn't be driving my car. Is that what you two are getting at?"

Fidgeting even more, Earl buttered another hush puppy, even though it was now cold.

"Mama, all we're saying, all we're trying to put across, is that we're worried sick that something really bad could happen if you don't start taking better care of yourself and maybe make a few changes. Is it so wrong for two children to worry about their mother?"

"Have you two forgotten that I also have another child, and you have an older brother, who most likely disagrees with everything you're saying?" she stated sarcastically.

"Of course not, Mama," Earl drawled in exasperation. "And I think Ty's just as concerned as we are, as Daddy would be if he was still here."

"Tyler minds his own business, like he should, which is one reason we rarely have a cross word."

"Yeah, all Ty has to worry about up there is his next party, and gettin' his name in the paper, and his next million, and . . . that Barry," Earl cracked indiscreetly.

Ella slapped her hand on the table, then began reaching for her pocketbook and light sweater next to her. "You'll not talk about your brother like that. I won't stand for it. And as for my condition, you let me worry about that, okay? When I'm no longer able to function normally and think I'm becoming a burden to you all, I'll be the first to make some changes, but till then, I'm still in charge of my life. Is that understood? This conversation has made me almost nauseous, so would you kindly pay the check? Goldie and I were planning to put out some marigolds in the side yard, so I'd like to go home."

By the time Earl had put some bills on top of the small paper tab and pulled himself up from the booth to give his mother a hand, she was already headed for the shiny black Lexus SUV parked outside.

"Why anybody in his right mind would want to drive one of these vulgar tanks," Ella grumbled as Earl almost hoisted her into the front seat of the enormous vehicle.

On the way back, Earl and Olivia didn't have much more to say, and Ella's mind was going a hundred miles an hour as she sat silently and gazed at a median in the road bursting with giant yellowbells. When the children dropped her off at the house after the fretful lunch, Goldie was already on her knees in the side garden loosening the soil with a spade, flats of marigolds spread out on the yard. Normally, Ella's role would have been to hand her the multicolored flowers and direct exactly where they should be placed, but this time she told Goldie that she had a sick headache and just to plant the marigolds as she liked. She then proceeded into the house without saying another word and collapsed in her favorite reading chair in the library next to a picture window overlooking a massive pin oak at the edge of the lawn. For a long while, she simply sat there, gently fondling her gold cigarette case and glancing wistfully from time to time at the huge tree. Finally, she got up, went to one of the mahogany bookshelves, and removed a flimsy photo album that she carefully opened on her knees, turning the brittle pages slowly till she came to a faded black-and-white picture of a young couple standing arm in arm on a beach in front of what looked like an immense, opulent, white hotel. Still rubbing the case, she stared at the photo as if mesmerized, tears soon forming in her delicate blue eyes. Closing the album and dabbing her eyes with a soft cotton hanky from her pocketbook, she next fixed her gaze on the framed picture of Tyler on a tea table taken when he graduated from Myers Park High School. Then she looked out again at the oak, which was full of tiny, silver-green leaves that shaded a large area of the lawn, and it was at that moment that Ella decided what she had to do, before it was too late, to come to terms with certain ghosts of the past that had haunted her for an entire lifetime.

Chapter 4

THE SQUAW

Unable to nap at the inn but determined to block out further memories of what her children had implied (if not threatened) over lunch, Ella decided that nothing would be more soothing and likely to take her mind off family problems than a warm shower. Afterward, she called downstairs for a bucket of ice, and, as she and Earl had always done when traveling, mixed a dressing drink to be sipped while deciding on which outfit to wear for dinner. She then knocked on Goldie's door to see if she was ready to go down for a cocktail on the front porch and to remind her that the dining room was rather formal. Predictably, Goldie's idea of formality was a brightly colored, belted tunic, a turquoise necklace, and ringlets of silver bracelets that made a stark contrast with Ella's classic pale blue linen dress, single strand of pearls, and light navy sweater she wore over her shoulders. Once, however, they were seated in old-fashioned rocking chairs and Ella noticed two young boys sitting on the banister decked out in the same jeans, open-neck polo shirts, and sneakers she'd become accustomed to seeing back home even at the club, she didn't give a second thought to Goldie's bizarre ensemble.

What she did think twice about, and what actually startled

her momentarily, was not only how much one of the boys had an uncanny resemblance to someone she had cared about deeply in her youth, but also the way the old but very dignified gentleman with them would occasionally glance over in Ella's direction as he and an attractive woman next to him rocked away and chatted while sipping drinks. The man, who was slender and had a full head of hair as silver as Ella's, was nicely dressed in a dark green jacket and dapper bow tie, and while it was always possible these days that the lady in a stunning yellow and white dress could have been his wife, Ella chose to believe that she was his daughter and the boys his grandsons. The question was soon mostly solved when another, younger man in a blazer showed up, squeezed the woman's shoulders and pecked her on the cheek, then began cavorting with one of the boys the way fathers and sons often do. Not long after, the same waiter in a white uniform who had served Ella her whiskey and soda and Goldie a Coke brought the gentleman a clear iced drink with a wedge of lime stuck on the edge of the tall glass.

"It'll be so good seeing Tyler again," Ella said almost wistfully to Goldie, making the move to prop one foot against the banister the way she once did, then deciding against it.

"Oh, yes, ma'am. I know how you always miss him."

"And Lord, I still worry my head off about him—even after all these years. Isn't that silly?"

"No, ma'am, I don't think it's silly at all for any mother to worry about her son, no matter how old he is. That just seems natural to me." She twirled the ice in her Coke with a finger the way she'd seen Ella do. "I remember how I used to worry myself sick when John would be late from school."

"If only Tyler didn't live so far away," Ella continued to ramble as if lost in her thoughts. "But, as you know, his work keeps him up there."

"Yes, ma'am. I'm sure you sometimes wish Mr. Tyler had a family to look out after him."

Ella snapped her head around at the Indian, her eyes wide open, and said curtly, "And what in this world ever gave you that idea?"

Goldie, who usually had a fixed smile on her auburn, smooth, almost sculpted face, grimaced, fingering her necklace. "Oh, you know what I mean, Miss Ella. If only he had a regular family, maybe you wouldn't worry so much."

"My dear, Barry is enough family for Tyler, and you should know that by now. Tyler's different from most folks, and not everybody needs a houseful of kids to be happy."

"Now, Miss Ella, you know I wasn't saying exactly that," she stumbled, "and I did like Mr. Barry that one time I met him at the house—I liked him a lot. A real gentleman."

"He certainly is," Ella proclaimed more calmly. "And he's very devoted to Tyler. That I don't doubt for one minute."

Goldie would have liked to explain further what she meant by the comment, but she not only knew never to pry too deeply into Ella's emotions, but she'd also learned that to argue with this stubborn lady was usually pretty futile.

Goldie Russell had been Ella's housekeeper and basic cook for over twenty years, but ever since Big Earl's sudden death from a massive stroke, she had also become something of a formal companion for Ella, who depended on her increasingly to help with various socials, to shop and tend the garden, and even to drive the white Cadillac when the weather was particularly nasty. Goldie was a robust, full-blooded Cherokee Indian, born and raised on the reservation up in the Great Smoky Mountain National Park not far from Asheville, and the story was that her first name had been derived from that of a grandmother called Golden Bird. When still a young woman with glistening, long, straight, black hair down to her waist, prominent facial features, and large hazel eyes, Goldie had first been noticed by Bud Russell one weekend at a bowling alley in Charlotte while she and a couple of friends were visiting the big city to participate in an arts and crafts fair. One thing led to another, and before the evening was over, the two had spent hours together eating hamburgers and drinking beer.

Bud worked for Big Earl as a pressman at Creative Graphics, a skillful, reliable, self-confident employee who liked his job, got along well with everyone at the company, and had no further ambition than to meet the right woman and one day start a family. Infatuated with Goldie and impervious to the ribbing by pals who couldn't begin to understand how a normal, good ole boy could be attracted to a "redskin," Bud made a couple of weekend trips up to Cherokee just to see her again, and take her out bowling in Asheville, and even go deer hunting with her in the mountains. Of course, Goldie's family and others in the tribe no more approved of her cavorting with a white man than Bud's parents and friends condoned his fooling around with some Indian. Neither, however, allowed these prejudices to affect their feelings for each other, and soon Goldie, who'd been working part-time in a gift shop on the reservation ever since finishing high school, was taking the bus down to Charlotte to spend weekends with Bud at his cabin on the Catawba River. The two bowled and fished together, and shopped at Kmart, and went to barbecues thrown by a few of Bud's friends who came to accept and like Goldie once they got to know her. Strangers in public who were cruel enough to voice derogatory remarks at the Indian either received a merciless tongue-lashing from Bud or picked themselves up off the ground.

To partially placate Goldie's family, the two were eventually married at a very ritualistic, colorful, and festive ceremony on the reservation with Goldie dressed in full tribal regalia, then again at a much more modest wedding in Bud's Baptist church out in Pineville. Big Earl was seriously reluctant to attend when both he and Ella were invited, but Ella insisted that it was the least he could do for such a hardworking, loyal employee, and nothing made Bud prouder than seeing the Duboses among the handful of well-wishers—especially when his own parents refused to show up. Ella even brought one of her caramel pound cakes to the wedding as a gift.

Bud and Goldie moved into a small house in a working-class neighborhood off Freedom Drive a few months after they were married, and Goldie assimilated happily into her new culture, cutting her raven black hair up to the neck, gradually forsaking some of her long, multicolored, belted smocks and beaded necklaces for tight jeans, cotton blouses, and gold chains like those worn by other young women around her, and learning to cook beef short ribs, fried chicken, stuffed bell peppers, buttermilk biscuits, and other Southern dishes that Bud and his friends loved to eat. At one point, she took a job doing custodian work at Mercy Hospital to help Bud save some money for their future, but when they learned she was pregnant, which thrilled them both beyond words, Bud put his foot down and demanded that she stay home and take good care of herself till the baby came.

Goldie gave birth to a healthy boy, but the delivery was difficult, and for reasons Goldie and Bud discussed only with a doctor, it was determined that the couple should never try to have another baby. The child had Goldie's bronze complexion and high cheekbones and Bud's deep-set brown eyes, and they named him John after her father, John Blacksmith. For the next number of years, the three led a very simple but happy life. Little John did reasonably well in school and learned to ignore careless remarks made by other kids about him being a half-breed, and even relatives up on the reservation, where the family visited regularly, gradually developed a certain pride in the boy. At home, Goldie even made sure that he learned to speak Cherokee and acquaint himself with tribal traditions.

He and Bud were as close as any son and father could be, going to ball games and the racetrack together, fishing in the crappiethons at Lake Wylie, and venturing across the state line from time to time to shoot ducks down in South Carolina. Unfortunately, it was during one of these duck-hunting forays that the tragedy occurred that would change Goldie's life forever. Bud and John had left home in the pickup one Saturday morning at the crack of dawn and were headed toward Fort Mill in dense fog when they collided head-on just across the state line with a tractor trailer transporting tons of auto parts. The driver of the eighteen-wheeler walked away without a scratch, but Bud and his son were killed instantly, their bodies barely recognizable when the state police arrived on the gory scene. The rig driver swore that the small truck had simply veered into the wrong lane, and since there were no witnesses or suspicious tire marks on the road to disprove his story, he was not even called in for further questioning. When Goldie received the horrid news, the shock was such that neighbors had to take her to the hospital emergency room for sedation, and after she was found the next day in the house on her knees with ritualistic blood smeared on her face from a self-inflicted hand wound, chanting incoherently in words nobody could understand, Big Earl was called to arrange for a doctor.

Big Earl and Ella both went to the funeral, and it was there that Ella, taking sincere pity on the devastated young Indian, told Goldie to call if she ever needed help or advice or even work. Bud had been meaning to take out some life insurance just six months before the accident, but since he never got around to it, Goldie would have been virtually destitute if Earl had not seen fit to provide a little financial compensation till she got back on her feet. As the months passed, Goldie did take on odd jobs at places like Winn-Dixie and Wal-Mart just to make house payments, hung out with a few close friends at the bowling alley and a diner where she used to go with Bud and John, and, on some weekends, got a kick out of going to the racetrack with two other Cherokees who also worked at Wal-Mart and were as assimilated as she was. But increasingly lonely and unable to meet another man who might be interested in getting to know her better, she developed a serious drinking problem, reverted to braiding her hair and wearing more traditional Indian outfits, and often astonished her neighbors by hanging bones, feathers, and other cryptic amulets in her windows and chanting quietly to a hand drum in the wee hours. Some thought she'd actually lost her mind, in fact, and were thinking of ways to encourage her to return to the reservation and her own people, when, one evening, Ella called to ask if, by chance, she might be available to do some housework a couple of days a week.

While the children were growing up and afterward, Ella had always paid a number of maids very well to clean, and polish silver, and do laundry, but, as she complained one day to Lilybelle Armstrong, colored help was just not what it used to be, and recently she'd come home to find Leanna watching TV when she was supposed to be ironing napkins, and she wasn't going to stand for it a moment longer. It was not long after that tirade that she suddenly remembered Bud's wife as a pleasant enough, honest-looking young girl and figured she might be needing a little extra work. Goldie found the opportunity to do some housecleaning for the elegant lady Bud had always called Miss Ella to be a gift from the Great Spirits, and while she was intimidated at first by the big home over in Eastover, Ella put her at ease by carefully showing her about and patiently explaining in detail what the chores would be.

Before long, Goldie had begun to pull her life together

again and felt right at home working on Colville Road, and while Ella found many of her mannerisms to be bizarre, she couldn't praise her Indian maid enough to the wary ladies invited routinely for lunch or tea and to her and Big Earl's close friends who came over periodically for dinner to eat Ella's renowned shrimp and oyster gumbo, cracklin' cornbread, and grasshopper pie. So pleased was Ella with Goldie, in fact, that she gradually entrusted her with more responsibilities, enticed her to work additional days for more cash as time passed, and, since she was winding down a little, essentially turned over most of the daily housekeeping, shopping, and even part of the cooking to the younger woman. Earl himself was basically indifferent to Goldie, perceiving her only as another commodity that made his wife happy.

By now, Goldie couldn't have been more content in her working routine. Ella knew that she maintained close contact with her relatives on the reservation and assumed she had a few friends in Charlotte with whom she socialized, but such was their proper relationship that Ella never asked much about Goldie's private life. What she did often worry about out loud to Big Earl was the possibility that Goldie might announce one day that she was returning to the reservation or that she was getting married again and couldn't spend as much time on the job.

The truth was that Goldie, her hair starting to gray and her weight more of a problem the older she became, not only had very few social outlets and certainly no prospects of marriage but, at least in her own mind, had adopted the house on Colville as her real home and the Duboses as her surrogate family. When Big Earl died and Goldie stayed a couple of nights in a back room at the house, it unnerved Ella to hear the woman's hushed grief chant and to find a weird collection of small feathers, beads, and shells in a bowl by the bed, but she asked no questions. Now Ella depended on Goldie even more than before for help and companionship, and while both Little Earl and Olivia viewed "the squaw" as little more than a harmless necessity for keeping up the big house, Ella's oldest and closest friends were fully aware of the strange but necessary bond that had come to exist between these two women whose backgrounds, lifestyles, and sophistication couldn't have been more different. As for Goldie herself, nobody on earth came to better understand and respect Ella Dubose's demanding, often condescending ways, and while the Indian was always aware how grateful she was to the other woman who'd virtually given her a new life, such was her nature and pride that she'd also evolved various means to handle Ella like few others could.

Just being in a plush milieu like the Priscilla for the first time was so overwhelming to Goldie that she was satisfied simply taking in the surroundings and watching the sophisticated guests come and go, but for Ella the experience was so nostalgic and bittersweet that most of her disoriented thoughts focused either on how much she missed the good times with Earl and the children or the best way to reveal to Tyler a truth that could no longer be concealed. Her reflections, in fact, might have brought on a bad case of nerves had they not suddenly been interrupted by a soft but nasal voice on her right as the family with the young boys made their way toward the dining room.

"Please excuse me," said the older man with the bow tie, leaning down and nodding to both women.

"Why, good evening," Ella responded cordially, obviously surprised.

"I'm Edmund O'Conner, and I hope you won't find me too presumptuous, but, to tell you the truth, my two grandsons here are absolutely intrigued by your friend's beautiful dress and jewelry." He turned to Goldie. "They aren't by any chance authentic Native American, are they?"

It was hard to tell by Goldie's expression whether she was slightly piqued or just shy, but she said nothing.

"As a matter of fact, they are," Ella answered forthrightly. "Yes, sir, my companion here is, in fact, a full-blooded Chero-kee Indian, and the tunic and all the jewelry couldn't be more traditional and genuine." She patted Goldie on the arm while looking at the gentleman. "Very becoming, don't you think?"

"Oh, yes, very," he agreed affably. "You see, one of the boys here is studying Native Americans in middle school up in New Jersey—we're from Englewood—and when we noticed the lady's turquoise and silver and the way she wears her hair . . ."

"Well, let me introduce you to my American Indian friend," Ella said proudly, gesturing to the boys who were standing back sheepishly with the couple. "This is Goldie Russell, and I'm Mrs. Dubose. We're from Charlotte, but Goldie was born and raised on the Cherokee reservation up near our national park in the Smokies, weren't you, Goldie?"

"That's right," Goldie finally murmured, smiling.

"Well, this is a rare privilege, indeed," said the older man, shaking hands with them both, then coaxing the two boys to step up to Goldie. "Again, I hope we're not intruding, but . . . Boys, say hello to Miss Russell, and you'll have something spe-cial to tell your friends about."

"Everybody just calls me Goldie," she said in a more re-laxed voice, extending her hand as all the bracelets jangled. "It's nice to meet you fellas."

"Do you ever wear feathers?" asked the boy whose dark, curly hair once again reminded Ella of the beloved boy she'd known in her youth.

"Tommy!" his mother scolded, visibly embarrassed. "You shouldn't ask questions like that."

Goldie cracked a big smile. "No, no, honey, no feathers or deerskins—though some of the men in our tribe do wear them at ritual powwows."

"Gosh," the youngster exclaimed, staring at Goldie with eyes of amazement. "My teacher told us about powwows."

"Okay, Tom, that's enough for now," insisted the older man, taking the boy's arm. "We've bothered these nice people enough, and it's time for dinner. Mrs. Dubose, I would like for you and Goldie to meet my daughter and her husband, Elizabeth and Sal Mariani. We're all here together on a vacation while the boys are on spring break from school. Are you down for long?"

"Maybe a couple of weeks," Ella said vaguely.

After everybody shook hands and the family proceeded inside, Ella reflected for an instant on how attractive and vigorous the older man still was. Then she patted Goldie again on the arm.

"It appears you're something of a celebrity to them, dear."

Goldie began to blush. "They're very nice people."

"Yes," Ella laughed. "Some Northerners can be interesting and charming. Not all, mind you, but some. I wonder how in heaven's name they knew about the Priscilla. Mr. O'Conner obviously has an Irish background, and . . . Mariani—sounds Italian."

Most of the rockers along the wide porch were now occupied by well-dressed guests chatting cheerfully while enjoying the glorious vista of the sea, and when Ella eventually placed her empty glass on the banister and allowed Goldie to help her up, she was aware of feeling delightfully tipsy and hungry as a bear. Wondering if the dining room had changed much, she was startled when a rather frail-looking but distinguished black man with gray hair and eyebrows stepped forward in a tuxedo as if preparing to seat the two women.

"Mrs. Dubose?" he said quietly. "Mrs. Ella Dubose from Charlotte?"

"Yes," she responded with more astonishment.

Breaking into a wide grin that exposed a mouth full of pearl white teeth, he leaned over and said, "Lord have mercy, ma'am, I saw that name on the list and wondered if that could maybe be the same Mrs. Dubose from the old days."

Ella studied his venerable face for a moment. Then she opened her mouth as if dumbfounded, extended her hand with glee, and exclaimed, "Riley! Well, I don't believe my own eyes. I really don't believe my eyes!"

"Yessum, I'm still here doing the same old thing, Miss Ella, and I knew that was you the minute I noticed you coming across the hall. Lord, Miss Ella, you haven't changed one little bit."

"Now, now, Riley, let's not go overboard. But I can tell you this is the biggest surprise I've had in ages," she continued, pumping his hand. "I never had any idea. . . ."

"Yessum," he repeated, patting his lower back. "A little creaky in the joints and gray as an old gander, but, yessum, I'm still around and guess I'll stay till they carry me out feet first. Here over forty years now." He grinned widely again. "And how's that nice family of yours doing, Miss Ella?"

"Well, Riley, Mr. Dubose passed on some years ago, and my son Tyler's become a full-fledged Yankee writer up in New York City."

"Umm, umm, you don't say."

"Yes, he has, and the other two children are just fine, and are in Charlotte, and have beautiful children themselves. And how's your family, Riley? Still throwing those big oyster roasts and fish fries?"

"Oh, no, ma'am, 'fraid not. The missus passed 'bout ten years ago—a bad cancer—and I lost my boy in a bad accident down at the mill in Georgetown a spell back. But my daughter, Essie, she's with her family over in Conway, and I see right much of all of them. Remember those spots I used to catch for Mr. Earl's breakfast? Well, I still love to fish in my spare time. I do."

Ella's face took on a more somber expression. "Times have changed, haven't they, Riley? There's not much left of the old days."

"They sho have, Miss Ella. Just look at what they done to this beach." He shook his head back and forth. "Not like the old days, as you say. No, ma'am. And wait till the season begins next month. But I gotta say things stay pretty much the same 'round here at the inn—thank the good Lord."

All this time, Goldie had simply stood and listened, but once Ella and Riley had finished reminiscing about better days, she was introduced to the head waiter as Ella's companion with no further explanations. Nor did Ella volunteer any particular reason why she'd stayed away so many years or why she'd now decided to return with this curious-looking other woman. What did impress her beyond words was that, from memory or by sheer coincidence, Riley seated them in the half-filled dining room overlooking the ocean at a table for two in the exact same area where she and the family used to take their meals morning, noon, and night. She immediately recognized on the wall the same colorful oil painting of sea oats and a pier, and even two large potted palms in the corners seemed familiar and were comforting.

After Riley handed them simple printed menus that listed mainly classic Southern dishes that changed daily, Ella wiggled her finger for him to lean down as if she had a secret to reveal.

"Perhaps I should tell you, Riley, that Mr. Tyler is planning to fly down and join me on the weekend."

"Why, you don't say, Miss Ella. That's wonderful news, just wonderful. Now I'll get to see him again—all grown up." He laughed. "Lord have mercy, the last time . . ."

"You probably won't even recognize him, and I'll keep it a surprise, but maybe you should know since we'll then need a bigger table."

"No problem, ma'am, no problem at all, and, yessum, it'll be a real pleasure seeing that young man again."

Chapter 5

KEYBOARD TINKERBELL

It had been months since Ella had seen Tyler, and while she was as excited as ever over the prospect of spending a few days with her older son, the circumstances that had prompted her to call him from Charlotte weighed heavily on her conscience all during Holy Week as she had gone about the same routine Easter rituals she'd observed for decades. Once Billy from next door had finally rolled one of the artificial Christmas trees into the library in preparation for the Ash Wednesday afternoon tea she always held for members of her church guild, she decorated it with hand-painted eggs, tiny fuzzy bunnies, and streamers of pastel ribbons. She attended the Good Friday service at church, and the next day, with Goldie's help, she conducted her traditional Easter egg hunt in the yard for children in the neighborhood. And, naturally, she went to church with the whole family on Easter morning, as was expected, followed by a festive lunch at Little Earl's and Betty Jane's home.

What was not routine, and what lunch with Little Earl and Olivia had helped trigger, was Ella's impulsive decision and determination to finally confront a shattering facet of her past that had remained a closely guarded secret and that, even in old age, still could not be erased from her mind. The secret, of course, was her certain knowledge that Tyler was not the son of Earl Dubose, a complex intuition harbored for half a century and based as much on the nature of her son's personality as on the logistics of his early birth. Many were the times she had been tempted to confess the truth to Earl or broach the subject with Tyler the way other devoted wives and mothers might eventually do. Fear, however, had always precluded any overdue, open declarations on Ella's part, not that she was exactly ashamed of this youthful reality or daunted by the possibility of retaliation, but because revealing such a fact might have caused her husband or son to question her moral creed in general. Over the years, Ella had simply learned to cope with the periodic anxiety and tame the guilt, rarely allowing the inner conflict to affect her genuine love and respect for Earl and the efforts she made to deal normally with her family. But now, forced to face her mortality and overwhelmed more and more by distant memories as the shadows closed in, it was her peculiar but earnest conviction that the fog of deception that had shrouded her life had to be finally lifted and that Tyler had every right to know why and how he came into this world. She also felt the desperate urge to get away from Charlotte and the family, to escape back to the region of her roots that held such vivid nostalgia and where, if only for a short time, she might wrap up some loose ends and perhaps find the emotional fulfillment needed to round out her life.

Ella's plan couldn't have been more bold, a concocted scheme to simply take off in the car with Goldie for Myrtle Beach, spend a couple of off-season weeks at the Priscilla without informing a soul in Charlotte, and convince Tyler to join her there for at least a few days. Friends had told her that, while the inn itself was still very nice, she might be shocked by the changes at Myrtle since she and Earl were last there. But no matter. Ella's mind was set, and when Ella Dubose set her mind to something, nothing could alter her intentions.

"It's something I need to do for several reasons" was her only explanation to Goldie, "and nobody except you and Mr. Tyler are to know—nobody. I'd like for you to go along to help with the driving and other things, and it might be nice for you also to get away. But if you can't, I'll do it on my own. I might even do a little fishing."

Goldie, who had never so much as seen the ocean but could remember hearing Mr. Earl and Miss Ella talking about the beach and grand hotel and going fishing back in the old days, was as perplexed by this announcement as she was convinced of Ella's strong resolve to take the trip. No doubt she was excited by the prospect of a vacation, but even if she'd had some good reason not to be away from Charlotte, which she didn't, there was no way she was about to allow this elderly lady whom she so admired and depended on to undertake an excursion by herself. As for all the secrecy, not to mention the worry this would cause Ella's family, Goldie knew it was not her place to pry—at least not yet.

"Fine. So that's decided," Ella said. "Now remember, Goldie, this is our little secret. It's nobody's business but my own, and I don't want any more problems than I already have."

"Yes, ma'am," Goldie answered, even more baffled by this last statement.

Ella's next move was to call Tyler, who, having undergone some time ago both surgery to remove a cancerous part of his colon and a subsequent round of chemo, had recently been in Paris with Barry mainly to recuperate. Somehow he had kept the news of his condition relatively quiet from most people, and, as if that ordeal had not been taxing enough, what he had facing him now was all the publicity deemed necessary to promote his provocative new memoirs. He loathed having to do all the interviews and media appearances, not only because he no longer had the physical stamina but because such tedious activity robbed him of the precious time needed to write what he considered to be the most challenging novel of his career.

In the past, of course, Tyler had allowed nothing to cramp his working habits, his social style, and certainly not his occasional extracurricular sexual habits even while leading a sedate and happy life with Barry Livingston. During the first year of his relationship with the younger, strikingly handsome man, there had been little urge to indulge in sexual promiscuity in Manhattan and on the beach at night out in Amagansett, and the two quickly established a respect for each other's disposition and professional needs that evolved into a solid, rare friendship. When, however, the bloom of carnal infatuation eventually faded, as it does in most passionate affairs, Tyler had reverted periodically to the same random flings with other young men that had once cost him a career and that he knew could be as precarious as zooming about the Hamptons in his snappy BMW convertible after one too many Negronis. Although sexual relations with Barry had long ago come to a halt, and although Barry himself had not exactly been twiddling his thumbs while on gallery trips or when Tyler spent days on end alone writing at the country house, these two men were totally devoted to one another in unorthodox ways that might make even their worst enemies envious. Despite the graying dark curly hair and slight jowls that had begun to betray a man in his early fifties, Tyler was still remarkably good-looking, and, actually, the six-year age difference between the two had never been an important factor. Nor did it really matter that Tyler's glittery image as a darling of New York's publishing world contrasted sharply with Barry's reputation as a social standoff involved almost exclusively with his shrewd art transactions when not relaxing or traveling with Tyler. Some viewed Barry as a snob. Both being highly successful, the two men lived well but not extravagantly, sharing basically the same tastes even as each exercised and enjoyed a certain independence. There had been testy moments over the years, to be sure, but none so dramatic or mordant as to alter their genuine affection and need for one another.

Most of this Ella had come to accept and understand about her son, and if other family members and friends in Charlotte disapproved of and disparaged a reputed lifestyle that Tyler had never made the least effort to conceal, they'd learned to keep their opinions to themselves. More cynical minds were no doubt convinced that Ella simply tolerated a revolting situation she could do nothing about, but, in reality, she was actually very fond of Barry and enjoyed his company when she visited the two in Amagansett. What not even Tyler suspected, however, was that there were much deeper, covert reasons why his mother had rarely ever found serious fault with her oldest son and his unusual ways.

Not that she had exactly spoiled Tyler when he was growing up or failed to enforce the same discipline on him as on the other two children. But what she had nurtured in him in ways that Big Earl was incapable of doing was the more sensitive, fastidious side of his nature that made him different from his siblings and, at least in his mother's opinion, superior to most of his classmates. Like other healthy young Southern boys in the early sixties, Tyler was automatically expected by his father to engage in sports and other virile activities, and although he loathed being on the Myers Park football team, he met the challenge the best he could and gained the necessary respect from Big Earl, his buddies, and a flock of adoring females who measured the worth of any man by his athletic abilities. Whatever resentment he felt playing the brute he kept as much to himself as he did the strange urges awakened in the locker room.

Ella had never been exactly the most literate or artistic mother on earth, but she had possessed enough insightful intention to recognize Tyler's special intellectual talents and do all she could to guide him in the right directions when he was young. Unlike his brother and sister, Tyler never seemed to have trouble maintaining top grades in school, resulting in his eventually being elected president of the Honor Society by his junior year and receiving a merit scholarship to attend Duke University after he finished high school. Aware of his instinctive love of music, Ella not only talked Big Earl into buying an upright piano but arranged for Tyler to take piano lessons every Saturday morning while most of his male friends were out hunting, pitching ball, or just racking around. And if Earl dared to dispairingly refer to his son as "Charlotte's Liberace" or "the keyboard Tinkerbell," Ella was capable of delivering a tongue-lashing that would put even the most uncouth slob in his place. She encouraged Tyler to read all types of books and helped him routinely with his homework to the best of her ability. She bought him records of classical music and jazz and would sometimes sit and listen with him. And, wanting him to be as socially well-rounded as possible, she even taught him a few expert dance steps so he could impress his partners and the crowd at school proms and cotillions. The bond Ella formed with her son was solid, and although the perception that Tyler was too much of a mama's boy and not enough a regular guy like most of his classmates could infuriate Big Earl, he knew that to interfere too much would only spark his wife's wrath and distance himself even further from his son.

The irony, of course, was that once Tyler had finished his higher education at Duke and come to terms with his sexual makeup, and finally fled the smothering cultural limitations of the South, his life couldn't have differed more from that of his mother. Nothing suited him more than the liberal climate of Princeton during his three-year tenure as assistant professor of English, and while he did enjoy weekend jaunts into Manhattan to dine in fine restaurants, attend operatic performances and the ballet, and indulge in the dissolute gay bar scene, on campus he was respected both by the faculty and his students as an inspired, conscientious teacher keenly devoted to his profession.

What little social life he led in Princeton revolved mainly around the occasional staid, quaint cocktail or dinner party at the home of a colleague or one of his few close gay friends. Most likely, all would have continued to go well, and Tyler might well have developed into a high-level academic, had there not been that one fateful, careless spring night when, deep in his cups after a lively birthday dinner for a faculty wife, he ventured into a downtown tavern, struck up a conversation at the bar with a handsome, well-built, equally smashed undergraduate junior named Mike who was on the university swimming team and, when last call was announced, persuaded him to return to his modest house just off campus for more boozing and a little jazz. Identifying himself not as a faculty member but a graduate student in English, Tyler knew he was taking a chance fraternizing too closely with the young stranger, but, after all, Mike had been openly receptive to the invitation, and, of course, nothing was more exciting about this type of seduction than the element of risk.

Back at the house, Tyler poured more Scotch for them both, put on a recent cassette of Sergio Mendes, and tried to show a convincing interest in Mike's major in business administration. And sprawled at one end of the sofa with his legs spread open on the coffee table, Mike couldn't have made himself more at home or seemed more at ease.

"So you're also on the swimming team?" Tyler eventually asked from the other end of the sofa, studying the other man's perfectly proportioned chest that filled out every inch of his polo shirt.

"Yeah," Mike slurred, taking another big slug of his drink and shaking his feet nervously. "Mainly fifty-meter freestyle,

but sometimes one hundred–meter butterfly. I'll swim butterfly next weekend at the meet with Penn."

"I'm impressed. That must take lots of working out," said
Tyler, who cared no more about swimming than any other
sport.

"I stay in pretty good shape," Mike almost garbled, his head
now swaying slightly back and forth as the alcohol began to
take its toll.

"I can see that," Tyler said, reaching over and smacking
him friskily on his firm pecs outlined in the tight shirt. "Great
build."

When Mike didn't react but just kept on shaking his feet,
Tyler next boldly squeezed his upper left arm and felt him instinctively flex his muscle.

"Hard as a rock," Tyler complimented, noticing in the corner of his eye a mounting bulge in the man's jeans.

"Yeah," was Mike's only comment as he partly drew his
legs up and perched his sneakers on the edge of the table, now
rocking his knees back and forth.

For an instant, Tyler debated what to say and do next.
Then, deciding to throw all caution to the wind, he whispered, "And that's not all that seems to be hard as a rock,"
reaching down and groping the exposed crotch.

Mike barely flinched, but then managed to groan, "Hey,
whatcha doing?" while still making no effort to offer much resistance.

"Just playing around," Tyler mumbled as he clasped the
husky bulge and the arousal became more and more pronounced in the tight jeans. "Seems like you're ready to explode. Does this offend you?"

"Hey . . . you didn't . . . I don't know about this," he pretended to object groggily, his eyes now closed and his head rotating around as he thrust his legs back over the table.

With no further comment or hesitation, and his heart

pounding, Tyler proceeded to unzip and loosen the jeans, manipulate the jockey shorts, and, spitting into the palm of his hand, grasp the thick shaft tightly and stroke it up and down.

"Feel good?"

When Mike didn't answer and Tyler could hear only his uncontrollable heavy breathing, he wasted no more time replacing his hand with his anxious mouth, and, in what seemed like mere seconds, Mike's whole body was in rampant convulsions.

Spent, the young man now did seem to pass out, or so Tyler thought till he zipped the jeans back up and began gently caressing his flawless midsection and chest.

"Hey, what the fuck's going on?" Mike suddenly grunted out loud, shoving Tyler's arm away, pulling his shirt back down, and struggling to pull himself up. "What the fuck are you doing?"

Startled but trying to keep his wits about him, Tyler immediately backed away and was calmly saying "Oh, come on, Mike. . . . Just a little fun . . ." when, with no warning, the other man took a drunken swing, landed a blow across Tyler's face, and bellowed, "Fucking faggot, keep your fucking hands off me!"

Now truly stunned, and wiping blood that was already trickling from his nose, Tyler carefully moved to the center of the room and said, "I'm sorry you feel like that, Mike. Maybe you'd just better leave."

Finally on his feet but tottering, Mike next lunged at Tyler, again blatted "Fucking faggot," and shoved him so violently against a tall bookcase along one wall that most of the books on the top two shelves came crashing to the floor, one cutting a nasty gash in Tyler's forehead. For a moment, he feared the rage would continue. Then, slurring "Fucking faggot" for the third time, Mike stumbled to the front door and out into the dark early morning.

Naturally, Tyler was pretty shaken up by the brutal experience, but, thankful that the consequences of his foolish behavior were no worse, and naively confident that the episode would just blow over, he concluded that the student must be struggling with his own demons and simply tried to forget it all. What he never suspected was that Mike would return to his dorm and relate how he'd been molested to his roommate, who, in turn, reported the incident to their hall counselor, who, in turn, decided to contact the town police. Unfortunately, an ugly scandal ensued, the news made both the Princeton and New Brunswick newspapers, and, in the long run, Tyler was given the option of facing morals charges in court and causing further embarrassment to the university or proffering his resignation and leaving town altogether. Not one of his colleagues offered departmental support or the least bit of understanding and sympathy, and since all but one happened to be Jews who, in their self-righteousness, turned against a close associate who now posed a potential threat to their security, Tyler, for the first time in his life, experienced a prick of anti-Semitism that would remain with him for years to come. Actually, the only person besides a couple of closeted gay friends he was able to discuss the problem with was his mother, and, within a couple of weeks, he had quietly resigned his position and wrapped up most of his affairs, rented a small apartment in Greenwich Village, and made the last drive from Princeton to Manhattan.

Wrecking his beloved career so carelessly, and aware of the improbability of ever securing another top academic job after all the adverse publicity and gossip, Tyler naturally went through a terrible period of recrimination and gloom. Once, however, he'd adjusted to life in New York, made a few good friends, and set out to write a long novel about a Southern family's struggle to survive the Great Depression, he began to realize that perhaps this was the direction he was meant to take all along. When the book was immediately picked up by a major publisher and went on to become a phenomenal mass-market hit, things would never again be quite the same for Tyler—professionally, socially, and, indeed, financially. Almost overnight, calls from agents and editors were routine, invitations to the town's toniest literary and social receptions flooded in, and when the second novel, a modern psychological romance set in the Garden District of New Orleans, proved even more successful and profitable than the first, reviewers wrote of Tyler Dubose as the dashing new Updike or Cheever.

Tyler took the celebrity and wealth in stride, moving uptown to a delightful duplex apartment just off Park Avenue, promoting his books on TV talk shows and at bookshops around the country, and, when not writing or working the bars for sexual gratification, hanging out at Elaine's and Studio 54 with the likes of Andy Warhol, Truman Capote, Bianca Jagger, Calvin Klein, and other bold-face decadents who found the handsome young Southern novelist with the melodious accent to be engaging company. Basically, Tyler was indifferent to all the attention, the one exception being that paid him the night he was introduced to Tennessee Williams at a crowded birthday reception held at the Gotham Book Mart in the playwright's honor. Williams, who had arrived alone and smashed in what could only be described as Fidel Castro army fatigues, was, in Tyler's opinion, not only the finest modern American dramatist but a veritable icon of the literary world. When he found himself sitting on a sofa next to the great man, every nerve in his body seemed to vibrate, and when Williams' lecherous good eye surveyed him from head to toe, it was all he could do to maintain his composure.

"Now, hold on just one second, young man, and let me guess," Williams drawled in his inimitable voice after taking a big slug of vodka. "Georgia. I'd say right off the bat that the accent's Georgia." He let out a short cackle for no apparent reason and stared into Tyler's dark eyes.

"You're close," Tyler stammered. "It's North Carolina, though I was actually born in Charleston."

"Ah, Charleston. Baby, that is one lovely, gracious town, and Dubose is one lovely, gracious name," he slurred, pulling on his tight jacket as if he might be uncomfortable. "I myself am from Mississippi." He cackled again inexplicably, then sipped more booze. "I can tell you must be in some field of the arts," he continued, obviously unaware of who Tyler was.

"Well, in fact, I am a writer—a novelist."

"Oh, that's grand, just wonderful." For a moment, he gazed out blankly into space, as if he were contemplating or remembering. "I'm also a novelist, but, I should add, a failed novelist. Heeheehee."

Tyler had absolutely no idea how to respond to that startling remark and weird cackle, so he tried changing the subject.

"Do you get back to the South very often?"

"Well, ya see, I still have a small cottage down in Key West that I use as a retreat from the tyranny of reality and when I'm on the verge of emotional collapse, but"—he giggled again, this time almost maniacally—"well, I've never considered Key West to be exactly a Southern locale, do you?"

"I think I know what you mean," was all Tyler could say.

"And, of course, no place on earth is still as dear to me as New Awyens, where I've spent a considerable amount of time over the years and still visit when I'm not drifting around—"

The sentence was cut off abruptly when Williams heard someone say, "May I wish the Bird a happy birthday?" and looked up at a stout, patrician-looking man whom Tyler immediately recognized as Gore Vidal.

"Well, heavens to Betsy, if it isn't dear Gore," Williams exclaimed as Vidal leaned down and pecked him on the cheek. "How ya doing, baby? Obviously in better shape than I am." He hooted loudly again. "Let me introduce you to this nice young gentleman from Charleston by the name of Tyler Dubose. Mr. Dubose is a writer—a novelist. Tyler, meet Mr. Gore Vidal, *eminence grise* of the literary world. Heeheehee."

"It's my pleasure," Vidal said in his dignified, deep voice, rubbing Tyler's shoulder instead of shaking his hand. "I read your first book. Well done."

Tennessee appeared a little perplexed as a stranger from nowhere handed him another drink, and he turned to Tyler. "Well, I guess I'm the only illiterate one around here. Baby, have you written something I should have read?"

Vidal cracked a wicked smile at Tyler. "The Bird here must have been asleep for the past couple of years."

"Baby, I've been asleep for the past *decade*," Williams pronounced in a shriek of laughter. "Between the liquor and pills and . . ."

"Well, I can tell you, my dear, you haven't missed much," Vidal said, leaving Tyler in even greater awe.

Once Vidal had moved on to socialize with others in the large room, Tyler, nursing his second gin and tonic, mainly sat and listened as Williams rattled on about his physical problems, and his recent mistreatment by the vicious press, and the role he himself was undertaking in his new play opening soon at a theater in the Village. Periodically, people would come over to wish him happy birthday, chat for a moment, and perhaps even compliment Tyler on his latest book, and, from time to time, Tennessee would interrupt one of his rambling stories and, out of the blue, ask Tyler some personal question about himself that had no relevance whatsoever to anything being said. Finally, at one point, when it appeared the playwright might actually pass out right there on the sofa in front of dozens of friends and associates who'd come to celebrate another year of his survival, he raised his eyes and took Tyler's hand.

"You're a very attractive and interesting young man, but I suspect something about you. Yeah, there's something that's just dawned on me. And what I suspect, what has become more and more evident the longer you sit and converse with me, is that . . . Well, how do I put it? The more we converse, baby, the more evident it becomes to me that you have already lost the capacity for surprise. Heeheehee."

Tyler sat stunned, unable to respond to the daunting remark as Tennessee casually sipped his drink, his expression almost glazed.

"Now, what I was wondering," Williams resumed in his distracted manner, "I was wondering if you might enjoy having a civilized dinner one evening with an elderly gentleman who needs a little good company from time to time."

And thus began a relatively close but strange friendship that would endure till Williams' sudden death over a decade later and that Tyler would one day recount in some detail in his memoirs. Since, at the time, Tyler was often seen in New York with Tennessee everywhere from seedy bars to deluxe French restaurants to front-row seats in theaters, it was naturally assumed by many that the two were involved in some sort of affair. It was true that, after many late nights of carousing and heavy drinking, when Tyler had to virtually put the playwright to bed in a stupor, it became almost routine for him to conduct the pill-taking ritual, then hold and hug Tennessee till he finally fell into a deep, drug-induced sleep. But, if his later revelations were to be believed, that was the extent of any physical intimacy between the two men. Tyler was no more and no less than what Williams often referred to as "a necessary companion," an arrangement that made sense given the novelist's penchant for much younger men and need for steady sexual diversity.

Of course, after Tyler and Barry Livingston were utterly smitten by one another at an exclusive party in the East Side townhouse of none other than the notorious and closeted lawyer Roy Cohn, the two soon began living together in Tyler's duplex and his social life settled down considerably. Eventually, he and Barry bought a secluded house out in the Hamptons, which was not only a perfect retreat from the chaos of Manhattan but the ideal place for Ella to visit from time to time. To be sure, every time she announced in Charlotte her plans to go spend a week up North, tongues wagged privately, especially those of family members and friends who simply could never imagine why Ella would want to subject herself to such degeneracy even if it did involve her own son. Elsewhere in the country, the gay lifestyle was coming more and more to the front as an inevitable fact of the modern world, but for Southerners like Little Earl and Betty Jane Dubose and Lily-belle Armstrong and a large clique of other Charlotteans still bogged down in bigoted morality, Tyler, despite his celebrity, was considered a disgrace not only to the community in which he was raised but to his very heritage. "First the squaw, next the Catholics, and now those two perverts," was the way Little Earl referred in disgust at one point to his mother's increasingly shocking fancies, and when, by some chance, the society column in the liberal *Charlotte Observer* once reported that Mrs. Earl Dubose Sr. on Colville Road was visiting her famous son and his companion at their home on Long Island, Olivia was so mortified that the following Sunday morning in church she was unable to walk up to the communion rail.

Not that Ella wouldn't have preferred a more traditional way of life for her son, or that she didn't have heated words with Tyler when, in his memoirs, he exposed enough about his family and growing up in the unsophisticated Queen City to warrant a good tar and feathering. But she made the best of everything despite the antipathy all around her at home, for she never forgot for a moment that there were probable reasons for Tyler's unconventional nature and personality that had never been discerned by anyone, factors that only she had understood and kept buried deep inside her as only a loving mother can do. That the two shared few intellectual, cultural, or even social interests was immaterial to them both and never seemed to affect their relationship in the least. Tyler simply respected and loved his mother for her practical sense and steadfast devotion, and even though they could argue and fight like cats and dogs, she not only admired his success and independence but always knew he was the one person she could turn to in times of critical doubts and adversity.

"Son, I know you're busy with all your highfalutin friends up there," Ella had said on the phone in her typical half-mocking manner that Tyler was completely used to, "but I was hoping you might be able to pull free in the next week or so and join me for a few days at the beach. It should be nice down there this time of year before the crowds arrive."

"Where, Mama?" he asked almost in dismay from the study in his Manhattan duplex, slightly irritated to have his concentration on the important new novel interrupted during the middle of the day.

"The beach. The Priscilla down at Myrtle. You certainly remember the Priscilla. Well, I tell you, Son, I've got to get out of here and away from your meddling brother and sister and all the rest for awhile, and, well, I thought how nice it would be to go back to the Priscilla after all these years. Goldie and I are driving down the first of next week, and I don't want a living soul—not a soul—except you to know where I'll be."

There was a long silence on the phone. Then Tyler, in his soft but startled voice, declared, "Mama, have you gone stark raving mad? What in hell's this all about?"

"Tyler, please mind your language, and I don't appreciate that insinuation. Of course I haven't lost my mind—not yet, at least. I need to go somewhere peaceful, and I also need to talk with you about some other things that have been on my mind. It would mean lots to me, Son, if you could spare a few days and fly down to be with me."

"Mama, I'm really involved in this book promotion," he reminded her firmly, well aware that such a thing actually meant little to his mother.

"Oh, honey, I know you must be busy as a bee and that this comes as a little surprise. But I haven't seen you in a coon's age, and you used to love the Priscilla, and we can fish and do things, and there really are some matters I can't discuss on the phone."

"What matters, Mama?" he tried to prod.

"Just some family matters I need to talk over with you. And I want to hear all about what you and Barry did in my favorite city."

Tyler was on the verge of resisting further when Barry, dressed in shorts, stuck his head in the door and silently pointed to a cup of tea in his hand as if asking whether Tyler wanted some. Rolling his eyes, Tyler signaled him to come in, then spouted over the phone, "Here, Mama, Barry wants to say hello."

"Hi, gorgeous," Barry almost crooned, sitting on the corner of the desk. "How's my favorite Southern belle?"

For a couple of minutes, the two made small talk, then Barry handed the receiver back to Tyler.

"I tell you what, Mama, would you consider maybe spending a little time in Amagansett instead? Actually, Barry's got to be out of town visiting galleries the rest of this month, so we could be pretty much to ourselves when I'm not in the city."

"Honey, you know how I dislike being in that house by myself, and besides, I have other important reasons for wanting to go back to the beach after all these years—reasons I'll explain if you'll come down. And we could fish, and eat crab cakes, and do everything we used to do, and . . . one day I'd even like to drive down to Charleston and look around. Of course, Goldie and I would meet you at the airport."

By this time, Tyler had learned how futile it was to debate his mother when she was about to get her dander up. Perhaps, since the two were so much alike in temperament, they often argued to the point where others thought they might actually hate each other, but, deep down, Ella believed that Tyler could do no wrong, and he, in return, was virtually incapable of denying his mother anything—no matter how unreasonable or absurd—that he felt would make her happy. Consequently, although her strange request that he drop everything and meet her at Myrtle Beach couldn't have come at a more difficult and inconvenient time, the slight sense of urgency in her voice was enough to convince him that he was truly needed.

"This all sounds crazy, Mama," he finally said, "but . . . well, next week's out of the question, since I'm scheduled for three TV interviews, but I guess I could fly down over the weekend and stay a few days the following week."

"You're an angel," she said as if addressing a child. "And we'll talk, and eat well, and maybe do a little fishing, and have a good time. I'll call the inn and make the reservation for you. But remember, Tyler, that Earl and Liv are to know nothing about this, and that I'll be incognito there in case they try to find me. Don't call me, Son. I'll call you. And don't forget to bring a nice jacket for the dining room."

After Tyler put down the phone, he explained what his mother wanted and was aware of Barry staring worriedly at him.

"Don't you think you're pushing things a little too far?" his boyfriend said.

"What can I do?" Tyler answered. "Something strange is up, and you know Mama."

"When are you going to tell her about your condition?" Barry then asked, rubbing the back of Tyler's neck affectionately. "She's bound to notice some physical changes."

"I don't know. Mama's tough, but I'm not sure how she could deal with something like this. Maybe the doctor will have some good news to report; then I can take it from there."

Chapter 6

GRITS AND GRUNTS

After her first dinner at the Priscilla, Ella was about to tell Goldie that she was tired and wanted to turn in early, when, as suddenly as on the porch earlier on, Edmund O'Conner approached the table by himself, apologized cordially for bothering the ladies, and asked if they'd had a good meal.

"Excellent, thank you," Ella said, once again admiring his radiant white hair and handsome outfit. "I had the she-crab soup and stuffed flounder, and Goldie had clam chowder and fried chicken. Delicious, overall, as good as Goldie does back home. Just wish we'd had room left for some of that blueberry cobbler."

"I agree with you completely," O'Conner said in his soft, articulate voice. "I also had the she-crab soup, then the deviled crabs, and I was telling my family that Southerners seem to have a way with crab that we Yankees just don't understand."

Ella chuckled, said that was not always the case, then asked if this was his first visit to the Priscilla.

"Actually, it is for me, but not for my daughter and her family. They started coming down here a couple of years ago when friends told them about the place, and, well, ever since I retired, they've been trying to drag me along. They love Myrtle Beach, especially when there're no crowds, as I gather you do."

Ella laughed again a little nervously, fingering the cloth napkin still in her lap. "Oh, heavens yes—the Priscilla, that is. Of course, Myrtle itself now appears to be vulgar honky-tonk, but, then, what isn't these days? If only you could have seen the beach back in the fifties and early sixties. But thank the Good Lord, the Priscilla seems to have changed very little since I and my family had so many happy times here. This is Goldie's first visit, isn't it, dear?" Goldie nodded her head and smiled. "There's really no place like it—especially if you're as old-fashioned as I am."

She laughed still again and was about to ask him to sit down when, gazing intently at her as a much younger man might stare at a beautiful girl, he disclosed that his daughter and her husband had decided to take the boys downtown to the Pavilion and wondered if he could buy the ladies a drink out in the lounge.

"Why, how gracious of you, Mr. O'Conner," Ella said in her refined, lilting accent, turning to Goldie. "Would you like that, dear, or were you planning to go straight up?"

Even if the offer had not intimidated Goldie, just the polite but firm tone of Ella's voice made it clear that the other woman's presence at such an occasion would hardly be appropriate, prompting Goldie to shake her head and say, "Thank you, but I do need to go up and finish unpacking our things."

After all three had told Riley how nice dinner had been and Goldie had said good night, Ella, with renewed energy, accompanied her attractive new friend to a small table in the quiet, paneled lounge not far from a talented black pianist with slicked-back hair playing soft, romantic tunes on a small grand.

"So you're from Charlotte," he began.

"Well, actually, I was born and raised in Charleston," she

said proudly, "but yes, I have to call myself a Charlottean. And your home is New Jersey?"

"For over seventy years."

"And I take it Mrs. O'Conner is deceased," Ella prodded politely after ordering a Grand Marnier on the rocks.

"Oh, yes, my wife passed away some time ago. Cancer. I continued my dental practice for a couple of years, then finally decided to retire."

"A dentist. Mercy me," she said.

"Yes. Periodontics. Over forty years."

"Well, Dr. O'Conner, I'm impressed. My husband was in printing and engraving, but, Lord, he's been dead now going on fifteen years. Hard to believe." She reached into her purse for the gold cigarette case. "Does this offend you?"

He frowned, took the lighter, and lit her cigarette. "Shame on you. You know it can stunt your growth."

Ella chuckled in her nonchalant way. "I've been giving it up for forty years and guess it's a miracle I've made it to seventy-three."

"Well, Mrs. Dubose, you have me beat by a couple of years, but I must say you look remarkable for seventy-three."

Blushing slightly, she took a big sip of her drink, breathed in deeply as the pungent liquor burned its way down her throat, then said playfully, "Get on with you, Dr. O'Conner. And, please, everybody just calls me Miss Ella."

For maybe an hour, she elaborated on who Goldie was and told the doctor all about Charlotte and her children and grand-children there, and he, in turn, related a few details of his long, rather routine but happy career and life in Englewood, his passion for tennis, and his active involvement in New Jersey's Democratic Party campaigns. While he talked, and the piano tinkled, Ella studied his features and mannerisms as carefully as she would have if he'd been fifty years younger: intense dark eyes shaded by heavy eyelids that betrayed his age; pinkish, smooth cheeks broken only by moderate crevices on either side of a small nose; a prominent dimple in his chin flanked by slightly puffy jowls that rested on the tips of his bow tie; thick, nicely groomed hair white as a cloud; a slow, slightly nasal voice; and the habit of waving an index finger while trying to make a point. As Ella perceived the man, he couldn't have been anything other than a highly capable, intelligent professional, and while she was under no silly illusion over either of their advanced years, she couldn't deny the mild flutter inside as they talked and he fixed his eyes avidly on hers.

"Do you by any chance fish, Dr. O'Conner?" she asked out of the blue.

Cupping his snifter of brandy, he seemed taken aback by the question, then, cracking a smile, confessed, "No, not really, not since I was a child."

"Well, I do, and I love it. Of course, it's been years since my husband, Earl, and I fished down here. Mercy, I doubt I have the strength to cast a line ten feet now, but I brought the rods along, and when my other son arrives on the weekend from New York, I certainly plan to give it a big try—if not before."

"Your other son?" O'Conner asked.

"Yes, I guess I got wound up about Charlotte and forgot to mention my older son, but Tyler is a writer up in your neck of the woods, and he's flying down to join me for a few days. I'd like for you to meet him."

The doctor appeared to be ruminating over what she'd just said. Then, waving his finger as a sign that something important had just dawned on him, he uttered the name Tyler Dubose twice and exclaimed, "I knew that Dubose rang a bell. Tyler Dubose. Of course, he's a famous author, and I read one of his novels a few years ago. I'll be damned. So he's your son?"

"He certainly is, and . . ." She laughed. "Yeah, Tyler's in

high cotton. Just published his memoirs, in fact—for better or worse. I'm pretty proud of him."

"And you should be. Does he have a family up North?"

After a long hesitation, Ella finally decided to tell the truth. "No, no, Tyler's different from my other son. He lives with another gentleman, if you know what I mean, and the two seem to be very happy."

"I see," O'Conner said, obviously not fazed by the revelation. "Does his sexual orientation bother you?"

"Not in the least." She chuckled again. "Oh, I'm sure it bothers my other children and most of my friends in Charlotte—and my husband was never exactly thrilled by it. But, no, I accepted the way Tyler is a long time ago. Actually, we're very close."

"As you should be. Fortunately, we're living in different times today, when that sort of circumstance no longer seems that earthshaking."

Ella laughed again. "You don't live in the South, Dr. O'Conner."

Now he let out a warm, confident chortle, and Ella wondered if his pearly teeth were false, unlike her own. Then she felt a tinge of self-consciousness, glancing furtively at her red nails, and wondering if her hair was still tidy and attractive, and hoping the liver spots on the back of her hands were not too obvious. Wanting to show him a photo of Tyler in plastic she always carried in one of her large, elegant pocketbooks, she began rummaging through a slew of items, one of which was her small pistol that she placed momentarily on the cocktail table. The doctor stared at the object in disbelief.

"Is that thing loaded?" he almost stammered.

"You bet your bottom dollar it is," Ella answered, still looking for the picture. "And I know how to use it if I had to." She picked up the pistol and waved it menacingly in the air.

"Is that legal down here?" he asked next, utterly flabber-gasted.

"Sure it is, honey, so long as you run down and get a per-mit. Why, everybody's got a gun, especially if you live alone the way I do. A man broke into one of my best friend's house not too long ago, and she blew his brains clear out. You never know." All at once, she came up with the photo. "Ah, here it is. Look how handsome my Tyler is."

After complimenting her on the photo, he once again gazed at her, smiled, and said, "You're quite a lady, Miss Ella."

Little did he know, of course, that even as a youngster growing up down in Charleston during the Great Depression and World War II, Ella Pinckney Hodges had always had a de-termined, often rebellious spirit that caused her archly conser-vative parents considerable concern but, along with her natural radiance and charm, gave her unusual distinction among those her age. Like many other prominent Charlestonians of the era who had been richer in plutocratic heritage than financial means ever since the days of Reconstruction, the Hodges lived in a large, ornamental Federal house on the city's lower penin-sula that went back generations in the family and had not been renovated in years. Ella's father, Archibald Tyler Hodges (or Archie, as he was known about town), had enjoyed notable success as a banker till fortunes were ravaged in 1929, but even in reduced financial circumstances, he and his wife, Tillie, who was, by birth, a Pinckney from Aiken, remained active mem-bers in Charleston's exclusive St. Cecilia Society, contributed generously to St. Philip's Episcopal Church, and still managed to provide their son and daughter the type of privileges that would enable them to associate with the right people and eventually enter into proper marriages worthy of the Hodges name and pedigree.

Since Ella just became more alluring and popular the older she became, she was certainly never at a loss in high school for beaus competing to squire her around at cotillions, beach parties out on Sullivan's Island, and plantation oyster roasts. At the top of her list of boyfriends was Earl Dubose, not so much because he was particularly attractive and the son of a relatively prosperous paper manufacturer who owned a pine pulpwood mill up near Georgetown, but because she thought he was the best dancer in all of Charleston County. Ella loved to dance as much as she loved to drink and have a good time, and she never had a better time than on those special occasions when she and Earl and maybe another couple would hop into his daddy's Plymouth convertible, head over to Folly's Pier Pavilion or Atlantic Boardwalk on Folly Beach, and dance the night away to the swing music of Artie Shaw, Harry James, Tommy Dorsey, and other big-band leaders touring after the outbreak of war.

Although Earl had been obsessed with Ella all during high school and would tell close buddies that he was going to marry that gal one day, she never considered herself exactly pinned to him and more than once had to make it clear that she wasn't yet ready for a steady relationship. Ella's much more conventional older brother, Sherman, with whom she'd never been particularly close, had already married a charming girl from a well-bred family in Mt. Pleasant, and, of course, nothing would have made Ella's parents happier than to see their carefree, often unruly daughter also settle down soon with a fine, respectable young man like Earl Dubose. But Ella had her own ideas and ambitions and dreams, and nobody was going to force or coax her to do anything she might end up regretting.

She, in fact, had never been truly serious about any boy, not, that is, till she met Jonathan Green at a fish fry on a lake during the summer of 1943 before both were to begin their senior year at Arcadia High. Jonathan, raised in Savannah, was a new transfer student whose father had recently opened a textile mill on an old rice plantation north of Charleston, and from the minute he and Ella were seated together and began chatting at the large communal wooden table, the two were smitten with one another.

"Grits and grunts" were the first words Ella remembered Jonathan uttering in his soft drawl.

"Beg your pardon," she said, passing a basket of cornbread to the boy seated on her left, who was talking loudly about baseball with a friend across the table.

"Grits and grunts," Jonathan repeated, an almost smug expression on his face. "Down in Savannah, we never eat fried fish without a big pot of grits. Grits and grunts, we call 'em."

"Why, I've never heard of such a thing," Ella exclaimed. "Fish with grits?"

"My mama makes the best, and these fried spots just don't taste right without some grits." He laughed while cutting into a piece of fish, then eating a forkful of coleslaw.

"Sounds kinda weird," cracked another boy across the table wearing a billed cap with the image of a swordfish on the front. "We don't eat grits like that here in Charleston."

"Nothing like it," Jonathan said in a friendly manner. "In Savannah, we even fix grits and grunts sometimes for breakfast."

"Then maybe you should go back to Savannah," the other boy muttered defiantly, picking up some fish with his fingers and popping it into his mouth.

"Oh, why don't you just shut up, Conrad?" Ella said, tossing a wadded paper napkin at him. "Don't be such a slob. Who says grits wouldn't be great with fish?"

Jonathan simply sat quietly, as if slightly hurt. Exotically handsome, with soft dark eyes, coal black hair that curled almost in ringlets, and a slightly remote attitude, he was the first boy Ella had ever met who could talk about something besides sports, cars, and clothes. For his part, he simply found Ella to be the prettiest, most outspoken creature he'd ever met, an intelligent young lady eager to ask questions and listen as he divulged his interest in Southern literature, cooking, and jazz.

"What books do you like to read the most?" she asked after the two had gotten up and moved to a bench near the water.

"Oh, Faulkner, and Rawlings, and Wolfe—I really like the novels of Thomas Wolfe. And I'm now reading a wonderful new story by this Georgia writer, Carson McCullers, called *The Heart Is a Lonely Hunter*—about a deaf-mute."

"*Look Homeward, Angel,*" Ella said almost shyly, lighting a cigarette. "We studied that novel in my English class, but I really didn't understand a lot of it—only the man's problems with his family."

Snapping repeatedly a twig he was holding in one hand, Jonathan gazed over the lake. "I think Wolfe's writing mainly about loneliness, and growing up, and . . . our need to escape to find ourselves." He flipped the pieces of the twig into the air. "I love that novel."

Ella stared admiringly at him, noticing his long eyelashes and how he blinked rapidly while talking.

"I guess you've read *The Yearling,*" she then said.

"Oh, yeah, we read that for class down in Savannah. Did you like it?"

"Oh, I cried my eyes out—just sobbed at the end."

Jonathan smiled. "Me, too, I must confess. I'd like to read more Rawlings."

Ella was on the verge of pursuing the subject when she heard the boy named Conrad yell from the table, "Hey, Ella, we're gonna go do a little shootin'. Wanna come?"

"Not this time," she called back, a look of embarrassment on her face.

"For a gal, you must be pretty good with a gun," Jonathan said somewhat in amazement.

"Just tin cans or duck decoys once in awhile," she admitted meekly, fearing his disapproval. "Hey, what's your favorite jazz and blues?"

"Oh, Bobby Johnson on alto sax," he answered without a moment's hesitation. "And Art Blakey's drumming. And have you heard this Count Basie? Wish I could play piano like that."

"You play piano?"

"If you want to call it that. Gershwin, Kern, things like that. I've played by ear since I was a kid. Do you play?"

"Oh, Lord, no. But I do love to dance. I'm really crazy about dancing."

He watched as she swept her glistening blond hair over one ear. Then he chuckled. "You've got me there."

"You don't dance?"

"About the way I play piano." He looked into her blue eyes, again smiling. "Maybe sometime you'll teach me a few steps."

Ella could have sat and smoked and talked with Jonathan all afternoon, and since he had mentioned at one point the possibility of the two of them getting together for a movie or some barbecue, her heart skipped a beat every time the phone rang over the next couple of days. That her friends didn't initially share her fascination with Jonathan might well have been due to their natural suspicions of any newcomer in their complacent, secure community. Another possible reason was the important fact that Jonathan happened to be Jewish.

Jonathan did indeed call Ella for a movie, and even though she continued to let Earl and other dates escort her from time to time to formal dances, big church picnics, and the like, it soon began to worry her family that she was spending more and more time with the Green boy from Savannah, who was rarely seen at football games and preferred reading books and listening to Count Basie records to duck hunting down on Goat Island. Together, he and Ella took long walks in Battery

Park and watched the black "basket ladies" demonstrate their skills with sweetgrass at City Market. She took him to see the rare artifacts and treasures of the Lowcountry at the Charleston Museum and the ornate plasterwork and domed ceiling in the spectacular Calhoun Mansion on Meeting Street, and he gave her her first glimpse of the interior of Beth Elohim Synagogue on Hasell Street, the birthplace of American Reform Judaism and one of the finest examples of Greek Revival architecture in the country. They ate she-crab soup and shrimp and grits at Henry's on Saturday afternoons, and when they wanted to splurge on Friday dinner, Ella would pick out one of her silk dresses and wear her lustrous hair down over her delicate shoulders and Jonathan would take her to Perdita's for the city's best flounder stuffed with crabmeat and roast squab with rice pilau.

Eventually, as Jonathan became more involved in various school activities and his classmates came to accept him as one of them, he and Ella would go horseback riding with friends, or attend war-bond rallies at the Citadel, or join others on Saturday nights at a popular jazz club on King Street where everybody drank lots of beer and Jonathan played Gershwin and Porter tunes on the upright piano. He and Ella did lots together, but, above all, they talked, and the more Ella learned about Jonathan and got to know him, the more appealing he became. Since he respected her the way young men were taught to do in those virtuous days, their intimacy was pretty much limited to innocent petting at the drive-in movie or on the beach and good-night pecks, but once, when they went to a tea dance at the elegant Fort Sumpter Hotel and were dancing especially close, Ella, smelling the clean aroma of Jonathan's neck and feeling his pronounced arousal, experienced frightening yearnings that made her shiver and perspire almost perceptably.

* * *

For a good while longer, Ella and Dr. O'Conner chatted casually about her early days in Charleston, and his wife's short career in the New York theater while he was in dental school at Seton Hall, and Sal's success as a highly respected estates lawyer in Englewood. Then, obviously determined to satisfy his curiosity about Goldie, he began to ask more questions about the unusual companion.

"I don't know what I'd have done without Goldie after Earl's death," she explained soulfully. "You know, she's pure Cherokee Indian with some strange ways, so we're different as night and day. But I've come to understand Goldie and think of her almost as family—somebody who's always there when I need her." She stopped a long while, reflecting. "Her life was so tragic when she was younger, and maybe she would have been better off and happier if she'd gone back to her own people after losing her husband and son. We'll never know. But I hope we've been the family she never really had." She paused again, a solemn expression on her face. "She probably doesn't realize it, but Goldie has taught me a lot over the years. Oh, sometimes her peculiar habits and customs make me want to wring her neck, but I'm used to it all, and don't forget that she didn't have much education, and . . . The point is, nobody's ever been more loyal to me, and, as I said, I've learned a lot from Goldie over the years—things my children and friends could never understand."

"I'd say you're very lucky to have her around," he said with a hint of envy in his voice. "Don't get me wrong. I couldn't ask for a better daughter and son-in-law than Lizzy and Sal, but, as you must know, they have their own life to lead. I guess my real salvation after Grace died was staying busy with my practice for a number of years, but since I retired . . . Well, you know, old friends and colleagues have a way of disappearing or dying, and a big house can get pretty empty sometimes." He smiled and raised his sparse eyebrows. "I'd like to believe I've helped a good many patients in my day, but, gloomy as it might sound, the one condition that not even the most brilliant medical doctor can cure is old age. And, frankly, that irritates me beyond words—irritates the hell out of me."

Ella reached again into her pocketbook for the cigarette case, but instead of opening it, she simply began rubbing it gently as she'd done so many times over the years.

"With all due respect, Dr. O'Conner, I've always refused to let that get me down, since you know as well as I do that there's not one thing on God's green earth we can do to change nature. If I allowed my age to get me down, I'd lose my mind— go stark raving mad. What's funny is that I never used to give age a second thought, or dwell so much on the past. But, you know, as we get older, age and time seem to become more important, and I do find myself thinking more and more about the old days. I don't like this, but there doesn't seem there's much I can do to control it." She paused. "In any case, contrary to what my younger children seem to think sometimes, I'm still in pretty good shape physically and mentally, so nobody's going to turn me into a feeble old lady till I'm good and ready."

"Miss Ella, the last thing I'd say you are is a feeble old lady, and the first thing I'd say is that you give new meaning to the term Southern rebel," he declared more cheerfully, obviously captivated by her spirited monologue. "And my instincts also tell me that you're a Republican."

"Staunch. Dyed in the wool. Have been my whole life, even when most Southerners were Democrats."

He simply laughed.

"Anyway," she went on, "I guess I'm content as long as I can maintain my independence. As far as I'm concerned, the one thing active oldies like you and me must hold on to as long as possible is our independence. I'm not sure about lots of things, but I'm absolutely sure that once we give up our independence, we're good as dead—finished."

"Aren't you forgetting something even more important?" he asked.

"What's that?"

"Control. The determination to maintain control over our lives."

"Same thing," she uttered casually, without thinking.

"Not really," he said, waving his finger in the air. "We can be independent but, without realizing it, allow others to make decisions that only we ourselves were once expected to make. That's losing control."

Ella's eyes began blinking rapidly, as if something had suddenly dawned on her. "Like allowing my children to decide whether I'm still capable of driving my car."

"Exactly," he confirmed. "Loss of control."

She stared admiringly at him. "Why, Dr. O'Conner, I do believe you have a little of the wise philosopher in you. You know, I never thought of it in those terms, but you're exactly right."

He laughed again, and when he asked if she'd like another Grand Marnier, she looked at her small gold watch and exclaimed, "Lord have mercy! Do you have any idea how long we've been sitting here gabbing? We're the only ones left."

"Who's keeping time?" he said. "I thought Lizzy and the kids would be back by now, but let me say, Miss Ella, I don't remember when I've enjoyed myself so much."

Ella was already gathering her pocketbook and reaching for her sweater when he stood up, took her garment, and gently placed it around her shoulders.

"Why, thank you, Dr. O'Conner," she acknowledged, now sounding almost like a schoolgirl. "And let me add what a delight this has been for me also."

"Sure I can't talk you into a nightcap?" he coaxed, taking her elbow.

"Mercy me, no, but thank you ever so kindly. Goldie must

be beside herself with worry, and, besides, I'm thinking about getting up bright and early and trying a little surf fishing since the weather's so beautiful." She turned to him as he pushed the button for the elevator. "Perhaps you'd like to fish with me one day. Shouldn't be too many people on the beach this time of year to interfere."

He smiled and squeezed her arm, which gave Ella a pleasant sensation. "I certainly would—so long as you don't expect too much from me."

After O'Conner got out on the second floor, Ella fumbled around for her room key, let herself in, and noticed immediately how Goldie had finished unpacking the bags and hanging dresses and other outfits in the closet. Then, as she was folding her sweater, there was a soft tap on the connecting door to Goldie's room.

"Yes, Goldie," she called just as the door opened, revealing the other woman in a rather crude brown and lavender shift that fell all the way to the floor.

"Just checking, Miss Ella."

"Thank you, dear. I hope you sleep well."

"Don't forget your pill. I put the bottle on the bathroom sink."

"You don't have to remind me, dear. Remember, I take one every night at home without anybody reminding me. But thank you just the same. Now, get on to bed. We may do some fishing tomorrow, and oh, yes, Goldie, do remind me in the morning to call that man in Marion about the dog."

Once Goldie had shut the door and Ella had put on her frilly nightgown, removed her makeup, brushed her teeth, and taken her pill, she decided to sit at the cracked-open window and smoke a cigarette before going to bed. As she listened to the pounding waves in the distance, she first reflected on the wonderful evening with Dr. O'Conner, which made her realize again how much she sometimes missed Earl and all the memorable times they shared together at this very location. Then, for no particular reason except maybe the mention of the dog or the pungent smell of the sea air, her thoughts shifted unchecked to a spring night back during the war on Sullivan's Island when she and Jonathan Green slipped away from an oyster roast, found a remote spot on the beach, and spread out a rough blanket on the sand. There, on their backs and holding hands, they talked and gazed up at the stars, and she remembered that Jonathan recited a beautiful passage about loneliness from Wolfe's *Look Homeward, Angel*. She also remembered the way they eventually cuddled and kissed gently, and how, despite the self-control that was expected, she yearned desperately for him to caress her more passionately and do whatever came naturally. Then, just as it seemed he might fondle her breast, there appeared out of nowhere a large white dog, a strapping, unruly Labrador eager to frolic and get as much attention as possible. At first, they looked about for the dog's possible owner and tried to shoo the animal away, but soon the blanket was a mess, and they were covered with sand, and Jonathan was laughing and playing with the beast as if it were his own. Eventually, the dog romped on down the beach, but by then the romantic mood was broken, so they whisked the sand off their clothes and slowly headed back to the party. Ella remembered how she hated that dog.

Chapter 7

NOBODY ARGUES WITH
A GUN

Before going down for breakfast, Ella picked up the phone and dialed the number the officer in Marion had jotted down on her pad. The man who answered the phone had a much deeper voice than Ella remembered, so she recounted the dog episode she was calling about and asked what had been done about the crime, adding "and I'm in no mood for a song and dance." Of course, she couldn't be certain whether the officer was telling the truth or not, but he did assure her very politely that he was familiar with the incident and that the license plate had been traced to a car over in Mullins. Ella again threatened to contact the ASPCA, but somehow the officer managed to convince her that the case was being investigated and that some action would be taken. Finally satisfied, she thanked him for being much more concerned and attentive than the other officer, asked his name, and said she planned to write a letter to the mayor of Marion complimenting at least part of his police force. No doubt the clever officer put down the phone and nonchalantly told his associates that he'd just pacified still another nut.

"They tell me the spots are biting," Riley whispered to Ella while she and Goldie were finishing a hearty Southern breakfast of fried eggs, country ham with red-eye gravy, grits, and hot buttermilk biscuits that Ella proclaimed to be as fluffy as the ones she baked.

"Then that settles it," she said excitedly. "It's a beautiful day, and we're going to do a little surf fishing. If I can't manage, Goldie will cast for me, won't you, Goldie?"

"I'll do my best, ma'am, but I never fished in the ocean."

"Well, I say it's high time you learned, don't you, Riley?"

"Yessum. Ain't nothing like it. And not many people on the beach yet to mess around."

Back in the room, Ella changed into a pair of khaki slacks, a blue and white striped shirt she didn't tuck in, and espadrilles. Then, while Goldie drove a few blocks down the beach to a tackle shop the desk clerk told them about to buy bloodworms and cut bait, she began the tricky process of rigging and oiling the rods just as Big Earl had once taught her how to do. A couple of guests did stare at the elegant older lady wearing a wide-brimmed yellow hat and her hefty Indian companion in plaid shorts with her hair braided in a ponytail as they traipsed through the lobby with fishing poles and a bucket, but Ella couldn't have cared less. Outside, next to their rented cabana, they sank two pole holders deep in the sand and baited the hooks with wiggly, slimy worms, and Ella, tossing her hat on a chair when she noticed the calm breeze, was relieved to see that the beach was still mostly empty. Wound up, she threw the canvas shoulder bag containing her personal items over one shoulder and, walking carefully in the sand, proceeded down to the water's edge.

The feel of the rod and line in her fingers was so familiar to Ella that she might well have been fishing the day before instead of for the first time in almost twenty years, but when she reared back, cast with all her might, and the rig landed only in the rough breakers, she realized angrily that she just didn't have the strength she once had. Goldie, on the other hand, who had not only grown up fly-fishing for trout in rivers on or around the reservation but also taken numerous weekend excursions with Bud when he was alive, sailed her line out maybe fifty yards like an old pro.

"Here, honey, cast mine out for me," Ella directed impatiently after reeling in, taking Goldie's rod to hold.

Goldie did as she was told, but no sooner had she landed the bait beyond the waves than Ella suddenly jerked Goldie's line and yelled, "Whoooa, I think I got one! Yep, I got one. He's on there."

While she was reeling the fish in, Goldie also suddenly pulled back hard on her line, exclaiming, "Me, too, Miss Ella! Me, too! I think I got one, too!"

"Spots!" Ella said elatedly, grabbing her writhing fish with one hand and removing the hook from its mouth like a real veteran. "Yep, they're biting. Nice size, too."

Goldie unhooked her fish with equal ease, then filled the bucket with water while Ella combed through the seaweed in a small container for a fat bloodworm and threaded one on a hook.

"What are we gonna do with these fish, Miss Ella?"

"If we get at least two more, we're going to take them to Riley and have him fry them up for breakfast, that's what. And if we have plenty, he can have some for himself. Here, honey, cast this out again for me."

By this time, a young couple walking on the beach stopped and looked with curiosity first at the fish in the bucket, then at the two strange women preparing to try their luck again. Within a few minutes, Ella pulled in another spot and Goldie followed suit, and, not long after, Goldie snagged a third, whooping with joy. Then, nothing. No more fish, not even a nibble on either line, as if the critters had all decided they were no longer hungry and simply swum away. Eventually, the women changed to cut bait, hoping to attract blues, or grouper, or anything, but, still, not a single bite.

"That's the way it goes," Ella remarked in frustration. "Maybe the tide's changing. That's what Mr. Earl used to think when they stopped biting."

"Do you know what my people would say? They'd say the sacred Water Spirit had moved the fish away so there'd be enough left in time of need. Once, they say, man became greedy about the fish, and all the rivers dried up, and soon thousands died of starvation. Now my people respect the ways of the Sacred Spirit, and nobody goes hungry."

"Makes sense," Ella commented wryly, still hoping for one more bite.

It felt so good fishing again, and even with the fish no longer cooperating, Ella loved just standing on the sparsely populated strand next to Goldie with her line taut, and the water lapping over her espadrilles, and her eyes focused on the distant horizon as the tepid sea breeze blew across her face. From time to time, she would shift her stance instinctively to maintain a steady balance in the wet sand, a move that somehow could evoke the days when she and Earl were young and the two would stand together for hours waiting for bites and talking about things that were important to them.

"Sometimes I wonder if Tyler's really enjoying himself," she remembered Earl once worrying when their oldest son refused to play with his siblings on the beach and sat quietly alone near the cabana either reading or tracing intricate designs in the sand. "He's not like the other two, you know. At times, I really don't think the boy's completely normal."

When Earl made remarks like that, Ella would feel a knot in her stomach, praying that her husband would just let the subject drop and accept his son as the individual he was.

"Of course he's normal, dear," she'd insisted. "He's just different from the other two, and you do forget that, after all, Tyler's older and gets bored easily. Maybe he'd like to fish."

At which point, she'd called to Tyler, who came running and anxiously took hold of his mother's rod. Ella remembered thinking that the gods were with them when, just as she was showing the boy how to take up slack on the line by reeling slowly and steadily, a fish hit the bait while her hand was still on the rod.

"You've got one, Tyler! Pull!" she'd howled, still helping him hold the rod. "Pull hard! You've got to hook him. Now, reel fast and keep the line tight. Keep reeling, honey. That's the boy. Don't stop. Keep reeling and watch your slack. You've got him, Tyler. Don't let him off."

"Keep reeling, Son," Earl had chimed in, placing his rod in the holder and stepping over closer as the two other children came rushing down to share the excitement. "Thatta boy, Tyler. Just keep up the slack and reel hard. Don't lose him."

When the fish came flopping through the sand, Earl had peered down anxiously. "A whiting! Son, you got a whiting— and he's a nice size. First one today. Can you beat that? Looks like we have a real fisherman in the family."

As Ella unhooked the fish and tossed him in the bucket, she hadn't known who was more thrilled, Tyler or his father. And now, still gazing over the sea at the horizon, she could still hear Earl's strong, approving voice and see him put his arm proudly around his son's small shoulders. At least for the moment, Tyler was indeed a normal boy.

No doubt the spell would have continued had Ella, all of a sudden, not become aware of how weak her knees were feeling and of the hot sun. When she mentioned this to Goldie, the Indian quickly reeled in her line and asked if Ella was sure she was all right.

"Oh, of course I am. These old knees are not what they used to be, and I'm just getting a little bit tired. Maybe, dear, if you could bring me one of those chairs from the cabana, I could get the weight off my feet and we could fish some more. I'm determined to get at least one more bite. "And, oh, yes, Goldie, also please bring me my hat. It'll ruin my hair, but it's better than getting blistered."

Goldie did as she was asked, and when Ella got settled, Goldie again cast for her, then resumed her own fishing.

The sight of a nicely dressed elderly lady in a big yellow hat perched in a chair at the water's edge with a fishing pole in her hands was enough to attract the attention of anybody strolling along the strand, not least a small group of ratty-looking young men and two skimpily clad girls, one carrying an enormous boom box and all guzzling beer from cans and using foul language that could be heard everywhere. At first, they simply meandered tipsily over to gawk in the bucket, then one of them poked a fish to see if it was still alive and yelled "Shit, man!" when it flopped about.

For a while, Ella refused to let the intrusion bother her, but when the rock music blasting on the radio began to shatter her nerves and one of the oafs hurled his empty beer can into the water, she reeled around in her chair, removed her large sunglasses, and lost all patience.

"Why did you have to do that? There're beach ordinances against littering, or don't you care? And would you please tell your friend to cut down that infernal radio so we can have a little peace?"

The man, who may have been twenty-five and wore a reversed baseball cap over his bushy hair, reached into an insulated bag slung over one of the girl's shoulders and popped open another can of beer. "This here's a public beach, old lady, and we got the right to play whatever music we want to."

"You don't have the right to get drunk and disturb others," she belted out angrily, "and you certainly don't have the right to throw cans into the ocean and fool around with our fish. Y'all have this entire beach to roam around, so we'd appreciate it if you and your friends would just move away and stop bothering us."

"*We'd appreciate it . . .*" He imitated her mockingly.

"What's wrong with looking at your goddamn fish, lady?" one of the man's pals bellowed crudely, picking a dead spot from the bucket by the tail and waving it back and forth in the air as if trying to impress the girls.

"Put that fish back down this instant!" Ella raved, laying the rod on the sand and reaching for her canvas bag hanging on the back of the chair. "And if you kids don't leave us alone, I'll have my friend there go up to the inn and call the police."

"*. . . and call the police,*" the same man mocked again, trying to mimic Ella's refined accent as his friends laughed.

All this time, Goldie had been ignored as she stood some feet away with her line still out, but when it became clear that this bunch of vulgar idiots had nothing better to do than harass an elderly lady, she reeled in and glanced about to see if there were any people close by on the strand. Normally, there would have been an attendant near the cabanas back near the dunes, but since only two others were yet occupied by older guests reading books or dozing, he was nowhere to be seen.

"Should I go up and get somebody at the inn?" Goldie asked Ella.

"No, not yet. I can handle this for the time being," she said confidently, clutching her bag tightly.

"Well, well, well, just looka there," one of the tipsy girls in a scanty gold bikini and lots of frizzy hair blared, noticing the large turquoise medallion around Goldie's neck and her braided ponytail. "Just looka there. If it's not Pocahontas herself. Hi,

Pocahontas, baby. Why aren't you in your teepee with the other squaws instead of down here at that fancy hotel with the rich palefaces?"

The man who'd picked up the fish suddenly began dancing in a circle and, patting his hand against his open mouth, whooping crazily. Then another man repeated the mockery, and everybody howled in laughter.

"Leave this lady alone," Goldie commanded of no one in particular, standing defiantly with her hands on her hips. "You don't have the right to talk to her like this."

"What's Pocahontas gonna do, scalp us if we don't behave ourselves?" one of the men now yelled sarcastically before slugging his beer.

"I can tell you one thing she ain't gonna do," another slurred. "She ain't gonna get very sunburned 'cause she's already got red skin."

The whole group howled again as Goldie simply maintained her stance and glared at them helplessly.

"I'm warning you kids for the last time," Ella declared with unusual fury. "You'll not ridicule and insult me and my friend like that, and you'll get out of here this very minute or there's going to be serious trouble."

The man wearing the baseball cap now testily poured some of his beer into the fish bucket, then garbled, "And what's Miss Gotrocks with the big fancy hat and Pocahontas gonna do to us bad ole boys? Is Miss Gotrocks gonna call the police and have us thrown in the clink?" He reared back again and pitched the can high into the ocean, the others cheering him on.

Turning around further in her chair, Ella reached into her bag, pulled out the small pistol, and waved it threateningly in the air. "I've had just about enough of this impudence," she announced slowly and dauntlessly, releasing the safety on the gun like a real expert.

The youngsters gawked incredulously at the weapon, and even Goldie appeared shaken.

"Whoa, lady," the lug in the cap muttered in disbelief, stepping back quickly with the others. "That's heavy duty, lady. That thing ain't loaded, is it?"

Her hand steady as a rock, Ella aimed the pistol at the sand not far from their feet and fired, the crack mostly muffled by the sound of the crashing waves. Instantly, one of the girls screamed and grabbed a man's arm.

"Is that real enough for you hoodlums?" she yelled at the top of her voice.

"Are you crazy, lady?" another man almost gasped, stepping back even farther. "Just cool it, lady. Cool it."

"Next time it'll be a foot or a leg," Ella warned, still waving the shiny weapon. "And I've got a permit for this, in case you're wondering."

"Let's get the hell out of here," said the girl who'd screamed, grasping the man's arm even tighter. "She's fucking crazy, Buck. Come on, let's go."

Gradually, they all began to move up the beach, swearing, and when they were some distance away, one of the men cupped his mouth with his hands and, in a slurred twang, yelled back over and over, "You're a crazy ole bitch, lady, a crazy ole bitch."

"Are you okay?" Goldie asked as Ella calmly placed the pistol back into her bag and reached for her cigarette case and lighter.

"Trash," she said with disgust, deciding the breeze was now too strong to light a cigarette. "White trash. It's those types that give the South a bad name. And let me tell you, if young people had behaved and talked like that in my day, if they'd even been seen dressed like bums, and drinking on a public beach in the middle of the day, and bothering decent folks like us, they'd have been locked up before you could say Jack Robinson."

Goldie, who'd been scanning the beach and was surprised that somebody from somewhere hadn't come rushing down after Ella fired the shot, reminded her that you see youngsters like that everywhere today.

"Miss Ella, would you really have shot them in the foot?" she then asked, still astonished by what had happened.

"Oh, of course not. I'm not that mean and stupid," she huffed. "The only thing live I ever shot was a squirrel in my pecan tree years ago. But you just can't reason with trash like that, and I had to show them the old gal meant business. Mr. Earl taught me one thing, and that's that nobody in their right mind argues with a gun."

Goldie picked up Ella's rod, reeled in the line, and asked if she wanted her to throw it out again. When Ella saw bait still on the hooks, she said it was hopeless, and that her nerves were now on end, and that she'd like to just sit in the cabana, have a nice drink, and read some of Tyler's new book.

Just as they were getting settled and Goldie was looking around for the attendant, down came Edmund O'Conner and his family headed for a cabana two down from Ella's. All were wearing bathing suits except O'Conner himself, who sported a ridiculous floral shirt, a pair of Bermuda shorts that exposed thin, pale, almost hairless legs, sandals, and a cap with a long bill that looked brand-new. The adults all greeted Ella and Goldie cordially and related how they'd just driven up to Little River to see the fishing boats while the two boys stood anxiously over the bucket staring at the fish. Then the two, followed by their father, made a dash for the ocean carrying an inflated raft, and Elizabeth and her father collapsed in chairs under an umbrella and began rummaging through canvas bags for suntan lotion, magazines, and a package of crackers.

Seeing how svelte and radiant Elizabeth still looked in her two-piece bathing suit as she rubbed lotion over her smooth arms and legs jogged Ella's memory of how attractive she herself once was when she knew Jonathan Green and envoked one particular summer day at Folly Beach with him and a group of friends. She remembered the heavy Coke cooler that Sam Ludlow had lugged down to the strand, and Bobby Fisher burying Mary Beth Williams in sand almost up to her face, and swing tunes playing on a bulky portable radio. But most of all she recalled Jonathan ribbing her about the fiery sun when they finally settled down on enormous beach towels.

"You're going to blister," he warned, pressing a finger into the pink skin of her shoulder and watching the spot instantly turn white.

"I don't blister," she said, "and I want a good tan."

"I'm telling you, smart aleck, you'll blister not tan in this blazing sun and need some oil."

"I hate that greasy stuff."

"So you want to burn and peel and look like some reptile?" he persisted, unscrewing the lid on a bottle of suntan oil. "Turn over."

"Jonathan!" she objected playfully, reaching to snatch the bottle from his hand.

"Just on your back," he said more forcefully, tugging at her arm.

After further coaxing, she finally uttered, "Okay, okay, you monster, but not too much—do you hear me?" and turned over on her stomach.

She could barely feel the hot oil he drizzled just beneath her shoulders, but when he began steadily rubbing it into her skin with soft, slightly circular strokes, she mumbled "Ummm" and cradled her head on her arms. Next she could feel a few drops of oil in the middle of her back as "In the Mood" played on Bobby's radio a few yards away, then again Jonathan's warm hands continuously and gently gliding over her vulnerable flesh.

"Feel good?" he asked.

"Ummm" was her only response.

"Don't go to sleep."

Never once inching beyond the edges of her one-piece bathing suit, he kept on rubbing her back, and when he finally stopped and dribbled more oil on both legs, Ella didn't budge or utter a word. Ever so slowly, he lightly kneaded and massaged the backs of her calves, causing Ella to yearn silently for more, and when, gradually, his hands crept up to her thighs and slid back and forth between the crevice of her legs, she thought every nerve in her body would explode. Only the interruption of Sam yelling "Anybody wanna Coke?" stopped the intensity of the sensation.

Sitting in the cabana waiting for Goldie to return, Ella glanced at the spidery veins that now covered much of her ankles. Then she watched wistfully as Sal frolicked with Tommy and his older brother in the water as they tried to catch waves with the raft, and, for a moment, she could see Big Earl with Little Earl and Olivia holding onto a big raft designed as a Confederate flag while she sat with Tyler and worried whether they were out too far. Reaching into her bag, she took out her compact, reinforced her red lipstick, and tried to neaten her hair with her fingers. Then she slowly rubbed the cigarette case and finally managed to light up a smoke.

After cavorting with the boys in the water, Sal, who had a handsome physique, pulled Elizabeth out of the chair, said he'd like to take a walk up the strand, and told Tommy and Rex to pitch ball for a while. By the time Goldie got back to say the attendant would be down shortly, the boys were bored with their game, so before their grandfather could warn them not to pester the two ladies, Tommy rushed up to Goldie and asked about her turquoise medallion. Obligingly, Goldie bent down, removed the medallion from around her neck, and handed it to the boy to admire.

"Can you make out the figure on the front?" she asked as the two boys fondled and studied the light turquoise excitedly.

"It's an eagle," Rex guessed.

"Not quite," Goldie corrected in her soft voice. "It's really a buzzard, which is as sacred to the Cherokee Indians as the buffalo. And this necklace was given to me by a medicine man when I was about your age. It's beautiful, isn't it?"

"Gosh," Tommy said. "A real medicine man like in my book?"

"Yes, a real medicine man who once helped cure me when I had a bad sickness in the stomach."

"Tom, you boys stop bothering that lady," O'Conner spoke up when he noticed the three talking.

"Oh, they're not bothering me one bit, Dr. O'Conner," Goldie assured. "I was just showing them my necklace."

"My teacher told us about buffalos," Tommy said, ignoring his grandfather. "They're out somewhere with the cowboys."

Goldie smiled and put her hand around the boy's shoulder as Ella looked on without saying a word. "Well, I guess they are today, but there was a time when the buffalo were very important to my people. Did your teacher tell you that?"

"I can't remember," the younger boy said.

"Tell us about the buzzard," Rex begged, staring intently at the medallion. "They're so ugly, aren't they?"

Now Ella smiled when she overheard the boy's comment and waved at Goldie to continue the lesson, aware that the youngsters must be about the same age as Goldie's son when he was killed.

"I tell you what, fellas," Goldie suggested, glancing back at Ella for reassurance. "Let's go sit in the sand, and have a small powwow the way we Indians do, and I'll tell you all about the sacred buzzard."

"Gosh," Tommy repeated as the three moved down toward the water and sat cross-legged in a small circle.

Both Ella and Edmund watched as the scene unfolded a few yards from them. Then, putting down his magazine, he pulled himself up from the chair, crossed in front of the empty cabana that separated his from hers, and said, "I do hope the boys are not annoying your companion."

"Heavens to Betsy, no. You see, Dr. O'Conner, I didn't go into any detail when I was telling you about Goldie, but she once had a son about that same age who was killed with his father in a tragic accident, so I think it might mean a lot to her to associate with the boys and tell them some of her wild tales. She's a very proud Indian, you know." She paused a moment. "Would you care to sit down here and keep an old lady company for a while?"

"I'd be very happy to sit down and keep a very attractive lady company," he said with a mischievous smile on his face, lowering himself into the deck chair and stretching out. "If you promise, that is, not to admire my brawny legs too much."

Ella sort of tittered, feigning embarrassment, then wondered out loud where the attendant could be.

"Can I buy you a drink?" he asked.

"No, sir, you cannot. But I can buy you one," she teased. "That is, if that confounded man ever shows up to take our order. It's been a trying morning, and I could certainly use a stiff drink."

"But it looks like the fishing was pretty good."

"Just fair, but fishing wasn't the problem. We had a very unpleasant incident with a bunch of young people down on the beach—ruffians who talked perfectly terrible to me and Goldie and caused a bad commotion. I just don't know what's happening to this young generation, Dr. O'Conner. No manners whatsoever, dressed like bums, and . . . their vulgar language is unspeakable, absolutely appalling."

"Yes, I know what you mean," he agreed, "and sometimes

I worry about Rex and Tom—though Elizabeth and Sal seem to be doing a pretty good job raising them."

Ella snapped her head around. "Why, I should say they are, Dr. O'Conner—at least from what I've noticed so far. Those two boys behave like angels compared with the riffraff we encountered this morning."

"Thank you, Miss Ella. That's encouraging. My wife, Grace, used to worry since Sal and Lizzy waited so long to have children. But Grace always worried much too much about everything and everybody—myself included."

"It sounds like she was a very good person."

"The best," he said almost somberly. "Grace was selfless. Yes, a very good and caring woman."

"My husband was also a big worrier," Ella began. "Earl worried about me and the children, and expanding his business more and more, and where we should travel next, and whether we'd end up having two dimes to rub together. Of course, there was really no reason in this world for Earl to push himself so, but he did, and I'm afraid that's what killed him. In fact, I know that's what struck him down—that and being overweight. Lord, Earl loved to eat good food, and now I have to worry myself sick over my younger son, Little Earl, who's also heavy and loves to eat as much as his daddy did."

O'Conner reached over and patted her gently on one hand covered with faint liver spots. "I bet you're a good cook."

"Well, I do love to cook when I have time, and I'm not too bad at certain Southern dishes, but, to tell the truth, I can't hold a candle to Goldie. She's become a genius in the kitchen, and I couldn't get along and entertain without her—not on your life."

He patted her again. "Let me ask you another question. Does it ever appear to you that seniors like us live too much in the past? I worry about that."

"Well, first of all, Dr. O'Conner, I dislike that term 'seniors' more than I can say. We're old people, so why not just call it like it is? Seniors: sounds like those in the last year of high school. In any case, sometimes I think I actually strive to live in the past. In fact, I guess I make every effort to live in the past since I understand the past so much better than the present. And I tell you, my era was so much more gracious and beautiful and . . . civilized than this vulgar age of computers and cell phones and jet travel and sloppy clothes and . . . racial violence everywhere you look. And, you see, Dr. O'Conner, I don't give a hoot if people think I'm old-fashioned and cranky and set in my ways. I think I've earned it, and I'm not about to change—not for one second."

He looked over admiringly at her. "You don't mind expressing your opinions, do you?"

"I should say I do not—not in the least." She laughed again. "At our age, honey, there's no time to beat around the bush." She then pointed at Goldie and the two boys at their powwow. "Now, those kids have all the time in the world to adapt to changes, and discover new horizons, and create memories—and that's their right. Me, I'm too busy trying to understand every aspect of my past and just survive in the present. Does that make one grain of sense?"

Before he could comment, they were interrupted by the uniformed cabana attendant apologizing and explaining that management up at the inn had called him on his cell phone to help move a large planter in the dining room. Ella decided she wanted a Zombie, and after she explained to O'Conner what the strong rum drink was and that she and Earl used to sip them before lunch, he said to make it two. By this time, Ella had forgotten all about the unpleasant episode on the beach, and the more she reflected on the evening before in the lounge and the charm of this Yankee doctor paying her so much attention, the more she began to feel like the permissive young lady who was once the belle of Charleston. She was on the verge of telling O'Conner more about those glorious days before her marriage, in fact, when they both noticed Goldie holding her arms out wide as if she were gliding in the air while Rex and Tommy watched and listened in utter fascination.

"And one day long, long ago," she was saying, "the Great Buzzard swooped down over the new earth where my people now live, and when his wings brushed the ground, huge mountains rose up in the mist and faded into the sky. For many seasons, my people lived there happily with the deer and buffalo and bear, but then evil strangers came to the mountains to dig for the shiny metal that glowed like the sun, and most of my people were taken away to a distant land in the West where many suffered and died of sickness. But a few escaped into the hills, and that's when the Great Buzzard returned. And when his wings touched one of the mountains, the mountain opened up, and on the other side were green fields and large rivers and forests and many deer and buffalo, and after my people passed through, the Great Buzzard closed the mountain so the Cherokees would be safe. Today, we call this land the Qualla Boundary, and we believe it is still protected by the spirit of the Great Buzzard—the same buzzard you see on my necklace."

When Goldie raised her arms again, Ella smiled warmly. "I'm sure she's telling the boys the Great Buzzard tale about how the bird saved the Cherokee tribe. Of course, it's all superstition, but, you know, I find it a very beautiful story. It's something, I can assure you, they won't be taught in school."

At that moment, Sal and Elizabeth returned from their walk and, intrigued, stood observing Goldie with their two sons till O'Conner waved them over and explained the curious powwow. In a short while, the younger couple reminded everybody that it was time to change for lunch, prompting Ella to ask them if they'd ever driven down to Pawleys Island to eat crab cakes and roam about the old rice plantations along the Waccamaw River. Elizabeth said they had indeed taken the boys to visit the venerable Hammock Shop at Pawleys on a previous trip, but when O'Conner professed total ignorance of these attractions, Ella insisted that he let her drive him down that very afternoon to visit the shop, as well as the nearby antebellum All Saints Episcopal Church. No mention was made of anyone else joining them, and when the expression on Elizabeth's face betrayed her doubts about this elderly lady and her dad zooming alone down Highway 17, all Ella did was take her arm and mutter, "Don't worry, dear, I drive all the time and have never so much as dented a fender."

Chapter 8

WACCAMAW NECK

Normally, Little Earl might go a couple of days without calling Ella, but since he and Olivia were determined to have their mother see the doctor whether she liked it or not, he'd phoned her repeatedly on Monday afternoon to tell her that she had an appointment with Dr. Singer and that they expected her to cooperate. When there was no answer, he'd figured she must be out with Goldie doing one thing or another, but when she didn't pick up even at night, he'd become alarmed and driven over to the house, only to see all the lights out and Goldie's old Chevy parked in the driveway. Letting himself in with his key, he'd gone directly to his mother's bedroom, and when she was nowhere to be found, he'd called Liv on his cell phone, asked if she knew anything, and told her she'd better come right over.

"What in hell's happening around here?" he said fretfully when his sister showed up. "What kind of stunt has she pulled now?"

"Well, I think it's perfectly obvious she's gone somewhere with Goldie," Olivia had reckoned in her simplistic way. "Lord, I hope she's all right."

"But where? Mama's never gone anywhere without telling

you or me, and if Goldie took her to the hospital for some reason, somebody would have called by now."

"Maybe she's really ticked off about us wanting her to go to the doctor, and, you know, when Mama's really mad, there's no telling what she might do."

"Oh, don't be silly, child. Mama's capable of doing lots of crazy things, but I can't imagine . . . Why, she'd never just pick up and leave, no matter what. Where would she go? Let's run next door and ask the Richardsons if they know anything."

When the neighbors appeared as surprised and concerned as Earl and Olivia, he'd suggested they return home and begin calling some of Ella's friends, which did little more than bring Lilybelle Armstrong, Jinks Ferguson, Lulu Woodside, and a few others close to hysteria. Then he'd decided to wait till the next morning, and if there was still no sign of his mother, he'd have no alternative but to notify the police and have them start a trace on her car. Which is exactly what was done the following day when it became clear that Mama Ella had simply disappeared. Obviously, the entire ordeal was not only a terrible worry for the family but an appalling embarrassment.

Of course, by the time the authorities had put out a routine bulletin with a description of the Cadillac, Ella and Edmund were sailing down the coastal highway in the car like carefree youngsters on their first sightseeing tour together of the South Carolina Lowcountry. Ella was now decked out in a colorfully designed silk blouse and white duck pants, and he was wearing a handsome safari jacket over a red polo shirt. At one point, she had apologized for her hair and said she would have to go to the beauty parlor at the inn, but he assured her it didn't matter to him what her hair looked like. Nor did it seem to matter much that Goldie and the others had been left to lounge, swim, or hold further powwows on the beach.

Since so little between Myrtle Beach and Georgetown had changed over the years, Ella recognized nearly every place name, historical landmark, and bend in the road, enlightening her companion about the great rice, indigo, and cotton plantations that once flourished from this area down to Charleston, the gracious mansions and glamorous way of life that existed all along the large inland rivers before the War Between the States, and, to be sure, the slave culture that made it all possible for the fabulously wealthy barons. Ella knew her Lowcountry history, and, as she related the facts and stories and myths, there was a melancholy nostalgia in her voice that suggested to O'Conner that she would love nothing more than to be able to return to those faraway days.

"There it is," she suddenly exclaimed, spotting The Hammock Shop on the left of the highway and turning into a complex of small wooden buildings nestled beneath gigantic oaks festooned with Spanish moss. "Finest rope handmade hammocks on the eastern seaboard, and the place looks almost like it did when I was here last. For years, they've also carried fine prints, and Lowcountry crafts and foods, and all sorts of fancy doodads, but I can recall when there was just one shop selling the hammocks."

Parking under a majestic gnarled oak, she suddenly seemed disoriented as she stared wistfully through the window at the ancient tree and had a vision of the time she'd stopped here with Jonathan Green on their excursion up to Myrtle. Clear as crystal, she could see him friskily leaping into one of the display hammocks strung between two of the old trees at the side of the shop and swinging higher and higher by sweeping his hand forcefully across the hard ground below. At one point, he reached up for her hand. She resisted at first, but when she finally relented, he playfully pulled her down on top of him and resumed propelling the two of them as they both howled with laughter. Then Jonathan stopped sweeping the ground, and, wrapped tightly in the coarse ropes, they simply lay in each other's arms as the hammock swayed slowly in the warm, humid air and they gazed up through the thick moss and listened to the crickets. Ella could have remained there forever, but, in a few minutes, a woman appeared from inside the shop, and accused them of not having any breeding, and told them in no uncertain terms that this was no playground and that the two would have to leave if they couldn't behave themselves.

Of course, this had all been shortly after Jonathan returned from the war and not long before the shattering episode that would alter the course of Ella's life forever. When he turned eighteen, Jonathan, like Ella's brother before him, had been called up almost overnight to serve in the conflict overseas and instructed to report to Fort Dix in New Jersey for induction into the army. Ella couldn't help but be proud of him as she and a few friends and his parents watched the train pull away from the station on a sweltering Charleston summer afternoon, but she was also heartsick, sadder than she'd ever been in her life as she caressed a cigarette case in her hand and wondered gloomily if she'd ever see him again.

It was during their last dinner at Perdita's that Jonathan had given her the gold-filled case with EPH monogrammed on top, and it was an evening that would remain as rooted in her memory as the faint tufts of dark hair on the backs of his almost delicate hands and the ruddy aroma of his skin when they danced close. As usual, they had both dressed appropriately for the rather formal occasion; on their intimate table along a wall were two votive candles that caused the crystal glasses and ashtray to sparkle; and in one corner of the restaurant, a small combo played soft popular tunes. Both decided to have Bulls Bay oysters as an appetizer, and though they were tempted to order the stuffed flounder once again, when the waiter described a special shrimp bog for two served in a copper casserole, they followed his recommendation.

"Do you promise to write?" Ella had asked about midway through the delicious bog, looking into his luminous eyes.

"Don't be crazy. Of course I'll write," he said nervously, reaching into the pocket of his jacket and handing her a small packet wrapped in brown paper. "And so you don't forget about me, here's something I got you."

For a moment, Ella simply sat and gazed at the case, rubbing its shiny finish and tracing the engraved letters on the lid with a finger. "Oh, it's beautiful, Jonathan, so beautiful," she then said, almost choking up and forgetting about the rest of her food.

"Not really much," he said nonchalantly. "Just something I thought you could use while I'm away."

She kept stroking the case, then reached over and squeezed his free hand. "Honey, it's the most beautiful thing anybody's ever given me. Thank you, Jonathan. It's something I'll treasure always. Believe me."

Drinking and talking late into the night, they had been almost the last customers to leave the restaurant, and before letting her out of the car at the house, Jonathan had pulled her over on the seat and, for the first time, kissed her really passionately. Ella's parents had lectured her repeatedly about getting too serious over a Jewish boy, but especially after that wonderful evening, the last thing on her mind were silly warnings that made no difference to her whatsoever. All Ella knew was that she'd never experienced such emotions over another human being, that the feeling was not just overwhelming but genuine, and that just the possibility of never seeing this boy again was too unbearable to even contemplate.

Although Earl Dubose was as anxious as other young men to serve his country in wartime, he was rejected at his physical because of poor eyesight and instead given a job helping to administer the city's gas-rationing program. For a while, Ella worked as a tour guide, escorting tourists through the historic cobblestone, palmetto-shaded streets and through some of the pastel-colored houses along Rainbow Row near her home, but when this began to bore her, she enrolled in courses in American literature and art appreciation at the College of Charleston, hoping to gain knowledge that would impress Jonathan when he got back. Although Earl had been as aware as everyone else of Ella's involvement with Jonathan, he had remained stubbornly determined to see her whenever possible and, one evening after a big oyster roast they attended up at Boone Hall Plantation given to raise money for the March of Dimes, had finally made his first move to be intimate with her when they parked outside her house.

"Do you realize, Peaches, how serious I am about you?" he openly declared, putting his arm around her shoulder and pulling her closer.

"Honey, you know I'm crazy about you too," she teased, inhaling his familiar scent, which had a woodsy quality and blended with the alcohol on his breath, "but I'm really not ready to be serious about anybody yet."

"Well, I just want you to know once and for all how I feel," he tried to stress, nudging her even closer when she didn't resist. "And there's something else I want you to know, and that's . . ." He cracked a mischievous smile and sort of chuckled ". . . well, sweetheart, one day I'm determined to marry you. Do you hear? If you'll have me, one day I wanna marry you. And that ain't the booze talking."

For a moment, Ella sat staring through the front window of the car, then, looking up tenderly at him, said, "Earl, that's one of the sweetest things anybody's ever said to me."

"Well, I've said it, so now you know."

And with no further hesitation, he clasped her head in his husky hand, and when he gently kissed her on the lips, Ella responded by putting her hand around the back of his neck and squeezing.

"That was nice," she whimpered, releasing him and reaching for the door handle. "But I mean it when I say . . . Can you understand why I'm just not ready to be serious about anyone?"

"Sure, honey, I guess I understand," he said quietly, the bulge in his trousers almost aching. "But I'm pretty patient, Peaches. I can be patient for as long as it takes."

Ella did genuinely respect and care for Earl. After all, he was a gentleman, he was fun, and never had there been a time when she didn't feel comfortable around him. Even at her young age, she was fairly certain that probably no man would make a better husband and father, but she also knew that her emotions were still too confused for her to affirm any further commitment. Of course, the major problem was that she simply was not in love with Earl.

Trained as a medic in England, Jonathan was eventually shipped to the Continent not long after D-day, and while he was not subjected to active combat, he was always close enough to the front lines to witness the horrors of war and watch the wounded die by the hundreds. He described much of the experience to Ella in the many letters he wrote from the battle zone, and she, in turn, never allowed a week to pass without sending him news from home that meant so much to him and assuring him how he was missed. Actually, it was through their steady correspondence that Ella began to realize to what extent she'd fallen truly in love with Jonathan. Now, she never for once doubted that he would return unharmed, and though she rarely mentioned Jonathan to Earl or her parents, and refused to even contemplate possible social and religious problems the two might be forced to confront in the future, her only dream was to be soon reunited with him and to pick up where they'd left off.

Little did she know that the worst problems concerning Jonathan would be neither social nor religious but directly related to dramatic events overseas that even Jonathan had little reason to anticipate. As it happened, after drinking heavily one night with buddies in a London pub shortly before leaving for France, Jonathan ended up going back to a jovial and handsome friend's flat close by to sleep it off. But there was more drinking when Sonny played swing on the Victrola, and lots of talk about being horny, and some horseplay, and, at one point, innocent frolic got out of control on the sofa and the two men found themselves unwittingly rubbing and stroking one another passionately.

"I don't know about this," Jonathan slurred fearfully when Sonny began grazing his neck with his lips, fighting the instinct to respond but aware of the wonderful sensation that ripped through his body.

"Just relax," the other man muttered, reaching down almost frantically to unbuckle Jonathan's belt. "God, I'm so horny and know you must be, too."

For a short time longer, Jonathan tried to disregard the impulses being awakened in him, but the more Sonny pecked his neck up and down and grasped at his rigid erection, the greater was the urge to reciprocate the lust and release desires that had either remained concealed or gone unacknowledged till this pivotal moment. Consequently, when Sonny blew spit into his hand, began steadily pumping Jonathan's cock, and guided Jonathan's hand to his own thick, swollen rod, all Jonathan could think about while caressing the man's strong body with his other hand was the helpless sudden longing to go a step further. Then, without warning, they both exploded almost at the same time. The following morning there was no mention of the erotic experience.

Recollections of this carnal incident did disturb Jonathan from time to time afterward, and maybe he would have been able to simply blame it all on booze and the trauma of war had it not been for a much more intense and revealing episode that occurred one night in Normandy when he and an older medic from Brooklyn who'd recently befriended him were billeted in a small, partially burned-out farmhouse. It had been another sickening day of dealing with the dead and wounded, the heat was almost stifling, and, after eating a few rations washed down with some apple brandy that an old Frenchman had given Roger, the two stripped to their underwear and stretched out on part of a singed rug in what used to be a dining room. Reeling slightly from the potent alcohol, Jonathan couldn't help but notice Roger's slight but solid build in the glow of a lantern they'd found, unaware that he was actually staring.

"How serious are you about this girl back in Charleston who keeps writing?" the older buddy asked at one point, lying on his back and blowing smoke rings in the air.

"She's a close friend," was all Jonathan could muster. "We're very close friends." He waited for Roger to continue, but when he said nothing, he asked in turn, "I guess you have a gal back in Brooklyn."

"No, not anymore," he answered, snuffing out his cigarette in a plate and taking another swig of brandy. "I figured a good-looking guy like you must have girls coming from all directions. Here, want another slug?"

Jonathan felt his heart beginning to pump faster and faster as he took the bottle. He was also aware of what was happening in his boxer shorts, so much so that he was forced to turn on his side and face Roger as he drank from the bottle.

"Got problems down there?" the other man then asked.

"What problems?" Jonathan stammered, but before he could think of an excuse, or shift around, or even get up, Roger reached up and grabbed him and pulled him down on top of him.

"Buddy, I've noticed the way you've been looking at me, and I think you need the same thing I need, and it's time we stopped playing games."

Every instinct told Jonathan to resist the lurid temptation, but when Roger held him close, and began licking his neck, and he felt the other man's hardness pressing steadfastly into his own, he could only yield to overwhelming desire as their lips met and tongues began lashing wildly. Now unrestrained, they kissed and groped and kneaded one another into utter frenzy.

"Are you all right?" O'Conner whispered to Ella as she continued to gaze at the old moss-covered oak that evoked just another memory of Jonathan.

"Of course I am," she said, snapping back to reality. "I guess I was just daydreaming. I do that sometimes."

More agile than a man half his age, he then rushed around and opened her door, after which they meandered through a number of the shop's rooms till his eye caught a beautiful old map of Georgetown with surrounding illustrations of rice plantations. Holding the map up for Ella to see, he commented that it might look good on the wall of the Marianis' den back in Englewood—a perfect momento of their trip. Ella agreed it was a lovely map; then she noticed the price on the back.

"Are they crazy?" she proclaimed indignantly. "Two hundred twenty-five dollars for a map! That's highway robbery!"

O'Conner simply laughed, told her to calm down, and said that would be a very reasonable price up North for a large antique map such as this.

"Well, this is not the North, and I think it's outrageous, and I intend to tell these people so."

Once again, he took her arm and said gently, "Now, now, Miss Ella. No need to make a scene over nothing. We both agree it's a beautiful map, and when it comes to my family and all that they do for me . . . I can afford it."

"It's not a question of affording it or not. I just don't like to be made a fool of," she huffed as he rolled up the map, nudged her toward the desk, and took out his credit card.

"Young lady," Ella said to the pretty clerk despite O'Conner's plea, "I just want to say that your prices have become disgraceful. This gentleman is visiting from up North, and I'm downright embarrassed over what he's being charged for this map."

The girl appeared taken aback for a moment as she secured the rolled-up map with a rubber band. "Oh, I'm sorry, ma'am, but I have nothing to do with the prices. I just work here. Would you like to speak with the manager?"

"No, no," O'Conner interrupted before Ella could get further worked up. "It's all right, miss. Don't worry about it."

He was coaxing Ella out of the shop when, abruptly, she turned back around and asked the clerk if she lived in the immediate area.

"Yes, ma'am. At Debidue."

"Well, then, dear, perhaps you could remind me of the exact turnoff for All Saints Church. I know it's close by, and I'd like to show it to my friend."

The girl gave the specific directions, Ella thanked her politely, and in no time she was steering the car slowly down a narrow dirt road shrouded by massive cypress and oak trees dripping with moss that O'Conner believed might well be leading into some spooky swamp.

"I take it you're Catholic," Ella commented casually as the car bumped over holes and crevices in the road and he gawked nervously straight ahead.

"With the name O'Conner?" he said. "Are you sure you know where we're going?"

"Positive," she reassured calmly. "I've been down here many times with my husband and children, and nothing's changed in Waccamaw Neck for three hundred years—unlike up in Myrtle. In case I didn't tell you, I'm Episcopalian, as is this lovely church you're going to see. Goes back to the French Huguenots who settled much of the Lowcountry and built rice plantations all along the Waccamaw and other rivers around here. That's one of the first things we learned as kids in Charleston."

Eventually, there appeared in the distance a handsome iron gate that was open, beyond which stood an imposing white stucco structure with classic Doric columns, a brick chimney, and ordinary frame windows like those found on any elegant Southern mansion. Since there was not even a lock on the front door, the two merely wandered in and gazed around the simple old interior decorated with little more than a small altar, straight pews made of cypress, a few old tablets on the walls, and a beautiful marble font to one side. Outside, the silence was broken only by the persistent trill of insects in the thick surrounding forest, and when Ella suggested they sit momentarily on a weathered bench near a small, iron fence–enclosed cemetery in the ancient churchyard, O'Conner almost felt he was in the midst of some desolate jungle.

"Lovely, isn't it?" she mused. "Few tourists ever see this church, but I thought you'd enjoy it. Time has stood still here."

"How did you first know about it?"

"Very simple. My husband's people were originally from Georgetown, and were communicants at All Saints. Of course, this isn't the same church that was built during Colonial times, which burned down, or the one that replaced the second after the war. Earl told me that at one time the church ministered to both planters and Negro slaves, and that, even after the war, the stained wooden slave galleries upstairs were considered to be the most beautiful in the whole South."

O'Conner grimaced. "Sounds a little perverse, wouldn't you say? A house of God ministering to black slaves, and people exclaiming about the architecture of their slave galleries?"

"Now, now, Dr. O'Conner," she objected with a trace of irritation in her voice. "I'm simply telling you the facts and not asking you to pass judgment on something that happened more than a century ago. Lord knows, slavery was terrible, and I don't have a prejudiced bone in my body against the Negroes, but there's nothing we can do to change history. Besides, you know, the North wasn't exactly innocent on the subject of slavery, but they don't teach that in the schools, do they? That used to just burn my husband, Earl, up."

Waggling his crossed leg up and down, he twisted his lips. "I'm afraid there's lots they don't teach in the schools today. We Irish Catholics know all about that." He paused a moment. "I can't believe that people still come all the way back here for church every Sunday."

"Have been for centuries—some of the finest families in the area." She pointed to the small cemetery. "In fact, Earl's grandparents are buried right over there, and I'll show you their graves in a minute. I once heard Earl himself say he wouldn't mind being buried here, but that wouldn't have made much sense since both his parents were buried in Charleston and we'd bought a plot for ourselves in Charlotte."

"So where was he laid to rest?"

"Oh, in Charlotte, but not on our plot as originally planned. You see, Earl loved to play golf more than anything in this world, so when he died suddenly, I finally decided to have him cremated and give him the sort of funeral he really would have appreciated. What I did was organize a big get-together at our country club, invite our best friends and his business associates, and do it up right—a fancy luncheon buffet with the dishes he loved, a jazz band playing his favorite tunes, the works. Then I contacted a close buddy of his who had a Piper Cub and gave him Earl's ashes, and while everybody was eating and listening to the music and talking about Earl, the plane flew overhead and his ashes were scattered over the club's golf course, and everybody clapped and made a big to-do over Big Earl. Needless to say, my two youngest children thought I was disrespectful and had gone stark raving mad, and I did find out later that there is an ordinance in Charlotte forbidding such things. But nobody caused any commotion and everything turned out exactly as I think Earl would have wanted it." She then appeared solemn. "I guess they'll just stick me in the ground all alone when my time comes."

With no warning, he put an arm around her shoulder, pulled her close, and, chuckling, said, "Miss Ella, you're quite a woman."

She didn't resist his gesture and simply responded alluringly, "Why, Dr. O'Conner, I can't imagine what might move you to make a statement like that."

"Oh, come on," he said, releasing her cheerfully. "We're both too old to play games. You must know you're a pretty unusual lady—and, as I said, still a very attractive one."

She pretended to blush. "Why, thank you, sir. That's the most gracious remark anybody's made to me in ages." She then glanced at her watch. "Lord have mercy, we better go take a look at those graves and get back to the inn. It'll soon be cocktail time, and the folks must be wondering what on earth has happened to us."

After they viewed the almost illegible Dubose headstones, he took her arm and was about to open her door when, in a split second, she reached for the side of the car, dropped her head, and mumbled, "Mercy me."

"Are you okay?" he called out anxiously, grabbing her around the waist as if she might fall.

For a moment, she remained silent and simply stared at the car as she tried to catch her breath, her eyes blinking rapidly. "I'm all right," she then muttered weakly. "Just a little dizzy spell. That's all it is, just a dizzy spell. Nothing to worry about. Maybe if I sat in the car for a minute and . . ." She handed him her pocketbook as he helped her down to the edge of the seat. "There's a small bottle of pills in here, and if you wouldn't mind . . ."

Nervously, he rummaged about in the large bag, past the gold case and lighter and wallet and gun and a few cotton hankies, and finally retrieved the small bottle, which he opened. She shook out a single white pill, placed it under her tongue, and sat quietly while he watched her carefully.

"How do you feel now?" he asked, bending down as the color began to return to her fragile face.

"Much better, thank you. I can't imagine what came over me, and I can't tell you how embarrassed I am."

"What are those pills?"

"Oh, they tell me I have a little heart murmur and should take one if I ever have a spell. Guess these things should be expected at my age, but it makes me mad as a hornet." She grabbed the car door and began pulling herself back up as he took her arm again. "I've had a lot on my mind lately and guess I just overdid it today. But I'm okay now. I feel just fine."

"Well, I'll tell you one thing, Miss Ella, and that's you're not driving back," he insisted, coaxing her around to the other side of the car.

For once, she offered no resistance, asking only if he thought he could handle her big car on the bumpy road. He informed her that he drove a large Mercedes himself, and had been driving down country roads and crowded northern turnpikes for years, and that she could just sit back and relax and let him take over.

"You're a very considerate gentleman, Dr. O'Conner," she said softly before he closed her door. "And I think we'll both be ready for a good honest drink when we get back."

Chapter 9

THE WHOLE OCEAN
OF TRUTH

When Ella and Edmund arrived back at the Priscilla, Elizabeth and Sal kidded her father about there maybe being a little romance in the air, then told him how the two boys seemed to have struck up a real friendship with Goldie. Ella made no mention to Goldie of her dizzy spell at the church, asking only if she'd given Riley the fish to clean and stating that Dr. O'Conner had invited them to join his family for drinks on the front porch before dinner. At one point, she thought about phoning Tyler to let him know that she and Goldie were settled and looking forward to his visit on the weekend, but since she still hadn't dressed for dinner and they were expected downstairs at seven, she decided to put off the call till the next day. What was now foremost in her thoughts was the wonderful afternoon she'd spent with Edmund O'Conner, his unpretentious sophistication, and the flattering remarks he'd made, all of which aroused in her certain emotions she hadn't sensed in years. On the other hand, she couldn't deny feeling tired after a strenuous day, and while nothing made Ella angrier than being forced to admit she simply couldn't maintain the same pace she did twenty years ago, she told Goldie that she intended to eat lightly, make it an early evening, and get a good night's sleep.

Most of the next day, in fact, she simply lounged in the cabana with her needlepoint and Tyler's memoirs, dozed, and, while Goldie either fished or told the Mariani boys more stories, analyzed what she must do during Tyler's stay. From time to time, Edmund, ignoring the much younger couple now occupying the cabana in between, would break the spell by wandering over to sit on the edge of her chair and chat. Now stuck to his rosy cheek was a tiny piece of Kleenex or toilet paper with a spot of dried blood, and, in the full light of day, there seemed to be a rusty hue to his white hair, suggesting for the first time that he may originally have been a redhead. Once again, Ella studied his dark eyes and thin eyebrows, then his hands—long, pale fingers, perfectly manicured nails, ashen hair on the knuckles—and, for a split second, she tried to imagine what it would be like if one of those hands were to accidentally brush against her breast. At times, he would talk seriously about small ailments, and politics, and his tennis game, but mostly he gabbed casually and cajoled her about her accent and Southern mannerisms, leading Ella to wonder if he was openly flirting with her. At first, such a possibility seemed far-fetched, but when he would gaze steadily into her bright eyes while making a comment, or laugh and touch her arm tenderly, she couldn't help but be seized by an undeniable thrill that made her feel very attractive and reminded her of youthful days so far in the past.

"I have a suggestion," she finally said at one point, adjusting the kerchief on her hair and popping him playfully on one bony knee.

"I have the impression you usually do," he jested.

"I think we should all go pier fishing tomorrow. I bet that's something y'all have never done, and I know it would excite Goldie. It's really loads of fun, and you're almost guaranteed to catch some fish. What do you say?"

O'Conner laughed almost like a child. "Sure, I'm game for anything, if they are, and I'm sure the boys would love the experience." He stopped a second, an apprehensive look on his venerable face as the breeze scattered his hair wildly in every direction. "But we don't have fishing rods."

"Lord, that's the least problem," she assured. "You can rent everything right on the pier—or at least you used to be able to. We could call to make sure."

"Sounds good to me."

"Fine," she said as if the proposition were already settled. "And now, I have another idea, if you don't think I'm being too presumptuous. Have you ever heard of Calabash, just up across the North Carolina border?"

He looked puzzled. "It seems I heard Sal and Elizabeth mention that. Isn't it a restaurant?"

"Not per se," she answered, an almost smug expression on her face. "Calabash is actually a small village with more seafood houses than you can count. Anyway, the last thing I want to do is impose on you and your family, but I was thinking that maybe it would be fun if we all drove up there tonight for some fried seafood and hush puppies. Ever eaten hush puppies?"

He broke out into a big smile. "No, I can't say I have."

"Well, I don't guess many Yankees have," she chuckled. "But I can tell you, honey, you don't know what you've been missing. Little fried balls of cornmeal, and there's nothing like them if they're light and crispy and well seasoned. Lord, I could eat half a dozen this very minute."

Before Ella could finish her discourse on hush puppies, Sal and Elizabeth returned from their swim, followed by the two boys, who'd been playing in the wet sand next to Goldie while she fished and intrigued them with tales about the buffalo. O'Conner informed them of Ella's two proposals, and when he mentioned Calabash, Elizabeth exclaimed that they'd indeed been there the year before, loved a particular restaurant called Pirates Cove, and thought it was a great idea for dinner. Sal added that he wasn't much of a fisherman, but since he knew the boys would get a real kick out of going on the pier, Ella and Goldie could count on them the next day.

Happy to have made friends with such a pleasant family that had what Southerners referred to as quality, not to mention being so attracted to Edmund O'Conner, Ella was excited as a schoolgirl as she poured a cool toddy, changed into an off white skirt and pink silk blouse for lunch, retouched her makeup, and thought about her beauty parlor appointment later in the afternoon. Then, just as she was wondering what she might be in the mood to eat and about to tap on Goldie's door, the phone rang. A woman's voice on the line apologized sheepishly for putting through an outside call, but, as she explained, her son in Charlotte was anxiously trying to reach her, and apparently there'd been a small incident involving the police, and perhaps Mrs. Dubose should take the call.

What had happened, of course, was that, by whatever chance or forensic maneuver, Ella's big white Cadillac had finally been located during the car trace and reported to the Charlotte police.

"Mama," Little Earl blatted on the phone, "would you mind telling us what in hell is going on? We've had the police in two states trying to track you down, and you're bound to know you've had us worried sick."

Ella simply held the receiver for a moment, thinking, then said in a low voice, "Earl, honey, I suggest first you calm down, and second, I'd appreciate you not using that tone of voice and crude language with me. I'm simply down at the beach with

Goldie on a short vacation and have my own reasons for wanting to be left alone for a while. Is that clear?"

"But for heaven's sake," he continued ranting, "the least you could have done was let somebody know where you were going. I mean, we didn't know if you were dead or alive."

"Well, Son, I'm very much alive and enjoying myself, so you can stop all your worrying."

Ella could hear him breathing heavily as he persisted in castigating her.

"Mama, have you lost your mind, just picking up and driving down to Myrtle Beach with that squaw without telling a single living soul?"

"Earl, I'll not have you referring to Goldie in those terms, and if you do so again, I'll hang up the phone this very minute. Is that understood?"

"Yeah, Mama, but this stunt you've pulled is just not normal—it's crazy—and, well, it's just one more example of why Liv and I worry about you so much. It's like those ridiculous Christmas trees, and the marijuana plant, and the staircase episode, and that gun and whiskey you carry everywhere, and . . . Well, Mama, we never know what you're going to pull next—and sometimes it gets to be downright embarrassing."

The Christmas trees Earl was referring to were the two large and medium-sized artificial trees on wheels that Ella kept in the house year-round and loved to dress with appropriate decorations not only for Christmas but for Valentine's Day, Easter, the Fourth of July, Halloween, Thanksgiving, and any other festive occasion that might inspire her imagination. No doubt the trees did cause tongues to wag, but this was a seasonal ritual that Ella had observed for years, one that gave her immense pleasure and that she had no reason to discontinue.

As for the staircase episode, this had to do with the dramatic circular mahogany staircase that once graced the house's elegant foyer and elicited awed acclamations from everybody who came to visit. The problem was that, even when Big Earl was still alive, Ella had always hated the staircase, not so much because it was difficult to carpet properly and keep clean but because it camouflaged a large space that she thought would be perfect for displaying such treasured possessions as her impressive collection of Oriental porcelain urns. She'd learned to just abide the thing, but, then, one boozy evening, a well-to-do guest who'd been marveling passionately over the staircase asked Ella if she'd ever consider selling it.

"Why don't you make me an offer?" she replied tersely to his and everyone else's astonishment.

The man, only half-seriously, quoted a handsome figure, never suspecting for a moment that Ella might actually agree to the sale.

"I'll tell you what," she said with conviction, stirring the ice in her drink with a finger. "If you can get the staircase out of here no later than tomorrow, it's yours."

The man didn't even question the urgency, and the following day, he, accompanied by a team of carpenters, dismantled the entire staircase and hauled it away to his mansion over on Queens Road West. Ella, in turn, had another, much more practical, straight staircase constructed along the wall, but before it was finished, her family and friends couldn't help but be startled and troubled by a ladder that had to be climbed to reach the second story of the house.

"I do wish you and Betty Jane and Liv would mind to your own business and, for heaven's sake, stop worrying about me so much," Ella continued with her son on the phone in utter exasperation.

"But that's the point, Mama: it is our business to be concerned about you, and it so happens that since you're so bullheaded, we've gone to the trouble of making an appointment for you to see Dr. Singer."

"You've what?"

"Next week, Mama. Dr. Singer can see you next week just for a routine checkup, and we expect you to show up. Liv says she'll even go with you."

After a long silence, Ella said calmly, "Well, you can just pick up the phone and cancel that appointment. Why, the nerve."

"Now, Mama, we're not going to argue with you till kingdom come about this. If you don't have the common good sense to take better care of yourself . . . I mean, look, just look, Mama. There you are . . . flying the coop down to Myrtle Beach without telling a single soul . . . with a heart condition . . . and driving around like you were thirty years old. . . . It's crazy, Mama. It's foolish and crazy and has us worried sick."

He was now breathing so hard that Ella could hardly catch everything he was trying to say.

"Now you listen to me, Son, and you listen to me good," she finally said slowly but sternly. "I have my own reasons for driving down to Myrtle, and I don't know exactly when Goldie and I'll be back home. But I've taken care of myself— and you and your brother and sister and daddy—for more years than I can count, and I can take care of myself now. I know y'all have my best interests at heart, but nobody—not you or Liv or Tyler or anybody—is going to dictate what I should and should not do. Is that understood?"

"But, Mama, the way you've been acting lately is just not normal," he panted, "and, frankly, we're almost at our wits' end—as I'm sure Daddy would be if he was here."

"Earl, leave your father out of this. Now, I have no intentions of seeing Dr. Singer till I need to see Dr. Singer, so you can just pick that phone back up and cancel that appointment. I'm trying to enjoy a little rest and relaxation, and I'm tired of talking about this mess. If I've upset you and the others, I'm sorry, but I'm late for lunch downstairs and so am hanging up.

For heaven's sake, Son, just stop worrying and don't bother me anymore. I'm fine, just fine."

Putting down the receiver, Ella felt her heart racing in anger, and she was just on the verge of telling Goldie that she had lost her appetite for lunch when, glancing down on the beach at a young couple frolicking like kids at the edge of the surf, the memory of her and Jonathan in front of the Ocean Forest Hotel was awakened as clear as crystal.

Like most soldiers returning from war in the summer of 1945, Jonathan had received a rousing welcome from the crowd that lined the platform at the railroad station, and the most excited among them was Ella, wearing a smart floral dress and her long blond hair tied in a ponytail with a light blue cord. To her, Jonathan looked thinner and more mature in his handsome uniform, but his mellow voice sounded just like before when he embraced his parents, and shook hands with a few men, and finally hugged Ella discreetly. She longed to kiss him, and touch his dark curly hair, and be alone with him somewhere, and when, before heading for his parents' big Chrysler, he whispered that he'd call her as soon as things calmed down, her head was spinning so fast that all she could do was light a cigarette and stare at a young Negro woman holding a screaming young child in front of a bathroom on the platform with a sign on the door that clearly read WHITES ONLY. The woman herself was almost on the verge of tears as the youngster jerked and howled.

"Is there something wrong with that child?" Ella finally asked with concern.

"She need to potty real bad, ma'am—real bad. I don't reckon . . ."

Ella tossed her cigarette on the tracks. "Give her to me," she said resolutely, "and you wait right here." With which she reached gently for the girl and disappeared into the bathroom.

Ella did detect some changes in Jonathan during the first

weeks after his return, particularly his periodic somber moods and the impression that he was drinking more heavily than she remembered. She attributed this, however, only to his rugged war experience and efforts to readjust to normal life back home. Still living with her parents the way most young ladies who were not yet married did, she'd been reasonably content making extra money by working part-time cataloging artifacts at the old Charleston Museum. Having convinced his family that he now needed his privacy, Jonathan himself had immediately rented a small row-house apartment up on King Street, talked his dad into buying him a used DeSoto, and, in return, agreed to begin working in management at the textile mill. He hated the job from the start, and told Ella that what he really wanted to do was go to college on the GI Bill, perhaps major in Southern history or literature, and get a good education before settling down. He never mentioned that his parents naturally expected him to marry a nice Jewish girl, and, as before, that was a reality that Ella still chose not to think about.

Nor had Jonathan given her the slightest reason to suspect that he might be missing another woman he'd met in Europe, much less struggling with much more alarming emotional matters. In truth, Jonathan had somehow managed to convince himself that what had happened on those two wanton nights overseas was little more than the need for solace amidst all the horrors of war and the consequences of too much alcohol, and the confidence that he loved Ella and was still attracted to her physically served only to foster any denial about himself and confirm his normalcy. It was true that he didn't seem to be quite as solicitous of her and social with others as he'd been before he left, but he still reached for her hand when they walked, and held her tightly when they danced, and enjoyed occasionally entertaining friends with his mellow piano playing and singing. And it was Jonathan, in fact, who came up with the suggestion that the two of them drive up the coast one Saturday morning, take a camera, and spend the day exploring Myrtle Beach, which was still an unspoiled community with charming family cottages, gracious hotels and rooming houses, and a relatively genteel ambiance that would one day succumb to resort vulgarity.

On the way, they had stopped not only to browse at The Hammock Shop on Pawleys Island but also to take pictures of the mysterious coves at Murrells Inlet shaded by giant live oaks dripping with Spanish moss, and when they reached Myrtle, hungry, they pulled into Mammy's Kitchen right in the center of town and ordered two fat hamburgers with french fries and Cokes. After lunch they roamed about the downtown Pavilion with others their age, then watched a couple of old salts catch spots on the long fishing pier. But what impressed Ella most was the spectacular sight of the Ocean Forest Hotel looming high and majestically above the dunes at the northernmost point of the beach. Out front were colorful cabanas filled with well-to-do hotel guests relishing the last days of summer, the same guests, Ella imagined, who would later dress for dinner and dance under the stars to the accompaniment of a famous band on the large dance floor she noticed in front of the wide front porch dotted with rocking chairs.

Anxious to dip at least their feet into the surf, they kicked off their shoes and socks, Jonathan rolled up the legs of his trousers, and, shyly, Ella held up the bottom of her gingham skirt with one hand while holding onto Jonathan with the other.

"You'll have us arrested for indecent exposure," he had joshed as the gentle waves broke over her feet and she noticed him staring at her smooth and alluring legs.

"Then maybe we'll get to see the Myrtle Beach jail, and you know what could happen in a jail," she said suggestively.

He laughed, then, taking her hand, began to gaze over the water at the horizon with a sudden solemn expression on his face. "You know what Newton said about the sea, don't you?"

"Who?"

"Sir Isaac Newton. He said, 'I feel like a little boy on the beach finding each shell prettier than the one before, while the whole ocean of truth lies undiscovered before me.' Something like that."

For a moment, Ella simply looked straight ahead, and when she turned to study his soft face and the ringlets of shining black hair that now scattered over his forehead, it seemed to her that his eyes were filling with tears.

"That's one of the most beautiful things I've ever heard," she said soulfully over the murmur of the breaking waves, squeezing his hand tightly.

"Miss Baker," he muttered. "Miss Baker taught us that in physics class, and I thought about it so often when I was over there."

Ella again remained silent for a while. Then, feeling his arm around her waist, she finally dared to ask, "Do you want to talk about what it was like, Jonathan?"

He hesitated, looking down and kicking the water. "Not really."

"You know you can talk to me about it anytime you want," she persisted, not so much curious about the details of his war experience as anxious to simply help him overcome any lingering trauma.

"Not a very pretty story," he said. "Most of it I just want to forget."

Deciding not to pressure him further, Ella reached for the Kodak in her big pocketbook, backed away, told him to say "Cheese," and snapped a picture. He then took one of her, and, stopping a man strolling on the beach, it didn't faze her to ask if he'd mind snapping one of them together in front of the hotel. Finally noticing the time, she reminded Jonathan that they'd promised to meet friends that night at the jazz club, so they returned to the car and drove straight back to Charleston without stopping.

And it was after that wonderful excursion, followed by another alcoholic, fun-filled session at the jazz club on a steamy August night, that Ella and Jonathan, letting down all defenses during a righteous era when even intimate fondling outside marriage was still considered wicked and dangerous, finally made love in the safe confines of his apartment. It all started innocently enough while they were on the second-hand sofa listening to Benny Goodman records, drinking Gin Rickeys, and discussing jazz while a rotating electric fan on a side table stirred the humid air.

"Lord, I love Hazel Scott's voice," Ella said, puffing on a cigarette.

"That's not Hazel Scott," Jonathan corrected. "That's Helen Forest."

"You're nuts!" she said playfully, reaching behind the sofa to place the needle back at the beginning of the record. "I know Scott's voice when I hear it."

Jonathan put his arm around her shoulder and squeezed. "Hazel Scott doesn't sing with the Goodman band, sweetheart. She sings with Duke Ellington and Dorsey. Forest sings with Goodman and Artie Shaw."

"But I recognize Hazel Scott's sexy voice, and I still say that's Hazel Scott."

Sipping his drink and aware once again how Ella's plump breasts more than filled out her pastel blue blouse, he pulled her closer, prompting her to drop her head onto his chest and utter "You know-it-all" while snuffing out her smoke in a large seashell on the coffee table.

"And her voice isn't as sexy as yours, honey, I can tell you that," he said a little unsteadily as the alcohol loosened his tongue even more.

With one large gulp, Ella finished her gin, placed her glass on the table, and, almost compulsively and without saying a word, reached up and pulled his head down so they could kiss like they'd never kissed before. Then, sensing that every nerve in her quivering body was on fire and forgetting every social principle she'd always followed scrupulously, she took his free hand and, as they continued to kiss passionately, pressed it against one of her firm breasts and sighed deeply when he began to clasp and caress her.

"Are you sure we should be doing this?" he asked cautiously, his voice still groggy but his heart pounding relentlessly and the tension in his groin almost aching for release.

"We're now adults, my love, and you should know how special you are to me," she whispered as the end of the spinning record repeated its scratchy monotonous sound over and over. "I want the first time for me to be with you, Jonathan."

Ella would have preferred to move into the small bedroom to continue the erotic ritual, but so eager was Jonathan to remove her clothing, and so unbridled were her own efforts to maneuver and stimulate him to the fullest, that they simply yielded to their passion right there on the tattered sofa while the dull repetition of the grating record droned on and on and the fan whirled a refreshing breeze over their perspiring bodies every few seconds. Then, after the frantic preliminaries were accomplished and they had probed the fleshy interiors of each other's mouths, there was a hiatus when Jonathan softly grazed her rigid nipples with his lips, and very calmly caressed the moist tissues of her groin with his delicate fingers, and, looking into her misty eyes at one point, uttered, "You're so beautiful." Even when she felt him enter her, producing a slight pain at first but then a rapture that made her entire body begin to erupt in spasms, she was aware how naturally gentle he was, how tenderly careful not to exaggerate his thrusts, how determined to prolong the adventure to her utmost gratification.

And when it was over and the two, drenched in sweet sweat and smoking cigarettes, lay crunched in each other's arms, Ella felt not a trace of fear or recrimination, only a fresh sense of joy that was more glorious and powerful than anything she'd ever imagined. As for Jonathan himself, the experience served mainly to exorcise whatever demons remained to threaten his normalcy.

Chapter 10

WISTERIA

The pungent odor of fried seafood literally filled the air as Goldie followed the Marianis' car into the sandy parking lot of Pirates Cove and pulled up next to another big Cadillac. Like most of the dozen or so other inexpensive, ultra-casual, family-style restaurants packed into the tiny hamlet of Calabash on the Intercoastal Waterway, this one catered as much to regular locals as to tourists from all over eager to visit the so-called Seafood Capital of the World. And, like most of the others, this pine-planked location decked out with fishing nets, an old rusted anchor, a huge salt-water aquarium at the entrance, and other maritime trappings adhered strictly to the same basic menu formula that had drawn customers back for generations: fried seafood with coleslaw, french fries, and hush puppies; fried chicken; some cut of steak; and pitchers of iced tea.

"My late husband used to say you could close your eyes while eating in any restaurant at Calabash and not know where you were," Ella whispered jokingly to Sal as a young hostess in jeans and a T-shirt showed them to a large, round wooden table under a pair of oars fixed to the wall. "He also said any dedicated alcoholic could die in one of these places," she added mischievously, referring to the policy of no booze.

"Can we sit next to Goldie?" Tommy pleaded with his father, not waiting for an answer before he and his brother plopped down on either side of her. Edmund, wearing a tan linen jacket, pulled out a chair for Ella, then sat down beside her, leaned over close, and quietly complimented her on her hair and perfume. When the waitress came to distribute menus and pour ice water, Ella debated with herself whether to take out her flask and offer a nip to O'Conner and the Marianis, but, considering the children and fearing what the others might think, she decided to play it safe. Even when she noticed a spoiled, antsy child cutting the buck at the next table, the most she did to calm her nerves was discreetly light up a cigarette and pray nobody stared daggers at her.

"Last year, we ordered the fried seafood platter," Elizabeth said, glancing at Ella and her father, "and that's exactly what I'd like tonight. You know, we just never have good fried seafood up in Jersey."

"Well, honey, you've come to the right place," Ella assured. "Frying seafood is an art down in this neck of the woods, and you won't find this even up in Charlotte. Calabash style: they say it all has to do with the fresh seafood, and light battering, and clean oil, and quick, shallow frying. Just hope it's as good as it used to be."

After lots of discussion of the menu, all the adults ultimately ordered the same platter with fish, shrimp, scallops, clams, oysters, french fries, and coleslaw, while the two boys, who hated seafood, said they wanted fried chicken and mashed potatoes. Soon, the waitress returned with two pitchers of iced tea and a big basket of oval hush puppies, but before she could leave, Ella grabbed her arm frantically.

"Honey, are those hush puppies fresh and piping hot?"

"Yes, ma'am."

"Well, you wait here just one minute. These folks are from up North, so they don't know much about hush puppies, and, even before I taste one, I want to tell you that if they've been sitting around out there and aren't really hot, I'm going to have to ask you to bring us some really fresh ones."

A little startled, the young lady looked Ella straight in the eyes. "Oh, they're right out of the pot, ma'am. They was just draining when I put 'em in the basket."

"Fine," Ella said, picking one up and taking a bite while the waitress and all at the table watched. She chewed, waited, then took another bite, her expression beaming more and more. "Good. Very good. Light and crisp and hot and . . . Do I detect a little onion?"

"Oh, yes, ma'am," we always make our hush puppies with onion."

"Well, thank you, dear. I didn't want my friends to be disappointed, and I hope you'll tell the cook that these are delicious."

Sal and Elizabeth sat intrigued with Ella throughout the entire evaluation of the hush puppies, then pretended to ignore Edmund when he grasped her hand romantically and proclaimed, "Miss Ella, you certainly put that young gal through the ringer."

"Well, as my husband used to say," she explained, passing the basket to Sal, "if the hush puppies in a place like this are not good, you can almost bet the other food will be no better. Of course, it's tricky working with any cornmeal, isn't it, Goldie?"

"Oh, yes, ma'am, especially cornpone and spoon bread."

"And, believe me, Goldie knows, don't you, Goldie?"

She then focused on Tommy and Rex, both of whom were now imitating Goldie by smearing dabs of butter on their small dodgers. "Did they tell you boys in school how the Indians taught the first pilgrims all about corn?" Before they could answer, she glanced back at Goldie. "Goldie, why don't you tell these folks about the Green Corn Moon and the Green Corn Goddess ritual up on the reservation?"

Goldie appeared shy. "Oh, Miss Ella, they're not interested in things like that."

"Sure we are, Goldie," Sal said in earnest, pointing a finger at his sons. "And you boys listen carefully so you can tell your friends."

"Well," Goldie began in her low, articulate voice, pushing up the silver bracelets on one arm, "my people believe that the Mother of Earth blessed the Indians with great hills of corn many, many ages ago before there were animals in the forest to hunt and fish in the rivers to catch, and then the Sacred Fire Kituhwa was sent to show us how to cook the corn to protect us from starvation. And so we honor every August as the month of the Green Corn Moon when the corn ripens, and at that time we hold a festival where young girls of the tribe pay tribute to the Goddess of Green Corn by dancing and letting down their long hair just as the ripe ears of corn let down their silks." She paused, as if wondering whether to continue. "Corn is still a very important symbol to the Cherokees. I remember how dried corn always hung in my mother's kitchen to protect the home, and today some of the tribal elders still bless a house by sprinkling cornmeal across the doorway during the full moon."

All eyes remained fixed on Goldie till Ella, a proud smile on her face, said, "I think the story about the girls letting down their hair is one of the most beautiful I've ever heard."

"I agree, Miss Ella," Elizabeth said. "I could listen to Goldie all night."

"Tell us some more stories, Goldie," Rex pleaded anxiously, tugging on her arm.

Sal and Edmund both asked Goldie a few practical questions about the exotic style of life and tribal customs on the reservations, and no doubt she would have related more fascinating tales of Cherokee culture had the food not arrived, along with another basket of piping hot hush puppies and more iced tea. Since Sal had never mentioned his job, Ella quizzed him for a while about not only estates law in general but certain legal technicalities involved in the transfer of real estate in last wills, but when the subject appeared to bore the others, she and the Marianis exchanged a few stories about traveling in Italy while Edmund simply listened and the boys whispered with Goldie. When, from time to time, Edmund would find something Ella said particularly amusing, he'd laugh and gently pat her arm, a gesture that never failed to titillate her and capture the younger couple's smiling notice. Everybody ate heartily, Goldie finally relaxed around the strangers and relished the boys' attention, and by the time the meal was over, Ella sensed that she was part of a respectable, congenial family—not unlike the one that had once brought her so much happiness. Then, when the waitress placed the bill in the middle of the table, Ella immediately reached over and grabbed it.

"Not on your life, Miss Ella," exclaimed Sal, wiggling his fingers in the air for her to pass it over.

"Why not?" she protested. "I'm the one who suggested we come here, so you are my guests."

Before the two could argue further, Edmund puckishly snatched the small sheet from her hand and said, "Nonsense, Miss Ella. No lady picks up my bill—not for me and my entire family. This has been a real treat and privilege, and this old fogy will not discuss it further with you naive upstarts." He leaned over close to Ella. "And I haven't even had a drink."

The others couldn't help but laugh, so Ella, not about to create a scene, simply looked admiringly at Edmund and said, "You're a naughty but very gracious man, Dr. O'Conner."

"Daddy, can we go to Fast Eddie's?" Tommy blurted all at once to his father as everyone got up to leave.

"Tommy, I don't think that's a good idea tonight," Sal answered, putting his arm around the boy's shoulder. "Remember we're going fishing with Miss Ella and Goldie tomorrow and need to get to bed early. Maybe later on in the week."

"Please, Daddy," Rex begged. "You promised. Can't we go for just a little while—please?"

Located on the main street of what was once known as Ocean Drive Beach before the small, independent township, like so many others, was incorporated ignominiously into North Myrtle Beach, Fast Eddie's had attained mythical status as one of the few remaining old-fashioned public dance clubs where people could still come to shag and slow dance to the music of Johnny Mathis, Nat King Cole, Ella Fitzgerald, and other stars of the fifties popular long before the appearance of hard rock and disco. Inside the concrete building was a well-stocked bar, Naugahyde booths, low lighting, a disc jockey at a tape deck, and an extensive wooden dance floor never without traces of sand. Without question, the vast majority of customers were middle-aged sentimentalists eager to recapture a glorious era when the shag and more romantic music dominated the late-night scene at the outdoor O. D. Pavilion only a block away near the water. But there was also always a surprising number of younger faces, and, since the place was so civilized and didn't seem to impose any underage restrictions on the clientele, it was not unusual to spot couples like the Marianis, with adolescent children in tow, either dancing or sitting quietly drinking and listening to the nostalgic music. Told about Fast Eddie's by friends at the Priscilla the year before, Sal and Elizabeth had gone to the club with the boys one night, and since Tommy and Rex had never been exposed back home to any such social arena, to them the place was an exciting live adventure they'd never forgotten.

"Son," Sal insisted, "I don't think a dance club is your grandfather's and Miss Ella's idea of a good time. Do you understand?"

"What kind of dance club?" Ella interrupted abruptly as she held onto Edmund's arm on the way to the parking lot.

Sal and Elizabeth described the setting and music, prompting Ella to stop and relate how she and Earl used to dance the evenings away at the old Ocean Forest Hotel and the Myrtle Pavilion, and any number of other nightspots.

"Why, I had no idea such places still existed," she exclaimed, "not since real dancing at the old Pavilions went out of style. Wouldn't you know it takes Yankee ingenuity to find out about something like that. Well, personally, I'd love to drop by this Fast Eddie's for old time's sake—so long as you promise there's none of that indecent, wild music you hear everywhere today." She looked up at Edmund and squeezed his arm. "Are we up to it, Dr. O'Conner?"

"I'm just along for the ride," he quipped, guiding her over to her car, where Goldie was waiting. "We only live twice, as they say."

When they entered the club, which was about half full of mostly older customers, Frank Sinatra was crooning "My Way" over the sound system, and a few couples were dancing cheek to cheek. After they'd arranged themselves in a large booth, Ella, Edmund, and the Marianis decided to order beers and told the waitress to bring Cokes for Goldie and the boys. Then, when a snappier tune sung by the Drifters was played, rousing Ella to beat time with her foot, a few people got up and, extending one hand to their partners, began to execute a special style of sliding footwork on the sandy floor.

"Now, that's the shag," Ella informed the others excitedly. "You know, they say the shag was invented here at O. D. Who knows if it's true, but, Lord, I'd like to have a dime for every time I shagged down here in the old days."

Paul Anka, Buddy Holly, Sarah Vaughan, Sonny Rollins, Bo Diddley—the songs played one after the next, some fast, some slow, and, at one point, Sal pulled Elizabeth up and caused the boys to snicker as they watched their parents move a little awkwardly about the dance floor. Then Elizabeth coaxed Tommy up playfully and tried to show him a few steps, and when the boy's confidence had been bolstered, he tugged at Goldie till she followed him reluctantly and danced surprisingly well to a rockabilly classic by the Everly Brothers. Next it was Rex's turn with Goldie, who, towering over the boy, seemed to lose herself in all the fun while those back at the table cheered them on. Throughout it all, Ella tapped her hand steadily on the table, but when the disc jockey slipped in a real oldie of Jo Stafford singing "Long Ago and Far Away," a chill went through her entire body as the song abruptly and uncontrollably evoked a warm evening in Charleston before Jonathan Green was drafted when the two attended a student war-bond dance in the ballroom of the Fort Sumpter Hotel.

All had been enjoyable, she recalled, till a husky, swaggering star on the high-school football team, soused to the point of tottering, tried to break in on Jonathan and Ella while they were dancing. At first, they simply ignored him, but when he persisted, Jonathan accused him of being drunk and impolite and said they'd like to be left alone. Insulted, the oaf whacked Jonathan's shoulder with the heel of his hand, which knocked him off balance and caused those in the immediate vicinity to back away in dismay.

"So I ain't good enough to dance with the Jew boy's gal," he had slurred, again pushing Jonathan back.

"Just leave us alone, Barney," Jonathan said, but no sooner had he uttered the plea than he was hit again.

Jonathan attempted to retaliate by shoving him away, but such was the other's brawn that it was like striking a tree.

"So the Jew squirt's looking for trouble," Barney garbled almost incoherently, socking him again on the shoulder. "Let's see ya defend yo woman, Jew boy."

"Okay, Barney, enough's enough," Ella exploded, turning

to those gathered around the fracas. "Would somebody please go find a chaperone this minute?"

"Oh, so now Miss Ella Hodges has to take up for her poor little Jew boy," Barney bellowed cruelly, reaching out to try to chuck her playfully under the chin.

She recoiled and, not caring how unladylike she might appear, swung her hand back as far as possible and slammed him in the face with all her might, declaring, "Barney, you're nothing but a crude slob!"

For a moment, he appeared stunned, and by the time he'd regained his stamina, two rugged-looking older men in tuxedos emerged from nowhere, sized up the scene, and, seizing him harshly by the arms, led him away as the lively music from the bandstand in the distance played on.

Ella remembered how she and Jonathan had gone to sit down awhile, and how she couldn't determine whether he was more angry or humiliated, and how swollen eyes showed he was doing all he could to hold back the tears. All she wanted to do at that moment was pull him over close and reassure him, but, instead, she simply took his hand and waited till the band again played the sort of slow, romantic music he liked so much. The tune the female vocalist sang was "Long Ago and Far Away," so they returned to the dance floor, and didn't say a word, and held each other more tightly than they ever had, and listened to the sad lyrics.

The nostalgia was broken when Stafford's final notes faded away, the familiar strains of Johnny Mathis's "Chances Are" began, and Ella once again felt Edmund take her hand.

"Shall we show them how it's really done by two old veterans?" he said wistfully.

Looking a little surprised as she wasted no time pulling

herself up on her feet, Ella answered, "Well, Dr. O'Conner, you've never mentioned that hoofing is another one of your talents."

"Oh, I'm no Astaire," he joked, "but Grace used to say that I could cut a pretty good rug if I was in the right mood."

And, indeed, it didn't take a moment for Ella to realize that the good doctor was as light and articulate on his feet as Earl had ever been, providing a strong lead that allowed them to move gracefully in sync with each other's steps and attract the attention of rather startled admirers all around the dance floor. Ella, of course, loved just the action of dancing again after so many years, but what confused her emotions was being held close by a man whom she'd come to really like and admire and noticing those little things that long ago had always sparked her most primal instincts—the clean aroma of soap on Edmund's neck, the warmth of his breath when he made utterances, the tight grasp of his fingers beneath her shoulder blade, and, undeniably, the erotic sensation of brushing repeatedly against his groin. Now, however, it didn't seem to matter that she was no longer the alluring siren once capable of arousing any male in her clutches, or that the ripe partner she was dancing with made no unruly attempts to caress and fondle with calculated prospects in mind. She remembered. Oh, she remembered all right. But time and experience and, yes, fragility had tamed such wanton impulses in them both, leaving mainly the placid yearning to thwart loneliness by sharing a few simple, unadorned pleasures in a world that was passing them by. Being wrapped in Edmund's arms did make Ella feel good and appreciated, but it also reawakened in her certain memories that she'd spent a lifetime trying to eradicate, memories that burrowed deep in her soul and threatened to haunt her forever.

"You're good," O'Conner proclaimed, breaking away slightly

and gazing into her face as Nat King Cole's "Too Young" began over the speakers. "You must have had plenty of practice."

"Oh, mercy, I haven't danced in ages, but, yes, I've always loved it ever since my high-school years in Charleston. And I might add that you're not so bad yourself."

"Well, I did have lots of practice with Grace when we were younger and socialized a good deal at my tennis club—a nice relief from cutting into gums day after day." He laughed, then pulled her close again.

"Why can't they write respectable music like this today?" Ella mumbled in his ear. "With words that really mean something?"

"It's just a whole other new generation, Miss Ella, and, let's face it, we're on the sidelines."

"Well, it doesn't mean I have to like and accept it."

Just as she was getting morose, Chuck Berry's "Maybellene" livened up the mood, stirring more couples to approach the dance floor but causing Edmund to break away and announce jovially, "Okay, that's too much for these old limbs."

"Oh, nonsense, Dr. O'Conner," she protested, refusing to release his hand. "We haven't even shagged yet, so here, let me show you how. Just follow me."

With which she began to shuffle confidently and slide her low-heeled pumps over the sandy floor while twisting the two joined hands back and forth in time with the catchy beat. In no time, he caught on to the technique, now seemingly no more aware than she that what they were doing could be a little too reckless at their age.

"Now, pull me to you," she then directed, "and grab me around the waist."

He complied, holding her in such an agile manner that the two, side by side and facing out, shuffled in place almost like runners getting ready to sprint. After a few moments, she reeled herself loose again and, never releasing his hand, resumed her stance facing him. It was at this point that she started to perspire and felt her heart thumping, so, exclaiming "Mercy me, mercy me," she finally nudged up against him and declared that perhaps it would be a good idea to sit down and rest.

Everyone at the table sat with dazed expressions except Goldie, who had stood up to watch with her hands clasped in front of her chest and a wide grin on her face.

"Hollywood, here we come," Sal exclaimed, patting his father-in-law proudly on the back as the older man helped Ella slide back into the booth and the two boys stared at her with twinkles of admiration in their eyes.

"That was lots of fun," Ella said to Goldie as they drove slowly down Ocean Boulevard back to the Priscilla, and her spirits would have remained high had she not caught the despised but unmistakable scent of wisteria that drifted from nowhere in the open window of the car and, brutally, forced her not only to relive once again that shocking night in Charleston when all hope of any happiness with Jonathan Green was devastated in a matter of minutes but also to soon make vital decisions that would determine the direction of her entire future.

The episode had unfolded no later than the steamy weekend following their intense lovemaking at Jonathan's apartment, and the locale was the rather grand two-story Georgian house on lower King Street of a newly married couple who'd hired a local band and invited lots of people over for a buffet supper and dancing in honor of some out-of-town friends. Jonathan hadn't been particularly anxious to attend the get-together, but after Ella had promised that they wouldn't stay till the wee hours, he had finally agreed to pick her up in the two-tone DeSoto. As usual, the party began on a quiet, dignified note as guests helped themselves to shrimp paste on toast, baked country ham, chicken perloo, benne seed biscuits, and many other Lowcountry dishes that filled a buffet table set up in the parlor. In fine Charleston tradition, there were also huge crystal bowls of lethal punch placed strategically in various areas on the first floor, explanation enough of why most of the revelers were well on the road to being smashed after the Oriental carpet in the spacious living room was rolled back and the band's tempo picked up. By eleven o'clock, the evening was in full swing, and nobody was living it up more than Ella Hodges as she and Earl Dubose or another dance partner did full justice to the jitterbug and Charleston.

Earlier in the evening, when the music was slower and more romantic, Ella had naturally taken every opportunity possible to dance cheek to cheek with Jonathan, since that was more his style, but once the action had picked up and one after another blade had asked her for a twirl around the floor, Jonathan seemed perfectly content in the next room drinking and chatting with a young man from Spartanburg who was enrolled in the history department at USC in Columbia. At one point, when Ella strolled in casually under the pretense of being exhausted and needing another glass of punch, she couldn't help but notice how glassy Jonathan's eyes were and the way his speech was slurred from the alcohol; and she couldn't help but notice how he weaved when he stood up to peck her on the cheek and ask groggily if she was having a good time. The handsome other boy, Jeremy, couldn't have been more courteous, and, in fact, Ella was just about to ask boldly if he liked to Lindy when Earl, also in his cups, suddenly appeared, grabbed her by the arm, and playfully pulled her back to the dance floor.

As the night wore on and the crowd got more rowdy, Ella did find it strange that Jonathan, who continued to spend most of his time huddled in conversation or tottering about with his

arm over the shoulder of the stranger from Columbia, was ignoring her and everybody else at the party. No doubt, she figured, he was simply learning everything about the university
he could from this student, and though he'd obviously had
much too much to drink, it made her happy to see him in a
better mood and once again enjoying himself socially. On the
other hand, she now looked upon Jonathan and herself as
much more than mere friends, considering what had happened between them just the week before, and while she accepted the fact that it wasn't in his nature to kick up his heels
the way she liked to do at affairs such as this, she still had to
wonder why he was paying her so little attention.

The harsh answer came after she and a group of friends
were gathered around the piano boozily singing "I Can't
Give You Anything But Love, Baby," and she noticed
Jonathan and Jeremy in the distance staggering down a small
flight of stairs that led to the garden in back of the house. For
a while, she tried to disregard the occurrence, then, out of
worry or curiosity, her instincts forced her to go check on
them. Outside, the humid air was not as stifling as indoors;
there was a strong fragrance of wisteria that crept up a wide
trellis at the far end of the walled garden, and the only light
was that reflected from the tall parlor windows. Standing on
the thick grass with her drink in her hand, all she could hear
at first was the muffled racket from inside the house, but
when she walked closer to the trellis, she detected low voices
garbled by what sounded like intermittent moans. Now a little frightened, she took a few more steps in the direction of
the sounds, and when she reached the trellis and peered behind it, what she could discern, what she could definitely
make out in the dim glow, was the unmistakable sight of
Jonathan eagerly caressing Jeremy's chest under his shirt as
they kissed passionately. At first the two were so wrapped up

in their lust that they didn't notice her, but when a massive shiver caused her to drop her cup and they heard the faint thud, they frantically broke away from each other and could only stare at her in terror.

"Ella!" was all Jonathan finally mustered as Jeremy nervously turned around and tucked his shirt back into his trousers.

For a moment, she simply stood and glared at Jonathan, so stunned in disbelief and embarrassment that she could hardly catch her breath, much less utter a word. Then, regaining what composure she could, she turned and walked rapidly back toward the house as her eyes began to tear uncontrollably. Inside, the gang around the piano was still singing upbeat tunes, and, after dabbing her eyes with a paper napkin, she spotted Earl, went up and took his arm, and discreetly coaxed him out into the hallway.

"Would you mind driving me home now?" she asked pointedly and undramatically.

"Why sure, honey," he agreed, studying her face carefully. "Are you okay?"

"Of course I am," she said softly. "I'm just hot and tired, and have had too much to drink, and I don't feel like hanging around here any longer. Do you mind?"

Earl didn't ask any more questions, but after they'd extended their thanks to Pinky Stoudemire and headed outside to Earl's car on the tree-lined street buzzing with crickets, Ella, helpless to control her emotions any longer, suddenly threw her arms around Earl's broad shoulders and sobbed like a distraught child, her whole body trembling.

"Hey, hey, sugar pie," he tried to console, holding her tightly, "what brought all this on?"

"Oh, Earl," was all she could mutter between gasps.

"What's wrong, sweetie? Is it Jonathan? Has Jonathan done or said something to hurt you?" he asked in an angry tone.

For a long moment, she fought the urge to relate what

she'd just witnessed in the garden. Then, taking the handkerchief Earl had given her, she backed away, wiped her nose and eyes, and repeated, "Honey, I've just had too much to drink and need to go home. Please take me home, Earl."

Having learned long ago not to pry too deeply into the causes of Ella's erratic moods, and that patience on many levels was the only way he might one day win her over, Earl simply put his arm around her shoulder, opened the car door, and said, "Hop in, sweetie."

Chapter 11

IN THE GAZEBO

After the numbing incident in the garden, Ella hadn't closed her eyes all night, and when her mother came into her room the next morning while she was dressing for early church and commented on how tired she looked, Ella simply passed it off as a consequence of too much late-night fun at the Stoudemires' home. Foremost in her mind, of course, was if and when Jonathan might call to account for his shocking conduct, or at least to suggest that the two have a long talk so he might offer some rational explanation that Ella could understand. But deep down she knew, her instincts told her, that Jonathan would not call, or come by, or make any attempt to justify such repulsive behavior. At first, she had been simply stunned, angry, and full of a desire for revenge against this man who had taken full emotional and physical advantage of her, then committed such an indecent act. What she now sensed most, however, was intense hurt and a gnawing need to comprehend why Jonathan could have done something so abnormal and scandalous. Things like that just didn't happen in Charleston, and if they did, she'd read somewhere how such people were locked away in jails or insane asylums. She desperately wanted to discuss it with her mother, or a close girlfriend, or even Earl, but just the humiliation and the prospect of appearing blind and foolish were enough to persuade her to keep the entire ugly story to herself. What did she expect, people would say, getting so tied up with a Jewish boy? Never did Ella feel so alone or cry so much in private, and perhaps the worst part, even worse than not grasping how such tragic realities can simply be part of life, was the frightening awareness that, despite all, she was still deeply in love with Jonathan.

Ella may have been youthfully naive in some respects, but she was not so vulnerable that she was unable to make strong, sensible decisions once determination had become a driving force. Which is why, not long after Jonathan's deception, and given a little time to calmly, carefully analyze her predicament and her future, she left work at the museum one day, called Earl, and asked if they could have a quiet dinner together at Henry's. By now, Earl had managed to buy a small but well-preserved Colonial house on Queen Street and was already making a moderate success of a small printing company called PrintCraft that he and a partner had begun in north Charleston in connection with his father's pulpwood enterprise. Although he was working almost day and night to build up more business, he didn't hesitate a second to agree to whatever Ella wanted to do, no matter how perplexing the request.

Charleston was still legally as dry as the rest of South Carolina when it came to serving alcohol in restaurants, but as with most other hedonistic locals, neither Earl nor Ella ever allowed the stupid law to stop them from carrying a flask or small bottle of bourbon to pour into glasses of ice water even under the indifferent eyes of waiters. And it was while Earl was doctoring her glass that Ella casually asked him a question that made him almost splash booze on the tablecloth.

"Earl, do you still want to marry me?"

He pushed his glasses back on his nose, then struggled to light her cigarette as he stared at her with a vivid expression on his face.

"Honey, are you serious?" he asked slowly in his deep, strong drawl, now nervously fingering the knot of his necktie.

Looking pretty as ever with her long blond hair tumbling radiantly over a pale yellow sweater worn around the shoulders, she fixed her soft eyes on him. "I wouldn't bring it up if I weren't serious."

He looked almost frightened. "Well, I'll be damned," he said more confidently, taking a long slug of his drink. "You know I do, Ella. You know I do. You must know I've wanted to marry you ever since we finished school, and I've never given up hope—not for one second."

"Well, I'm finally ready to talk about it, so let's talk about it."

The old black waiter, wearing a tuxedo, served her bowl of she-crab soup, then placed Earl's small raw oysters nestled on cracked ice in front of him.

He reached over and took her free hand. "Do you mind me asking what's brought this on so suddenly?"

She lowered her head and pretended to be rearranging the white napkin over her simple pink and white dress. "It's not so sudden, not really. I've thought about it lots of times. You've always been special to me, Earl—you should know that by now. Maybe I just had to grow up and get a few crazy things out of my system. Does that make any sense?"

He looked at her knowingly. "Are you talking about Jonathan?"

"That's over," she answered bluntly, stirring her soup gently with the spoon. "All over."

"Because he's Jewish?"

"Don't be absurd. Of course not. But what I now realize is that Jonathan has been just a long infatuation—maybe like you and Mary Beth Williams when you were seeing so much of her. He's different, you know—hard to understand. And, of course, the war changed Jonathan a lot—everybody's aware of that. Lord knows what all happened over there, but he's never been the same person, and maybe I've just been feeling sorry for him. He could be fun, but, whatever, it was just an infatuation, and now it's over. We all have to grow up and start thinking like adults, don't we?"

She began looking anxiously about the room. "Honey, do you think we could get some more water?"

Earl signaled the waiter, and when their glasses were refilled, he reached inside his plaid jacket for the flask and again spiked both drinks.

"I do want to thank you, honey, thank you with all my heart for being so patient with me all this time," she continued. "I mean, we've been through right much together, and had some great times, and you're the one person, the one living soul, I've always known I could count on and trust, and, well . . . What I guess I now realize most, Earl, is that I'm always happy and relaxed and not at all upset when I'm with you. And I'm ready to settle down—it's time we both started to settle down a little. I think I'm really ready to settle down and start leading a more mature life. Am I making any sense?"

He reached over and took both of her hands, and she could feel that he was trembling slightly. "Are you trying to say what I think you're saying? Are you saying, sweetheart, that you'll actually marry me?"

Ella smiled, then kissed one of his hands. "Do you think we could make a go of it, Earl? Do you think we could really make it work the way I've always dreamed marriage should work?"

He squeezed her hands tightly. "I know we can make it work, sweetheart. Why in blazes wouldn't it work? As far as I'm concerned, we were made for each other. I knew that the first time I laid eyes on you, and my feelings have never changed—not one iota. I love you, Ella, and I want to share everything with you, and raise a good family we can be proud of, and grow old as the hills with you."

Ella sat still for a long moment, relishing his comforting words, and praying he wasn't going to ask if she was deeply in love with him, and trying to forget all about her secret sadness. She then again looked him straight in the eyes and gave him a mischievous smile.

"Then I'd say we've just made a very important deal."

Earl's face was now as flushed as a child's with excitement. "Do you really mean it, Ella? You're not putting me on, are you?"

"Stop asking me so many crazy questions," she said, laughing. "How could I have any doubts about the best dancer in the entire South?" Then she looked at him tenderly, and, for an instant, the idea of being truly intimate with Earl made her tingle inside as she watched him rake his fingers through his straight, brown hair and beheld him in a strange new light.

"Hot damn!" he blurted out uncontrollably, jumping up from his chair to hug her tightly while a much older couple at the next table watched with surprise and the waiter rushed over anxiously to remove what was left of the soup. "We're gonna get married! This sweet little lady here has just agreed to marry me!" he gushed openly to the other couple, who broke into big smiles and discreetly extended their congratulations.

Ella began to blush from embarrassment and coaxed Earl back into his chair.

"Wait, just wait till I tell Mama and Daddy," he exclaimed next, reaching for his drink as the waiter asked if they were ready for the shrimp Newburg they'd both ordered. "You've always been their favorite, you know, and they're gonna be so thrilled—tickled pink."

"Same with mine," she added joyfully. "Especially Mama. She never stops talking about what a handsome gentleman you are and what good manners you have."

The waiter returned with plates of steaming white rice, then very ceremoniously spooned richly sauced shrimp from a chafing dish over the mounds and sprinkled a little paprika over each serving. Impressed, they each tasted the dish and proclaimed it excellent, but tonight their concentration was hardly on the food, delicious as it was. Earl was simply ecstatic and eager to discuss their future together. No matter that she still hadn't uttered the four-letter word he was yearning to hear. Such, he reasoned, was just not in Ella's nature. Her emotions were more complex, though she now experienced a wonderful sense of relief that almost managed to erase much of the anxiety that had been threatening to devour her. Then Earl became very serious, almost solemn.

"I want you to know, Ella, that you've just made me the happiest man in the world—my biggest dream come true. And I'll make you a good husband, sweetheart—that you can bet your life on. I have some big ideas and career plans, you know, and now you'll be part of everything. One day, you'll be really proud of me. I'll show you. I'll make you the proudest gal in South Carolina—in the whole South." He then hesitated and frowned. "But you know something? This is an occasion for champagne. We ought to have champagne right now to celebrate something this important. It's ridiculous, plain down ridiculous we can't order a damn bottle of champagne in this backward state." He stopped again, taking another big sip of his drink and buttering a lukewarm biscuit. "Okay, sweetheart, so when do we tie the knot—before you change your mind?"

"What about tomorrow?" she teased, her small mouth stretching to a wide grin. "In the Gazebo. Not too many people."

She was referring to the most romantic spot and number

one marriage site in the city, a gazebo in White Point Gardens, overlooking the harbor, where nuptials were an old Charleston tradition.

"Wouldn't that be rushing it a little?" he joked. "I hear you've got to reserve that place ages in advance."

"Not if you know the right people," she whispered. "And my sweet daddy, he knows the right people."

"You're serious about this, sugar, aren't you?" he said excitedly, grabbing her hand again.

"Well, as you know, I've never been one to beat around the bush."

After their plates had been cleared from the table, the waiter appeared with a small pecan pie with a single lighted candle stuck in the middle. Everyone around them began to clap cheerfully, and, utterly surprised, Ella and Earl both beamed.

And, as luck would have it, Archie Hodges did indeed learn that, due to an unexpected cancellation, the Gazebo would be available on a Saturday just two weeks away, and that the assistant priest at St. Philip's was free to perform the ceremony. Since Ella had made it perfectly clear that she wanted a simple wedding that would not cost her parents an arm and a leg, it was decided that no more than about forty family members and old friends would be invited and that she would wear a modest off white linen dress with matching veiled hat, elbow-length gloves, and low-heeled pumps. At first, she had no intention of including Jonathan's name on the guest list. When, however, she realized the gossip this could cause given her close friendship with him, she sent him an invitation, almost certain that he'd find a legitimate excuse not to show up. Not that anybody had ever believed for a moment that Ella might actually one day marry a Jew, but for her to ignore a man she'd been dating on and off for a long time would not only have been abnormal but possibly solicited more questions than she cared to answer.

After a frantic two weeks for all concerned, Ella and Earl were married on a bright, warm day amidst a rainbow of fresh flowers that filled the Gazebo and to the music of a small string orchestra that Archie Hodges had engaged. She was given away by her proud father, while Earl's served as his best man, and both mothers cried profusely. When the ceremony was over and Jonathan surprisingly appeared with a few friends to congratulate the couple and wish them luck, a terrible anxiety seized Ella that she had a hard time camouflaging. She wondered if he'd also attend the punch-and-buffet reception sponsored by her parents at St. Cecilia's, but he never came. For the honeymoon, Earl had wanted to book a wildly expensive suite at the Ocean Forest Hotel up in Myrtle Beach, but Ella found that extravagant, so he settled for a beautiful oceanfront room at the equally exclusive but more reasonably priced Priscilla Inn not far away.

Like most normal young men of his chaste generation who were expected to conform to rigid principles of morality—especially in a town like Charleston—Earl Dubose had never once crossed the limits of sexual boldness with a woman till the night he made love to Ella on their honeymoon. Not, by any means, that he'd been idle while forever hoping that Ella would eventually tire of infatuations with other men like Jonathan Green and finally focus more serious attention on him. Rarely was Earl without a date at all the social functions and athletic events he attended with those he'd known in high school and an ever-growing contingent of new friends, and because he was an ardent football fan, a great dancer, and obviously setting out to make something worthwhile of his life, he was both liked and respected by virtually everyone in the smug community—and, of course, Ella championed him as much as anybody else did. If, during the past weeks, he'd had reason to ask himself over and over if this wonderful girl, this apple of his eye, had truly fallen in love with him, any worries were usually dispelled by the certainty that marriage itself would magically bring happiness to them both.

After the reception, the two had changed into more casual clothes at Earl's new house and driven directly up to the Priscilla, and, no surprise to Ella, he had not only reserved one of the inn's best-appointed front rooms but arranged for an elaborate seafood dinner and a bottle of illicit French champagne and a vase of two dozen red roses to be wheeled in on a candlelit table covered with starched white linen. And except for his switching on the console radio to hear the outcome of a baseball game played earlier over in Columbia, the evening couldn't have started out on a more romantic note as the two discussed the quaint wedding ceremony, and beautiful music, and how nicely all the guests were dressed.

"I hope you realize what a happy man you've made me," he repeated for the umpteenth time, holding up his champagne glass to ting hers before diving into the fresh stuffed flounder they both loved to eat.

"You're so sweet, honey," she said, taking a large gulp of wine, then reaching over to take his hand. "I thought the reception was particularly gracious, and I think everybody we know was there."

"Well, almost everybody," Earl said flippantly, pouring more champagne from the ice bucket into her glass.

"What do you mean?" she hedged, pushing the fish around her plate.

"Your old flame, Mr. Green. I didn't see Jonathan at the reception."

Ella had feared that mention might be made of this, and she was ready. "Oh, you know Jonathan and how antisocial he can be—especially since the war. But he was at the ceremony, you know."

"Yeah, I saw him standing with Ruth Ann." He piled a

portion of potatoes au gratin on his fork and wolfed it down. "Strange guy, I gotta say, and, to be frank, I and a few others have never understood your fascination with him."

Ella didn't know whether to interpret that comment as a sign of anger or jealousy or suspicion, but, in any case, she felt a chill run down her back as she debated once again whether to confess right up front her one serious fling with Jonathan and relate what had happened that shocking night in the Stoudemires' garden.

"Honey," she said instead, "can we now just drop the subject of Jonathan and everybody else and maybe talk about fixing up the house?"

He reached over and began rubbing her arm. "I say we stop talking, period, and interrupt this delicious supper with a little cheek-to-cheek dancing." At which he got up, turned the dial on the mahogany radio till he heard Frank Sinatra crooning a romantic ballad, and, extending both his hands to her, said, "May I have the honor, Mrs. Dubose?"

All of a sudden, the warm, salty breeze drifting through the windows turned slightly chilly, and before they could clasp each other in the middle of the thick carpet, torrents of rain and gusty wind outside forced Earl to rush over and close all the windows before also switching off the electric ceiling fan overhead.

"So much for a walk later on the beach," Ella said, reaching again for her glass.

"Who needs to walk when we can dance?" he declared suggestively, pulling her close again so that, at intervals, her knee lodged between his strong legs as they steadily moved to the romantic music.

"Lord, you feel so good," he said at one point. "You always have."

"So do you," Ella purred in his ear, stroking the back of his neck and feeling a surge of warm exhilaration race through her vulnerable body as he slowly ground his stiff shaft against her.

Jo Stafford was singing "It Could Happen to You" on the radio when, aroused beyond control and forgetting all about the small green hummingbird cake on the table, the two finally shuffled over to the double bed and, Earl still in his checkered bow tie and Ella in her baby blue cotton dress, began making more fervid love. Then, when she commented playfully that her dress would be destroyed, Earl yanked back the bedspread, cut off the one burning floor lamp, and stripped to his underwear at the same time she slipped out of her dress and folded it neatly over the back of a chair. From then on, it was only a matter of nature taking its course as the callow young couple explored and caressed and groped each other in a frenzy, and if, while Ella felt Earl deep inside her, she had to fight inexorable thoughts of Jonathan that flashed involuntarily through her disoriented brain, not even this troubling psychological distraction could altogether alter the powerful gratification that she craved and that Earl was capable of delivering in full measure.

Afterward, as they lay on their backs in each other's arms covered by the bleach-scented sheet, Ella could hear Earl still breathing heavily through his nostrils as she smoked a cigarette and reflected on how happy their marriage would be. Outside, the rain continued to pour, and one candle on the dinner table still flickered its warm glow.

"You know what?" she asked, nestling her head on his chest and tapping an ash into the ashtray.

"Hummm?" he sort of gurgled, nudging her softly with his hand.

"You're the best thing that's ever happened to me."

She waited for him to comment, but when he said nothing, she noticed he'd fallen sound asleep.

Chapter 12

THE QUEEN CITY

Since Earl had a new business to supervise, the honeymoon had lasted only four days, but they were four wonderful days filled with lots of surf fishing, scouting the area's historic landmarks, sharing memorable meals in the inn's elegant dining room or at a couple of seafood houses, and, of course, making love. Back in Charleston, they settled into Earl's charming small house that boasted the original cypress floors and even had an ornate wrought-iron piazza overlooking the street, and Ella set about to redecorate the rather shabby parlor when not still cataloging at the museum three days a week, activities that at least partly kept her mind off Jonathan and the bitter emotional problems that lingered so privately and tenaciously in her soul. The phone never rang that she didn't flinch. She never ventured out to shop that she didn't fear running smack into him. And not a day passed that she couldn't help but wonder what was happening with him.

Tragically, the truth was revealed to all just a few weeks after the honeymoon when Ella and Earl arrived one Friday evening for a dinner party at Wade and Trudy Yarborough's lovely home just a couple of blocks away on Broad Street and noticed everybody gossiping somberly.

"Sally Burnside says it was his maid who found him, and called the police, and then told her maid," Mary Beth Williams was informing Mark and Zizi Campbell at the punch table.

"Well, it's awful, perfectly awful," Gladys Buchanan whimpered, arranging a few cheese straws on her small cocktail plate.

"What's awful?" Earl asked out loud as he dipped the ladle into the punch bowl and filled a glass for Ella.

"Just goes to show," Ransom Meade remarked dubiously, raising his eyebrows to Patsy Costner while pressing the dimple in the knot of his necktie. "Just goes to show."

"Dammit, what's happened?" Earl repeated impatiently as Ella stood silent. "What in hell y'all talking about?"

"Jonathan Green," Zizi whispered, dabbing her scarlet lips with a cocktail napkin. "We're talking about poor Jonathan Green, precious."

She then went on to relate that, evidently, Jonathan Green had been discovered dead in his apartment earlier in the afternoon, a pistol in his hand. The police had no doubt that it was a suicide, and the details would be in the next day's paper. Of course, everybody knew that Jonathan had never been the same since returning from the war, and that he usually seemed down and depressed, and that he had never really been able to readapt after all he had witnessed and experienced overseas. Since it was certainly no secret that Ella and Jonathan had been particularly close friends and that she'd always gone out of her way to make him feel welcome in Charleston, special sympathy went out to her from everyone in the room.

"I'm so sorry, angel," Mary Beth tried to console, even though Ella had shown little emotion and was too numb to cry. How she got through that dinner was a miracle that would baffle her for years to come, but what she would never forget was how much it meant having Earl by her side. Later that evening in the bathroom at home, when it truly dawned on her that Jonathan was gone forever, she finally released all the grief and longing pent up inside and cried uncontrollably.

After a brief funeral held at Beth Elohim that Ella and Earl and a number of other former classmates attended, Jonathan was buried in the synagogue's cemetery on Coming Street in a plot under a yellow pine tree that his father apparently had to negotiate at the last minute. Earl didn't think it was appropriate to join the few family mourners at the graveside, but when Ella made it clear that she wanted to pay last respects to her friend, there was no further objection. Ella maintained her composure at the cemetery, but it was while she and Earl were standing in the background that a wave of nausea came over her the likes of which she'd never experienced before.

Normally, she would have attributed the seizure to her shattered nerves over recent events, but it happened again a few days later while she and Earl were having breakfast, and then she knew . . . she knew without question that she had to be pregnant. For a few moments, the sudden awareness filled Ella with the same immediate sense of joy that any woman feels when she first realizes she's going to create a new life and give birth, but then, forced to confront the truth of who the father of this child most likely was, she was gripped by a thrust of fear and dread that threatened not only any happiness over the momentous fulfillment but even the future of her marriage. Throughout the entire morning she wrestled with the terrifying crisis, crying herself almost sick, but gradually summoning up untapped inner strength and courage that even she never knew she had. Then, acknowledging the dearth of viable options, she finally made the sensible decision to simply accept all consequences, go see Dr. Crawford for confirmation of her condition, and surprise Earl with the good news.

Arriving home from work the night after her consultation,

Earl noticed she had an especially radiant smile on her face as she kissed him, then proceeded to mix two bourbon and waters.

"So why the big grin?" he asked repeatedly as she stood stirring her drink slowly with a finger.

"I have some terrible news," she finally said dispassionately.

"Good Lord, what?"

"Well, I saw Dr. Crawford today, and he said we'd better start looking for a larger home." She patted her stomach.

Earl froze for a few moments, then rushed across the parlor to hug her tightly, sloshing part of his drink on the carpet. "Oh my Lord, sweetheart! I can't believe it! Is it true? Is he sure? Oh my Lord. And are you okay?"

Ella laughed. "Honey, I don't think doctors are ever wrong about these things. And don't be silly. Of course I'm okay."

By the time, in spring, Ella gave birth almost three weeks early to a healthy, beautiful boy with dark hair and certain facial features that resembled those of Jonathan, she had virtually reconciled herself to the probability of the infant's real father and to the dreadful secret she knew she'd have to harbor for many years to come. Earl, to whom all babies of course looked alike, wanted his son to be a junior in fine Southern tradition, but when Ella said that she'd really had her mind set on naming their first boy after her parents, he agreed to call the child Tyler Pinckney Dubose. Ella adored her baby, as did Earl and the doting grandparents, and there wasn't a relative or friend in town who didn't consider Ella to be an exemplary wife and mother whose family came before all else.

It was also at this time that Ella hired her first black maid to do housekeeping twice a week, the same competent, kind Venus who'd been cleaning for her mother the past couple of years. And it was about this time that she developed a keen passion for cooking, which quickly made her one of the most popular young hostesses in Charleston. Although Earl worked late many weekday evenings, they did enjoy entertaining on weekends throughout the winter, and while the dinners were hardly the unbridled, wee-hour affairs they used to so relish, nobody invited to the Dubose home wanted for plenty of good Southern food, premium booze, and lively conversation.

Just when Ella was adjusting to marriage and motherhood, and the secret she harbored was becoming less painful, Earl came home one night and, while she was in the kitchen mixing the dough for a batch of buttermilk biscuits, mentioned that his father knew a man up in Charlotte who'd been a salesman at a small printing operation for some years and was now looking for a partner to help finance and create what he envisioned to be the city's largest and most prestigious printing and engraving company.

"Jay Rutherford's his name," Earl explained further, watching her measure the baking powder as he twirled the ice in his whiskey, "and can you believe Charlotte still has no quality printers like those in Atlanta, Columbia, or even Raleigh?"

"What are you trying to say, honey?" Ella asked worriedly, now adding baking soda to the flour in her large bowl.

"What I'm saying, Peaches, is that in this business there's so little growth potential in Charleston, and, well, Charlotte just might be the big opportunity I've been looking for."

"Hand me that can of shortening, please," she directed, taking a sip of bourbon from her glass on the counter.

"Anyway," he continued, "I like this Jay fellow so far, and he's got some big ideas about this company he wants to start up there, and I thought we might drive up and meet him face-to-face."

Ella began cutting the shortening into the flour with a steel pastry cutter, then stopped and asked him to keep cutting while she stuck her head in the living room to check on Tyler.

"Are you talking about us maybe leaving Charleston, and our families and friends, and this wonderful house?" she called from the other room.

"Now, now, sweetheart, don't jump the gun," he said as she returned. "It's just a possibility I'd like to look into, and, besides, we might enjoy taking a ride up to Charlotte."

Ella slowly poured buttermilk into the dry ingredients and began mixing the sticky dough with her other hand. "That could be a pretty big risk, wouldn't you say? Leaving everything and everybody we've ever known and moving to a strange town."

Earl grasped her around the waist and kissed her on the back of her neck as she now mixed with both hands, signaling to him to pour in a little more buttermilk. "Honey, you know I'm no fool and would never jeopardize you and me and Tyler—not on your life. But I've got big plans for us, and who knows, this might be just the right opportunity. Don't you think it's worth at least investigating?"

Flouring her hands, she began patting out the dough, then, handing him the biscuit cutter before reaching for her Lucky Strikes on the windowsill, instructed, "Here, buster, start cutting 'em out—straight down—and put them on the baking sheet." She took a long puff, pecked him on the cheek, and said, "If it means that much to you, I say let's drive up to Charlotte and meet this guy."

And, sure enough, Earl and Ella couldn't have been more impressed by Jay Rutherford and his ideas, and after Jay and his charming wife had given them a thorough tour of Charlotte, Ella and Earl not only took an immediate liking to the couple but fell in love with the Queen City—its lively downtown area, its majestic churches and many schools, its imposing homes on wide streets with towering dogwoods and maples, and its overall genteel Southern atmosphere. Jay even showed them the large, vacant, red-brick building out on Providence

Road he had his eye on for the company. Back home, the two weighed the pros and cons of the matter for almost a month. Earl discussed a buyout with his willing partner at PrintCraft and a loan with his father, and although Ella still had a number of reservations about the move, she admired her husband's ambition and knew he was determined to take on the challenge if she agreed. They were still young, and it could be an exciting venture, she reasoned, and, after all, if things didn't work out as anticipated, they could always return to Charleston.

The Rutherfords couldn't have been more cooperative helping the Duboses find a modest but attractive home in Charlotte's Dilworth area, and by the time Ella learned she was again pregnant, they had already made a number of good friends and become active members of St. Martin's Episcopal Church. Jay and Earl named their company Creative Graphics, both worked long and hard to produce the finest products possible and attract the city's most upscale corporate and private customers, and by the end of the first year, they had purchased two more high-performance presses and almost doubled profits. Nonetheless, Earl and Ella led anything but an extravagant existence, and if sacrifice meant not shopping for new clothes, limiting entertaining to a few friends invited in for cocktails and gumbo from time to time, no cleaning maid, and riding the bus to church to conserve gasoline in their old Ford, the Duboses made plenty of concessions while Earl was struggling to build the business.

Ella gave birth to another boy who was indeed named Earl Preston Dubose II, then, the following year, to an adorable girl they decided to call Olivia Louise after the two grandmothers. As the children grew and developed, Ella and Earl became more and more aware of distinct personality differences between Tyler and his younger siblings, the most obvious being his stubborn independence and exceptional intelligence. Tyler was a much more sensitive, delicate child than the other two, and although Earl wondered at times if he was completely normal, Ella indulged his every idiosyncrasy and flooded him with enough love and attention to make any boy feel special, all the time safeguarding the shameful secret that might well have helped to explain the boy's peculiarities but that she knew could never be revealed without the risk of dire consequences.

After a few more years of phenomenal business success, during which time he and Ella fully adopted Charlotte as their home town and the children fared well in school, Earl was finally in the financial position to take a mortgage on a large, beautiful, Colonial home on Colville Road in what many considered to be Charlotte's most prestigious residential area. Long before, he had promised Ella that one day he'd make her very proud and comfortable, and while, by this time, her genuine love and respect for Earl hardly had to be enhanced by the acquisition of an expensive house and a new white Cadillac De Ville, there could be no doubt that she came to relish in Charlotte the same gracious lifestyle she'd known while growing up in Charleston. Eventually, they joined the Myers Park Country Club and transferred their membership to the newly built and more convenient Christ Episcopal Church, and it was at this time that Earl developed his passion for golf. Ella hired a maid to clean twice a week, and once, when the children got a little older and school was over for summer, they even indulged in the luxury of taking a steamship to Europe from New York and spending a couple of weeks in London and Paris to expose themselves and the kids to all the cultural attractions these glamorous cities had to offer.

Otherwise, their choice vacation venue became the same Priscilla Inn at Myrtle Beach where they'd spent their honeymoon. Popular with many well-to-do Charlotteans, the Priscilla now had true sentimental value for Ella, and she loved everything about the place. She loved sitting peacefully in a rocking chair on the porch or in a beach cabana doing needlepoint and watching Earl and the children battle the waves. She loved surf fishing with Earl for spots and whiting on cloudy days, or driving up to Little River to see the fishing boats and eat fried flounder at Captain Jule's Seafood House. But most of all she loved dressing for dinner at the inn, then, while Tyler, Little Earl, and Olivia played bingo or canasta with other young folks in the supervised Card Room, going up to the Ocean Forest Hotel for an hour or so to dance with Earl under the stars just as she once imagined doing with Jonathan when they were so young and in love.

As the years passed, going to the Priscilla evolved into a summer ritual for the Dubose family—especially after Ella hired Goldie and had someone she could trust to watch over the house. And even after the children, one by one, left home to pursue their own lives and Ella and Earl were free to board other ocean liners and tour the capitals of Europe, nothing remained so special to them both as returning time and again either alone or with friends from Charlotte to the Priscilla for a week or two of total relaxation, good fishing and golf and eating, and maybe roaming about a few of the old, deserted rice plantations hidden amongst giant moss-covered oaks on or around the Waccamaw River. While they still had parents alive in Charleston, they sometimes drove down to spend part of a day, but once most of the close relatives were gone, they no longer had much reason to make the trip.

Jay Rutherford died of cancer in the late sixties, but not before Creative Graphics had become the largest and most successful printing and engraving operation not only in Charlotte but in the Carolinas. Ella had hoped, of course, that Earl would gradually slow down and delegate more responsibility to his office manager and plant foreman, but even after Little Earl joined the company and was being trained to one day take over from his father, Big Earl continued to work at the same compulsive pace he'd maintained since the beginning. As a result, it was really no great surprise to anyone when, on his way out to the car one day with a buddy to play a few holes of golf at the club, he complained of dizziness for a few moments, then collapsed on the pavement. Ella was called immediately to meet the ambulance at Mercy Hospital, but when she and Goldie arrived, she was told that her husband had apparently died instantly of a massive brain aneurysm. Goldie went all to pieces, but, as always in times of crisis, Ella maintained the composure and strength of the proverbial steel magnolia till decisions had been made and she was left to grieve in private. The sorrow and heartbreak she felt over losing Earl couldn't have been more absolute, but what disturbed her most, and weighed strangely on her conscience, was how vividly the tragedy evoked that terrible evening in Charleston long ago when everybody learned that Jonathan Green had shot himself.

Chapter 13

FEEDIN' THE CRABS

"Ty," Little Earl was saying to his older brother on the phone, "she just took off, took off like a shot with Goldie like some mad woman. And when the police finally tracked 'em down at Myrtle Beach, she acted as if nothing had happened—nothing at all."

"Well, you know Mama," Tyler said dispassionately, pretending that he was unaware of any shenanigan but a bit surprised that they'd already caught up with her. "If she's anything, she's a maverick with her mind set. We all know that."

"Is that all you gotta say?" Earl drawled impatiently, taking a defiant stance. "I don't think you got any idea what she's been puttin' us all through lately, and there for a while we didn't know whether the woman was dead or alive. I mean, Ty, I got a big business to run down here, and things like the church, and Little League, and obligations at the club, and I sho don't have time to go chasing round two states for Mama and Goldie."

"So what do you expect me to do?" Tyler asked calmly, sitting on the deck of his beach house with some medical papers spread out on a table and refusing to reveal that he knew about their mother's spree and actually would be seeing her in a few days.

"Well, the first thing you might do is try to convince Mama to see the doctor, which she refuses to do even though we've already made an appointment for her. You know she's got that heart condition, and all we need down here is for her to have something like a bad stroke. As a matter of fact, we sometimes wonder if her sick spells are nothing but little strokes. And I gotta tell you, Ty, she's really been acting weird lately, like she's confused, or has something bad on her mind that's driving her crazy, or is on the verge of Alzheimer's."

"I can't force Mama to do anything," Tyler said nonchalantly, frowning at the lab reports before him, "and don't you think you're maybe overreacting? Mama has her own strange reasons for doing things, and it doesn't mean she's having strokes or losing her mind. I talked with her right after Barry and I returned from Europe, and she sounded pretty healthy and normal to me."

"Normal? You call gettin' in the car with that squaw and driving all the way to Myrtle Beach without telling anybody normal?"

"Believe me, Earl, Mama has her reasons. And you have no right to talk about Goldie like that. We're lucky Mama has her."

"Yeah, it's easy for you to say that sittin' up there seven hundred miles away while we have to suffer the consequences for everything down here."

"I don't appreciate that insinuation, Earl," he snapped, pressing lightly on what he suddenly detected as a mild pain in his lower abdomen.

"Listen, ole buddy, I know there's no love lost between the two of us, and this sho ain't no social call. All I'm asking is that you talk with Mama and get her to see Dr. Singer. Is that too much to ask? I mean, let's not beat around the bush, Ty. We know you've always been Mama's favorite, so maybe she'll listen to you and make life a little easier for us."

"Earl," Tyler finally said caustically, looking up from the disturbing figures on one report, "I don't see any need for spite and sarcasm, so let's try to remain civil, if that's okay with you."

"I'm always civil, so stop trying to give me bullshit," Earl almost exploded, panting the same way he did when he spoke with his mother at the inn.

"I won't continue this conversation till you calm down."

"Goddammit, Ty, don't tell me what to do."

"Then stop raving like some maniac, dear boy, and let's try to have an intelligent conversation."

"And don't call me *dear boy*. Nobody calls me *dear boy*."

Tyler let out a gruff laugh. "Sometimes I think you're the one who's got problems, Earl, not Mama."

"Whatta you mean by that crack?"

"Forget it. Just tell me exactly what y'all expect from me."

"I just told you. Mama's as much your responsibility as ours, and the least you can do is talk some sense into her about going to the doctor. Is that too much to ask? And it's also driving me nuts the way she wheels around in that car by herself, so you could have a few words with her about that. And if she won't listen to you . . . Well, we might have to take some drastic steps."

Tyler remained silent for a moment as he continued to press on his gut, then uttered a sigh of frustration. "Okay, Earl, I'll have another talk with Mama, but I'm warning you not to threaten her, not unless you care to bite off more than you can chew. You forget Mama's a tough gal, and you also forget I wouldn't do anything in this world to hurt her."

"Are you implying we would?" Earl grumbled.

While her two sons were sparring about their mother's future, Ella's mind couldn't have been further distracted from the subject as she excitedly surveyed the fishing pier while waiting on the Marianis and Goldie to rent poles and buy bait. Although it was still early, at least half the rickety, wooden benches were already occupied, and as she meandered farther out with rod in hand, observing the mostly rugged, silent, stone-faced men and women with lines in the water, she hoped that all the empty buckets and chests were not an indication of how the fish were, as Big Earl used to say, "cooperating." Sighting an empty bench facing north, she balanced her rod against the railing, sat down, adjusted her floppy red hat, and unzipped the front of her cotton jacket.

"Don't waste yo time, little lady," she heard the scruffy, middle-aged man over on her left grouse loudly. "So far, ain't nothing much out there worth baiting yo hook for."

"No luck?" she called back, noticing the equally harsh-looking woman seated next to him threading a bloodworm on a hook.

"Naw, nothin' to speak of. Been here since seven and think we're just feedin' the crabs."

"Maybe when the tide turns—" Ella began just as he suddenly jerked the rod back very dramatically, waited a second, then began reeling in steadily.

"Ain't nothin' but a puny spot, I can tell you that right off the bat."

And sure enough, what he pulled in was a spot no bigger than a small hairbrush. Still, the woman with a cigarette dangling from her crimson lips put down her rod, quickly unhooked the fish, and tossed it into a plastic bucket.

"Gimme a shrimp," the man then directed. "Maybe there's a hungry flounder foolin' 'round somewhere out there."

Just hearing the word "shrimp" triggered still another memory for Ella as she pressed both hands down on the rotting bench, gazed blankly at the small whitecaps on the water, and was forced to remember the one and only time she was ever disloyal to Big Earl, back in the fifties. The episode occurred not long after the family had moved into the big house on Colville, and no doubt nothing would have ever happened if any one of many circumstances had been different. First, since Earl had been working harder and longer than ever building up the company, including some weekends, he was usually so preoccupied and exhausted when he got home that rarely did he even feel up to giving the children much attention or indulging in much of the close intimacy with Ella that had once been so vital to their marriage. Gradually, she had learned to condition herself to this troubling reality, but many were the nights in bed when, hearing Earl begin to snore almost the second his head hit the pillow, she yearned to be held and caressed and made to feel like the attractive, vigorous woman she still was.

Earl had not been really that anxious to attend a dinner dance with two other couples at the club one Saturday evening, but when Ella reminded him that plans had been made weeks in advance and that she had already engaged someone to stay with the children, he, as usual, agreed to do anything that would make her happy. One of the young couples, Dennis and Naomi Chapman, had moved to Charlotte from Atlanta just the previous year when he was made executive vice-president of Wachovia Bank, and while Ella viewed Naomi as a social-climbing snob with little if any notable family roots to justify her pretensions, she genuinely liked Dennis, who was Hollywood handsome and sharp as a tack, utterly down to earth, and almost as good a dancer as Earl. It was, in fact, after the two had executed a stylish tango that had everyone at the table, even Naomi, clapping wildly, that Dennis happened to mention an associate at the bank who'd just returned from Wilmington and brought him a whopping ten pounds of the most beautiful fresh shrimp he'd ever seen—right off the boat. Ella's only reaction was to criticize the mushy, disgraceful shrimp found in even Charlotte's best seafood markets and to proclaim how she'd just given up trying to make a decent shrimp remoulade or shrimp bog.

"You want some good shrimp?" asked Dennis, seated next to her at the table.

"Oh, Lord, I wasn't implying . . . ," Ella stammered, trying to ignore his leg touching hers.

"Don't be silly. We'll never use up ten pounds of shrimp, even freezing most of them in water. Tell you what. I'll drop off a couple of pounds tomorrow or the next day."

Sunday passed, but, sure enough, late Monday morning, long after Earl had dropped the kids off at school and taken off for Greensboro to inspect an expensive new press he and Jay were thinking about buying, Dennis showed up at the house with two plastic cartons of large shrimp already frozen in water. Since Ella still hadn't found a good housekeeper, she was alone and busy arranging spice bottles in a kitchen cabinet while music played quietly on a radio perched on a shelf. He was dressed in the sort of conventional, dark-vested suit and conservative silk necktie expected of most bankers, which contrasted starkly with her casual, open-necked, collared blouse worn outside beige linen slacks. After chatting awhile at the kitchen table about the trick of freezing shrimp in water and her problems fixing up the new house, she finally asked if he'd like a Bloody Mary or a bite of lunch.

"Gotta watch my time," he said, tapping his wristwatch while gazing intently at her eyes. "Appointment this afternoon with a real-estate developer who's applying for a whoppin' loan."

"Oh, then don't let me keep you," Ella said, exchanging provocative glances with him and admiring his long dark eye-lashes that seemed to flutter inordinately.

He chuckled quietly. "Well, he's not due till midafternoon, so . . . Hell, I could use a good Bloody Mary on a sweltering day like this—if you don't mind." He loosened his necktie. "Earl coming home for lunch?"

"Earl's in Greensboro today, and the kids don't get home till about three," she informed him, reaching into the refrigerator for a can of tomato juice, then stepping into the den for a bottle of vodka on the bar. "Mild or spicy?" she asked next, holding up a small bottle of Tabasco.

"Now, whatta you think, honey?" he teased suggestively, pounding his fist in the air and laughing. "Would an expert tango dancer want anything mild?"

They both laughed, and Ella once again admired his handsome face and wide smile when she handed him the drink and sat back down. "You don't meet many dignified bankers who can do a mean tango, I can tell you that."

"Honey, banking ain't got nothing to do with having a little fun from time to time," he jested, drinking a big gulp and, eyes wide open, exclaiming, "Oh boy, sister, you're not just a great dancer but really know how to make a damn good drink."

They made more small talk awhile longer, and when Ella saw that his glass was almost empty, she got up and poured another round from the pitcher.

"Listen," he said suddenly, pointing to the radio. "Buddy Holly. 'Peggy Sue.' You like this rock 'n' roll?"

"Some of it's pretty good," she admitted, noticing now the way his alluring brown eyes seemed to be devouring every inch of her upper body.

"What say we give it a quick twirl?" he then asked, standing up, taking off his jacket, and extending his arms.

"Oh, Dennis, are you crazy?" she whined, observing how stocky he looked in the tight vest.

"Come on," he insisted, obviously feeling his drinks. "Let's see if your shag's as good as your tango."

"You shag?" she asked excitedly.

"Try me."

For a second, the proposition frightened Ella, but then she reasoned that Dennis was such a decent gentleman. So, giving in to the alcohol and the urge to indulge in a little innocent frivolity, she uttered, "Why not?"

The problem was that a little innocent frivolity quickly developed into a passionate adventure as the music changed to a romantic Peggy Lee ballad, and he pressed his strong body securely against hers, and she could feel his heavy, warm breathing on the side of her face. At first, she resisted the temptation to allow the dance to continue as they swayed together on the kitchen floor to one of June Christie's sultry songs, but when he began to nibble on her neck and ever so gradually maneuvered a hand across her firm breast, she was simply unable to control the shiver that raced through her body and the craving to act.

"Let's don't let this get out of hand, Dennis," she muttered, relishing the torrid sensations that had been virtually smothered by Earl for weeks.

"Is there somewhere else more comfortable where we can sit down?" was his only comment as he continued to caress her.

For another instant, she tried to imagine the dangerous consequences of their reckless behavior in the full light of day, but when it dawned on her that what they were indulging in was no more than fervid lust and that, if anything, Dennis had as much or more to lose if the frolic were ever exposed, she broke away from him momentarily, locked the kitchen door, and simply pointed to the entrance to the den. And there on the sofa, while the music played, and without so much as a prolonged deep kiss or any other gesture of amorous affection, and each of them still half-dressed, they made erotic love that left them both panting like exhausted animals. When the escapade was over, Ella did fix him a ham and cheese sandwich, and they both agreed, like any sensible, confident human beings with successful marriages, never to repeat the chancy diversion. And they never did, remaining close friends for many years, till Dennis, after becoming the highly respected president of the bank, died of complications from diabetes. The fact that Ella felt little shame after the wanton encounter did bother her for a couple of weeks, not so much because she had been unfaithful to her neglectful husband but because it reinforced the reality of how much she truly enjoyed just the act of sex itself. But not one to dwell on inconsequential foibles, she never again gave much thought to the incident except when the subject of shrimp came up.

"Ready to catch a shark?" she heard Edmund asking behind her as he squeezed one of her sides, balanced his rented rod on the railing, and pulled a small plastic bag of bloodworms out of the pocket of his Windbreaker.

"So far, things don't look too promising," she grumbled as he edged next to her on the bench. "Wouldn't you know it?"

A few yards away, Sal and Elizabeth claimed the first empty bench they saw, and still farther out on the pier, Tommy and Rex watched Goldie carefully as she baited the hooks on her line, then those on the rods rented for the boys.

"That weight on your line's too heavy," Ella told O'Conner, pointing to the small tackle box Goldie had left beside the bench. "Hand me a Number 2 weight, if you would."

"How can you tell?" he asked, fascinated by her instinctive know-how.

"Just look at the tiny whitecaps. It's pretty calm out there, and the tide's out. A Number 3 will just sit, stuck in the sand. Earl taught me that." She tried and tried to unhook the metal catch for the new weight but couldn't budge it. "Rats! Here, see if you have more strength than I do."

After he'd released the catch and secured the new weight,

time came for them both to cast. Ella, as expected, didn't land her rig very far, which made her almost curse, but Edmund sailed his out as if he'd been casting his entire life.

"Well, knock me down!" she exclaimed, reaching over and squeezing his upper arm playfully to feel his muscle. "I thought you said you'd never done any fishing to speak of."

"They don't call me Charles Atlas for nothing," he laughed, handling his reel like a true expert.

"Dad, look, look!" they heard Elizabeth yowl a couple of times farther down the pier as Sal pulled in what looked like a nice-sized fish.

"I'll be damned," Edmund proclaimed, noticing the two boys rush over to see what their father had caught. "And we haven't had a nibble."

"Honey, that's the way it goes," Ella said. "I can remember sitting right on this very pier and watching people reel in dozens while we didn't have the first bite. Used to make Earl furious—mad as a hornet."

"You and your husband must have fished a lot together."

"Yeah, lots. Surf, pier, deep sea—you name it." She suddenly jerked her line and concentrated for a second, but then reeled in the slack calmly, a look of disappointment in her expression. "And you or your wife neither one ever liked to fish?"

He chuckled. "You couldn't get Grace near the water. Grace was terrified of water—any water. I recall one summer, when Lizzy was small, we decided to take her down to the Jersey shore so she could see the ocean, but Grace wouldn't get near the water, much less go in swimming. Then, years later, when we learned about Grace's illness, I thought a Caribbean cruise might be good for her, but . . ." He looked solemn for a second, then smiled again. "She was so uncomfortable on the boat that she spent all her time in the cabin and begged to get off in Ft. Lauderdale. We never really analyzed the problem in detail, but I think Grace was simply terrified of drowning." He paused again. "Can you beat it? Eaten up with cancer and scared of drowning."

"Maybe she had a bad experience as a child."

"Well, in any case, what Grace was certainly not frightened of was the tennis court, and I'm here to tell you that that woman could hit a tennis ball like—" All of a sudden, he pulled hard on his line and cried, "Heeey, what do we have here!"

"Snag him!" Ella shrieked, glancing up at the line. "Now, wait a second to see if he's on."

When the tip of the rod fluttered, O'Conner pulled again and began reeling steadily as Ella and the two salts at the next bench peered over the railing.

"Goddamn crab," bellowed the leathery man fishing for flounder.

Edmund continue to reel, but when the crab was about halfway out of the water, it released its hold on the bait and plummeted back down into the ocean.

All Ella and Edmund could do was howl with laughter and listen as Elizabeth screamed mockingly, "Big deal, Dad, big deal!" By the time he'd reeled in the rig, Ella had already secured her rod between her knees, reached for another slimy bloodworm with her scarlet nails, and proceeded to cut the creature in half on the railing with a small knife. "You thread it," she then directed him, wiping the disgusting blood off her fingers with a small towel she'd brought from the inn.

"Did you and your wife ever do much traveling—besides that unfortunate cruise?" she then asked after he'd cast out again.

"Right much, especially after Lizzy was grown and away at school—Douglas in New Brunswick. You see, Grace always loved the theater and was actually a fairly talented dramatic actress in New York before we got married and Elizabeth came along. Naturally, we used to go into the city whenever there was something special on Broadway or Off Broadway Grace wanted to see, but what she really loved to do whenever I could take off from work for a few days was drive to various cities and towns and attend repertory theater. Frankly, I never really cared that much for plays and musicals, but Grace did, so we traveled everywhere—as far away as Cincinnati and Virginia and even Chicago. Now that I think about it, it seems that when we weren't playing tennis or involved with some political rally we were usually sitting in some theater soaking up Williams, or O'Neill, or Chekhov. Must say the experience taught me a lot." He now appeared lost in his own memories. "My one real regret is that I never took Grace to London for the theater. That's something I know she always wanted to do, but with my practice, and Grace always worrying about Lizzy . . . And then, of course, it was too late to do anything."

Ella sat silent listening to his story and staring impassively at the distant whitecaps enlightened by the warm, soft morning sun. Then, without turning her head, she said, "You must have been very much in love with Grace."

"From the moment we first met at a church social. Yes, I was very much in love with Grace. She was a good woman and a good mother—the best. Believe it or not, I never looked at anyone else. She was that type of woman."

Ella was seized by a strange quiver as she paid close attention to Edmund's words, prompted not so much by their touching implications and his candid honesty as by the way they forced her to confront once again certain enigmas in her own soul that had remained unaddressed for so many years.

"I can tell it must have been much the same with you and your husband, Earl," he then said, reaching for her hand and gripping it tightly.

"Yes, Dr. O'Conner. Earl and I were very close, and he was the most loyal husband and friend and father a wife could ever hope for. Oh, we traveled the world together, and overcame lots of crises and disappointments, and, I think, did a pretty good job bringing up three fine children, and . . . Lord, we danced our feet off every chance we got. You see, nobody on earth could dance like Earl—no reflection on you, of course. He put his heart and mind into every step, it seemed, and he could dance all night, any style, any step. It all came so naturally to him, and I used to say that Earl had been born with rhythm in his soul, and feathers on his feet, and magic in his fingers. Oh, we danced everywhere—on ocean liners, and Paris ballrooms, once at a little square in Venice, at the club in Charlotte on weekends—but mostly I remember how we danced down here in the Lowcountry. We made quite a couple, if I say so myself." Her eyes began to mist when she stopped talking, and Edmund couldn't tell whether she'd continue or not. "But there was a problem, Dr. O'Conner. A big problem." She hesitated again, as if debating whether to continue. "I've never uttered this to another living soul and don't know why I'm confiding in you at this point in time, but the problem, the honest, shameful truth . . . the truth is that I was never in love with my husband." She tried to wipe her eyes with the sleeve of her jacket. "Maybe that's hard for you to understand, Dr. O'Conner, and I'm not sure I understand it myself, but that's the way it was." She finally looked tearfully up at him. "You must think I'm an awful woman."

He grasped her hand even tighter and waited a long while to reply, obviously puzzled. "I believe I can understand. At least I can try."

"Please forgive me for being so blunt," she came close to fully sobbing. "I don't know what came over me, confessing something like that to you out here on a fishing pier. You must wonder where my manners are." She wiped her eyes again. "Why aren't these confounded fish biting?"

"Do you mind if I ask you just one very personal question?" he then said softly.

"Of course not."

"Were you ever in love with someone else?"

She again held back a moment and could feel her heart thumping rapidly. "Well, as a matter of fact, yes. Oh, yes, I was. Many, many years ago when I was a young lady. Yes, I was very much in love with a boy when I was young, but he died, Dr. O'Conner. He died when we both were very young."

"Do you care to talk about it?"

She sat silent, wondering what to say. "Not much really to talk about. It was so long ago, and we were so young, and, of course, there was the war."

"So he was killed in the war?"

Ella pretended to reel her line to take up slack and give herself time to think. "No, he was overseas, but he survived that. Were you in the war?"

"Not that one. I missed it by about a year. My war was Korea—two long years." A downcast expression came over his rosy face. "Not that anybody remembers that war these days."

"Well, I remember it," she began, ready to relate how one of Earl's closest friends was killed in Korea when a sudden pull on Edmund's line made him jerk the rod back and exclaim, "Wow! What do we have here?"

He waited a moment, as Ella had coached him, and when the tug was even stronger, he began reeling frantically while she cheered him on.

"A blue!" she blurted out even before he'd hauled the big fish all the way in. "I swear if you don't have a big blue— caught with bloodworm and at this time of year. Just look at that!"

"Watch his teeth!" yelled the man from the next bench, perching his rod on the rail and rushing over. "Them blues'll take yo damn finger off. Mean as snakes. Here, lemme unhook him for ya."

By this time, Goldie and the Marianis had noticed all the action and dashed over to gawk and praise.

"Gosh, Paw!" Tommy marveled at his grandfather, watching the gasping fish flop around on the partly rotted planks of the old pier.

Elizabeth, beaming, told Sal to go get the bucket with the spot, but after a short discussion about what, after all, they were going to do with these and any other fish they might catch, Ella suggested they simply give them to the scraggly couple at the next bench, who didn't hesitate to accept. Then, with everybody's hopes sparked by O'Conner's bonanza and the turning tide, the fishing recommenced in earnest, and, in almost no time, Goldie and the boys had snagged a few more spots, while Sal pulled in a good-sized whiting. Ella still didn't get so much as a nibble, and when Edmund hooked another crab, she said jokingly it served him right.

"I don't remember when I've had so much fun," he said at one point, placing one arm loosely around her waist. "I hope you realize that getting to know you and Goldie has so far been the highlight of our vacation."

"Oh, don't prevaricate, Dr. O'Conner. To tell you the truth, sometimes I worry that we've been intruding on your family's privacy."

"Nonsense. I've never seen the boys have more fun, and, well, Lizzy and Sal are infatuated by you both—as is this old geezer."

She laughed, invigorated by the tepid salt breeze gently blowing her shaggy cloth hat and relishing the feel of his arm.

"I guess we're doing okay."

"I beg your pardon," he muttered, puzzled.

"We're doing okay. For our age, I guess we're both doing okay."

Now hardly aware of his line in the water, he fixed his eyes squarely on her face. "Old age has nothing to do with anything, except maybe a little loneliness. I truly believe that."

Ella didn't react for a long moment, her mouth twitching

nervously. "You're probably right, and I guess I'm just a fool to dwell on something I can't do one thing about. But the truth is . . . the truth is I really don't like being old. Maybe I could accept it better if only I could block out the past. Oh, it's pretty easy dealing with the little aches and infirmities, and I've even learned to adjust to lots of today's crudeness and sloven ways. But what's hard, what's really painful about being old, is re-membering when you were young. For years, that didn't affect me much, but now, at this stage, it does. It does affect me, and I don't seem to be able to control it."

He grasped her waist gently. "Remember what I told you about not losing control of anything?"

"But sometimes I do feel so confused and helpless when the past closes in," she almost sobbed.

"At least you know you don't have Alzheimer's," he quipped.

"I'm serious about this, Dr. O'Conner."

"So am I. You must have lots of unpleasant memories."

"That's not really true, not true at all. I have mostly won-derful memories, and I guess that's part of my problem—knowing those wonderful times are gone forever. That a way of life is gone forever. Sort of silly and childish, isn't it? But yes, you're right, I do also have a few very unpleasant memories that sometimes I wish I could forget—just erase from my mind. As I said, that used to not bother me so much, but lately I seem to dwell on them. Does that ever happen to you?"

O'Conner reflected for a moment. "Not really. An Irish father who drank too much and neglected the family. Being jilted by a special sweetheart in high school. Having to work at a gas station to help put myself through college. Korea. Grace's long battle with cancer. Sure, I've got my share of sour memo-ries, but, you see, Miss Ella, I take a very philosophical ap-proach to it all and try not to dwell on it. I'm certainly no wise man, but I do believe that painful memories—like the good ones—are part of what makes us who we are, and that we must use them to our advantage so long as they don't take control of us. About the only thing I know lots about in this world is teeth, but I am convinced that if we try to block out all the painful memories of our past, we also run the risk of blocking out the most wonderful parts of our lives. To put it another way, I guess, we diminish our humanity."

Ella sat deadly still. Then, as if overtaken by an awesome sense of relief, she looked into his eyes. "I must confess I never thought about it in those terms, Dr. O'Conner."

He pulled her closer to him. "I think you sometimes underestimate yourself."

Then, with no warning, he leaned forward and kissed her tenderly on the cheek, adding, "Hope you're not offended by me doing that."

Although her free hand was partly stained with dry blood from the worms, she wiped her fingers unmindfully over her chin and red lips. "Can I confess something else to you?"

"The last I heard, we still at least have the right to free speech."

"Well, I'm mortified to admit this, but it just dawned on me . . . something just dawned on me. I suddenly realize, for the best of me, I can't remember your first name."

He broke into a big smile that made the creases next to his nose more pronounced. "Edmund."

"Of course. Edmund." She repeated the name in her soft accent. "Now I remember. How silly and thoughtless of me. Do you mind if I call you Edmund?"

His smile became even more pronounced. "I thought you never would."

Chapter 14

A DISTANT CLAP OF THUNDER

That night, after dinner, Ella and Edmund decided to take a walk on the solitary beach while the Marianis were up roaming around the Pavilion and Goldie was watching a movie on TV. Luminescence from the moon, almost full, gave the strand a slightly eerie glow and the foam on the gently breaking waves a sparkle that seemed to flicker from nowhere, and, if viewed from a distance, the elderly couple, holding hands, would have appeared to be just two young lovebirds on a romantic nocturnal stroll along the sand.

"I think it's finally catching up with me," Edmund was saying.

"And what could that be?" Ella asked, waiting for some engaging answer or gesture.

"The fried food," he moaned.

She hesitated as if disappointed, then laughed. "That can happen."

"Oh, don't get me wrong. I love it. The problem is, I love it too much."

She chuckled again. "Doesn't faze me, honey, but, then, I've been at it my whole life. Maybe your system has to get used to it. Are you upset?"

"No, no, just a little indigestion." Now he laughed. "Those flounder strips taste almost as good now as they did at dinner. I'll take a couple of Rolaids later on."

"Maybe we should go back."

"Would you mind? Sorry to be such a rotten date tonight."

"Oh, don't be silly," she said, squeezing his hand. "We have to expect those boring little inconveniences. And besides, I've enjoyed every minute of this evening."

When they reached the wooden stairs that led back up to the inn's planked terrace, Edmund stopped abruptly, faced her, and looked directly into her eyes.

"Would you consider this old geezer foolish if he said he'd like to kiss you good night?"

Ella stood motionless for a moment as she returned his gaze.

"Why, I'd be honored, Edmund," she whispered over the murmur of the waves as they lapped faintly but steadily in the distance.

Then, slowly and gently, he kissed her on the lips, sending a shiver through her as she held him tightly and relished a sensation she hadn't experienced in many years.

"That was nice," she said calmly, still holding onto him and wondering if he noticed her slight quivering.

"Well, it just confirms what I said about you being a very exciting lady."

"Thank you, Edmund. And you're quite a beau yourself," she sighed. "Now, you better go take care of that edgy tummy."

When they passed through the lounge and heard the piano music, he wondered out loud whether a brandy might be better than Rolaids, but Ella, now acting more protective than excited, insisted that what he really needed was a good night's sleep. After leaving him in the elevator, where he pecked her on the cheek, she returned to her room and could hear Goldie's TV still playing next door. She put on her own set and began nervously changing channels, but when nothing caught her interest, she sat in the comfortable chair without undressing and tried reading more of Tyler's memoirs. Distracted by what had just occurred with Edmund, however, and not the least bit sleepy, she decided that what she wanted, after all, was a snifter of Grand Marnier. Throwing the light sweater around her shoulders and checking her lipstick and the number of cigarettes in her case, she went back downstairs and was about to take a seat at a small table when, realizing how nice it would be to sit outside in a rocker, she asked the waiter to bring her cordial to the porch.

At first, she thought she was alone, but as soon as she'd taken a chair and lit a cigarette, she noticed a relatively young couple seated farther down the porch with drinks in their hands and their feet perched against the banister. They seemed to be arguing about something and were so absorbed in their squabble that they were unaware of, or impervious to, the presence of anybody else.

"Dammit, I've tried to explain it all, and you just refuse to listen," the man was declaring loudly enough to be overheard, his chair rocking steadily.

"Oh, I understand. I understand all too well—more than you think," the woman said in an equally angry drawl, staring straight ahead at the water.

"God, you're impossible," he ranted.

"Because I tell it like it really is?"

"You're crazy, Zelda. I mean, you get these sick ideas in your head, then accuse me of—"

"Would you please keep your voice down?" she asked more quietly when she suddenly noticed someone seated a few chairs away. "We're not at some tobacco auction, you know."

Ella tried to ignore the altercation and let her mind reflect on the mellow piano music in the background, and her lovely evening with Edmund, and her plans for Tyler after he arrived, but when the words again became more heated and foul and almost threatening, she was about to move back into the lounge when, very abruptly, the woman bolted from her chair and, obviously in a rage and crying, fled back inside. For a few moments, the man remained seated, rocking anxiously back and forth and drinking, then, with not so much as a glance at Ella, he too jumped up and hurried into the inn.

Anyone else would simply have been relieved to be left in peace and allowed to relish the balmy night and pleasant thoughts, but what the awkward incident aroused in Ella was the most painful of all her haunted memories, an episode from the early days in Charleston that had been even more traumatic than the near certainty about Tyler's real father and that she'd spent much of a lifetime struggling to forget. It, too, had involved Jonathan Green, but unlike her one indiscretion that, she was convinced, had resulted in the birth of a child whom she came to love more than any soul on earth, this unspeakable event had had such emotional reverberations that any woman less strong and resilient would have allowed it to totally destroy her.

The truth was that, unbeknownst to Earl, her parents, and the group of friends who'd been at the Yarboroughs' home the evening everyone learned about Jonathan's suicide, Ella had actually been the last person to see him alive. As it happened, the day before the stylish dinner party, and just a couple of weeks after her honeymoon, Ella's phone rang around noon, while she was sanding some antique wooden orbs to be used on the ends of curtain rods. At first, there was silence on the line, but after she'd repeated "Hello" a couple of times, Jonathan finally identified himself in a slurred voice, said he needed to talk with her, and asked if she were alone.

"I want to try to explain," he mumbled, leading Ella to believe he'd been drinking.

"I think it's a little late for explanations," she responded frostily, her stomach already churning.

"Please, Ella, all I ask is to talk to you for a while and for you to give me a chance to—"

"Jonathan, we have nothing to talk about—nothing at all. And why aren't you at work?"

He hesitated. "I told Dad I hadn't been feeling too good, and he said to take the day off and rest. But I need to talk to you, Ella, and . . . we've been through too much together, and . . . I know I should have called before now. . . . Ella, I don't have anybody else I can talk to—nobody else. You've got to talk to me, Ella."

"Have you been drinking, Jonathan?"

"If I could just come over for a while so we could talk. . . . I've got to try to make you understand. I need help, Ella, and . . ." He seemed to choke up, as if he might burst out crying. "You're the only person I can turn to, Ella. Please let me come over."

Hearing Jonathan's voice again stirred confused feelings of fervor and anger in Ella, but when, after he pleaded over and over and she decided he was truly desperate, she realized she had little alternative but to act against her better instincts. And besides, she couldn't help but be curious.

"You can't come here, Jonathan," she finally said. "I'll come up to your place. I can't stay long."

Since Earl always needed the car for his work, Ella had taken to riding a bicycle around town when not working part-time at the museum. Jonathan's apartment on King Street was no more than seven or eight blocks from her house, and she managed, even after taking time to change her blouse and brush her hair, to ride there in about twenty minutes. The front room of the apartment was in disarray, and the first thing she noticed was a half-empty whiskey bottle on top of the cluttered desk. What really shocked her, though, was Jonathan's haggard appearance, especially his glassy eyes and dull curly hair, which looked as if it hadn't been washed in days. Also, a slightly foul odor filled the room, suggesting that there might be garbage back in the small kitchen that he hadn't bothered to take out. She wondered if he might try to hug her or kiss her on the forehead the way he used to do, but he made no move to show any affection.

"Can I fix you a drink?" he asked groggily, reaching for the bottle and pouring a few shots in a glass for himself.

"Not this time of day. Aren't you starting a little early?"

He had no reply and only pointed to the deep, cracked-leather, burgundy chair where he and Ella had frolicked more than once shortly after he returned from the war. "Have a seat," he muttered, almost stumbling into the desk chair. "You're wonderful to come. This can't be easy for you."

"It's not."

"I know how badly I hurt you."

"I just don't understand, Jonathan."

He looked down at his drink. "Did you ever tell anybody—about what you saw in the garden, I mean?"

"No. How could I?"

"Not even Earl?"

"Not even Earl."

He finally looked directly at her. "You have no idea how sorry I've been about that and . . . how humiliating and frightening it's been for me."

"It should be," she said coldly, tapping her fingers on the arm of the chair. "And don't talk to me about humiliation. You told me you could explain it."

"I can't really explain it, Ella. It just happened."

"Disgusting things like that don't just happen, Jonathan. There has to be reasons." She paused a long while. "Just tell me one thing. Had that sort of thing ever happened before? Tell me that."

He dropped his head again and waited. "Yes. Overseas.

The first time in London. You see, a bunch of us were drinking one night at this pub, and—"

"I don't care to hear the gory details, Jonathan," she interrupted abruptly. "All I want to know now is if anything . . . just tell me if anything like that ever happened here in Charleston before that night in the garden."

"No, no, Ella, I swear. Never." He struggled to convince her. "I give you my word. And that night at the party . . . I don't remember much, except all the drinking, and the noise, and meeting that guy, and looking up and seeing you out there. How I could have done that? How I could have been so stupid and . . . weak? I'm so confused about it all, Ella."

"But what about me, Jonathan?" she protested strongly, trying to hold back tears. "Did I really mean so little to you? I mean, how did I fit into this sick nightmare? How could you have taken advantage of me the way you did, then do something so disgraceful? It's just not normal, Jonathan. It's so sick and disgusting, and I just don't understand it."

He poured himself another drink, his hand shaking, and ran a hand frantically through his bedraggled hair. "Don't you think I've asked myself that question a hundred times, Ella? Don't you think I've been terrified of . . . But it had nothing to do with the way I felt about you—you've got to believe that. You've always been so special to me, Ella."

She suddenly got up and began pacing the room, banging her hand fitfully against her hip.

"Special! Special!" she screamed. "You've got some gall saying that, Jonathan. We did things together I'd never, ever done before, and a week later, just one week later, right there with all our friends at someone's home, I catch you in that disgusting act. And you have the gall to tell me I was special." Her cheeks were now almost blood red. "Do you know . . . can you imagine how shocked and deceived and humiliated I felt that night in the garden? I just want to ask you that. I cared about you, Jonathan, I really cared about you and thought we had something good going for us."

"But you married Earl," he said, raising the glass again to his lips.

Impulsively, Ella reached over and, with one powerful swipe, sent the glass flying across the room. "You're drunk, and don't you so much as mention me and Earl. That's none of your business, none of your concern at all."

He placed his knuckles against his mouth, bit hard on them, then began to sob helplessly. "You don't understand, Ella. It's something I don't seem to be able to control. I've tried, but it's something I can't control."

"What I understand, Jonathan, and what apparently has never entered your selfish brain, is that you're a sick man who could have done me more damage than you could ever imagine."

"I know I've hurt you, Ella, and I'm trying, God knows I'm trying with all my might, to say how sorry I am."

Defiantly, she stood with both hands on her hips and stared down at him. "You still don't understand, Jonathan. You still don't understand that it's more than that—a lot more. What you don't understand . . . what apparently hasn't dawned on you, Jonathan, and what probably wouldn't make a particle of difference to you, is that I could be carrying your child. Has that ever so much as dawned on you? Are you really that selfish and stupid?"

He sat silent, still gnawing on his knuckles as she glared at him. "Oh, God, Ella," he finally uttered.

"You need help, Jonathan," she persisted, "and I'm not the one who can help you."

"I'm so sorry, Ella," he cried even more painfully, evidently shocked by the realization of the harm he might have caused.

"Stop saying you're sorry. It's too late for that now. You're really disturbed, Jonathan, and you'd better do something about it before it's too late. See a doctor, or talk with your daddy or the rabbi or another close friend, but you'd better do something to straighten yourself out before they lock you up and throw away the key."

His head weaving slightly, he grabbed his forehead with one hand, began to open the desk drawer with the other, then, as if suddenly aware of what he was doing, closed it quickly.

"I don't have anybody else to talk to, Ella. Nobody," he repeated. "I thought you might understand and help. . . . I don't blame you for being so mad. . . . I don't know what's wrong with me."

"Listen, Jonathan, I'm leaving," she announced firmly, opening the front door as he remained in the same stance at the desk, his head in his hand and his eyes cast downward. "And I'd appreciate you not calling me again."

"Please don't go, Ella," were the last garbled words she heard as she closed the door.

Outside, she realized she was trembling as she stood holding the handlebars of her silver bicycle propped against a side of the building, and, for an instant, she wondered if she'd been too harsh with Jonathan, if maybe she should calm down, and go back in, and hold this boy who'd governed her emotions for so long, and try to show a little more compassion and understanding.

Tears were now streaming down her cheeks, but, regaining her composure and resolve, she finally pushed the bike out to the sidewalk and was about to climb onto the seat when she heard, like a distant clap of thunder, a muffled blast from inside the apartment that made her stop in her tracks and snap her head around. At first, she imagined it could be some object that had crashed to the floor, or even an electrical fixture or appliance that had exploded, but Ella was not a fool and had heard enough gunshots at reckless beach parties and on duck hunts and in her own backyard during tin-can target practices to recognize the unmistakable crack of a pistol.

Her heart thumping, she dropped the bicycle in the middle of the sidewalk, raced back to the door, and, when she frantically opened it, her worst fears were confirmed by the sight of Jonathan's motionless body sprawled faceup on the ragged carpet near the desk, a gun still in his right hand and the chair toppled over one leg.

"Jonathan!" she screamed. "Oh my Lord! Jonathan!"

His eyes were wide open, and there was already blood flowing from his mouth and all around his head. Hysterically, she shouted his name over and over, but when it became obvious that he was dead, she stood dazed for a few more moments, called out his name more gently, then, after slamming the door behind her and mindlessly scanning the empty street, jumped onto the bike and began peddling as if racing the devil himself.

Headed toward her house on Queen Street, she suddenly turned on Calhoun toward the Cooper River, then, frenetically and aimlessly, peddled as hard as she could down Meeting Street past Beth Elohim, then by the Confederate Museum on Market, and down Anson past the Old Powder Magazine, and through Rainbow Row, and along East Bay past the lavish Edmondston-Alston Mansion till, unable to go any farther, she pulled into Battery Park, where she and Jonathan had walked so often and where she and Earl had been married in the Gazebo just a few weeks before. Panting for breath, she collapsed on a bench beneath a giant palmetto and simply sat, in shock, staring helplessly over the harbor. She wanted to cry, but now the tears wouldn't come. She tried to remember what all she'd said to Jonathan back at the apartment, but her mind was blank. She wondered if what had happened could be only a terrible nightmare, but when the image of Jonathan's face kept reappearing vividly and mercilessly in her mind, the reality of the tragedy was only confirmed over and over.

After sitting at least an hour and calming her nerves enough to think halfway lucidly, Ella finally considered calling Earl at work, or her parents, or a close girlfriend, or the police. But then she knew, she knew for certain, that she couldn't call anybody, not that afternoon, not that night, not ever. The lives, and reputations, and futures of too many people were at stake, and to implicate herself further in a predicament that had already caused enough emotional and possibly other unforeseen damage that could affect not only herself but those dearest to her could only make matters worse. Jonathan was gone, a victim of postwar trauma in everyone's eyes, and while she tried to rationalize that she was not directly responsible for his death and that his role in her life had ended well before this horrible catastrophe, she already recognized that her knowledge of why he had really killed himself, along with her unwillingness to help him more in his struggle to defeat his demons, were grounds for a sense of guilt that would torment her periodically for years to come. She refused to analyze it further, so, drumming up what little strength and courage she had left, she got back on her bike, peddled slowly straight up Market Street, and tried to concentrate on what she might fix for Earl's dinner.

Once he arrived home, it took all the stamina Ella could muster to act and talk normally while they had their usual cocktails and listened to the radio.

"Three thousand letterheads," Earl said excitedly, sitting in his deep leather armchair and lighting a cigarette. "Sutter Advertising's put in a whopping order for three thousand letterheads. And that ain't bird feed—not for a small company like ours."

Ella, her legs crossed and a foot bobbing up and down nervously, sipped her drink. "Oh, honey, that's grand, just grand."

"A few more orders like that, and maybe we could even buy another press."

"You'll do fine, honey," she tried to reassure in a calm tone, lighting up another Lucky and praying this conversation wouldn't continue.

"Talked to Daddy, and he says two or three more accounts like this could put us on the road."

"And your daddy knows what he's talking about," she struggled to comment further, a sudden serious expression on her face betraying the turmoil raging inside.

Earl got up to sweeten his drink just as Jimmy Dorsey's band struck up a swing tune on the radio, but before reaching for the bottle of Old Crow, he leaned down and kissed her gently on the forehead. "Cat got your tongue, Peaches? I won't talk any more business."

She laughed haltingly. "Just a little tired, and a small tummy upset."

"Busy day?"

"Yeah, sort of. Working on those curtain rods, and I went over to Happy Home to look through fabrics." She turned her face up and kissed him on the lips. "Hope cold fried chicken's okay with you tonight."

"Anything you do is okay with me," he whispered, kissing her again. "But I did see Wade today, and don't forget we're due at their place for dinner tomorrow night."

Ella was unable to eat more than a couple of bites of chicken and potato salad, her only excuse being that too much country ham at breakfast hadn't sat well with her all day. As he often did in the early days, Earl made amorous overtures when they went to bed, but, for once, she pretended to be exhausted, yearning, instead, to break down, tell him about Jonathan, and have him simply hold her tightly while she cried her eyes out.

The following day, Earl reminded her of the dinner party

that evening at the Yarboroughs'. At first, she said she still wasn't feeling up to snuff and wondered if they could back out gracefully, but when he informed her he'd told Wade that he and Trudy could count on them not just to be there but to bring a few bottles of liquor and wine, Ella agreed they had to show up. Too depressed to go to work, all she could dwell on that entire long, frightening day was whether anybody had yet found Jonathan.

Chapter 15

DEFEATED SOUL

Since it was pouring down rain on Friday afternoon, Goldie drove the car to the Myrtle Beach airport to meet Tyler's plane from LaGuardia and dropped Ella off at the curb so she wouldn't get soaking wet and mess up her hair. Learning that the flight was delayed, Ella just suggested that they find a bar where she could sit down and have a relatively quiet drink while waiting when, out of the blue, she heard somebody on the concourse call her name. Turning around, she saw a rather exotic woman on the arm of a distinguished older man in a tan jacket pushing a cart with two expensive-looking leather suitcases and a couple of shopping bags.

"Well, I don't believe my eyes, Ella!" the other woman drawled dramatically, opening her arms for a big hug. "How in this world are you?"

Her hair, dyed a luminous cinnamon, appeared to have just been fluffed at the beauty parlor, and, even with all the heavy makeup, the taut skin around the eyes and on the neck made it obvious to anyone that this was a face that had been subjected to various surgical procedures more than once. She wore a lightweight green suede suit with leather buttons on the jacket, a knotted gold bracelet, and an enormous diamond ring that only drew attention to her mottled, slightly gnarled left hand.

At first, Ella didn't recognize the woman. Then, studying her reconditioned face more carefully, she said, "Why, Naomi Chapman. How are you, dear?" embracing her cordially but guardedly. "And what in heaven's name are you doing in this airport?"

"Oh, honey, we're on our way back to Atlanta," she explained slowly, taking the man's arm again and looking suspiciously at Goldie. "Ella, I don't think you ever met my husband, Lyman Spangler. Lyman, this is Ella Dubose, originally from Charleston, and we knew each other years ago in Charlotte before Dennis died—back longer than I care to remember." She let out a silly laugh. "I'm sure you've heard me mention the Duboses."

"And this is my companion, Goldie Russell," Ella told her casually, patting Goldie proudly on the arm.

"Pleased to meet you," Naomi said, nodding her head.

"So you're still in Atlanta?" Ella asked.

"Oh, heavens yes, honey. Couldn't live anywhere else, especially since both the children and three grandchildren are there. Can you imagine? Anyway, after Lyman here retired— he was in real estate out in Buckhead—we bought this precious cottage down here at Tilghman Beach—oceanfront, five bedrooms, and, as I'm sure you know, Tilghman is still very family oriented and pretty private, with no honky-tonk, and no pavilion, and, at least so far—thank the Good Lord—no coloreds. We really love the place and usually have a few nice houseguests come down whenever life in the big city just gets too much." She stopped only to laugh again and apologize. "Mercy me, where are my manners? I haven't even asked what you're doing in this airport yourself. And how is Earl, and those adorable children of yours? Are you still in that lovely big house on . . . oh, yeah, I remember, on Colville Road?"

Ella explained patiently that Earl had died some years ago. Yes, she still lived in the same house and was down at the Priscilla on a little vacation. The children were all fine, and, in fact, she was waiting on Tyler to arrive any minute from New York. Naomi wondered if she had time for a quick cup of coffee so they could really catch up on each other's lives, but when Ella said they were rushing to the gate to meet her son, Naomi gave her another hug, mentioned her married name again, and told her, made her promise, to call and come by the house for at least a drink anytime she happened to be back down in the Myrtle Beach area for any length of time.

"Awful woman," Ella snarled as she and Goldie were forced to head in the direction of the gates and forget about trying to find a bar. "Common as dirt. I didn't like her in the old days, and I still don't. So pretentious and unattractive. Her first husband was a very respectable gentleman, and I could never figure out what in this world he saw in that phony woman. Maybe I was a little rude, but all I wanted was to get away as quickly as possible."

Goldie laughed. "Maybe you shouldn't be so critical, Miss Ella. She was just trying to be nice."

"What do you mean, woman?" Ella said impatiently. "Nice? You saw her. You heard the way she talks. She's not worth our time, believe me, dear."

Proceeding to the waiting area at the gate, Goldie grabbed a *Charlotte Observer* at a concession, but Ella, commenting that the last thing she cared about during her vacation was reading about the horrors and corruption and violence in the world, settled into one of the uncomfortable chairs and took a small piece of needlepoint from her pocketbook. Although she couldn't have been more worked up over seeing Tyler again, the first time since he was in Charlotte for Christmas, what was weighing heavily on her mind was the main reason she'd coaxed him to join her and the mission she'd mapped out in her mind.

Repeatedly, she'd debated with herself over whether she was doing the right thing and how any revelations about his real father might affect their close relationship. But in the end her conscience still dictated that she simply had no right to continue living such a terrible lie and that this was something that had to be resolved before it was too late. Not that Ella had ever been really that righteous and religious, despite her active involvement in the church. Her faith had always been steadfast and consoling, but it had also been a very private, objective matter based more on the moral principles it taught than on any mighty inner strength and promise of pearly gates it might provide. Unlike most of her more zealous Catholic friends, conditioned to expiating guilt as a necessary step on the rocky road to salvation, Ella perceived her own guilt as a normal problem, with no religious overtones, to be tolerated and confronted realistically when the right time came.

As to exactly when and how she would broach the critical subject, she'd mulled over every possibility imaginable and ultimately came up with a plan to drive down to Charleston with Tyler, visit Jonathan's grave in Beth Elohim cemetery, and, as straightforwardly and undramatically as possible, inform him of the truth over lunch, maybe at Henry's. That she'd not been to the grave herself since that sad day of the funeral all those years ago was a daunting prospect she knew she'd find disturbing, but if the venture proved to her son just how serious she was about correcting, even at this late date, a deceit that might help explain a good deal about his personality and life, it would be worth any nostalgic suffering she herself might be forced to endure.

The moment Tyler came through the gate, the first thing Ella noticed was that he seemed to have lost weight and his hair was less luxuriant than before. Unlike the majority of other casually dressed men deboarding, however, he was wearing his customary tailored dark blazer and silk necktie and carrying a handsome leather-trimmed garment bag over one shoulder, so even though Ella thought for a moment that he felt much too thin when he hugged her tightly, then the grinning Goldie, she was certain there wasn't a thing wrong that plenty of wholesome Southern food wouldn't remedy. Little could she have known that, after hearing from the oncologist shortly before leaving that the most recent blood-cell count was less promising than one had hoped, Tyler had considerably more to be worried about than just weight loss.

"Y'all didn't have to come all the way to the gate, for heaven's sake," he told the two ladies, his arm still around his mother's waist.

"Well, to tell you the truth, honey, we hadn't planned to," Ella admitted, "and we had to do some real sidestepping. Do you remember that Mrs. Chapman in Charlotte—Naomi Chapman, married to the bank president? Well, I never cared much for her, and, of all people, we would have to run smack into her with her new husband right here on the concourse. Of course, nothing would do but for her to want to get chummy again, so we made up a big excuse about rushing to meet you, and . . . Lord, she's the crudest and ugliest woman I ever laid eyes on."

Tyler chuckled. "Now, now, Mama, you know people can't help it if they're ugly."

"I know she can't help it," Ella huffed, "but, as my daddy used to say, she could at least stay home."

Both Tyler and Goldie roared with laughter as he pulled his mother closer and exclaimed, "Mama! You never change."

Driving back to the inn, Ella was excited as she told Tyler all about the inn, and the dining room, and Riley, and the interesting Northern family they'd met and would probably have drinks with before dinner. He'd notice, she emphasized with outrage in her voice, that Myrtle Beach had changed disgracefully since he was last there, but the Priscilla was still delightfully old-fashioned, and she'd booked him a nice oceanfront room down from hers, and the mobs hadn't yet arrived to ruin the fishing, and lots of traditional seafood houses were still around. Tyler, who did feel an emotional contentment being back around familiar sites and smells and thick accents in the region where he was born, pretended to be as animated as his mother, but so reduced was his energy after the hassle of airports and delays and the flight that all he really wanted to do once they'd arrived at the inn was lie down, regain his strength, and try to figure out what all his mother had on her mind.

Since it was still too wet to sit on the porch, everybody met in the lounge for cocktails except the two boys, who were playing video games in a remote room for children off the lobby. The Marianis, duly impressed and a little nervous to be in the company of a celebrity author, paid most attention to Tyler and were relieved to find that he was just as friendly and down to earth as his mother.

"So, Dad says you're not married up in Manhattan," Sal said carelessly.

Tyler took a sip of his daiquiri, then cracked a sly smile. "Well, not legally."

For an instant, there was dead silence at the table. Then, when Elizabeth popped her husband's shoulder reproachfully and said, "Sal, you're such a dope," everybody burst out laughing.

"Honey, would you please behave yourself around these nice Yankees," Ella told Tyler, holding a cigarette up for Edmund to light.

"Watch your language, Miss Ella," the older man teased before turning to Tyler. "Maybe you'd better remind your mama that the war's been over for a good century, and that there really is life above the Mason-Dixon Line."

"Maybe you can finally convince her," Tyler cracked, wrapping an arm tenderly around his mother's shoulder.

"Why, I don't know what you two are talking about," Ella said smugly.

"We understand that you and your friend have been to Paris," Elizabeth broke in just as the waiter placed a small bowl of pickled shrimp on the table and asked if anybody was ready for a sweetener. "Sal and I have always wanted to go to Paris."

"Oh, listen," Ella exclaimed suddenly as she turned her head to look at the piano player and smiled. "Jo Stafford. 'Long Ago and Far Away.' "

For a few moments, everyone remained silent till, finally, glancing at the others, Tyler said warmly, "Pull out of it, Mama," and added, "In case you haven't noticed, my mama is a hopeless sentimentalist."

"I'm nothing of the sort," she grumbled, turning back. "I just happen to appreciate a little decent music—not this junk you hear everywhere today."

"I'll second that," Edmund said, raising his glass to Ella.

"You were going to tell us about Paris," Elizabeth pursued, pushing her glowing sandy hair back over an ear.

Although nothing irked Tyler more than having to relate abstract impressions of places and events with which others had little way or reason to identify, his skills as a novelist allowed him to do just that when necessary. Consequently, and out of courtesy, he drummed on a while about where he and Barry had dined in Paris, and the museums and galleries they revisited, and a concert they attended, and the city's inimitable light that never ceased to mystify him.

"I hear they've got some pretty raunchy nightclubs over there," Sal said.

Tyler tried not to frown. "Not our scene. Sorry, but you'll have to get somebody else to tell you all about the tits and feathers."

"Tyler!" Ella exclaimed, slapping him on the leg while the others roared with laughter. "When you were young, I'd wash your mouth out with soap for saying things like that. Have you lost all your manners?"

But it did please Ella seeing her son get along so well with the new friends, just as nothing could have made her prouder than watching Riley's reaction outside the dining room to Tyler when the two shook hands again for the first time in many years and began to banter.

"Lawsy me, Mr. Tyler," Riley gabbled, "last time I saw you was when Buck was a calf, and now they say you're in high cotton up there in Yankeeland. Umm, umm, I do say."

Laughing, Tyler grabbed his thin arm and squeezed it. "Well, Riley, they tell me you're still managing to rule the roost here just as you always did."

"Oh, get on with you, Mr. Tyler. They gotta have somebody to keep these good folks full and outta trouble, and I reckon I'll be around till they carry me out feet first. Umm, umm. And this hair sho can't get no whiter."

"Too many late nights chasing those fillies, I bet."

Riley leaned over in spasms of laughter, his whole fragile body shaking. "Get on with you, Mr. Tyler. If that was only half-true, these ole bones would probably be in better shape— I can tell you that. I reckon you left yo missus back up North."

"Which one you talking about, Riley?"

The head waiter buckled over again as if his sides would split, then pointed at Tyler's midsection as they moved toward the dining room. "I can tell you one thing, Mr. Tyler, and that's that they sho don't feed you too good up there in New York City. But, yessir, we'll take care of that right off the bat."

Once inside the gracious room, which was at least half-full and quiet, Riley, dressed in his usual neat tuxedo, resumed his more dignified demeanor as he led the three to a choice table overlooking the water, leaned down as if to reveal a secret, and whispered, "You folks might want to give serious thought to the okra fritters and crabmeat casserole this evening. Uh-huh."

Both Ella and Goldie took the recommendation, but Tyler, who had no real appetite, ordered only a shrimp cocktail and salad with the excuse that the wretched lunch on the plane had left his stomach a little queasy. Since he didn't feel at ease discussing serious family matters or even his and Barry's trip to Paris in front of Goldie, conversation revolved mainly around what the two women had been doing all week and the friendship they had developed with Dr. O'Conner and his family. Of course, Ella was discreet about her budding attraction to Edmund, but such were her glowing appraisals and compliments every time she referred to him that it didn't take Tyler long to suspect that his mother might actually be involved in a little innocent romance with the doctor. When he glanced over at Goldie, she simply winked at him.

As usual, Edmund dropped by the table after the meal to ask if he could twist a few arms to join him for a cordial in the lounge, explaining that Elizabeth and Sal had decided to turn in early with the boys since the weather was still so rotten. And, as usual, Goldie thanked him in her retiring way, then declined on the grounds that there was a program on TV she wanted to watch. Ella had hoped that Edmund could get to know Tyler better, but, having studied her son's pale complexion and vapid eyes during dinner, she couldn't have been more solicitous when he announced that he was really beat after a hectic week and the flight down and would have to leave tonight's carousing up to the "younger folks." As a result, Ella and Edmund were once again left to exchange more stories and memories and, at times, to be relatively intimate, and while she was tempted at one point to relate the true story about Jonathan Green and the reason she'd pressured Tyler to make the trip down, her troublesome secret was still much too personal and deep rooted to share even with this remarkable man who no doubt would sympathize and offer to help.

Although Tyler himself did feel lousy while he undressed

and swallowed a handful of pills, he had already drifted back under the wistful spell of the Lowcountry and, as the mild sea air and sound of breaking waves stirred his senses, opened himself up to disparate memories of youthful days much as his mother was prone to do. Almost instinctively, he could remember romping alone through tall sea oats in pursuit of hermit crabs while his father and brother pitched ball on the beach. As if it were only yesterday, he could feel his mother's soft hand as the two of them walked along the wet strand looking for unusual seashells, and smell the faint stench of pulpwood mills while crabbing with the family near Georgetown, and hear the strange Gullah lilt of old black basketwomen selling their handicrafts at lean-tos along the road at Pawleys Island. And, he realized, there was still something enchanted about this isolated region so haunted by the ghosts of its glorious and withered past, something that beckoned to the defeated soul and offered a mysterious solace that was as soothing as muted thunder over the horizon announcing a warm summer rain or a breeze whistling through the giant fronds of a palmetto.

Chapter 16

IMPERFECT BOND

On Saturday, the sun returned as brilliant as before, and, after a good night's sleep, Tyler not only felt and looked better but had enough appetite at breakfast to eat scrambled eggs, a couple of buttermilk biscuits, and even some grits. Not wanting to push his luck, however, he rebuffed his mother's plan to put in a morning of surf fishing and asked if they could simply relax on the porch and catch up on things while Goldie tried her luck with one of the rods. True to her sartorial form, Ella was now dressed in shocking pink linen slacks and a silk paisley blouse, while he wore a more practical pair of white duck shorts and a green short-sleeved shirt that exposed his ashen arms and legs.

"I was glad to see you eating a decent breakfast," Ella said. "You look like you've taken off a little flesh."

"No harm done," was his only comment.

"And a little sun wouldn't do you any harm," she added, pressing one of his pale knees with a finger.

"Stop worrying about me."

"Well, I do think you owe me one explanation," she continued to carp casually as they rocked.

"About what?"

"That book. Your memoirs. Don't you think you went a little overboard with the family and some of our close friends?"

He chuckled. "Oh, don't be silly, Mama. There're no secrets that everybody at home doesn't already know about. All I did was tell the truth."

"Well, some things—like poor Olivia's skin problem as a child and your daddy's and my disagreements—are private matters, in my opinion. And you have no right, no right whatever, to ridicule the way Rose-Ann Beale used to take communion at home after Rufus died."

"Oh, Mama, I didn't identify her by name, and besides, who wouldn't like to read about an eccentric grand dame who used to take communion every Sunday with coffee and Ritz crackers while watching a church service on TV?"

"Well, Rose-Ann is a Presbyterian, and even if she now knew night from day out in that awful nursing home, she wouldn't consider her ritual the least bit strange. Of course, those Presbyterians do things different than we do, and she was always quick to explain to anybody that she didn't have to dress up, and go to church, and be served grape juice and a special wafer to find meaning in Holy Communion. And, as far as I'm concerned, that was her privilege."

"She's certainly not going to be reading my book, and I doubt there are many relatives today who'd take offense."

"You'd be surprised. Now listen, I don't mind you telling all those shady stories about yourself—that's your right—but when you implicate the family and our friends . . . well, Son, it's just a question of good manners, that's all."

Ella's tone was in no way hostile, but, accustomed to being mildly chided by his mother over any number of similar matters, Tyler knew the only defense was to simply change the subject again and shift the train of conversation to herself.

"Darling, I don't think my book is the reason you asked

me to join you down here on this crazy expedition. Earl did call me, and he says you're giving them a hard time back in Charlotte. Is that what this is all about?"

"Why, the nerve! Me giving them a hard time! They're the ones driving me up the wall, trying to force me to go to doctors for no earthly good reason at all and acting like I'm on my last leg. Well, I'm not going to any doctor till I need one, and nobody's going to stop me from driving my automobile, and that's that. The nerve of your brother and sister."

"Honey, you really should have checkups from time to time."

Ella slapped the arm of her chair. "Now, don't you start on me—not for one second. That's one reason I had to get away from them for a while, and you're the one person I thought would understand. Anyway, that's certainly not what I want to talk about now. I've been thinking, thinking hard, and one thing I do have to talk over with you is what all of mine you might want when I'm gone—things out of the house, I mean. Earl and Liv both already have more than they know what to do with, and . . . what I want to do is draw up a specific list to be added to my will and make sure you get what you're entitled to before they snatch everything up. We need to discuss these things. Not that I'm planning to fall over dead anytime soon, mind you, but I would like to just get my affairs in order since . . . you never know."

Tyler simply made light of the issue by saying that he and Barry couldn't cram another thing in the apartment or house and that, yes, she did seem to be jumping to unnecessary conclusions. He also couldn't help pondering the stark possibility that, given his precarious physical condition, his mother might well outlive him.

"Well," she continued in her determined manner, "I do want you to have my antique screens and the mahogany dining table and china cabinet—that table, you know, has been in my family for four generations—and, of course, I know you want that Grand Baroque silver, and my Belgium lace tablecloth, and . . . the others would have no use whatsoever for those Alsatian wineglasses, or—"

"Mama," he interrupted her endless roster, patting her on the arm and not wanting to offend her, "I think it's going to be a long time before you have to worry about disposing of all those lovely things, and—" he falsified a short titter—"as I've always said, you'll probably outlive me at the rate you're going."

Ella said he was being absurd, and that she wanted him to think seriously about this since she planned to begin drawing up her list as soon as she got back home. Then, as quick to end this conversation as she'd been to start it, she broached the subject that had been distracting her all week.

"Son, I think I mentioned on the phone one reason I thought it would be nice for you to come down, and what I'd love for just the two of us to do one day is drive down to Charleston for old time's sake, and look around, and maybe have lunch at Simon's. Wouldn't you enjoy that?"

"Isn't that a pretty long drive just to have lunch?"

"Of course not, and it wouldn't be just to have lunch. Sometimes I think you forget that you were born in Charleston, and never got to know the town, and . . . It's such a lovely old town, and I do have lots of wonderful memories and would love to visit a few places, and see the old house again after all these years, and show you some interesting things. Do you remember the one time we took y'all to Simon's when your grandmother was still alive?"

"Afraid not," he replied, wondering where this could be leading.

From seemingly nowhere appeared an unfamiliar receptionist in a blazer and tie who bent over politely and informed Ella that she had a phone call at the front desk.

"Weren't you told, young man, that I'm not accepting any calls?" she scolded. "Whoever it is, just tell them you have no idea where I am. Is that understood?"

As the man apologized and slinked away, Tyler said in exasperation, "But Mama, it could be important."

"Nonsense. It's just that meddlesome brother of yours pestering me again, and I'm in no mood to put up with his hogwash. Now, as I was saying, Henry's and Simon's down in Charleston were always very special to me—so gracious and civilized and with the nicest waiters you could ever imagine. Lulu Woodside told me not long ago that Simon's had changed a lot since the old days, but I can't believe she's right. Things don't change much in Charleston. Charlestonians hate change."

Tyler figured his mother was simply indulging in another of her many nostalgic fantasies, but while the last thing he felt like doing during this short stay was traipsing around a city he'd visited maybe twice as a child and with which he had no real emotional ties, if the excursion meant that much to her, he wasn't about to protest and disappoint her.

"When did you want to drive down, Mama?"

"When do you have to go back to New York?"

"My return ticket is for Wednesday.

"That's absurd," she said. "When are we going to fish, and go down to Murrells Inlet, and eat at the Sea Captain, and . . . I'd really like you to get to know Dr. O'Conner and his family better."

He smiled and looked suspiciously at her. "You seem quite infatuated with this Dr. O'Conner. Could there be a little romance brewing?"

"Oh, don't be ridiculous, honey," she muttered coyly. "He's simply a very nice and intelligent gentleman. And, buster boy, he also happens to admire your writing, in case he didn't mention it last night."

"He did, but what he mentioned most was you." He reached over and stroked her frail, rosy cheek. "I do think you're blushing."

"I certainly am not, and you've lost your mind. Why, the very idea, at my age. In any case, why don't we drive down on Monday if the weather's still nice. That would give you all day tomorrow to rest up, and maybe we can go up to Captain Jule's at Little River for dinner. You remember Captain Jule's and the crab cakes. Riley says the place is still where it always was, right on the water, and I think Goldie would also enjoy it."

"Is Goldie having a good time?"

"I think she's having the time of her life, and it's really pathetic to see what those two Mariani boys mean to her. But she deserves a good time."

Before lunch, Tyler and his mother took a long walk on the beach, during which he recounted more of what all he and Barry had done in Paris the month before and made her yearn to return to some of the restaurants where she and Earl had had such wonderful times. Tyler was now aware how just being far away from New York's high life and his work and the tedious book promotion was already doing psychological wonders to restore his strength and reduce his anxiety, and while he did miss Barry, who was working a few galleries in Chicago, being with his mother again, and returning to a way of life that was altogether different and less stressful than the one to which he'd become so accustomed, provided a mental respite that was even coming close to making him forget, or at least ignore temporarily, the medical problem that had been tormenting him. For her part, Ella treasured every moment with her son, utterly convinced by now that her furtive plan to divulge the truth about his background would not only reveal to him a facet of her humanity that he may never have perceived but also erase the one obstacle to their perfect bond. It could also, she realized, have the opposite effect. That each of them was harboring a secret that could prove caustic to the other was a factor in the relationship that simply had to be played out in the fickle game of fate.

Returning to the porch, Ella immediately spotted Edmund, Elizabeth, and Sal, who, explaining that Goldie had taken the boys down to the other end of the beach to look at huge jellyfish some people reported had washed up on the sand, insisted that the two join them for a Bloody Mary. After Sal had arranged the chairs in a circle so everybody could talk better, Edmund told about finding a notice from the management slipped under the door of his room announcing an after-dinner combo dance on the outdoor terrace for guests scheduled for Tuesday evening—weather permitting. Tyler, of course, found the event a little too quaint for his taste, but when Ella said that was the most charming idea she'd heard in years, and typical of the inn's old-fashioned sophistication, he kept his opinion to himself.

"Have you ever seen your mother shag?" Elizabeth asked Tyler mischievously.

"Oh, God, don't tell me. Where?"

"Can you shag?" Edmund asked him, friskily twisting his own hand in imitation of the dance gesture. "Miss Ella taught us all about it."

"I guess I still know how—at least I used to before I drifted off the straight primrose path of my youth."

The Marianis sniggered nervously at the suggestive remark, but Ella burst out laughing.

"Don't tell me you've been showing yourself," Tyler pretended to scold his mother, cupping the back of her neck with his hand.

"I most certainly have not. The shag happens to be a very respectable dance, and these folks found this wonderful club over at O. D., and, yes, I did show them a few steps. I forgot to tell you, but it was just like the old days when I and your daddy danced all over this beach."

"Your mother can really cut a rug—I can vouch to that," Edmund added gleefully, staring at Ella as she blushed and began to change her expression.

"Oh, I know all about Mama's dancing," Tyler said.

"You know nothing of the sort," she corrected. "You never saw me and your daddy shag down here and at O. D. and Cherry Grove when we were in top form. You were just knee high to a grasshopper." She paused a long time, as if lost in her recollection. "Lord, we used to dance our heads off, me and Earl, and Bobby Foster, and lots of other boys out on the island, and over at the pavilion, and in the grand hotel, and . . . It was all so lovely and gracious, and, mercy, did we have fun— good, clean fun with nice people from good families. . . . The tango and Charleston and shag and slow dancing and . . ."

Ella now seemed to be laughing to herself and was holding her drink out over the arm of the rocker when, in a split second, her hand began to shake uncontrollably and she dropped the glass on the deck, her eyes blinking rapidly.

"Mama!" Tyler called out anxiously, jumping up and leaning over her while Sal reached down to pick up pieces of glass. "What's wrong, Mama? Are you okay?"

Ella seemed to be in a trance. Then, as suddenly as the spell had come over her, frightening everyone and leading them to worry that maybe she might be on the verge of a mild stroke, her eyes appeared to focus again. She looked at Tyler as if perplexed, then at Sal squatted on the floor, then at the front of her blouse, then, in her normal tone of voice, declared, "Mercy me, what a clumsy fool I am. Y'all must please excuse my manners. I am mortified, truly mortified."

"Are you sure you're all right?" Tyler questioned again, holding her hands.

"Oh, stop fussing over me, Son. Of course I'm all right. Haven't you ever lost your grip and dropped a drink? And Sal, please stop fooling with that glass. You're gonna cut yourself, young man. Tyler, go find that waiter and ask him to clean this mess up—and to please bring me another drink."

All the while Ella was apologizing and dictating, Edmund sat watching her carefully, first with a wry expression on his face, then with a bewitching smile.

"Now, I have a proposal to make," she announced as if nothing unusual had just happened, glancing over at Edmund. "Tyler's only here for a few days, and I don't think any of us want to sit around here on a Saturday night, so what I'd like to do is invite you all to go up to Captain Jule's at Little River for dinner as my guests—and no wrangling from you this time, Dr. O'Conner. That is, of course, unless you folks have other plans."

"Or unless I shoot Mama first," Tyler quipped just as he returned and caught the tail end of her invitation.

"Oh, hush," Ella said as she reached into her pocketbook for a mirror to check her hair.

"That's very nice of you, Miss Ella," Sal said, virtually agreeing to the idea. "We've heard about that restaurant."

"Haven't been there for ages, but I know it used to be awfully good, and you really can't beat the scenic atmosphere—right on this charming inlet."

"Maybe we should get a sitter for the boys this time," Elizabeth said to Sal, implying that they were both ready for a little break from responsibility.

"You know the boys are welcome to come," Ella assured them politely.

Tyler, who disliked children any time, any place, and under any circumstances, no matter how well behaved, couldn't have been more relieved when Sal seconded his wife's idea. Not that he was so anxious to spend an entire evening with these strangers with whom he had nothing in common and who would no doubt throw dozens of trivial questions at him about his work, and social life, and who knew what else. On the other hand, eating meals with Goldie, much as he liked and admired her, was equally awkward, so, aware that his mother was most probably arranging the evening mainly for his benefit, he had little option but to go along with the plans and try to enjoy himself. What did puzzle him a bit was why, after implying that she had important matters to discuss when she insisted he fly down, his mother wasn't making more effort to be quietly alone with him. Surely she had more on her mind than minor problems with Earl and Liv and what was going to happen to her silver service and Alsatian glasses.

As it turned out, the early dinner at Captain Jule's, around a table overlooking small boats in the inlet and dozens of seagulls perched complacently on mooring stumps, couldn't have been more delightful, and after a couple of martinis, neither Tyler nor his mother were even aware that the distraction was providing the illusory escape that both of them needed for altogether different reasons.

Chapter 17

AWENDAW

"Do you remember the time you caught your first whiting?" Ella was asking Tyler as the two stood together in the surf on Sunday morning with their lines out in the water while Goldie helped the Mariani boys build an elaborate sand castle a ways back.

"I do. How could I forget? I think that was one of the few times Daddy was really proud of me."

"Now, why would you say that? I noticed you made a number of cracks like that in the book."

"Oh, Mama, we all know that I was never exactly Daddy's favorite, and that, no matter what I did, I could never come up to his expectations. Why try to deny it?"

"That's ridiculous. It's simply not true. He cared a great deal about you. He may have had his strange ways of showing it, but he loved you dearly, Son."

"Yeah, okay, if you insist. Maybe if I'd performed better on the football field, or played golf with him, or wooed a few more gals in high school. . . ."

"That's just not true, Tyler. He always knew you were different from the others, but there wasn't a thing on God's green earth he wouldn't have done for you."

"Yeah, like show a little pride in my work, or come to my defense over the mess at Princeton—just a phone call to talk it over. Some father."

"That's not fair, Tyler. He tried but simply couldn't understand things like that. Earl was a good man, and I don't see why you have to be so negative and hateful toward him now that he's dead."

"Mama, don't you think it's a little late to argue about a subject that—" He suddenly pulled his rod back forcefully. "Whoa, whatta we have here?"

"I could kill you!" Ella wailed excitedly as he took up slack in the line instinctively and waited. "Is he on? Make sure he's on, honey."

Tyler again felt the familiar tug on the line and began reeling like an old pro. "Yep, he's on, and he's fightin'."

"A spot—and a good size," she exclaimed, happy for her son, as the fish flopped across the wet sand. "You dog."

Tyler caught a couple more, as she did, but after another hour of fishing and chatting about more pleasant topics pertaining to Charlotte and Amagansett, he said his back was starting to ache and wondered if they could call it a morning and stretch out in the cabana. Once seated, he immediately fell sound asleep, and, not wanting to disturb him, Ella moved over to join Edmund, who couldn't have been more pleased to have her company while he kept an eye on Goldie and the two boys still constructing their giant castle.

"Wish I could sleep as soundly as Tyler," he said, rubbing lotion on his hairless legs.

"He's been under lots of pressure promoting his new book—which I'll give you to read when I'm finished. That's one reason I wanted him to fly down and relax for a few days." Her expression became more pensive. "Lord, I do worry about him, and . . . Do you think Tyler looks well?"

Edmund wiped his hands on a towel, then touched her

arm. "Now how would I know, since I've just met him? But I do find him very attractive and dignified and think maybe you're being too much of a protective mother."

"Maybe you're right, but sometimes it's so hard for me to realize that my boy's getting old, and how hard he must work, and . . . I think he looks tired."

Edmund squeezed her arm. "I guess we all expect our children to remain young and energetic forever, just the way we ourselves once thought we'd stay young forever. But, you know, Miss Ella, there's lots to be said about leaving youth behind and enjoying the golden years."

"Like what?" she objected, snapping her head around.

He smiled, which always deepened the crevices on either side of his nose and made his eyes more puffy. "Like sitting with a mature Southern belle on a warm beach and having a meaningful conversation."

"Oh, get on with you, Edmund," she drawled, pretending to blush.

"I'm not just trying to flatter you, my dear, and you must know you're still a very lively and attractive woman."

"Why, I know nothing of the sort," she said, eating up every word he was saying. "But thank you all the same, dear."

For a while longer, she continued to worry out loud about Tyler, never realizing just how exhausted her son really was and that he would not only doze in his room most of the afternoon but, once he'd dutifully nursed a cognac in the lounge after dinner, knock off nine solid hours of sleep that night.

As a result, by the time he and his mother were ready to make their excursion to Charleston the following morning, Tyler felt the most rested he'd been in weeks and was actually looking forward to the drive. Ella, on the other hand, had never been more nervous and frightened as she tried to imagine how the day would go and whether, after all, she would have the courage to carry out a decision that might finally clear her conscience but could possibly prove devastating to her son and their rare relationship. Tossing and turning during the night, she'd resolved more than once to forget about the plan, let well enough alone, and simply enjoy the nostalgic visit while showing Tyler around the town he'd never really had much chance to know and appreciate. But the more she fought the moral dilemma, the more she knew she had no alternative if she was ever to fulfill this vital obligation to her son and find peace within herself while there was still a little time left. And even more wrenching was the sincere need, the strange compulsion to pay her respects to the memory of a love that, no matter how guileless and far-removed and painful, had never ceased to play a disguised but critical role in her emotional character.

Over Tyler's protests, Ella got behind the wheel of the car with the excuse that she could probably still make the drive to Charleston almost blindfolded. And, sure enough, as she barreled down U.S. 17 past Murrells Inlet and Litchfield Beach and Pawleys Island toward the old rice port of Georgetown, it was as if time had stood still for the past century. Signs on either side of the road pointed to Wedgefield, Arcadia, Hopsewee, Fairfield, and other famed but deteriorated antebellum plantations hidden along the Waccamaw, Sampit, and Great Pee Dee rivers where slavery once produced half the country's supply of "Carolina gold" and made possible a lavish society of wealthy rice planters that, virtually overnight, became extinct forever. Crossing the broad Pee Dee at Georgetown, where he'd crabbed and collected oysters in tidal creeks as a youngster when the family made short expeditions down from Myrtle, Tyler immediately recognized the thick, sweet scent of pine sap that filled the air of this diminished burgh that had boasted such glory at one time, and when they entered the Cape Romain Wildlife Refuge, brimming with giant long-leaf pines, moss-draped oaks, inky swamps, and exotic brown pelicans, Ella was so overwhelmed by vivid memories of the isolated region that she barely noticed two elderly black women crouched in front of a lean-to display on the side of the road, coiling, in the old tradition, sweet-grass baskets and place mats with metal spoon handles.

"Let's stop," Tyler announced, prompting his mother to slam on brakes, then slowly back the car up.

"Oh, honey, we can buy those by the dozens at the City Market in Charleston," she said as they approached the stand.

"No mo," one of the women uttered passively, overhearing the comment and not bothering to look up from her stitching.

"What do you mean?" Ella asked as Tyler reached for a mat hanging on the stand and began inspecting it.

"No mo basket ladies at da market. No ma'am. Dey gone."

Ella now noticed that the woman had hardly a tooth left in her mouth. "Gone where?"

"Dead."

"But there've always been basket ladies at the Charleston market."

"No mo, ma'am. An' we 'bout da only ones lef' up here."

"Why, I can't believe that."

"These mats are exquisite," Tyler said to his mother, running his fingers over the tight, smooth surface of the one in his hand.

"How much?" Ella asked the woman.

"Ten fo da small, twelve fo da big."

"Why, that's highway robbery," she hooted. "We used to buy those mats for a dollar apiece."

"Dat's da price, ma'am. Da grass, it's scarce as hen's teeth dees days."

"Well, I've never heard of such a thing."

"Dat's da price, ma'am."

"Oh, Mama, stop quibbling," Tyler whispered, taking bills from his money clip to pay for two of the mats. "This is not 1950, and you just don't find this type of craftsmanship today."

Back in the car, Ella was still ranting. "The nerve! I'll bet you fifty dollars spot cash the market in Charleston still has plenty of basket ladies selling mats for half that price. You know the problem, of course. They catch a few gullible Yankee tourists driving through here to Florida who don't know any better, then think they can charge anything they like."

Tyler laughed as he watched his mother fuming at the wheel, the dark spots on the backs of her hands accentuated by sunlight coming through the window. "That's absurd, Mama. I hate to guess what handmade mats like these would cost outside the area, even if you could find them."

"We're not outside the area. That's the point."

Just as they were skirting Bulls Bay, she heard a faint ringing from the satchel at Tyler's feet.

"Lord, don't tell me you have one of those confounded portable phones like Little Earl uses."

"Couldn't get along without it," he said, reaching quickly into the bag. "Hi. I thought it might be you. Well, at the moment, Mama's driving like a maniac through no man's land on our way down to Charleston. Fine, much better. Here, say hello to Mama. It's Barry, calling from Chicago." He tried to give her the cell phone, but she refused to take a hand off the wheel.

"Don't be ridiculous. Not on the highway."

"At least say hello," he insisted, holding the phone in front of her mouth.

"Hi, honey. Your boyfriend here is driving me crazy, and I don't approve of these new contraptions."

"No, she hasn't changed one iota," he continued with Barry. "How are things in the Windy City? That's too bad, but you sort of expected it, didn't you? Yeah, he called shortly before I left, and we had a long talk. I'll explain to you later. Don't worry. Same here."

"Well, that sounded very mysterious," Ella commented when he clicked the phone off. "Worry about what?"

"I'll tell you about it later," he said curtly, opening a map and studying it carefully. "I remember Awendaw. Didn't we once go there to eat fried oysters?"

She didn't respond, her mind suddenly seized by just the mention of the town's name and the memory of a weekend oyster roast she once attended there at a ramshackle clapboard cottage with Earl and lots of other local and out-of-town young people while Jonathan Green was overseas. It was an early, hot fall evening, she remembered, and there was music on a radio or Victrola, and everybody was drinking and dancing outside on a rickety deck overlooking a pit down in the sand where oysters and corn were being cooked under wet burlap. At one point, Ella had been slow dancing with a smashed, handsome feller from Columbia named Randy when he persuaded her to wander with him down toward the bay to look for sea turtles somebody had mentioned. At first, it seemed like a harmless ramble, but when they eventually reached a small tract of sea oats near the bay, Randy put an arm around her waist and, with no warning, pulled her close to him and proceeded to kiss her passionately. Caught totally off guard, she wasn't even able to resist till he, not satisfied with the kiss, began to try to fondle a breast.

"Stop it, Randy!" she said playfully, pushing him back.

"Oh, come on, honey, let's have a little fun," he coaxed, grabbing her again more forcefully. "Nobody's watching."

"I said no, Randy," she exclaimed loudly. "We don't act like that down here. What's come over you?"

"What's wrong with a little fun, Ella?" he persisted, wrestling with her till they lost their balance and tumbled to the sand.

"Randy, stop it this minute! Stop this right now," she

screamed as he pinned her down and tried to kiss her again and run a hand up under her flimsy cotton blouse. "You're drunk!"

"Oh, I know you wanna play around as much as I do," he said, his breath reeking of liquor. "I could tell up there, sugar."

When Ella next felt his hand creeping up one leg under her skirt, she again bellowed "Stop it!" over and over and began to sob uncontrollably, unable to break his hold or budge under his heavy body.

Then, as abruptly as the drunken assault had started, she felt his weight lifted and heard a dull thud and another voice roar "Bastard!"

It was Earl, and by the time she could focus on the two tussling and jump up, Earl had slammed the other boy again so fiercely in the face with his fist that blood was already streaming from the edge of his mouth. Randy tried to fight back, but he was no match for Earl, who continued to pummel him and yell "Goddamn bastard!" till Ella finally reached for his flailing arms and begged, "That's enough, Earl! Stop, Earl! You're gonna kill him!"

"Had enough, buddy? Had enough?" Earl howled as Randy pulled himself up unsteadily, touched his mouth, and looked at the blood on his fingers. "You ever touch this little lady again—you ever get near her—and you won't have a face left. Got it?"

Trembling, Ella walked slowly on Earl's arm back to the party and never saw Randy again. Earl didn't ask why she'd gone with him down near the bay in the first place, and not till some years later did she finally try to explain the awkward episode. Nor did Ella ever ask how Earl had known where the other two had gone and happened to show up when he did.

★ ★ ★

"Yeah, I think it was some sort of diner in or near Awen-daw," Tyler was saying. "Remember?"

Ella continued to stare blankly at the highway, as if hypno-tized.

"Remember?" he repeated, now glancing over at her sus-piciously and touching her arm. "Did you hear me, Mama?"

"Oh, sorry, honey," she finally reacted. "Guess I was day-dreaming. What were you saying?"

"Aren't you getting a little tired of driving? Maybe you should let me take over."

"Oh, stop babying me, honey. I'm doing just fine. And, be-sides, we'll be in Charleston before long, and you wouldn't know one street from the next."

Chapter 18

THE YELLOW PINE

The air was now sultry as Ella drove through Mt. Pleasant, and when they crossed the Cooper River on the Grace Memorial Bridge and caught a first glimpse of Charleston's low skyline pierced by innumerable church spires and steeples, Tyler commented how the historic town resembled an antebellum watercolor come to life in pastel shades.

" '*It was many and many a year ago, / In a kingdom by the sea . . . .*,'" Ella began reciting wistfully.

"That's Poe. 'Annabel Lee,' " he exclaimed in utter surprise. "How do you know 'Annabel Lee'? It's one of my favorite poems."

"You don't remember when I used to quote it to you as a young child? I'm not totally illiterate, you know. Every youngster of my generation who grew up in Charleston had to memorize that poem. '*I was a child and she was a child, / In this kingdom by the sea. . . .*' You know this was the place he was describing."

"Who told you that?"

"Oh, honey, every Charlestonian learns that Poe spent time on Sullivan's Island when he was in the military, and that that's the kingdom in his poem."

"Well, I'll be damned," he declared in even more astonishment. "I taught 'Annabel Lee' and always just took for granted the kingdom was purely imaginary."

"Shows how much you know with your fancy PhD. Maybe my recitations rubbed off on you, after all. '*But we loved with a love that was more than a love.* . . .' " She hesitated again, her expression changing as her eyes caught another quick glimpse of the harbor speckled with small shrimp boats, and she seemed to be trapped once more in some obscure memory. "Yes, it's a very beautiful poem, and this really is a kingdom by the sea."

"Mama, I do believe you're a hopeless romantic."

"And what's wrong with that?"

"You and Daddy must have had some wild times here back in the old days."

"Well, I wouldn't exactly call them wild, but, yes, we did have some wonderful times—us and all our friends. You can't imagine. Nothing like the slovenly, revolting things young people do today to entertain themselves. You see, we had refinement and manners in those days, and we cared about tradition, and family, and the way we dressed, and a bad war that had to be won. Not easy times, mind you, and we never knew who the next boy would be who wouldn't ever come home again from overseas. But we still managed somehow to have decent fun. We threw big barbecues and oyster roasts out on the islands, and we all participated in social benefits for the war effort, and we hunted ducks, and we danced—Lord, did we dance. It seemed like we never stopped dancing—at beach pavilions, and clubs, and hotel ballrooms, and grand homes—anyplace there was a band or piano or radio or record player. Nothing like this crazy, disgusting disco stuff they call dancing today. No, no. We did swing, and the shag, and the tango, and lots of romantic cheek-to-cheek slow dancing, and maybe the reason we drank and danced so much was to forget about what was happening in the world. . . . But yes, sir, those were wonderful times, and I think about them a lot today."

During her dreamy discourse, Tyler just sat and stared at his mother in awe, and when she had finished, all he could say was, "I wish I could have been part of that generation, Mama."

"Well, to a small extent, you were," she said ambiguously, "and I think some of our values rubbed off on you."

Leaving the bridge, Ella saw the turnoff for East Bay Street, but since this main artery had been transformed into a busy thruway skirting almost the entire east side of the peninsula, she cut off on Charlotte Street, admitted she was a little confused, and, pulling over in exasperation, told Tyler he'd better drive while she checked the small map in her pocketbook. Then, once they'd reached Meeting Street and she recognized the Charleston Museum and, across the street, the splendid Federal-style Joseph Manigault Mansion with its ornamental gatehouse, she began to feel at home in the city.

"I thought you remembered your way around so well," he kidded, cruising slowly down the street past more historic houses and a few modern hotels and shops and noticing the distinct aroma of jasmine in the air.

"Just hush and drive where I tell you," she snapped. "Some of these commercial places that have popped up on this street are a disgrace. But it's all coming back to me. Stay on Market till we get to Tradd."

The farther down the lower peninsula they drove, the more Ella seemed to remember every street and landmark and opulent mansion, some of the houses with Colonial clapboard sidings and pitched roofs, others in the Georgian style with flattened white columns and box chimneys, and a few boasting elaborate wooden Italianate balustrades, graceful verandas, and highly ornamental wrought-iron gates and fences. Tucked into narrow alleys off cobblestone lanes were exquisite gardens with old magnolias, wisteria trellises, flowering azaleas and camellias,

and camphor bushes, and when Tyler turned onto Tradd and
Ella spotted the large Federal-style home with iron balconies
where she was born and raised, she let out an audible gasp.

"Lord have mercy, just look at how those rich Northerners
restored and fixed the place up," she said almost sadly after directing Tyler to stop in the middle of the quiet, tree-lined
street. "I told your Uncle Vance and Aunt Sally we should
never have sold that house after Missy died, but they had their
mind set on living in Atlanta, and, to be frank, my dear brother
never really appreciated this town's unique history and charm—
and Sally, coming from Sumpter, of all places, certainly never
did. Anyway, I think they just saw a fast buck in selling the place,
and, at the time, your daddy and I were in no financial position
to put up much of an argument."

She sat staring pensively at the house a few moments
longer, then asked, "You don't remember visiting Granny
here, do you?"

"I think I faintly recall the iron fence and playing in the
yard with Liv. Out of curiosity, why didn't you and Daddy
bring us down here more often? I never realized just how
amazing this town is."

"Oh, all your friends were in Charlotte, and you remember
how Paw Paw and Granny were always coming up to visit, and
I guess once most of our relatives in Charleston were gone,
there wasn't much reason to go back and visit—even when we
were down at Myrtle. Now I wish we had. Maybe if we'd been
able to hold on to the old house . . . Lord, I hate to guess what
the place is worth today. But I've seen enough. Now, go down
here, and turn right, and we'll go up to Queen and look at the
house where you were born."

Although Ella's and Earl's small Colonial house now
seemed a little run down despite what looked like new iron-
work around the second-floor piazza, it had nevertheless been
well enough preserved to arouse an overwhelming store of

happy and sad memories for her. Aside from its interesting architecture, the place, of course, meant little to Tyler, but as the two sat quietly in the car, wiping scant beads of perspiration from their foreheads and watching two children as they cavorted with a young woman in the front yard, it wasn't difficult for him to imagine the thoughts and impressions that had to be racing through his mother's sentimental mind.

"Getting hungry?" he asked, hoping to disrupt her concentrated gaze at the house that he perceived as more troubling than gratifying.

She remained silent for a long moment, then reached nervously into her pocketbook for a cigarette. "Before we go eat, there is one other place I want us to visit. Someplace I think you should see."

Slowly, they weaved their way back uptown, past the stately Greek-Revival St. John's Lutheran Church on the corner of Clifford and Archdale, and, a bit farther, the overtly Gothic-style Unitarian church rebuilt shortly before the War Between the States. Then, when Ella spotted a small cemetery set unobtrusively off Coming Street, she told Tyler to pull up in front and get out of the car.

"There's a grave I want to see," she explained vaguely, opening her own door with some apprehension. "The grave of a very dear friend I was in school with during the war. And I'd like for you to see it too."

Tyler, who'd decided simply to humor another of his mother's quirks, was on the verge of asking casual questions when, pushing open the small gate, he was surprised to notice the Star of David engraved on most of the tombstones.

"Is this a Jewish cemetery or something?"

Ella stood looking about, as if wondering exactly where to go or what to look for.

"Yes, it is. The cemetery for Beth Elohim over on Hasell Street. Been here for centuries."

"You had a close Jewish friend in high school?" he asked next in some amazement. "I never heard you and Daddy mention having any close Jewish friends when you two were young."

"Well, I did," she said, her voice fluttering and her heart racing. "Green. Look for a marker that says Green. Jonathan Emanuel Green."

"Was this one of the classmates who didn't come back during the war?"

"Green," she repeated, ignoring his question as they moved slowly in the shadows of tall trees down a narrow gravel row on the right. "So many graves now. So many more than at the funeral. I remember his was under a pine, a yellow pine. It all looks so different now, with so many graves. I don't remember so many graves. Green. Jonathan Green. There has to be a marker."

Baffled by this whole uncanny pursuit, and beginning to feel tired, Tyler questioned with a little impatience whether she had ever visited the grave before, only to have her mumble something about not being in the cemetery since the day of the funeral years and years ago.

"I'm not saying you're crazy, Mama, but are you absolutely certain we're in the right cemetery?"

"Don't be insolent, honey," she said anxiously, grasping her pocketbook with both hands as she raised her head and stared up at a towering pine that blocked all but a few rays of the hot sun. "Over there near the fence. I think that's the tree. A yellow pine. It must be over there, under that tree. I remember it was a yellow pine. Lord, look how big it is now."

And, sure enough, when they walked a few steps farther, there were three markers next to one another, all with the name Green, and the smaller, most timeworn one on the left, with both a Star of David and an American flag engraved at the top of the marble, read "Jonathan Emanuel Green. 1925-

1945." Transfixed, Ella simply stood staring at the old stone now streaked with specks of moss, her heart pounding, and, as her mind traveled back, she could still see the small group of family mourners in black gathered around the shiny coffin and hear the low, indecipherable words of the rabbi as he read aloud in Hebrew.

She could also feel Earl's arm, which she clutched as they stood solemnly in the background with a few other friends, and even the same faint sensation of nausea she'd experienced on that terrible day now returned momentarily as the vision intensified and she was forced to revisit the tragedy.

"Young," Tyler said as his mother took his arm. "Only twenty years old."

"Yes, only twenty."

"I notice the flag. I guess he was killed in action?"

"No."

"Then how did he die?"

"You would have liked him," she averted the answer, rousing more curiosity and suspicion in Tyler.

"He must have been a very close friend—maybe a serious boyfriend, though I still can't imagine you having a Jewish boyfriend."

This was the moment Ella had dreaded for so long, the moment she'd rehearsed in her mind dozens of times when, standing with her son at the grave itself, she would reveal the truth to him about his real father, relate the story in some detail, and only pray he was strong enough to accept the fact and understand her need to make the disclosure. Then, fearing he might find such a dramatic confession in the cemetery to be too corny and in poor taste, she decided to wait till they could sit quietly over lunch and discuss it objectively like intelligent adults. Still, the urge to answer all his questions and get everything off her chest right away threatened her more sensible resolve, and perhaps she would have yielded to her impulsive instincts if Tyler, shifting from foot to foot, had not abruptly dropped her arm, moved over to perch on the edge of a tombstone in the next plot as if he were bored or too tired to stand, and said, "Come on, Mama. We didn't drive all the way down to Charleston to roam around some Jewish cemetery."

"Just hush," was her only comment.

"What in heaven's name, anyway, made you think about coming back here after all these years?" he then asked in genuine curiosity, watching her turn away and head back down the path. "And why did you want me to see this boy's grave?"

Again, she was tempted to stop and explain right then and there, but, instead, she said, "Let's go have some lunch at Simon's. I'll tell you about it then."

Still a little perplexed, he didn't balk when she again got behind the wheel, but he was aware during the short drive to the colorful historic district that his mother was acting more moody and preoccupied than usual. Whatever was causing her to brood, however, seemed to disappear when, pulling into a parking lot on Market Street, her eye caught something diverting at the entrance to the old City Market bustling with tourists and locals alike shopping for fresh produce, sacks of rice and pecans, and all sorts of crafts and cheap antiques.

"Uh-huh, looka there sitting in that lawn chair. Just look at that. A basket lady. I told you so. And I bet there're half a dozen more inside the market selling your mats at half the price you paid. I told you that colored woman back on the highway was trying to pull the wool over our eyes."

She pulled down the car visor overhead, reached into her pocketbook, and proceeded to carefully retouch her lipstick while looking in the small mirror.

Tyler was still chuckling about the basket ladies when they arrived at Simon's and, much to his liking, were greeted at the door by a good-looking young man in a cream-colored suit who asked, "Two for lunch?" Inside the restaurant, the venerable tile floors, ceiling fans, polished mahogany bar, bentwood chairs, and heady seafood aromas were almost exactly as Ella remembered them, and when an older, dignified black waiter with three service stripes on the arm of his uniform approached the table to take cocktail orders and hand them menus, she commented to Tyler that if she closed her eyes, she could easily be having lunch here fifty years ago. "I'd almost forgotten how gracious life in this old town can be," she then added, "and a place like this makes me wonder why we ever left." She nodded in the direction of a young couple close by sharing a large platter of shrimp perloo. "Just look how nicely they're dressed. That's the way we always dressed here."

"Snap out of it, Mama," he said playfully. "You must not have noticed those yahoos with a boom box coming out of the market, or heard the racket in the video shop across the street."

"I try to ignore things like that," she declared contemptuously, lighting a cigarette, then thanking and smiling at the waiter when he placed a whiskey sour in front of her and a glass of iced tea for Tyler.

"Listen, Son," she continued in a serious tone, determined once and for all to broach the subject she could no longer allow to devour her, "I need to tell you about something else . . . something difficult I should have told you years ago . . . the real reason I wanted us to drive down here today . . . something important that I can only pray you'll understand."

Prepared for still another of her exaggerated dilemmas or intrigues, he looked directly into her eyes while taking a sip of his tea, but before she could proceed with her daunting revelation, the waiter returned to take their orders. Too distracted to study the menu carefully as she normally would, Ella told him she'd simply have baked oysters, and some red rice, and coleslaw, and when it was Tyler's turn, he explained that he wasn't very hungry and ordered only a bowl of chicken-and-rice soup and another glass of tea.

"Why, that's ridiculous," she said. "First you don't have a cocktail, and now you only want soup. What's wrong with you? No wonder you've taken off flesh and look so pale."

"That's really all I want, Mama, and, besides, I'm driving back and don't relish the idea of being stopped for some reason by some redneck cop with liquor on my breath."

"That's not a very nice comment to make," she said. "But anyway, you didn't eat much the other night, and I noticed you didn't have sausage or bacon for breakfast. You used to love sausage and bacon. Don't tell me you're on some ridiculous diet."

"No, no, believe me, I'm not trying to lose weight."

"Well, what is it, then? Nobody comes to a place like Simon's and orders just a bowl of chicken soup. Why don't you also have the shrimp and grits, or at least a crab cake? Goldie commented on how pale you look, and it's no wonder—not eating right."

He began shifting nervously in his chair. "I'm not a child, Mama, so stop worrying about me. I just don't have that much appetite these days. What's so urgent you had to tell me?"

"I'm still your mother, and I do worry when you don't eat right. Of course, Edmund says I'm just being overly protective, but . . . are you sure you're feeling okay, Son?"

Tyler again smiled mischievously. "You ole vamp. I think there's more to you and Mr. O'Conner than meets the eye."

"Mind your own business. Edmund happens to be just a very respectable gentleman and a nice new friend. Stop changing the subject."

Tyler had been telling Barry the truth when he said he and his mother had never kept vital secrets from one another, secure as they both had always been in their special relationship based on mutual trust and understanding. And he had indeed fully intended to tell her about his problem, but only at the right time and under the right circumstances to avoid upsetting her any more than necessary. No doubt if he'd been even remotely aware of what she had concealed from him his entire life and was now prepared to confess and discuss, he would have postponed his own grave news for a more appropriate setting and let her vent what was on her mind. When it became obvious, though, that she would continue to badger him about his looks and behavior throughout lunch as only a caring mother can do, he made the split-second decision to simply clear the air by revealing frankly the predicament he knew they'd both have to face sooner or later.

"To be honest, Mama, no, I haven't been feeling that great for quite a while, and I do have to watch what I eat. I've put off discussing it to keep you from worrying, but the truth is, Mama, I've been pretty sick for the past few months." He hesitated, sipping his tea. "It's the colon."

She seemed alarmed for a second, then, waving her cigarette in the air, said, "Oh, my friend Jinks Ferguson had a touch of colitis a few years ago and got over it in almost no time."

"It's not colitis, Mama. I'm afraid my condition's more serious."

Tapping her cigarette in the ashtray, Ella now appeared dazed, as if somebody had suddenly slapped her in the face for no good reason. Then, staring intently at him and forgetting all about her own mission that she'd come so close to fulfilling, she took a deep breath and asked calmly, "How serious?"

"Pretty serious, Mama. They found a bad growth back in January, and performed a small operation, and thought that would do the trick."

"You had an operation and didn't let me know?"

"What good would that have done, Mama? You would have just gone hysterical."

"Don't be absurd," she said more calmly. "I'm never hysterical."

"Well, anyway, I was functioning pretty normally for a while, but then there was some radiation and chemo—the same old story—and . . . I had a long talk with the doctor right before I left, and the upshot is the cancer has apparently continued to spread beyond—"

"Don't use that word, Son. Please don't use that awful word. We've never had anything like that in our family—not your grandparents, or their parents, or—"

"We have to face facts, Mama, and it won't help for you to go right away into denial about this. Either we can discuss it like adults or we can't. Can you talk about it sensibly without getting emotional?"

Ella reached again for her drink, and he could see her hand was starting to quiver slightly.

"All I'm saying, Tyler, is that we have no history of that in our family, and that maybe those doctors of yours are wrong. Doctors can be wrong, you know. Terrible mistakes are made every day. I read in *Reader's Digest* about people suing doctors for everything they're worth for making dreadful mistakes."

She stubbed the butt out in the small crystal ashtray, her hand now visibly shaking. "You should have told me about this. I deserve to know. We've never kept things like that from each other."

"I just didn't want you to worry yourself sick, and I kept hoping to get better reports. Now they want to do further treatment. Barry's the only one who'd been aware of it all."

She began twisting her small sapphire ring. "I knew, the second I saw you at the airport, I knew you didn't look right."

The waiter returned with the food. Ella thanked him politely, but she made no move to taste her oysters.

"You need to see another doctor, maybe one at Duke or Chapel Hill," she pronounced firmly. "They're the best at Duke and Chapel Hill—some of the best doctors in the country."

Picking up his spoon, Tyler smiled. "My doctors are all at Sloan-Kettering, Mama, and it's common knowledge that that's the finest cancer center there is."

"It can't be any better than Duke," she protested with desperation now in her voice. "People come to Duke from all over the world, and . . . I just wouldn't trust those New York hospitals. I hear they're like factories up there. Patients like guinea pigs. You need to be down here where we can watch out for you till you get well. Barry could come with you, and . . . Goldie and I . . . I have a close friend at the church whose son is a highly respected doctor in Chapel Hill, and . . . you need personal attention. . . . Why, we could fix you up with the best at Carolina or Duke; then, when you're cured of whatever's wrong, you could come home for a while and recuperate in the house—with Barry right there too."

Frustrated by his mother's refusal to face reality, yet feeling equally guilty over causing her such obvious distress, Tyler had no alternative but to play down the gravity of his condition for the moment and pretend to concede to her blind notions. The tragic irony of the situation, he also realized stoically, was that if the prognosis of his disease was as dire as the doctor had led him to believe, the time would come when, despite his long-standing objection to living in the South, and his antipathy toward most of his relatives, he might actually prefer to return home and spend his final days with his own people.

"Well, let's hope things improve after this upcoming treatment," he tried to reassure her blithely, "and that this time next year we can look back and wonder why we worried so. It's amazing what modern medicine can do. Now, Mama, eat those oysters before they get cold, and, for heaven's sake, tell me what you had to say that's so earthshaking. I'm tired of talking about sickness and health."

Ella did eat an oyster, plus a forkful of slaw, but her mind was so agitated and confused, and she felt so defeated, that all she could do beyond that was stare down at her lunch and try to collect her thoughts. She had been so determined, so close to divulging the most tormenting secret of her life, but now, in just minutes, other unexpected and shocking forces had come into play that at once nullified the need to reveal this frightful truth and called for still another fiction to disguise the one that had to remain concealed. No matter how upright her motives, Ella knew that she was caught in a web of deceit, but she also realized that, somehow, exposing even the most painful secret was utterly inconsequential and futile when the very life of her son could be at stake. Where moral responsibility had been the motivating pressure behind her original intentions, maternal instincts now dictated the course of action. If Ella had ever been convinced of anything, she was convinced that Tyler would need her support and trust in the upcoming days as much as he'd depended on her when he was a child, and, at least in her eyes, this renewed need far outweighed any purpose he might derive from learning about the man whose grave he'd just visited.

"I didn't have anything really earthshaking to say, honey," she finally responded in a halting manner. "Only that it's always disturbed me that you've had so few emotional ties with this wonderful town where you were born—or, for that matter, any place in the South. You can't ignore your roots, Son. All we really have in the long run are our roots and our past, and many of yours are right here. That's the main reason I wanted you to see Charleston again."

He smiled again. "You do sound like Scarlett O'Hara."

"Don't be impudent."

Although Tyler was a bit perplexed by her cliché, he decided it was easier to indulge her fancy than to question her logic. "I guess that's why you wanted to visit that old friend's grave."

Her insides churning, it took all Ella's emotional strength to drum up the will to respond without wincing.

"Yes, he was part of my past here, and we should never forget anybody who played a role in our past." She stopped to reflect, her eyes blinking rapidly as she pushed rice around in the small bowl with her fork. "You would have liked Jonathan Green. He was a fine young man."

After lunch, Ella suggested they drive down to Battery Park past the Greek-Revival Edmondston-Alston Mansion with its three-story piazza overlooking the harbor, but when she saw White Point Gardens, where she'd been married in the Gazebo and where she'd fled from Jonathan's apartment that dreadful afternoon, the memories became so overwhelming that, instead of stopping to walk around and take in the spectacular view of Fort Sumpter, she told Tyler just to head back to Myrtle Beach so they'd both have time for a good nap. During the drive, Tyler kept expecting his mother to ask more questions about his medical problem, but the subject was never once mentioned again, as if she'd erased it from her mind or it simply didn't exist.

Chapter 19

MAGIC

Sitting alone in a deep, cushioned cane chair at one end of the reception hall, Edmund O'Conner looked up from his book when Tyler greeted him and said that they were just returning from their excursion to Charleston. Ella did appear to Edmund to be more preoccupied, or maybe tired, than usual, but when he explained that Sal and Elizabeth had already left to take the boys downtown for the early dinner theater extravaganza at Dixie Stampede, she didn't hesitate a second to insist that he join the three of them later in the dining room.

"Oh, I don't want to intrude on—"

"Don't be silly, Edmund," she said. "You certainly can't eat by yourself, and we'd be more than happy to have you at the table."

"On one condition," he accepted cheerfully. "That I order us a nice bottle of wine tonight."

"How gracious of you," Ella agreed, still acting and sounding a little wrapped up in her thoughts. "Now we're both off to stretch out awhile, if you'll excuse us."

Upstairs, Tyler did go sound asleep almost immediately, while Ella, hearing Goldie's TV set, wasted no time tapping on the door.

"I need to discuss something important with you, dear. Can you come in for a minute?"

"Yes, ma'am," Goldie said, cutting down the TV and setting a glass of Coke on the bureau before stepping through the doorway.

"It's Mr. Tyler," she said straightaway, lighting a cigarette and sitting on the foot of the bed while Goldie stood in the middle of the floor.

"Is something wrong, ma'am?"

"Yes. I mean, I think so. I don't know for sure, but I think Tyler's very sick, Goldie."

The Indian, clasping the long shell necklace around her neck, bent over as if trying to hear better. "Did you say sick?"

Ella tried to control her emotions, but, as her voice became more and more flimsy, it became obvious she was on the verge of tears.

"My boy's sick, Goldie," she began to sob, her eyes watering as she instinctively flicked an ash off her dress.

"What do you mean, Miss Ella?"

"Tyler's sick—he's not well."

"He seems fine to me—except he's lost some weight and—"

"I tell you, Goldie, he's not well, and he's already had an operation, and . . . I don't know what's going to happen to him, and . . ." She choked up even more and began coughing. "Goldie, you're the only person . . . the only person I know I can talk to about it."

When she continued to cough, Goldie asked if she was all right, to which Ella responded "I'm smoking too much," then began sobbing.

This was the first time Goldie could remember seeing Ella cry since Big Earl died, and, for a moment, she didn't know quite what to do or say. Then, forsaking all strictures that, for years, had governed much of their stilted personal relationship, she moved over, took the cigarette from Ella's fingers, snuffed it out in an ashtray, and awkwardly held her head against her body while the older woman wept uncontrollably.

"What is it, Miss Ella?" she asked calmly after a long wait.

"The colon. He has bad problems with his colon," Ella finally said, dabbing her eyes unwittingly with a piece of Goldie's coarse dress and withdrawing her head from the other woman's gentle grasp.

Goldie, backing away while Ella fingered the sides of her hair and began to regain her composure, appeared baffled. "I'm not sure what that is, ma'am."

"Oh, of course you do," Ella said impatiently, now coughing again. "Everybody knows what the colon is, woman. It's down near . . . It's part of the . . . You know, it's in the pit of the stomach—where you get colitis from eating the wrong things."

"Oh," Goldie muttered, again fondling her shells.

"But it doesn't matter. Tyler doesn't have just colitis. He could have something much worse, we think, and he's going to have to have all this treatment to cure it, and . . . well, he might be coming down to spend some time with us in Charlotte. I want him to see one of our fine doctors up at Duke or Chapel Hill, but whether he does or not, there's a good chance he'll be spending some time at the house. And maybe Barry will come too. I don't know what's going to happen. . . . I just don't know, Goldie, but . . . I haven't had time to think it all out. I need time to think it all out."

Goldie had a worried look in her dark, glistening eyes that betrayed her confusion over Ella's ramblings, but never one to pry too deeply into highly sensitive matters, she asked simply, "What can I do, Miss Ella?"

"Well," Ella continued, getting up, lighting another smoke,

and coughing again as she paced the floor, "what I need to know, Goldie . . . all I'm wondering is whether you'd be able to spend more time at the house if we needed you."

"Why, you know I would, Miss Ella. You know I'd do anything to help you and Mr. Tyler. You should know by now you don't even have to ask."

"Thank you, dear," she resumed in her normal tone of voice, as if another major problem had been solved and a potential catastrophe averted. "Of course it may never happen. He may be just fine. But if he did come, it's good to know I can count on you." She took a long draw and stared out the window. "I've been beside myself with worry and really don't know how I'll deal with this."

Goldie moved over behind her and put her hand around her waist. "We'll just take it a step at a time, won't we? And I'll do some special chants for him. I will."

Ella held her gaze out the window, then said calmly, "Sometimes I don't know what I'd do without you, Goldie. You're a good woman."

"We've been through lots together," Goldie hemmed, not knowing really how else to react to the compliment. "I know I'm not too smart, but—"

"Don't say that, Goldie," Ella declared, turning around abruptly. "Never say that again. You're one of the smartest women I've ever known, and don't you forget that."

"Thank you, Miss Ella," she said meekly, stepping away.

"But please, dear, please don't mention any of this to Mr. Tyler or anybody else."

"Oh, no, ma'am. It's our little secret. I know that."

"And oh, yes, Goldie, Dr. O'Conner's folks have gone downtown tonight, and I've asked him to join us for dinner so he won't be alone."

"You like Dr. O'Conner a lot, don't you, ma'am?"

Ella cracked a smile. "Nobody fools you, do they, Goldie? What do you think of him?"

"Oh, I think he's a wonderful man," she said with conviction, now twisting what looked like some style of green leather hair band she'd pulled out of the pocket of her smock.

"Not that there's anything really serious between the two of us, you understand," Ella assured guardedly, touching her hair again.

"Oh, no, ma'am. But if you don't mind me saying so, I have noticed the way he looks at you real special sometimes."

"Do you really think so?" she hedged, her eyes fluttering.

"Oh, yes, ma'am, and the way he touches you sometimes."

Ella snuffed out the cigarette in the ashtray in her hand. "Oh, get on with you, woman. You forget how old I am, and Dr. O'Conner's just being nice and friendly. When you get to be my age, dear, you no longer expect moonlight and magnolias, and, well . . . to tell the truth, I've scarcely looked at another man since Mr. Earl passed away."

"Oh, nobody could ever replace Mr. Earl, I know that," Goldie said, sitting in the straight chair at the dressing table and wondering just how far she could pursue the intimate subject. "But if you don't mind me asking, ma'am, don't you ever miss having a man around the house? I know I do sometimes."

Normally, Ella would have dismissed such a probing question from Goldie as an intrusion into her private world, but given her anxiety and confusion now over so many matters, and the compulsive need to confide certain emotions in someone she knew she could trust unequivocally, she lowered her defenses a little.

"Maybe the companionship at night," she confessed almost shyly. "Of course, I'm used to having you around most days, and, as you know, I do stay pretty busy. But, yes, sometimes I do get a little lonesome at night."

"I hope you know if you ever needed me at night . . ."

"Oh, I don't mean lonesome like that, dear. Don't forget I've learned to be pretty independent. It's just that some nights I remember what it was like when Mr. Earl was still alive."

"That's when I miss Bud most, too."

Ella raised her head and stared intently over at the Indian. "I've never asked you this, Goldie, but haven't you ever thought about marrying again?"

Goldie sat twisting her hair band. "Oh, yes, ma'am. I thought about it."

"Then why didn't you?"

"One reason is 'cause nobody ever asked me. Oh, I went out with some fellas a long time after Bud and John died, and I used to talk with my Spirits, but you see, ma'am, I think the Great Spirits intend for us all to have only one really special person in our life, and that person can never be replaced in the same way—no matter who else comes along. I had Bud, and you had Mr. Earl, and I always knew how much in love you were with Mr. Earl."

Ella sat perfectly still, her eyes again fluttering rapidly. "Wasn't there ever anybody special before Bud, Goldie?"

"No, not really. Oh, I went out with one fella on the reservation for a long time, but"—her expression became almost solemn—"the minute I met Bud, I knew. . . . I knew this was the man who was intended for me. Maybe we were just young and kinda crazy, but . . . No, ma'am, there was only one Bud, and I never could love another man the way I loved him."

Ella still didn't budge for a moment, her mind bursting with thoughts and realizations and questions about what all Goldie was saying. Then, as if coming out of another trance, she slowly got up from the bed, patted Goldie on the shoulder, and said, "I'm glad we had this little talk, dear. Now we really must start thinking about getting ready for dinner."

"I thought I'd wear my flower tunic and glass bead necklace tonight," Goldie said proudly, looking for Ella's nod of approval.

"That would be nice, dear."

When Goldie left the room, Ella collapsed in her chair at the window, her nerves a bit more relaxed but her breathing still slightly labored as she reflected on what Goldie had said, and all that had transpired in Charleston, and what she must do next. Foremost in her mind, naturally, was Tyler's health, but once she'd rationalized further that his condition would no doubt improve with the right medical treatment and personalized care, what now began to dominate her thoughts impulsively was the image of Jonathan's grave and how the visit had only served to revive still more tangled memories that often seemed to threaten her very sanity. Desperately she tried to sort out the complications swirling in her brain and dispel the anxiety, but the more she analyzed the confused crises, the more she was trapped between the present and the past, reality and fantasy, truth and fiction. Suddenly she felt so alone, more alone than she'd ever been in her life, and even though the mild salt breeze was blowing through the window over her entire body, her fragile face was soon drenched in perspiration that caused her makeup to run down her cheeks. She considered taking a shower, but too weak to go through the ordeal just yet, and now having a hard time catching a deep breath, she pulled herself up, took one of her tiny pills, and lay flat on the bed.

The next thing she realized, Tyler was standing over her repeating "Mama" while Goldie wiped her forehead and cheeks with a cool towel. What had happened was that Goldie, not having heard from Ella as evening approached and unable to rouse her when she finally entered the room again and found her on the bed, had panicked at the sight of her sallow complexion, fled down the hall, and pounded frantically on Tyler's door, waking him up.

"Are you okay, Mama?" he kept asking as he held her hand and gently shook one of her arms. "Wake up, Mama. Are you okay?"

Ella focused on him, then wondered aloud why Goldie was wiping her face with the towel. "What's happening?" she asked groggily, as if not sure where she was.

"Are you feeling all right, Mama?"

She still didn't budge for a few more hazy moments, then, gradually making the effort to get up, muttered "Mercy me, I must have dropped off. What in heaven's name are you two doing in here?"

Tyler studied her pasty face now caked with uneven makeup. "You did more than drop off, Mama. You were in a dead sleep and had Goldie worried to death."

"Why, that's ridiculous. I guess I was exhausted from the trip and just having a good nap, that's all. Doesn't anybody have the right to take a good sound nap?"

"Miss Ella, are you sure you feel like going down to dinner tonight?" Goldie asked with grave concern. "Maybe you'd like to just rest and let me order you some soup or a salad."

"Are you crazy, woman?" Ella protested in her typical manner, pulling herself up. "I feel fine now, and we do have a date with Dr. O'Conner. Mercy, what time is it?" She glanced at the bedside clock. "Good Lord, it's after six, and I haven't even changed or . . . We should be downstairs right now for drinks. Tyler, you're not even dressed yet. Go get dressed, Son, and call . . . No, I'm sure Dr. O'Conner's already on the porch, so Goldie, why don't you call down to reception and tell them to inform Dr. O'Conner that we're running a few minutes' late."

Eventually, all four were gathered for the ritual cocktail hour, plus a quick review of the trip to Charleston, but once Riley had seated them in the dining room, Goldie and the two men couldn't help but notice Ella's strange, withdrawn mood generated possibly by the straight Jack Daniel's on the rocks she'd downed on the porch. Even more unusual was the need for Goldie to suggest certain dishes when Ella seemed indifferent to the menu, and since she now hardly opened her mouth to make some pronouncement, or to criticize, or to exclaim about one thing or another, conversation amongst the other three was awkward. Normally, Goldie was hesitant to relate any stories or express opinions to anyone for fear of appearing foolish, but when, to break the silence at one point, Tyler asked what she'd done interesting during the day while he and his mother were away, she now seemed eager to describe a rather bizarre episode that had occurred on the beach.

"I was taking a long walk, and there was this man fishing by himself, and when I went up to peek in his bucket, we started talking, and soon he told me about his wife who used to always fish with him but who had died not long ago. He acted real, real sad and down in the dumps, so I told him he should remember that his wife's spirit was right there with him while he fished and that he shouldn't feel alone. Then I explained how a sacred chieftain of my tribe once told us that if you weighed someone the second before they die, then weighed them again the second afterward, there would be a difference of about one pound, which proves that we really do have a soul, and that it weighs about one pound, and that it leaves the body the instant we die. Then I told him about my husband and son, and how a day never goes by that something doesn't make me aware of their spirits, and that the same is true with him. I think it made him feel lots better."

The other three sat staring at Goldie as she picked at her crabmeat cocktail till Edmund asked, "Do you really believe that, Goldie?"

"Of course she does," Ella answered quickly, a restored

glow in her face and sudden change in her mood as she sipped the French Chablis that Edmund had ordered. "And I do too. Why didn't you ever tell me about that, Goldie?"

"I don't know, ma'am. But that's what our great chieftain said, and I know he was right."

"If you say so, Goldie," Tyler mumbled skeptically while reaching for a biscuit.

This time after dinner, Ella didn't insist that Tyler come along when Edmund suggested cordials in the lounge, not only because she knew he needed rest but also because she felt she'd explode if she went another day without unloading some of her emotional troubles on someone besides Goldie who might understand. No, Edmund O'Conner was certainly not the old friend or confidant she might normally turn to in time of desperation, but somehow instinct informed her that, in a short space of time, this intelligent, gentle doctor from New Jersey who had shown such affection and made her feel so young and special again was also that rare individual capable of listening to another's tribulations and genuinely caring.

Pulling out Ella's chair at a small table in a corner of the lounge, Edmund nodded at the piano player in approval of the tune "September Song."

"You don't seem to be your animated self tonight," he then said after the waiter had taken their orders, reaching for her hand as she gazed impassively at a large urn against the far wall. "Is something wrong, or are you just worn out?"

She sat motionless in the dim light, the high cheekbones of her venerable face and angle of her jaw now transmitting a serene dignity and veiled beauty he hadn't noticed before.

"My boy's sick, Edmund," she finally declared somberly.

"What do you mean? He looked fine enough at dinner."

"Tyler's not well. I knew he didn't look right and was behaving strange when he arrived, but . . . He told me about it today in Charleston." She squeezed his hand. "I have no right

to burden you with my problems, but I've got to talk to somebody or I'll go out of my mind." She was on the verge of
choking up.

"How serious?"

"I don't know, but it doesn't sound good," she almost
sobbed.

He hesitated, as if wondering how bold his next question
might be. "I hope it's not this AIDS that's so affected the gay
community."

"No, no, heavens no. Tyler would never have something
like that. No, it's his colon. They discovered something bad in
his colon, and they did an operation, and he's been on chemo-
therapy, and lost weight and some hair, and has so little energy,
and they say it's spreading. He told me all about it today."

"Cancer," he said bluntly.

Ella grimaced. "Oh, I hate that horrible word."

Edmund frowned. "I don't want to alarm you, but that can
be wicked stuff if they don't catch it early."

Her eyes began to water, and her voice wavered. "And do
you know, in his condition, he still flew all the way down here
to be with me. Can you imagine that? He's putting up a good
front, but . . . I'm just praying those doctors are wrong. No offense, but doctors can be wrong about lots of things, you
know. Edmund, I'm just beside myself, but I won't, I can't
show it in front of him. He has enough on his mind without
worrying about me."

She held back as long as she could, then, biting her thumb
as her voice broke, began crying again helplessly. "I just don't
know what I'd do, Edmund, if I lost Tyler. He's everything in
the world to me, and I don't know what I'd do if something
happened to him."

He put his arm around her delicate shoulder and pulled
her close. "Now, now, Miss Ella, nothing's going to happen to
your son," he said reassuringly. "Today they can work miracles

with things like that, and he's still fairly young and fit, and . . .
don't you worry, there's no need to worry till you know a
good deal more about his condition. And remember, it doesn't
help to let yourself get so upset."

For a long while, they tried to discuss what little she did
know of the situation, but since so much deliberation of ominous medical problems such as this is usually frustrating guess-
work, the most O'Conner could really do was suggest how he
might try to handle things if this were his daughter's or Sal's
case, convince Ella to remain positive, and give her all the
compassionate support he could muster.

"I don't think you realize how special Tyler is to me," she
said next, fighting the urge to reveal the real reason she'd taken
him back to Charleston and to share her most dreaded secret
with this man she'd come to trust. "It's not that I don't love my
other two children just as much, but, you see, things have always been different with Tyler—different from the day he was
born." She let Edmund light her cigarette, then took a large
gulp of Grand Marnier as if attempting to work up more
courage. "And there are reasons, Edmund . . . There are important reasons why Tyler is like he is and so different from his
brother and sister."

Edmund, sensing that she was attempting to relate a good
deal more about her son than the sad news of his poor health,
pulled her closer and kissed her tenderly on the cheek. "If you
need to talk about anything else, Miss Ella, I'm here to listen."

Suddenly, she pulled back, looked up at him, and said
sternly, "Oh, honey, please stop calling me Miss Ella. I feel like
I've known you a century, and my name is Ella. Simply Ella."

He chuckled and again pecked her cheek. "Okay, Ella, if
you say so."

Across the room, the piano player had just begun the first
notes of "It Might As Well Be Spring," and whether it was a
certain memory evoked by the music, or the effects of alcohol,

or simply her overwhelming compulsion to confront the truth, Ella was moved to finally broach the subject that had remained inviolate for so many long years.

"Do you remember on the pier when I told you about a boy I knew who died when I was young in Charleston?"

"I do, the one you said you were in love with during the war."

"Well, Edmund, I killed that boy. I killed the one person I was ever truly in love with, and today I visited his grave for the first time. I visited Jonathan's grave with Tyler."

O'Conner's expression didn't change as he cupped his brandy snifter in his hand, either because he might have misunderstood or because he simply didn't believe what Ella had just said. "Can you tell me about it?" he then asked dispassionately.

With which Ella, at first in a halting manner, then more and more impetuously, began a long discourse on Jonathan and herself that included virtually every facet of their affair and didn't end till their last encounter at his apartment, the funeral, and the certainty that he was Tyler's father. Forcing herself to recount many of the facts was, of course, painful, yet when she had finished the difficult narrative, it was as if at least part of the weight that was burdening her entire being had been lifted.

"I was sure you didn't mean you'd actually killed the boy," was Edmund's first comment, a hint of relief in his voice.

"But I did, Edmund," she professed quietly but firmly. "As sure as if I pulled the trigger myself on that gun, I was responsible for Jonathan's death, because, you see, I didn't even try to understand his problem—I didn't even try. All I could think about was myself, and how I'd been hurt and taken advantage of, and what was going to become of me and maybe a child. I couldn't see how desperately Jonathan was reaching out for help, and that I was the only person he could turn to. Oh, I know I was young and naive about lots, but the thing is I turned my back on a boy I loved dearly. I condemned him for something he couldn't help, and I've had to live with that nightmare—year after year and each and every time I looked into Tyler's face. I've had to live with that my whole life, Edmund. And it wasn't so much guilt as disgust. I was disgusted with myself."

"Were you sure Jonathan was the father?"

"Ninety-five percent sure. A woman has instincts about these things, and the timing was right, and, besides, all I had to do when Tyler was growing up was look at him and listen to him to see the resemblance."

"And you never told anyone, including your husband?"

"How could I? You don't understand what it was like living in a closed, bigoted society like Charleston in those days. First of all, no respectable girl could risk letting it be known that she was . . . crossing the line of intimacy. And it was inconceivable . . . it was unheard of that a proper lady with my upbringing would become really serious about a Jewish boy, much less even think about marrying him and having his child. That's just the way things were in Charleston when I grew up, and I had to think about my family, and my future, and, of course, Earl's reputation. No, no, no, a scandal like that would have destroyed me and lots of other people, so I had to keep it all to myself—all to myself. Oh, years later I was tempted more than once to confess everything to Earl, but, you see, wonderful as he was, Earl could never have understood and accepted that—I knew he never could. It would have killed him."

"Forgive me for asking, Ella, but if circumstances had been different, would you ever have eventually married this Jonathan?"

She took the last swallow of her drink and breathed deeply. "I don't know. I can't answer that. I used to wonder about that a lot, but, of course, given the truth about him, I doubt it. I was a pretty strong-willed lady, but not that strong."

"And you were planning to finally tell Tyler about all this?"

"I almost did this afternoon. I came within an inch of my life. I mean, I had to set things right before any more time passed, and was on the verge, right on the verge of explaining everything to him, since there are probably good reasons why his life turned out the way it did, and he deserves to know— it's his right to know. But then, before I had a chance, he began telling me about his condition and—"

Choking up again, she mindlessly reached for the cocktail napkin and dabbed her eyes as he put his arm back around her shoulder.

"Do you know what hurts most, Edmund?" she continued. "What hurts most are all these secrets and little deceits. It's bad enough that a good part of my life has involved a big cover-up, but now I realize my own son—the person I always trusted above all others—is just as capable of concealing important things from me as I have from him. Is it all one big lie, Edmund? Are our lives just one big, nasty lie?"

He signaled to the waiter to bring two more drinks, then sat perfectly still for a moment without commenting.

"You're being pretty tough on yourself," he finally said, "and quite frankly, I don't think you're being very realistic. Now, tonight you've opened up on some important matters that happen to hit a nerve with me, so I'm going to do the same with you to make a point. What I haven't told you— what I really had no reason to mention this past week—is that Elizabeth is not my biological daughter. She was adopted. After Grace and I were married, she discovered she could never have children, so, after quite a few years and some very difficult deliberations, we eventually decided to adopt Elizabeth when she was only three months old. We originally intended to tell her the truth when she was a child, but Grace always worried so that we never did, not till she was a teenager and we thought she could accept and adapt to it better. Others might say we were wrong trying to protect her by this deceit, and I can't deny it was a little traumatic when we finally decided to let her know. But I can honestly say that, not long afterward, the bond with our daughter became only tighter, and today she and I couldn't be more close. Of course, the circumstances with your son are different, no doubt, but the general point I'm trying to make is that sometimes secrecy and lies might be justified to prevent unnecessary hurt and grief and can work toward everyone's benefit." He paused and cracked a smile. "Actually, I wouldn't be in the least surprised if Lizzy and Sal hadn't been talking behind my back for some time about what to do with me when I get too decrepit to live alone in that house. And I understand. They're being realistic and want to spare me anxiety as long as possible." He pulled Ella close again. "Same with your other children, I'd guess."

She rested her head on his shoulder and dabbed her eyes again. "I never thought of it in those terms, Edmund. Thank you for sharing that story with me. And maybe you're right. Maybe there're lots of things that are better left hidden and untold and . . . magical." Her thoughts now seemed to be drifting again uncontrollably. "But I like magic, and glamour and romance, and beautiful memories of days when everybody was young, and nobody was ever sick or old, and the air always smelled of jasmine and the sea, and we all danced . . . danced in the moonlight on warm sand or a green summer lawn to soft music—the softest music in the South, the softest music in the entire world. Me and Earl and Jonathan and Tootsie Middleton and a handsome boy named Preston Goode and crazy Dee Griffith—we had such wonderful times in those days, so much fun, and it was magic—pure magic." She began gnawing nervously on her thumb, as if remembering something altogether different or maybe even regretting what she'd just said. "The Depression, the war, friends going away and never coming home—remember how we wanted it all to end, just end so we could get on with our lives? But when it was over, I don't think I ever stopped looking back at those days, because, you see, I think we lost something fine—innocence, purpose, hope, something important that could never be recaptured. Oh, Edmund, I guess I learned how to live with it as life went on, but, you know, I can now wake up in the middle of the night, or hear some song, or see an old friend, and those magical days come back to me so strong and so fresh that I actually become the young lady I was back then."

She didn't budge for a while longer, lost in her boozy recollections and dreams. Then, raising her head from Edmund's shoulder, she reached again for her liqueur and took a long, burning sip.

"Do you often get this wrapped up in nostalgia?" he asked gently, studying the changes in her expression as she listened to the amorous music. "You should be careful. It can devour you, you know."

"I wish this night could go on and on," she said wistfully, ignoring his statement and apparently having erased all worries from her confused mind.

"That would be nice, Ella," he agreed suggestively, now stroking her dainty arm. "And it could, if you'd like."

She looked up at him as if he were one of the beguiling phantoms from her past or in her imagination. "I'd like that very much, Edmund. Maybe for just a little while."

After they'd finished their drinks, he pulled out her chair, and just as she linked her arm through his on the way to the elevator, they could hear the distant squawking of a lone seagull through the open doors to the porch.

Chapter 20

SHARKS' TEETH

Ella was still sleeping off her wanton late-night session with Edmund when she was awakened by another early phone call put through from Little Earl checking to see how she was and asking if she'd decided when she and Goldie would be back home. The first thing she groggily told her son was that making these unnecessary calls was just a foolish waste of good money and that there was no need in this world for him to worry so about her. Then, in her disoriented state, she said carelessly that they would probably drive back shortly after Tyler returned to New York, unless, that is, she could convince him to stay a few days longer.

"Tyler?" Earl asked, obviously startled. "Is Tyler there with you?"

Suddenly realizing her blunder, Ella acknowledged calmly that, yes, his brother had flown down as a last-minute surprise, and she was enjoying his company.

There was a long silence of anger or frustration on the phone.

"Mama, what's going on? Would you please tell me just what in hell is going on? First you disappear and force us to get the state troopers to find you, then you try to refuse phone calls, and now you tell me that Ty has shown up at the beach. I just want to know, Mama, what's going on. I think your own family has a right to know, and I don't think we can take much more of this craziness."

"Please calm down, Son," she pronounced more coherently. "As I said, Tyler's visit was pretty spur of the moment, and, as you know, we haven't seen one another in ages."

"The little bastard. I talked to him just a few days ago, and he didn't say a goddamn word about flying down there."

"Listen, Earl, I'm in no frame of mind to talk at this hour, and even if I were, I will not stay on the line if you have to use that type of uncouth language. Now, why don't you go by and check the house, and I'll call to let you know when we'll be getting back. I have a sick headache, Son, and have too much on my mind to argue with you this early in the morning."

After she hung up, Ella remained in bed awhile longer, nursing her hangover and staring blearily at the ceiling as her head throbbed and she thought about having to confront the folks in Charlotte on numerous matters. Then she tried to recall exactly what she'd told Edmund the night before and what all had transpired between them in his room, and struggled to come to terms once again with Tyler's ominous predicament, and the persistent vision of Jonathan's mossy grave, and changing her will, and poor Goldie's future when there was nobody left to . . . The thoughts and images and worries whirled frenetically, and she wished she could just turn over and sleep all day. She then wondered if maybe she was drinking too much at night, and whether she should invite Edmund to visit her in Charlotte. Was this the evening for after-dinner dancing announced on the leaflet stuck under the door? What should she wear? Memories of the way Earl used to wring her into elegant, dramatic dips when they danced the tango at the old Ocean Forest Hotel flashed in her mind . . . the same place where Jonathan had rolled up his trousers and she her skirt so they could wade in the water and . . . that night, that awful night in the garden with the strong smell of wisteria . . . If only she could go back to sleep, and sleep all day, and stop remembering and worrying. But now there was hammering on the deck in front of the porch, and she could also hear the faint but infernal sound of Goldie's TV in the next room, so she pulled herself out of the bed, and gazed at her drawn face in the bathroom mirror, and swallowed two aspirins, and reached for her makeup. She also noticed a nagging ache in her lower back.

Tyler, in contrast, felt the best he'd felt in days, due not only to all the sleep but also, more surely, to the diminishing wretched effects of the chemo he'd undergone not long before leaving. He even once again ate what Ella considered to be a sensible Southern breakfast, which proved, in her opinion, that his condition was not as serious as the doctors had led him to believe and that all he needed was plenty of rest and good food and to be around his own people. What she didn't know, in her denial, but what Tyler had been told candidly, was that any full remission of his cancer was now highly improbable, and that the only advantage of periodic chemo would be to ease symptoms temporarily and delay the inevitable. Yes, he might have good days when not undergoing treatment, but, unlike his mother, Tyler had learned to be an unflinching realist about most things in life, and the one person he could never deceive was himself.

"Tyler seems to be in much better spirits today," Edmund was saying to Ella as the two sat in her cabana and watched Tyler and Goldie fishing together. She was now dressed in bright yellow slacks, a blue and white striped gondolier shirt, and narrow-brimmed beach hat, and he had on the same Bermuda shorts he'd worn every day.

"It does him good being home again," she said a little awkwardly. "He's been away a long time, and now he needs to be home. This is where he belongs. You see, Tyler's not well."

Edmund took her hand. "I know. You told me all about it last night."

Ella looked a little astonished. "I did?"

"You did. I guess we both had a bit too much to drink, but, yes, you did tell me about Tyler's illness, and Jonathan, and certain secrets, and how you all loved to dance when you were young. I believe you got a lot off your chest last night."

She sat looking straight ahead, her eyes blinking rapidly. "Oh, of course, and you told me about Elizabeth. I remember now. I do hope I didn't bore you with my problems, Edmund."

"You never bore me, my dear." He squeezed her hand. "I haven't had an evening like that since Grace died and just hope you enjoyed it as much as I did."

She blushed slightly, as if momentarily embarrassed by the recollection of their reckless frivolity. "Yes, Edmund, it was wonderful," she then professed openly. "You're a good man, and I always enjoy being in your company. You see, honey, you make me feel young, and I used to worry . . . What really bothered me was that I'd never be touched again, except by the undertaker."

He laughed. "Well, I'd say we both can still cut the mustard—as we used to say."

She pretended to blush again, then took her cigarette case out of her bag, put it back, and proclaimed, "I've gotta quit." Next she looked down at his stained shorts and asked in jest if they were his only pair.

"I'm afraid so," he confessed with some shame in his voice. "Lizzy's already lectured me about them."

Ella laughed. "Earl was the same way. He'd come down here with a half-dozen pairs of shorts I'd bought for him and wear the same tan ones day after day—to fish, to play ball on the beach, even to swim in. Said they were the only pair that didn't . . . bind him. Drove me crazy. You men are all alike—all of you except Tyler. But, then, he goes overboard in the other direction. Tyler's obsessed with clothes."

"Sort of like his mother," he teased.

"Why, that's not true. I go ages without buying a stitch of clothing."

"I guess we old geezers don't give much thought to things like that."

"But you usually dress beautifully. And stop calling yourself an old geezer."

"Well, if that's true, you can thank Grace and Lizzy. They bought every outfit I own."

"By the way, isn't this the night they're having the combo on the terrace after dinner?" she suddenly remembered.

"That's what the leaflet said. Eight to ten thirty."

"Well, then, why don't we all have dinner together again? Tyler has to go back tomorrow unless I can convince him to stay longer, and if you think the others might enjoy it . . . I could arrange it with Riley, and . . . I'll even order a bottle of champagne. Of course, I don't want to sound pushy . . ."

He popped her on the leg. "No lady buys me champagne—let's get that straight right now. I'm the one who orders champagne, but, sure, that's a great idea, if you think Tyler wants the company."

"Oh, he seems like his old self today, and I think a little celebration with good company would do him good. Don't worry about Tyler. I know him like a book, and he's better now, already so much better. This trip is doing him good. Just look at him out there fishing with Goldie. Reminds me of when he was a boy and would stand for hours waiting for a bite."

O'Conner's face now took on a very dubious expression,

but, not wanting to upset her, he kept his thoughts and opinions to himself.

Ella reached again for her cigarettes, and this time she let him light one, her normal mood now fully restored.

"I have another suggestion," she then said.

"I hate to guess."

"Don't be a smart aleck. I think we should go shopping while Sal and Elizabeth and the boys are down roaming around Brookgreen Gardens. I'd like to buy something for Goldie, and maybe we can find you another pair of shorts. I just saw an ad for the Gay Dolphin down near the Pavilion. Been there for decades. They have lots of junk but used to also have some pretty decent things. We could run down there and be back here in plenty of time for lunch. We don't wanna just lie around here all morning like two old fogies."

After Edmund walked down to tell Tyler and Goldie their plans, the two took off again in the Cadillac and were soon browsing through the massive gift emporium stocked with everything from elaborate toys to gutsy shells and figurines to beach clothing. Almost immediately, Ella's eye caught a handsome, rather expensive silver and turquoise bracelet in the jewelry section, and after she tried it on to judge its size, she told the clerk to gift wrap it for Goldie.

"What in God's name are those?" Edmund asked at another counter, pointing like a child to some ivory-looking spikes.

"Sharks' teeth," the clerk informed. "Genuine sharks' teeth."

"Well, I'll be damned. How ghastly!" he bawled.

"Oh, we must get a couple for the boys," Ella said friskily. "Every young boy should have a shark's tooth, and actually" —she fondled the daunting object in her hand—"you know, I think they're quite lovely."

After rummaging from one counter and display to the

next like two witless teenagers, Ella finally spotted a stack of men's shorts in every color imaginable and held up an aquamarine pair to examine.

"These are nice and exciting," she declared. "What's your size?"

"Not on your life!"

"Just hush up, honey. Now, tell me your size."

Reluctantly he pondered the question. "You know, I'm really not sure. Thirty-six. Thirty-eight. It's been so long. . . . Grace and Lizzy always handled that sort of thing."

Ella waved down a clerk and asked where a fitting room was, and when she was told there were no fitting rooms, she first expressed outrage, then, looking about, directed Edmund to step behind an unattended counter in a corner and try on the fanciful shorts while she stood guard. Naturally, he balked at the idea, but when Ella coaxed him over and over, he sheepishly did as he was told, slipped out of his old shorts, and quickly stepped into the new pair over his boxers as she watched and snickered.

"No time for modesty. How do they feel?" When he hesitated, she stepped behind the counter and pulled at the waist. "Don't suck it in, honey. Just relax. Yep, these are fine, just perfect. And I love the color. So summery. These'll knock 'em for a loop back up in New Jersey."

O'Conner looked truly shaken and embarrassed as he reemerged from behind the counter with the new shorts in his hand, but when Ella reached into her pocketbook and said the shorts were her treat to him, he protested vehemently, took out his credit card, and quipped, "I take full responsibility for what happens when the young ladies see me in these."

Laughing and glancing at her watch, Ella was about to say they'd better be getting back for lunch when they passed a small rack with a few travel books on the Lowcountry and a selection of popular paperback novels.

"Well, I swear," she exclaimed suddenly, reaching anxiously for one of the paperbacks. "Would you just look at this. If it isn't one of Tyler's books. Why, he'd be tickled pink."

Noticing that there were three copies, Edmund took them all, said he was going to ask Tyler to autograph them, and proceeded to a young cashier whose long frizzy hair was dyed almost orange with a thin green streak down the middle.

"The author's my son," Ella whispered to the hip clerk as she rang up the sale and began to put the books into a bag.

"Uh-huh," the girl muttered coolly, implying that she didn't believe for one second the quaint older lady wearing a stylish gondolier shirt, expensive slacks, and small sapphire earrings.

"I said the author of this novel is my son," Ella repeated.

"Yeah," the girl said in a churlish tone, chewing a piece of gum.

This riled Ella, so, determined to put the ill-mannered clerk in her place, she took out a credit card, tapped it on one of the books, then held it up.

"If you can read, young lady, you'll see that my last name is Dubose, the same name as the author of this book."

Still smacking her gum, the girl glanced at the card, then at Ella, and repeated "Uh-huh."

"Do you think one day, dear, by some miracle of nature, you might have a son who's a famous author?" Ella asked defiantly.

Noticing the small handle of Ella's gun in the pocketbook, the girl didn't answer, finished bagging the books with the receipt, turned her back, and walked away.

"Twit!" Ella blurted quietly to Edmund as they headed for the door. "And that's what passes for youth today."

"Now, now, Miss Ella," he said, chuckling.

Back on the beach, Tyler and Goldie were having just fair luck fishing, but at least his energy level was now sufficient to allow him to enjoy the sport he'd loved since childhood, and if Ella hadn't mentioned to Goldie that he was not well, she would never have suspected a thing. Although conversation between the two was limited, this did give Tyler the opportunity to ask a few questions about his mother that only Goldie might be able to answer.

"Have you noticed any peculiar changes in Mama over the past months?"

"Oh, Mr. Tyler, I'm so used to your mama that I don't pay much attention to what she does," she hedged.

"No changes in her mood, or the way she talks? You know, Mama is not far from seventy-five."

"But your mama's a very strong lady, you know." She appeared a little nervous as she slowly took up slack in her line. " 'Bout the only thing I've noticed is she does seem to talk about the past lots more than she used to when Mr. Earl was alive. I think she still misses your daddy a lot. But guess that's normal when you get her age."

"Well, my brother and sister seem convinced she's going off her rocker and could keel over any minute."

"Oh, if you don't mind me saying so, Mr. Tyler, that's ridiculous. I think they just worry much too much about your mama, and that upsets her—that I know."

"They say she acts really crazy sometimes at home."

"Now, why would anybody say that? Miss Ella can get a little confused, but there's not one thing wrong with her mind. Oh, sometimes . . . sometimes I notice she's thinking hard about something, or lost in her thoughts, and sometimes I wonder if she's real sad about something—maybe about your daddy. But then she snaps out of it, just like that, and is her old self again."

"She seems happy enough down here, I'll say that."

"Oh, I think your mama's having a wonderful time—especially now that you're here. And she gets along so well with

Dr. O'Conner and his family. They're real nice people, don't you think?"

"Very nice." He cracked a smile. "And I think Mama's particularly taken with Dr. O'Conner. Haven't you noticed that?"

She began to blush. "Oh, Mr. Tyler."

"I think it's great."

"We just wish you didn't have to rush back tomorrow."

"I do too, Goldie, but I've got some problems with my health that need to be taken care of."

She didn't know how to react, so all she said was she was sorry to hear that and hoped he was going to be all right.

Now Tyler reeled in his line slightly, debating what to say next.

"We never know what's going to happen, do we, Goldie? And my only concern is that Mama's always well looked after, no matter what. The main reason I flew down was because she didn't sound right and seemed to need me. Now I think there's something important she's not telling me—maybe something about Little Earl and Liv that bothers her. Whatever, Goldie, I just hope you'll always be there to help and watch out after her. You know she trusts you and depends on you like nobody else."

"Oh, you never have to worry about that—not after all she's done for me. Your mama means more to me than anybody in the world, and I'll always be there when she needs me—that I can promise you. But nothing bad's going to happen, Mr. Tyler. I talk with my Great Spirits every single night and ask them to watch over us all, and nothing bad's going to happen—not to you or Miss Ella or me or anybody."

Chapter 21

PREVARICATION

After lunch, Ella, Tyler, and Goldie made the short drive up to Little River in hopes of watching some of the shrimp boats unload their haul on the old wooden docks shaded by heavy festoons of Spanish moss dripping from the gnarled oaks, but when a rugged character with a bushy white beard and sores on his face told them they were too early, they decided not to wait around but, instead, to return to the inn for Ella's beauty-parlor appointment and a rest. Just being in the locale and talking about white shrimp, however, not only evoked once again for Ella her indiscretion with Dennis Chapman that passionate afternoon in Charlotte long ago but also reminded her of the crazy way Big Earl used to haggle with shrimpers over price right on this same dock.

"Four dollars a pound with heads, five without," she remembered one old salt specifying in his gravely drawl, perched behind a giant bin full of white shrimp packed in ice.

"What if I get three pounds?" Earl had tried to bargain.

"Same price."

"What about five pounds?"

The man chewed over the offer. "Three-fifty with the heads, four-fifty without."

"I'll give you three for five pounds—with the heads."

"Whatta you think this is, captain, charity? We can ship these whities frozen up North and do better than that."

"Not with the heads. Makes no sense to ship shrimp with the heads. Too much waste. Even I know that. I'll give you three dollars a pound with heads."

"Three twenty-five."

"Three. Five pounds. Just medium-size are okay."

The man glared daggers at Earl, then took a plastic bag and began grabbing shrimp with his rough bare hands, letting the larger ones fall back into the bin and weighing the bag on a rickety metal scale.

"Fifteen dollars, captain," he huffed, tying the top of the bag.

Ella had a big smile on her face. "And I don't think Earl would have paid one penny more."

"One penny more for what, Mama?" Tyler asked from the backseat as Goldie pulled out onto the road back to Myrtle and glanced worriedly over at Ella.

"For the shrimp, of course," Ella said, unaware that the story was only in her mind. "That man wasn't too happy."

Silent, neither Tyler nor Goldie tried to pursue the details of the memory, and in a matter of seconds Ella was commenting on a large grove of palmettos off the side of the road.

"I plan to wear my black and gold tulle outfit with the puffy sleeves tonight," she then announced.

"Oh, I like that dress, Miss Ella," Goldie said.

"Son, I do hope you brought a nice suit."

"Mama, we're at the beach, for heaven's sake, and I've already told you once I brought only jackets. A double-breasted blue blazer should be appropriate enough."

There was no further reference to anyone's mode of dress, and, after they arrived back at the inn, it was as if Ella had managed to block from her thoughts any worry about Tyler's illness as she had her hair done in the late afternoon and made preparations for their early dinner with the Mariani family. Deep down, of course, she was devastated by the possibility that the disease ravaging her son might worsen, and even if this painful realization made the gravity of the problem about his real father seem even less important, it also presented a dilemma over which she had absolutely no control and one which could very well cause what rational equilibrium she still possessed to snap.

Fortunately, most of these dire matters were neutralized the moment she heard a knock on the door and a young man from reception presented her a vase of exquisite yellow roses with a card that read "Never trust a man in aquamarine shorts. Humbly yours, The Yankee." Never could she remember being so touched, and her spirits soared even more when she later found herself seated next to Edmund in a circle on the porch at sunset, sipping a restorative Jack Daniel's and chatting congenially as she and the others admired the decorative pennants and tapers flapping in the warm breeze on the terrace below and watched the members of a small combo getting set up for after-dinner music and dancing. At one point, the two boys, dressed in jackets like their father and grandfather and again sitting on either side of Goldie, became particularly restless, so, though she'd planned to wait till dinner to surprise them and Goldie with the gifts she'd bought with Edmund, Ella dug into her pocketbook and produced the sharks' teeth and bracelet, which thrilled the three to no end. Once all the excitement was over and Goldie had said the bracelet was the most beautiful she'd ever owned, Ella was generally her normal talkative self. If, on the other hand, she was led by Sal or Elizabeth to relate more facts about the Lowcountry, or reminisce about her background in Charleston, or kid Tyler about some aspect of his growing up in Charlotte, her thoughts could drift unchecked, giving the others the impression that she was a little disoriented or momentarily living in another world.

Since this was still the off-season, the dining room, as usual, was only about half-full of mostly middle-aged or elderly guests, but when the Priscilla sponsored this type of evening once a month with after-dinner dancing on the outdoor terrace, the kitchen always tried to come up with a few special regional dishes that would be dramatic to serve and would appeal to all the guests. This evening the distinctive appetizer was tiny crab and lobster cakes with mustard sauce on a bed of red and white coleslaw, the main course an elaborate chicken perloo studded with country ham and various herbs, and dessert a rich Huguenot torte. Predictably, Tommy and Rex opted for fried chicken wings and chopped sirloin steaks, but everyone else followed Riley's advice and ordered the specials. Originally, Ella had wanted to have champagne with dinner, but when Tyler, seated next to her, suggested they drink a more sensible California chardonnay with the food and save the bubbly for the terrace, she proudly deferred to his idea. Like the two boys on either side of her, Goldie drank Coke, though it was obvious by the way she glanced at the wine being poured that she would have given her eyeteeth for a glass.

"Can you tell us more about this new novel you're working on?" Sal asked Tyler at one point.

"Well, I'm not sure myself exactly what it's about, to tell the truth." He dodged the question, hesitant, as he always was, to discuss his work with anyone.

"I so much enjoyed the one you set in New Orleans," Edmund said, having already had the three paperbacks for him to sign delivered to the room with a note enclosed. "You really made me feel the spirit of the place and the people, and you had me on the edge wondering what was going to happen to that rascal who walked out on his entire family."

"Thanks," Tyler said meekly, now only picking at the rice in his perloo since his appetite was again dull. "I love New Orleans."

"I'm embarrassed to admit I haven't yet read any of your books," Elizabeth confessed, her smooth face especially radiant with a mellow suntan and her lightweight cream suit and tiny sapphire stud earrings in perfect taste that impressed Ella. "But from what Dad's told us, most of your stories take place in the South."

"I guess so," he confirmed. "All but one, in fact."

"But you haven't actually lived in the South for a long time, have you?" Sal asked with genuine interest. "Do you still consider yourself a Southern writer?"

Ella, who hadn't missed a word, glanced across the table. "Why, of course he's a Southern writer. His background and roots and traditions and . . . everything is Southern, so of course he's a Southern writer—no matter where he lives. Aren't I right, Son?"

"I never gave it that much thought, Mama," he answered with some embarrassment, looking back at Sal as the other man nodded to the waiter that he'd had enough perloo. "But I have spent lots of time all over the South and Southern subjects do interest me most, I suppose. You see, I'm convinced there's nobody . . . there're no people on earth more complicated—more corrupt, dishonest, and complicated—than we Southerners, and that makes for very good subject matter."

"Really?" Elizabeth said with a startled look on her face just as Riley approached to pour a little more wine into Ella's glass.

"Why, that's a terrible thing to say, Son," Ella declared indignantly, having either utterly forgotten expressing the same sentiment to Edmund the night before or too ashamed to agree now. "There's not a word of truth in that ugly statement."

"Sure there is, Mama," he said, pointing to his own glass for more wine, then directing his attention again at the Marianis. "Don't get me wrong. I'm very proud of my Southern heritage, but beyond all our graciousness and refinement and respect for tradition is a certain psychological fraudulence that could be connected with what Southerners had to contend with following the Civil War—the way they came to distrust all outsiders and even each other."

"Ridiculous, perfectly ridiculous," Ella grumbled. "I think you've lost your mind."

"But isn't a degree of dishonesty a fairly common trait in most folks?" Edmund interjected while studying with curiosity the rich torte placed in front of him.

"Probably," Tyler continued, the alcohol loosening his tongue more and more. "But with Southerners, prevarication and deception seem to be more than just a harmless trait. It's almost a natural instinct that can cause tremendous damage, as I see it. Oh, I'm not saying it's necessarily an evil instinct since, from all I've observed, Southerners lie as much to themselves as to others, which, at least for a novelist like myself, is what makes them so fascinating. And you don't have to read just my stories. Read Faulkner, or Tennessee Williams, or Eudora Welty, or most of the other great Southern authors. Not that I'm in their class, mind you, but I do believe they were all aware of this instinct and, painful as it might have been, exploited it fully to get to lots of truths." He stopped to drink more wine. "And, since you asked, I guess that's basically what I'm trying to deal with in this new book I'm working on—prevarication."

All the while Tyler was finally sharing some of his ideas and convictions, only Edmund understood the solemn expression that came over Ella's face.

"I never realized you hated the South so much," she said in a tone that could be interpreted as defensive, outraged, or gravely distressed.

"Oh, Mama, that's not at all what I'm saying—and I'm certainly not accusing you personally, of all people. I'm proud to be a Southerner, and it's ridiculous to say I hate the South. I'll probably be buried here when my time comes."

"Well, I must say you have a strange way of expressing it in front of these nice people," she scoffed, cutting a dainty bite of dessert with her fork. "And, after all, you haven't even seen fit to live here for almost thirty years."

"Now, that's another story, and you know the reasons why as well as I do, so don't you prevaricate, honey." He smiled and patted her lovingly on the arm.

"Why, I never prevaricate, and . . . just imagine what these fine friends of ours must think."

Of course, Tommy and Rex had paid no attention at all to the serious conversation, but Goldie, despite having to answer dozens of witless questions the boys shot at her, couldn't have been more conscious of what was being said across the table.

"I don't think it's exactly a sin to sometimes color what we say," Sal asserted, his cheeks now flushed from the wine. "Like Dad said, that's pretty normal for everybody."

"Please, dear," Elizabeth said, "not in front of the boys."

"All I'm talking about, sweetheart, are little falsehoods, innocent falsehoods people come up with to avoid hurting others—or to protect them. You, of all people, should know about that."

Not aware that her father had informed Ella of her adoption, Elizabeth glared daggers at her husband, as did Edmund, not because it had ever been a big issue but because she simply considered it to be a private matter hardly appropriate for discussion with strangers.

"I'm not interested in little white lies," Tyler persisted, adjusting the dimpled knot in his necktie. "What I like to explore are characters who prevaricate almost pathologically, the ones who can cheat even on those they love and respect the most." He leaned forward over his plate to prevent the boys from hearing his small diatribe. "I mean, everywhere you look—the papers and magazines, TV, movies, government, and the divorce courts . . . everywhere it's the same deceit and hypocrisy and willingness to con others that's been around for centuries—and, believe me, nobody excels in the practice like us gracious Southerners. Well, people get hurt and damaged, and the worst part, the really frightening part, is that nobody seems to care. Routine behavior, and nobody cares a whit." He leaned back. "And that's what I try to write about."

For a moment, everyone remained silent, staring at him, till Edmund spoke up.

"And, if I might ask, would you include yourself in that dubious cast of characters?"

"I'm a Southerner, aren't I?" he jested, the wine loosening his tongue more and more. "And I'm involved not only in a serious personal relationship with someone but with any number of professional people. So of course I'm as guilty as everyone else, though I'd like to think I'm at least aware of my ability to commit fraud, and that I'm learning to care about it. That seems to be the point, Dr. O'Conner. We're all guilty. Nobody's innocent. And, as I see it, what matters is how we confront the truth and try to rise above it."

"I'll buy that," Edmund declared, nudging Ella's arm discreetly. "You're quite an outspoken philosopher."

"Believe me, I'm no philosopher, Dr. O'Conner, just a writer searching for good material to write about."

During this weighty dialogue, Ella hadn't uttered a word, and now, her eyes blinking rapidly as if dazed, she began very quietly to hum the words of a song to herself, evidently lost in another far-off memory.

"Mama?" Tyler asked softly, touching her hand.

When she kept humming the melody, Edmund shook her other arm gently, trying to break the reverie. "Ella, Miss Ella, what in heaven's name are you singing?" he asked as Sal and Elizabeth watched nervously.

She stopped only when, in the distance, the small band outside struck up the first chords of an old dance tune, suddenly turning her introspective mood into one of gaiety.

"Listen," she stammered, snapping back to reality. " 'Slow Boat to China.' " She then pushed away the rest of her torte and reached into her pocketbook for her compact. "Why don't you folks finish up so we can go outside for some champagne and a few twirls?" She turned to Tyler and popped him cheerfully. "And maybe, young man, you'll even show me if you still know how to shag."

Chapter 22

LAST DANCE

In the faded black-and-white photograph, six young people, gathered closely around a table next to an imposing column in a glamorous ballroom, pose for the camera while other faces in the near background look on. Everyone is smiling. Visible on the tablecloth is a centerpiece of flowers, different styles of cocktail glasses and a few bottles, packs of cigarettes and ashtrays, and three small women's purses, and, in the far distance, the blurred, cropped image of a bandstand reveals only four fingers cupped around the midsection of a saxophone. Earl, Jonathan, and Bobby Foster are all dressed in vested suits and neckties and look trim and handsome, despite Earl's mussed hair after maybe five or ten minutes of lively dancing with Mary Beth Williams, who has a particularly wide grin on her pretty face. Ella, wearing a crepe de chine dress with ruffles around the neck and jewel earrings, holds a cigarette in one hand and Bobby's arm with the other, but the way her eyes are cocked slightly to the left, where Jonathan is seated next to buxom Sally Van Every in her low-cut dress and ornate pendant, recalls that he has asked Ella to dance just before the photo was shot. The group's mood seems overly cheerful, most likely because everyone is tight and anxious to return to the dance floor.

Reaching into her pocketbook for her cigarettes, Ella gazed down long and hard at the old picture illuminated by the flickering glow of a torch lamp on the terrace, remembering uncanny details of the shot and debating whether to pull it out and show it around the table as she'd intended before leaving the room for drinks and dinner. What had compelled her to remove this photo, plus the one of her and Jonathan in front of the hotel and a couple of others, from the album back home was a move she'd never stopped to analyze. Maybe her subconscious reason had been to allow Tyler to see his real father once she'd revealed the truth to him. Perhaps she'd simply wanted to take along on the trip a few sentimental mementos of those magic times in the region when she was so free and happy and . . . young. Furtively, she studied the photo again, gripped by a pang of nostalgia that threatened to engulf her. Then, her fingers tingling, she tucked it back next to her compact, took out the cigarette case, and waited for Edmund to give her a light.

By the time Ella and her crowd had arrived on the terrace, most of the tables arranged around the edge, each covered with colorful cloths secured with clips, were already occupied, and since each seated only four, Sal had kindly volunteered to join Goldie and the boys at a table nearby. Although most of the other guests were undeniably of another generation, a few of the younger couples, including the one whom Ella had heard arguing on the porch, appeared to be about the same age as Sal and Elizabeth, or at least old enough to know and appreciate the vintage upbeat tunes and romantic melodies performed by a formally dressed four-piece band at one corner of the terrace.

At bars, clubs, and resort hotels all over Myrtle Beach, clods decked out in jeans, tank tops, and sneakers were no doubt listening and gyrating to hard rock, disco, country-western, and other styles of music that Ella had told Edmund were more appropriate for "orangutans in heat," but here at the Priscilla the scene was a veritable time capsule of a more civilized era not that long ago when respectable dress and polished manners were hallmarks of polite society and the most popular music was easy songs by Sinatra, Peggy Lee, Dionne Warwick, and even the Beatles. That the inn had a virtual monopoly on a sizeable clientele that relished and demanded this old-fashioned, exclusive, downright corny ambiance was not so much the result of some stubborn determination to preserve a gracious Southern way of life as long as possible as of the pragmatic realization that there was still enormous profit to be made in a unique enterprise such as this. Ignoring for years most modern trends and innovations, the inn furnished the fantasy, attracting well-off guests from all over and confident that as long as there were Duboses and Marianis eager to dance to live outmoded music under stars at the edge of the sea, and exploit their dreams, and order lots of French champagne and cocktails, special events such as this were worth every hour of inconvenience and extra operating costs.

"This is the way it used to be up at the old Ocean Forest Hotel," Ella reminisced, gazing up at the half moon as the waiter filled glasses with champagne and the piano carried the melody of "Lullaby of Broadway." "Isn't this charming?"

"Okay, Mama, I can take a hint," Tyler remarked, holding out the palms of both hands in a gesture to dance. "I'll be fading soon, so if you'd like to play Fred and Ginger . . ."

It had been years since Ella had danced with her son, but after they glided smoothly over the floor a few minutes, she looked up at him and said, "Well, you certainly haven't lost your touch. Almost as good as your daddy."

Soon Edmund was dancing with Elizabeth. Then Sal broke in on his father-in-law, and Elizabeth later attempted to shag with Tommy and Rex when the band played "My Blue Heaven." Ella and Edmund demonstrated what the rumba was all about, and at one point, Tyler even grabbed Goldie and led her in his version of the jitterbug. Ella and Tyler prompted a round of applause with their dexterous execution of the shag, but, when she became a little dizzy, she was finally persuaded to stay seated, sip her bubbly, and tell more beguiling tales about the old days.

"From what you and Daddy used to say, y'all must have really kicked up your heels during the war," Tyler said, his fair cheeks now rosy.

"Lord, we could carry on like this till the wee hours of the morning—me and Earl and Betty-Sue Alexander and that sweet Tootsie Middleton and Jonathan and a boy named Ashley Lockhart. . . . Ashley went overseas right before Jonathan, and . . . he never came back. We never saw him again. That's the way it was during the war. Boys left on the train, and we never knew if we'd ever see them again except with a flag draped over their coffins. So we all drank lots while they were here, and listened to the radio, and collected newspapers and tin cans for the Allied Relief program, and hoped we didn't see the man delivering telegrams. That's the way it was. And everybody danced. Mercy, did we dance—at island beach parties, and at hotel proms, and in living rooms, and any place else where there was a radio or record player or band. Jimmy Dorsey, Benny Goodman, Guy Lombardo—the big bands, they all came down here, so far away from the war. Because, you see, there was a war we believed in that had to be won, and nobody knew what tomorrow would bring, and friends were being killed, or they'd come back and were never the same." She paused to take an unsteady sip and reflect further. "Things happened to boys over there, terrible things, and some who

came home were almost like strangers, and just wanted to forget, and get drunk, and dance. So we all drank lots, and paid no
attention to the liquor laws, and danced our feet off, and . . .
Lord, did we have fun."

"And fooled around lots, I bet," Tyler cracked without thinking. "I bet there was plenty of hanky-panky even back then."

Ella sat staring at her glass for a moment, then looked up at
him. "Why would you make such a remark? We didn't behave
like that in those days. In those days, we had different values,
didn't we, Edmund?"

He waved his finger at her and smiled knowingly. "Don't
get me in trouble."

"From what I've read and seen in films, everyone in those
days seems to have been pretty prudish," Elizabeth commented.

"Not prudish, my dear, just proper," Ella corrected, glancing at the champagne bottle on ice in the bucket. "Do we
need another bottle?"

"Let's not overdo it, Mama," Tyler said, raising up the half-
empty bottle and gesturing to Sal across the way about a refill.
"Nobody's up to carrying you to your room."

"Hush up," Ella said playfully. "I know my limit, for your
information, and I'm sober as a judge."

All the merrymaking and banter continued awhile longer,
but when the bottle was empty, and the boys got restless, and
the crowd began to thin out, Sal announced that it was time to
call it a night since they planned the next morning to drive
Edmund up to see Sunset, Ocean Isle, and a couple of other
North Carolina beaches. Tyler, also, now looked exhausted
after being in such high spirits, so even though all the alcohol
made Ella feel she could keep going till dawn, she finally
winked hopelessly at Edmund as Elizabeth took her father's
arm and Tyler said he would hold his farewells till breakfast.
Goldie, of course, was still glowing from all the excitement, but
when Ella grabbed Tyler's arm as everybody headed up to the

porch, Goldie still watched her like a hawk in case she happened to stumble on the steps.

Back in her room, alone and tipsy, Ella's mood was still elevated as she prepared to undress and thought about Edmund and what a wonderful evening everyone had enjoyed. Then she couldn't help but notice through the connecting door the faint, uncanny sound of Goldie chanting one of her bizarre prayers, this time a clear, steady descant that, as Ella listened, somehow seemed to be mysteriously directed at her and had an almost consoling effect. Opening a window wide to a tepid breeze and the comforting sound of waves breaking, what she detected next were the distant strains of "Sentimental Journey" being played down below by the band. This, in turn, reminded her that Tyler would be leaving the next day, and when she began dwelling on Tyler, there was little she could do to keep the reality of his precarious condition from surfacing ominously in her disoriented mind. Being forced to consider how serious his medical problem might be only stirred again unbearable emotions about the secret she'd failed to reveal to him, and reflecting on this dilemma only compounded her confusion over him, and her family, and her friendship with Edmund, and the swarm of crushing memories and dreams that seemed to control every instinct more and more.

Holding onto the back of the large chair as the music resonated, her head reeling, Ella seemed to forget where she was, and began crying helplessly. Then, as if a strange voice inside were coaxing her to come to grips with her anxiety, she suddenly felt the urge to go back downstairs, exactly for what reason she didn't even try to figure out. All she knew was she had to follow the impulse, and return to the music, and listen to this beckoning voice in her soul.

So without even locking the door or taking the pocketbook that contained her compact and cigarettes and bourbon and gun and photographs and other items she deemed essential to human survival, she made her way to the elevator, and across the dim reception hall redolent of sweet myrtle and old cypress, and down to the terrace where only a few couples were left drinking or slow dancing before the band decided to end the session. For a moment, she simply stood in the background and watched and listened. Then, compelled by the strong intuition, she went over to the weathered stairs leading down to the beach, mindlessly stepped out of her low crocodile pumps, and, grasping the rail carefully, proceeded to make her way down to the strand dimly lit up by the soft glow of the half moon. At first she felt a little frightened, but when she recognized the muffled sound of "I'll Be Seeing You" now being played by the combo, she wrapped her arms around herself, closed her eyes, and began swaying in place on the sand to the soothing melody. Slowly she wavered, then turned and moved to and fro to the distant beat of the music, then stepped from side to side in cadence with the languid words of the song reverberating in her mind.

"May I break in?" she then thought she heard a voice asking over the gentle modulation of the waves.

"Who's there? Who's that?" she mumbled in a frightened tone.

"Don't you recognize me, Ella?"

"Who is that?" she repeated to herself, her feet still moving.

"It's me, Ella," the voice rang more sharply in the silver realm of memory.

"Jonathan?" she muttered as the music played on from above. "Is that you, Jonathan?"

"Can I have this dance, Ella?"

"Is that really you, Jonathan?" she asked again, extending her arms to him. "Oh, Jonathan."

"I've come to say good-bye, Ella," he said in his soft, familiar accent, holding her and looking into her eyes. "We never really got to tell each other good-bye, and the time has now come."

"Oh, Jonathan," she repeated wistfully. "Can you ever forgive me?"

"I'm not asking for forgiveness, sweetheart. I'm just here to say good-bye."

"I'm so sorry about everything, Jonathan, and I've never stopped remembering our wonderful times." She began to sob, feeling the back of his curly hair and recognizing the clean scent of his neck. "I've never forgotten anything."

"You have to forget, Ella. It's time to forget and say good-bye to me and the past."

"But that's all I have left, Jonathan—my memories. The only thing I have are my memories."

"That's not all you have left, Ella. You have a son, and Tyler's soon going to need you more than he ever has. Nothing is more important now than Tyler."

"I've never told him about you and me, and there's so much about him that reminds me of you."

"That doesn't matter anymore, Ella. I no longer matter. All that matters now is Tyler and what you do with the rest of your life. You've been trapped too long, Ella, but now you're free."

"You can't leave me, Jonathan," she whimpered, feeling him pull away. "I feel so alone and need to remember you and those days."

"Those days are over, Ella," he said in a mature tone as she reached out and watched him gradually fade, a warm smile on his smooth, youthful face. "You're needed, and you still have a life to finish. You have to let go now, Ella. The past is over, and you're finally free. You're free, Ella."

"Don't leave me, Jonathan. Please don't leave me."

"Good-bye, Ella."

"Jonathan . . ."

"Good-bye, Ella," he repeated faintly, his voice soon silenced by the steady drone of the lapping waves.

Feeling an arm trying to clutch her waist as she continued to sway back and forth, Ella opened her terrified eyes and hazily saw Edmund standing next to her still dressed in his dark green jacket and tie.

"Easy, my dear," he tried to console, holding her tightly as her stockinged feet slowly stopped moving in the cool sand. "You must be having a bad dream, but it's now over, it's all over."

At first she said nothing. Then, beginning to realize who was now speaking, she put her arms around him and began crying and trembling uncontrollably.

"It was Jonathan. I saw Jonathan, and we danced, and talked, and . . . then he disappeared. He just disappeared."

"There, there," he said, handing her the handkerchief from the breast pocket of his jacket. "You just imagined it all."

"But I did see Jonathan," she sobbed hysterically. "It was him. It was Jonathan, and he hadn't changed one bit, and we danced and talked and then . . . then he told me good-bye and just disappeared."

"Maybe he was trying to tell you something important," Edmund whispered, patting her back gently. "But it's all over now, my dear. Your dream's over."

"But it wasn't a dream, was it? He was there. Jonathan was there. He'd come back to help me and tell me what I had to do about Tyler, and my own life, and—"

"It was a dream, Ella," he interrupted, trying even harder to break her trance. "You're tired, and you had a vision, but Jonathan's gone now, maybe gone forever, so why don't we go back upstairs and sit down?"

"He just disappeared," she persisted. "We were dancing and talking, and then, like a ghost, he just faded away and kept telling me good-bye."

For a few more moments, Edmund simply stood and held her till the weeping and quivering began to subside and she gazed down at her feet.

"Oh Lord, look at my stockings," she stammered with embarrassment when they finally turned to head for the stairs. Just look at my stockings, Edmund."

"Forget about your stockings. We can buy some more."

"What are we doing down here on the beach, Edmund?" she then asked feebly. "And where are my shoes?"

"You were just wandering. I called the room over and over, and when you didn't answer, I came looking for you and spotted you down on the beach. You could have stumbled, you know. I guess we all had a little too much champagne tonight. Your shoes are up here on the deck."

Now holding his arm tightly as they negotiated the loose sand, her voice strengthened and she started to act in a more normal manner. Up on the terrace, the music had stopped.

"Mercy, down on the beach this time of night. I must be losing my mind or something."

"You're not losing your mind, my dear. I think you've just had a good deal of pressure on you, and we had a big night, and it all got the best of you for a while."

After they'd retrieved her shoes, Edmund suggested they sit on the empty porch and talk, and the first thing Ella did was pull off her mangled stockings and slip barefooted into her pumps.

"Are you feeling better now?" he asked.

"Oh, I'm fine, Edmund. "It's late, and I'm a little tired, but I'm fine."

"Maybe you just had a little too much champagne tonight," he hinted casually.

"Don't be absurd. I'm sober as a judge," she said as if now oblivious to what had happened on the beach.

He simply chuckled and took her hand as they rocked slowly and remained silent for awhile.

"I'm thinking about all I intend to do when I get back home," she finally uttered on a much more serious note. "I have lots to take care of, and my major concern is Tyler. He could be sicker than he lets on, you know, and I've got to be there when he needs me. I plan to have a long talk with his friend, Barry. Barry and I need to have a long, serious talk."

"Do you think you'll ever have that long talk with Tyler about his real father?"

She sat reflecting, then said with conviction, "Oh, no, Edmund, that's no longer important. That's all in the past, and I know now I have to be realistic and deal with the present and future. You were right when you said some secrets should remain secrets. No, what matters most now is for Tyler to get well, and I think he's going to need me. I think he's going to need me and Goldie a lot. And if he won't come to us, I'll go to him."

"You're a good mother," Edmund said, squeezing her hand, then remaining silent while they both rocked. "Do you care to discuss what inspired you to go on the beach?" he eventually asked. "You seemed pretty lost in your thoughts or memories down there."

Ella again hesitated, as if she'd already forgotten the episode or was debating whether to comment. "Well, you see, Edmund, I think I've been lost in my memories and dreams for far too long, but all that's going to change. It has to change. Remember what you also said about losing control of things at our age? Well, I think I did lose control. I lost control of the past, and what I'm starting to realize . . . what's dawned on me, Edmund, is that losing control over something like that is really what makes us old. You know, it's not loneliness, or aches and pains, or even the loss of dear friends and relatives. It's getting bogged down in our memories and hopeless fantasies—that's what drains the most zest out of life at our stage of the game. Am I making much sense?"

He leaned over and planted a kiss on her cheek. "That's probably the most sensible thing I've heard you say." He dropped his head on the back of the chair. "Now, can I ask you a bold question?"

"You can ask me anything, Edmund."

"I know you'll be frank, but is there any chance . . . Once you've had time to take care of all you have to do back home, I was wondering if there's any chance we might see each other again. Just shut me up if I'm making a fool of myself, but I could fly back down to visit you, or perhaps you'd like to come up and see where this old codger lives. I figure we don't have much to lose, and we do seem to get along well, and" —he laughed—"I think we both realize the grass is no greener on the other side of the fence for either of us. Right?"

It was now she who took his hand and turned to face him in the dim light. "Are you propositioning me, Edmund?"

"I guess that's exactly what I'm doing," he laughed again, wagging a finger in the air in his special way.

"Well, I can tell you I'd be insulted if you weren't," she said, nervously touching the side of her mussed hair. "Of course, I have no idea how much I'll be involved with Tyler and Barry in the coming weeks, and there's lots I need to work out with my other two children." She hesitated a few seconds, as if already wrestling with an important decision. "I might even get myself one of those pocket phones. But yes, Edmund, nothing would make me happier than for us to continue this friendship. You're a very special gentleman, you know."

"Flatterer!" he exclaimed playfully, turning around only to see that the lounge was now closed. "Confound it! A nightcap would have been nice."

His remark apparently triggered some urgent awareness in Ella's mind, for, dropping his hand, she suddenly leaned up and began searching frantically every area of space in and around the chairs.

"Is there something wrong, dear?" he asked worriedly, looking about to see what could possibly be bothering her.

"Yes, there certainly is. Where's my damn pocketbook?"

DANCING IN THE LOWCOUNTRY

James Villas

ABOUT THIS GUIDE

The suggested questions are included to enhance
your group's reading of James Villas's
Dancing in the Lowcountry.

DISCUSSION QUESTIONS

1. A very special Southern society plays an important role in the evolution of Ella Dubose's life. How is Ella both a heroine and victim of that society—as a young lady and elderly woman—in all its different ethical and moral manifestations?

2. Much as she's portrayed as an old-fashioned Southern lady caught up in the clutches of her past, in what ways might Ella be construed as a modern woman?

3. Ella's younger son, Earl Jr., and her daughter, Olivia, do not come across as very sympathetic characters. Do they have any redeeming qualities, and if so, what are they?

4. Nobody can doubt that Ella's and Goldie's relationship is highly unusual and complex. Exactly what role does Goldie play in Ella's life and the psychological development of the narrative? Does Ella truly believe herself to be superior to Goldie, and is Goldie truly subservient to her domineering mistress?

5. Is Ella immoral—both as a young, carefree girl and a mature married lady? In what ways?

6. Was Ella truly in love with Jonathan, or has she always been in love mainly with an idea—or a fantasy? Likewise, did she ever really love her husband, Big Earl?

7. Before—and even after—his traumatic awakening about his sexual identity, were Jonathan's emotions over Ella ever genuine? Is it realistic to believe that he was ever really attracted to her sexually?

8. What strength does Ella possibly gain for her lifelong obsession with Jonathan's memory and the past?

9. What are the true reasons for Ella's special bond with her gay son, Tyler?

10. In what ways does Tyler stand apart from the other characters in this novel, even while serving as a motivation for much of the action?

11. What is most important to Ella: romance and passion, marriage, or motherhood? Could this eccentric lady have survived without any one of these factors?

12. In what ways is Ella's relationship with Edmund at once totally different and quite similar to those with Jonathan and Big Earl? Has there been any development in her emotional makeup over the decades?

13. Edmund purports to understand Ella, and the reader suspects that, in a short period of time, he may indeed have plumbed the depths in her confused soul that have never been explored. If so, how does he accomplish this?

14. Determined as Ella is to finally reveal hidden truths to Tyler about the past and his identity, she ultimately decides that his precarious welfare is more important than her need to resolve an overwhelming ethical dilemma. Is she right or wrong in her decision?

15. Can Ella be deemed a loving, responsible wife and mother?

16. Nothing ever seems to be as important to Ella as her pocketbook. What might the pocketbook be said to symbolize in this novel?